PRAISE FOR
NICOLE DIAMOND AUSTIN

"In the Bible, Caiaphas is the Holy Temple high priest who turns Jesus over to the Romans. That's about all most of us know. But in this rich, subtle, and thoughtful historical novel, we meet a serious and learned man facing impossible choices. Author Nicole Diamond Austin describes the growing tensions between the Temple priesthood, Jesus and his followers, and the Roman authorities, giving dignity and humanity to the individuals in all three groups. I found myself fascinated by Caiaphas' extraordinary life and the rich, beautiful traditions he served. I highly recommend *The Gospel of Caiaphas*. It's a generous, moving, and impressive work."

— MARTHA JEAN JOHNSON, *THE QUEEN'S MUSICIAN: A NOVEL*

"Nicole Diamond Austin builds a rich backstory for the Biblical high priest Caiaphas, rooted in historical research and thoughtful invention. This riveting tale is flush with an impressive level of detail about family life and temple practice during the Roman era, offering a vivid picture of the experiences of the Jewish people during the time of Jesus. I was especially captivated by the women whose essential partnership supported the work of the priesthood not only in household management but in their wise council and engagement with the political and social challenges of the day. Readers will love this achingly beautiful depiction of what might have transpired within the Jewish priesthood during the conviction of Jesus and the tragic destruction of the temple in Jerusalem."

— MEREDITH STORRS, BRAVE AND BELOVED: A BIBLE STUDY FOR WOMEN EXPLORING THE WISDOM AND DIVERSITY OF WOMEN IN THE BIBLE

"Nicole Diamond Austin's *The Gospel of Caiaphas* draws richly on often scant historical sources to build a pressure-cooker first-century world for her central character to emerge. As he grows and ages, Austin's Caiaphas collides centrally with the power of Rome's empire, and despite the politics and colonial impulse that animated the time and that animates the dramas of this novel, this gospel also imagines a life—and so a time—filled with love and duty, learning and unlearning, great loss and great intrigue. This book reminds us that though myth and magic and mystery are at the heart of any *gospel*, religious stories operate in service of the actual human lives, in all their fullness and complexity, that the narratives set in motion."

— SCOTT KORB, LIFE IN YEAR ONE: WHAT THE WORLD WAS LIKE IN FIRST-CENTURY PALESTINE

THE GOSPEL OF CAIAPHAS

NICOLE DIAMOND AUSTIN

MEDITERRANEAN SEA
↑ SYRIA
GALILEE
Ptolemais
Capernaum
Gamala
Bethsaida
Sea of Galilee
Sepphoris
Tiberias
Cana
Nazareth
SAMARIA
Caesarea
Apollonia
PEREA
Mt. Gerizim
Lydda
Jericho
Jerusalem
Bethany
Bethany
Valley of Elah
Bethlehem
JUDEA
Dead Sea
Hebron
N
IDUMAEA
Region Map

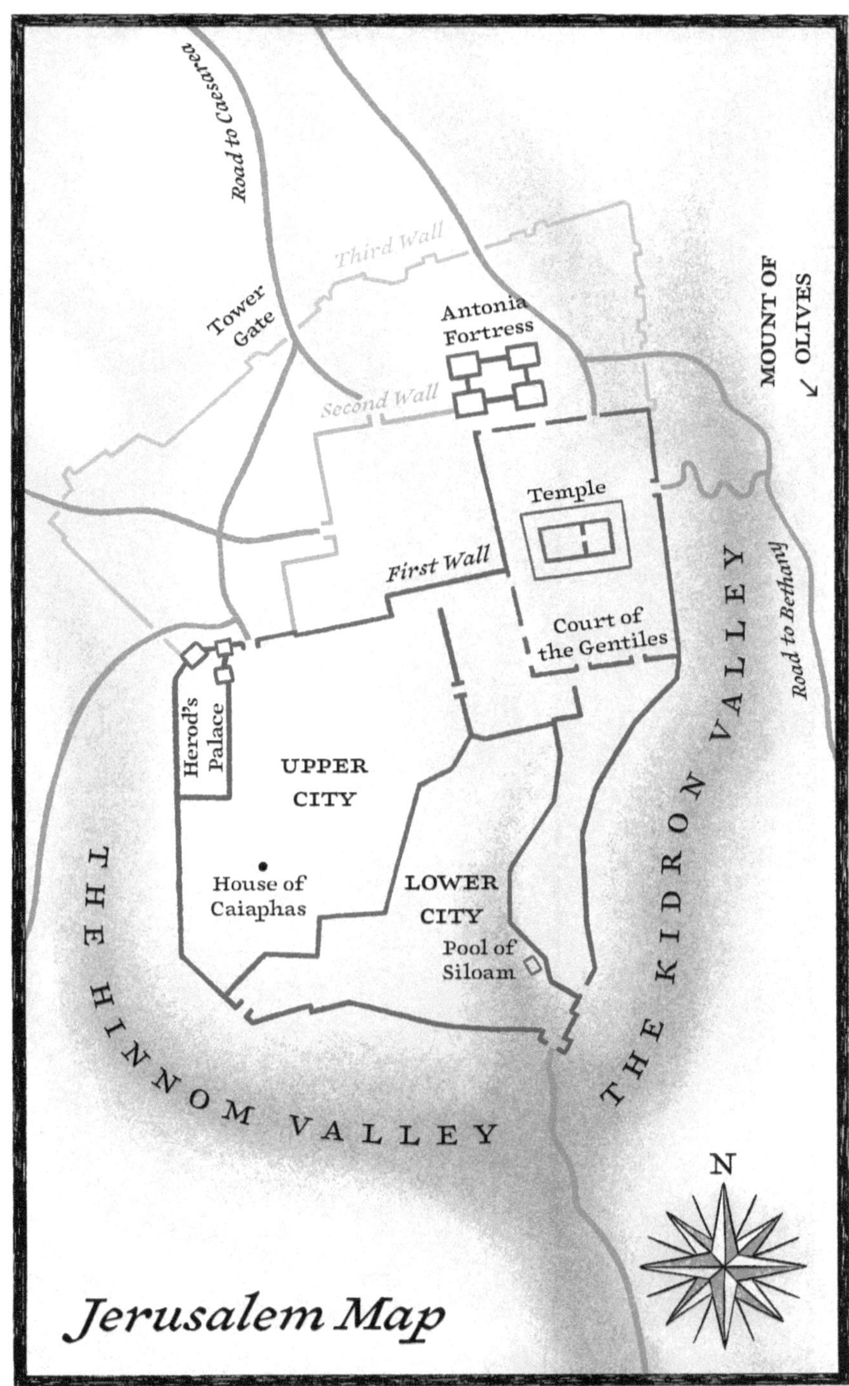

Jerusalem Map

Holy of
Holies
Salt
Chamber
Gate of
Kindling
Sanctuary
Place of
the Hearth
TEMPLE
Offering
Gate
Wash
Basin
Chamber
of Hewn
Stone
Altar
Place of
Slaughtering
PRIESTS' COURT
COURT OF THE ISRAELITES
Chamber
of Oils
Nicanor Gate
Chamber
of Lepers
WOMEN'S COURT
Chamber of
Nazarites
Chamber
of Wood
N

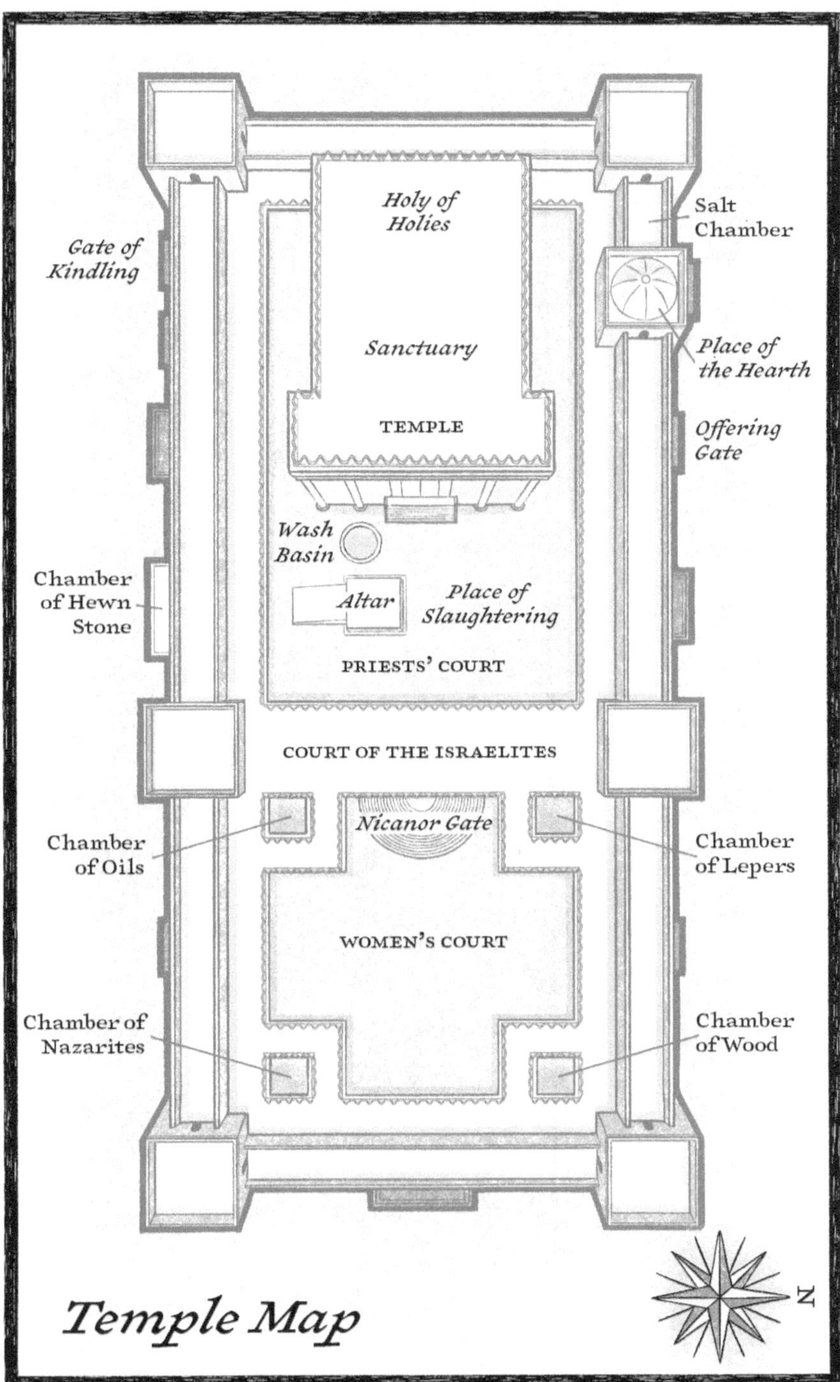

Temple Map

ROMAN LEADERSHIP

GOVERNORS

- Coponius
- Marcus – Marcus Ambivulus
- Rufus – Annius Rufus
- Gratus – Valerius Gratus
- Pilate – Pontius Pilate
- Felix – Marcus Antonius Felix
- Festus – Porcius Festus
- Lucius – Lucceius Albinus
- Florus – Gessius Florus

KINGS

- Herod – Herod the Great or Herod I
- Archelaus – Herod Archelaus, son of Herod the Great
- Antipas – Herod Antipas or Herod the Tetrarch, son of Herod the Great
- Agrippa – Herod Agrippa or Agrippa I, nephew of Archelaus and Antipas, grandson of Herod the Great
- Julius – Marcus Julius Agrippa or Herod Agrippa II, son of Agrippa

EMPERORS

- Caesar – Augustus Caesar
- Tiberius – Tiberius Caesar Augustus
- Nero – Nero Claudius Caesar Augustus Germanicus
- Vespasian – Caesar Vespasianus Augustus

Family Trees

THE HOUSE OF ABEL

Abel ┬ Hadassah

Caiaphas

THE HOUSE OF BOETHUS

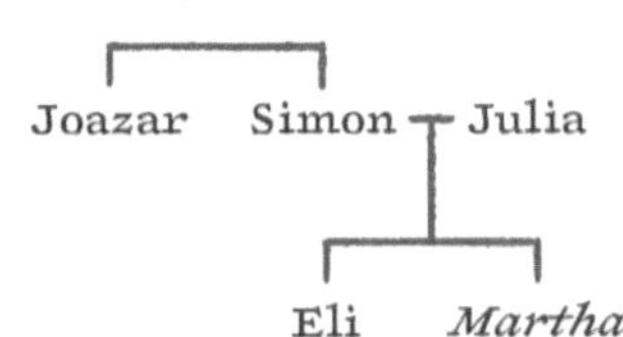

THE HOUSE OF ANNAS

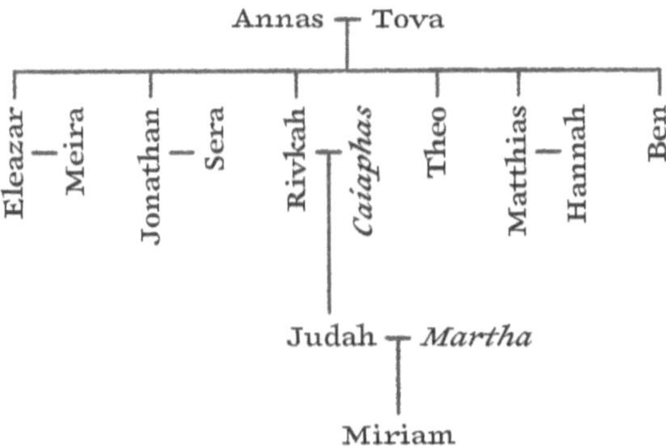

THE HOUSE OF HILLEL

Gamaliel

Joshua

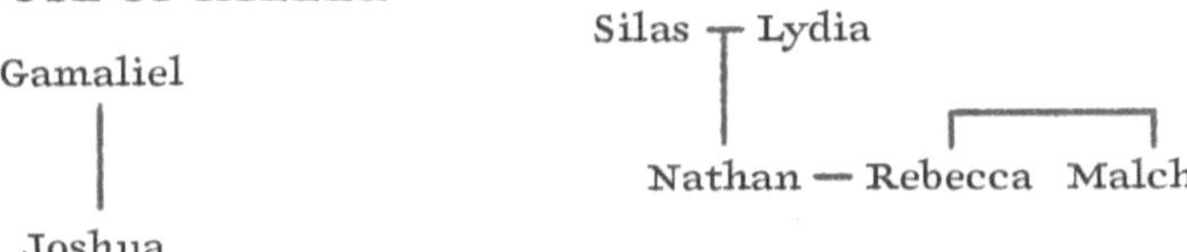

NOTE: Names in italics appear within more than one family tree.

"Then one of them, named Caiaphas, who was high priest that year, spoke up, 'You know nothing at all! You do not realize that it is better for you that one man die for the people than that the whole nation perish.'" – John 11:49-50

"We often forget that Caiaphas had a history before he met Jesus."
– Helen K. Bond, *Caiaphas*

PROLOGUE

Joseph Caiaphas sat upright in bed, shaking and trying his best not to cry out. He knew from past experience that his father Abel would not take kindly to a middle-of-the-night interruption. Worn from the previous day's work at the temple, his father needed rest. His mother Hadassah would come to him if he called, he knew. But he would not make her suffer his father's anger for babying her only child again. His father already felt that he was coddled, that because there had been so many pregnancies before him that had not resulted in a child, his mother made too much of him. With her frailty, it was best that she remain asleep as well. No, he would not make a sound.

But the vision that had roused him from sleep would not leave his mind. Pressing his hands against his eyes, he tried to block out the things he had seen, as if he could push them away by the pressure of his palms. Still he saw the flames, rising higher, and heard the screams as people scrambled in different directions, fleeing both the fire and the soldiers who descended upon them. The setting was always the same. He was standing in the Women's Court of the holy temple, facing west. As the dream began, he walked slowly through the gate to the Court of the Israelites. His father, a priest and a member of the temple guard, had taken him there once before, to show him where the priests performed their daily duties of slaughter and sacrifice. In the dream, however, Caiaphas was alone.

As he looked out over the temple courtyard toward the Priests' Court, his nostrils began to fill with the smell of smoke. It was not the typical odor of the temple, saturated with animal fat crackling on the flames of the altar, the aroma of roasted meat commingling with incense offerings of myrrh and frankincense. This burning was pungent, bitter, almost choking. He looked to the north and saw flames licking up the side of the wall, threatening the sanctuary with their ferocity and power. And then he was running, frantic, trying to escape. Suddenly the Women's Court was filled with Roman soldiers and civilians, screaming, crying, running everywhere. And still the burning continued, bringing with it a fear and a dread that caused him to wrench himself from sleep, choking back sobs, desperate to forget what had just seemed so very real.

The first time he had this nightmare, he cried out in terror, and his mother came to him, stroking his head and singing a soft, low melody until he fell back asleep. In the morning, his father called for him. Together they walked through the Lower City where they lived toward the Pool of Siloam, where his father often went to escape the crowded streets with their merchants and the din of daily life before heading to the temple. Abel had once told his son that he was able to breathe better there. Caiaphas felt honored to be joining him on this excursion.

"Joseph." Abel's voice was stern. "Tell me what happened last night. Your mother says you dreamt of the temple."

Caiaphas shared the details of his dream with his father. His voice shook slightly as he recalled how scared he had been, how alone he had felt. But now that he was here in the bright sunlight with Abel, he felt sure that all would be well. His father was a godly man, he knew. God had blessed their family. Surely, his father would be able to explain this dream, make sense of it, and reassure Caiaphas that there was nothing to fear.

But as he spoke he could see that Abel appeared neither calm nor reassuring. In fact, he looked around to make sure that no one was listening to the things Caiaphas told him.

When Caiaphas finished relaying the events of the dream, he looked up at his father with trepidation.

"Is that all, son?"

"Yes, father."

"All right. Now listen carefully to me. You must never tell anyone of this dream. If it is indeed an omen, it is a terrible one. It would not do for you to be tainted by it." His father paused as he gazed across the still water of the pool, which lay shimmering in the early morning light. Its perimeter was set with large rectangular paving stones, made from the same limestone used to construct the temple that lay to the north of where they now stood. Abel looked down at the stones, cold and hard beneath his sandals, and then glanced back up at his son.

"Joseph, you know that the temple was destroyed once, many years ago. God has allowed us to rebuild a new temple in his honor, and to worship him there. As a guard and priest, it is my duty to protect the temple from any harm. Defending it, and all it represents, is the greatest responsibility of the priesthood." Abel sighed deeply, and continued tracing a path around the pool. Caiaphas fell in step beside him. He heard the emotion in his father's voice over the gentle lapping of the water at their feet against the stone steps beside them.

"My boy, I wish more for you than I have been able to achieve in my lifetime. You are the son of a priest, albeit of a lower order, and an intelligent child, one who has the potential to be great. I have spoken of your abilities to my fellow priests. It is my hope that you will one day take your place among us." Abel's face twisted with a peculiar mixture of pride and resolve. His next words came out with quiet force. "But you must be strong, you must be unshakeable, and you must be prepared to serve God and the temple above all else. Do you understand?"

Caiaphas nodded, his eyes wide. His father had never spoken to him like this before. He knew that the temple was important, of course. He knew that God was mighty and that the temple housed the Holy of Holies, where God descended and honored his people with his presence. He had never actually considered that his dream might come true. Suddenly he felt very small, and even more afraid.

But he was also honored by his father's words. Could it be that he might someday follow in Abel's footsteps, or even that he might surpass him? As they continued to walk in silence, circling the pool, Caiaphas looked up at the sky. Crystal clear on this fall morning, it mirrored the water below. Caiaphas found its vastness soothing as he breathed deeply, his small chest filling with cool, damp air. He would do what he could to be worthy of his father's hopes for him. He would strive to represent his family, and his people, well. And he would speak no more of his visions.

PART I

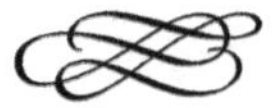

The day began like any other. Caiaphas rose with the dawn and helped his mother grind the barley for the day's bread. Once his father had balked at his doing this type of women's work. But Hadassah reminded him that she was frail, and that her son was a capable helper for her. Without servants, they were required to do all of the daily chores themselves. She could hardly spare him for decorum's sake. He was only ten years old, not yet a man in the eyes of God. Surely this work was a way for him to honor his parents as the Scriptures commanded. Abel, careful to protect his wife from overexertion, let the matter rest. Still, Caiaphas always tried to complete the task before his father arose.

This morning Caiaphas had just finished when a flurry from the courtyard caught his attention. His father was greeting two men with both a deference and a familiarity that told him who they were before he saw their faces. Annas would have been a hard man to miss anywhere. Rugged and broad, despite being of a priestly class where he had never worked a field or pulled a plow, there was a power to him that filled any space he inhabited. It was his voice that carried across the courtyard and his laugh that echoed through the open door, as he chided Caiaphas's father about his tousled hair and still sluggish manner.

"Abel, be careful, or people will think you have been too much at the wineskins." Annas slapped his father on the back with a force that made him fall forward slightly before righting himself. Annas was the only man Caiaphas had ever seen speak to his father like this. He was always taken aback by the way his usually stern father tolerated and even seemed to appreciate the other man's teasing. Despite being a learned and holy man, Annas was never one to stand on ceremony when he was not serving in his official capacity in the temple.

"Annas." Joazar, the other man who had entered their home, spoke quietly, but there was a reprimand in his voice. The son of Boethus, a former high priest of the temple in his own right, Joazar was the current high priest. His status gave him authority over all of the other priests, palace guards, and scribes, not to mention the entire Jewish community in Jerusalem and beyond. Favored by Herod the Great, who had taken his sister as a wife, he fully understood his place in both religious and high society. Joazar was a perfect counterpart to Annas, every inch an elite member of an elite Jerusalem family. Caiaphas thought he looked like one of the wax candles used at the temple, tall and thin and sallow, with an austerity that seemed out of place in the humble courtyard in which he now stood. Joazar's long fingers played with the edges of his robe as he looked at Annas with some disapproval. "We must remember our purpose."

Annas demurred, nodding even as his eyes twinkled. "Of course, Joazar. Of course, you are right."

"My lords, welcome to our home. May I offer you some food or drink?" Hadassah appeared through the open door of the main room, making her way toward the three men with the graceful delicacy of one whose every movement had to be calculated to utilize the least amount of energy. If she was surprised at seeing two high-ranking priests in her courtyard before the sun was barely up, she gave no indication. She smiled. She was beautiful, in her way, with soft, tender eyes and a small mouth that turned up like the scarlet poppies that bloomed in the hills surrounding the city. Annas's grin was back, bolder and broader than ever, but when he spoke, his voice was gentle and warm.

"My dear Hadassah, you look well. Thank you for allowing us to descend on you unannounced this morning. We must speak to your husband, if you can spare him."

As usual, Joazar's tone was more formal than that of his companion. "Thank you for your kind offer. But we will not trouble your household very long." He bowed slightly, as if to dismiss her.

Abel took this cue and put his hand on his wife's shoulder. "My dear, we will retire upstairs to talk. I will return to you when we are finished with our business." She nodded, and the three men walked across the courtyard to the steps leading to the second floor of their home. Upstairs, there was a small room that provided a degree of privacy, though their voices would drift down to the main courtyard unless they spoke in whispers.

As the men made their way up the stairs, Caiaphas suddenly realized that they were not alone. Three children close to Caiaphas's age had joined them on their errand. They now stood in a small cluster near the edge of the courtyard, staring at him. The eldest was his friend Eleazar, the son of Annas. Eleazar was a smaller version of his father. Although he was only a few years older than Caiaphas, he already looked as if he could snap him in two. Fortunately, like his father, Eleazar was good-natured and warm-hearted. He and Caiaphas had spent time together in the temple courts while their fathers were both busy with official responsibilities. They had raced up and down the long staircase leading to the fourth gate, collapsing at the base of the stairs when winded and watching the merchants and pilgrims pass by while they caught their breath. Now Eleazar looked eagerly at him, waiting for an opportunity to approach. Caiaphas couldn't help but smile as he contemplated what fresh news or joke his friend might have to share.

The other two children were younger, one boy and one girl, and looked to be the same age. The boy was frail, with very dark hair. Although it was clear that he and Eleazar were related, it seemed as if Eleazar had gotten all of the vigor of his father's personality, while this younger boy had received very little. He looked serious, and shy, and his gaze drifted downward as he stood in the shadow of his older brother.

The third child was a girl. Although at first she seemed to be a slightly smaller replica of her twin brother, a second glance made it clear that she was anything but. Unlike her brother, she stared straight at Caiaphas, her dark eyes shining and laughing, as if she knew a secret and would tell him if only he asked. As he continued to look at her, she tossed her dark curls and then smiled as he looked away, unsure of himself.

Eleazar broke the silence. "Greetings, Joseph Caiaphas, son of Abel." He strutted forward. Both his tone and his demeanor made it clear that he was impersonating the high priest. "It is a fine day, is it not? And how is your household this morning? Sheep behaving themselves? Goats in line?" And then he laughed, clapping Caiaphas on the shoulder and grinning at him.

Caiaphas grinned back at his friend. "Welcome, Eleazar." He looked over at the two younger children, who had followed Eleazar across the courtyard. "What business does your father have here? And are these your brother and sister?"

Eleazar looked back at his siblings with a half-glance. "Caiaphas, meet the twins. This one's Jonathan." He gave his brother a little shove, which Jonathan barely acknowledged. "They asked to come along today, I'm afraid, so I need to mind them. Fortunately, my mother kept the little ones at home. Important errands are no place for babies."

The girl's eyes darkened. "Perhaps you'd need to mind Theo if he were here. But I can mind myself." She turned her gaze to Caiaphas, who was again struck by her shining eyes. "I'm Rivkah. I'm eight. And you're Joseph. The temple guard's son. I've heard about you."

Caiaphas blushed. Heard about him? From whom? What had she heard? Suddenly, he felt Eleazar's eyes on him and pulled himself up. "It's nice to meet you both. You are welcome here. Let me go to my mother and see if we have some of yesterday's bread to share." As he turned, he replayed his words and was mortified. Yesterday's bread?

Already they could tell that his family's home was humble. Why did he have to reinforce the idea by offering them scraps? These were the children of Annas, who lived in one of the most beautiful homes in the Upper City. They did not have to grind barley for their mother, nor scrape together food for their guests. He wanted to go hide in a corner and cower in shame.

His mother saved him. She entered the courtyard, carrying a platter. He rushed to help her and set it down on a cask in the shade of the eaves. On it were dried figs, almonds, and some of the very bread he had mentioned. It was a handsome, if modest, offering, and he was relieved. "Children," Hadassah gestured. "Come and rest yourselves in the shade and take some food. The men may have no need of it, but I am sure your young bodies could use nourishment after the walk here."

The children murmured their thanks. Rivkah tugged Jonathan's hand, and together they knelt at the makeshift table. Caiaphas gave his mother a grateful smile, which she returned. It was hard on her son, being their only child. She was grateful to see him engaging with other children. She was no playmate for him. Even if she had the strength, there was much to do to run her household.

Hadassah contemplated her son as he took the figs and bread and sat with the others to eat. He was a handsome child, if slight, standing straight and tall, with light brown hair and deep hazel eyes. Unlike her, he had suffered no ill effects from the labor and delivery that had nearly taken her life. He had come early, and she was unprepared. So many times before, when her womb had begun to swell, she had found her hopes dashed. In this pregnancy she had barely allowed herself to believe that he might emerge, alive and whole. All the while she was laboring, she prayed to God, "Please let my child live." And live he had.

Her husband was both proud and afraid when he was born. They had all but given up hope for offspring. This child, a boy, seemed such a miracle that they did not know how to be worthy of it. Abel lay awake many nights, worrying about his son's future. Already Hadassah knew that he had been talking to the more prestigious priests at the temple about Caiaphas's intellect, his potential, his need for training. He was a quick child, eager to learn, eager to please. His ability to memorize Scripture was profound. Hadassah had taught him what she knew. But he had long ago exhausted her meager knowledge. By rights he should have been already learning at the temple with the other boys. But they had made the choice to keep him home to help her, a decision she knew weighed heavily on her husband. They were doing the best they could. Someday perhaps he would be able to take his rightful place at the temple, learning along-side other young men of the things of God. But for now, it was not to be.

Her reverie was broken by the voices from the chamber above, which increased in volume as the discussion became heated. Annas's voice echoed through the chamber and across the courtyard. She saw the children's heads lift and listen.

"Joazar, you must see reason. These zealots are dangerous. Copo-nius will not look kindly on our failure to control our own people. You more than most know what is at stake if we are not able to settle this peacefully."

"Annas, believe me. I do understand the danger here. But we must proceed cautiously. It would not do well for us to meddle too much. We cannot afford to further rile Judas of Gamala and his followers. The less we have to do with them, the better for us."

Caiaphas heard Abel clear his throat. When he spoke, Caiaphas could tell that his father was speaking in his official capacity, not only as a man of God but as a guard. "Gentlemen, I hear both of your concerns. It is wisdom that leads you to look ahead to the possible outcomes of this trouble. Of course, I offer my services to help in whatever way is necessary. If there is any question as to the safety and security of the temple, I am prepared to do whatever I can to protect it, and to enlist my fellow guards in the endeavor. But while the zealots are still quietly plotting, I am not sure there is much we can do."

Caiaphas understood enough to know that his father, always measured and precise, was offering sound advice to the two high-ranking priests who had come to call. He was proud that Abel's opinion had been sought out by these men, and that they seemed to value his perspective.

Eleazar nudged Caiaphas. "Do you think the zealots will rebel? I've seen them, meeting in the streets and huddled in doorways, always looking over their shoulders. Judas and his men are plotting something, for sure."

Caiaphas shrugged. He knew very little of the troubles that the men in the upstairs chamber were discussing. The fact that he was so often at home with his mother sheltered him from the turmoil brewing. What Caiaphas knew was this: When Herod the Great died, it was his son Archelaus who inherited the city of Jerusalem. But Archelaus was not looked on with favor by the emperor in Rome, and was eventually deposed and replaced. When Coponius was put in charge of the region as governor instead, the emperor instructed him to assert and strengthen Rome's hold on the region by implementing new taxes on the people. Caiaphas knew from conversations overheard between his parents that Joazar had been trying to work with Coponius and Cyrenius, a Roman senator, to appease the Roman empire, to demonstrate that there would be no trouble from the Jewish people. But a group of Jewish rebels, led by the man named Judas, balked at the Roman taxes and was threatening to revolt. Joazar was doing everything he could to reassure the Roman authorities that the Jews would cooperate peacefully. But the murmuring in the streets suggested otherwise. There was cause to be concerned if the zealots decided to escalate their grumbling to more violent activities.

Joazar's tone was approving if cautious as he considered what Caiaphas's father had said. "You are right, Abel. But we must be ready in case Judas and his men take action. I appreciate your willingness to help keep the peace. It is essential that we handle this ourselves rather than allowing the Romans to intercede. We have seen all too clearly their version of handling affairs in our land."

Even without being able to see him, Caiaphas could imagine that Joazar's fingers had gone back to plucking at his robe. There was an edge in his voice. Joazar's rule as high priest had not been without its troubles. Joazar had in fact been deposed as high priest ten years before by Archelaus, under suspicion of supporting rebel forces. He had only regained the high priesthood recently since Archelaus's removal. Older and wiser now, he was determined to keep his post this time. He wanted there to be no misunderstanding with the Romans that he was more than willing to take their side against the zealots if need be.

Annas's voice was soothing now, as he sought to reassure his friend and fellow priest. "Joazar, it is a different time. Coponius and Cyrenius are men of honor, even if they do not know our God. They know that we are doing everything we can to make sure these taxes are collected without incident. And if anything were to arise, we know we have men like Abel ready to come to our defense." Caiaphas could sense without seeing the smile on Annas's face as he must have been looking at his father.

"Now, we have taken enough of Abel's time, and we must be getting to the temple." The swish of garments and the descending footsteps told Hadassah and the children that the meeting was coming to a close. Rivkah grabbed one more fig, then rose to her feet, dusting off the edges of her skirt and shaking it slightly. Caiaphas and the other boys rose as well. By the time the men reentered the courtyard, Annas's three children had made their way to the doorway that led to the street.

"Thank you, Abel." Joazar had fully regained his composure and nodded at Caiaphas's father as he and Annas turned toward the door. "I hope this will be the last time we need speak of this unfortunate business. Thank you for welcoming us at this early hour. I know you of all people understand the need for decorum and care in these matters. Your advice is invaluable."

Caiaphas's father nodded as he led the two men across the courtyard. "It is my pleasure and honor to serve God and the temple." He stopped and bowed slightly. "Peace be with you."

Annas gestured to Eleazar, Jonathan, and Rivkah, who quickly trotted behind him. Rivkah took one last look at Caiaphas, standing beside his mother, a look that made him stand up straighter and his breath catch in his throat. "Come along, children." He turned to Caiaphas's father. "Peace be with us all, Abel." And with that, they were gone.

Abel sighed deeply and walked back the length of the courtyard toward his wife and son. Caiaphas saw now that he looked worried. His shoulders, usually held high, slumped slightly as he turned to his wife.

"Hadassah, the news is not good. The zealots are drawing more men to themselves daily. I fear that Joazar may not be able to keep the peace. The Romans will surely intercede if things get any worse."

"Then we must pray that this Judas and his men will have a change of heart, husband." Hadassah's voice was delicate, but firm. She spoke with the conviction of one whose deepest prayers had been answered by God.

"Yes, my love." Caiaphas's father sighed again as he looked at his son.

"Joseph, listen to me."

"Yes, father." Caiaphas did not know what Abel was about to say, but something about his father's tone made him want to cover his ears and run.

"My son, I do not know what the future holds. We live in uncertain times. But these men, Joazar and Annas, they are good men. They care deeply for our people, and for God's honor. I have labored alongside them at the temple for many years, and they have seen firsthand my loyalty and my devotion. If anything were to happen to me…"

Here Hadassah interrupted him, gently placing a hand on his. "Abel. Don't scare the child."

Caiaphas's father shrugged her off, and looked straight into his son's eyes.

"If anything happens to me, these men will make sure that you and your mother are safe and cared for. They have assured me of this, and I trust them with my life."

Hadassah had tears in her eyes as she again placed her hand on her husband's. "Please, my love."

Caiaphas's father nodded. "All right. Now I must go to the temple, to confer with the other guards regarding our defenses and to make arrangements as necessary. I will return this evening." He gave his wife a gentle kiss on her forehead and placed a hand on her cheek. "Do not trouble yourself, my dear. Your prayers are powerful, and I have no doubt of their worth. Pray them now, and try not to worry." He turned and made his way toward the chamber on the other side of the courtyard to ready himself for the day ahead.

CHAPTER 2

In the days that followed, there was a hush in the air. Hadassah spent her spare moments hunched over in the corner of their courtyard, her prayer shawl draped over her shoulders, murmuring words of prayer and petition to God, for safety, for security, for peace. Abel, when he was at home, was unusually quiet. When he spoke, there was a shortness to his words. Caiaphas knew better than to ask either of them whether there was any news. But even without asking, he couldn't help but overhear the updates his father brought home to his mother. The zealots had taken to gathering in large groups just outside the gates of the temple. Joazar and Annas continued to fear that at any moment their fervency might erupt into violence. There were rumors that Coponius and Cyrenius were planning to enlist Quirinius, who governed the nearby territory of Syria, to send Roman legions in to suppress the zealots. Joazar was doing everything he could to stop that from happening. But without the might of an army of their own, the priests had only diplomacy on their side, and Judas had already made it clear that he was not willing to back down or compromise. Most thought it was only a matter of time before the zealots made their move.

Abel looked tired, and older than his forty years. The lines around his eyes seemed more pronounced. Caiaphas could tell that he had not been sleeping well. Every morning he rose early, dressed quickly, and hurried to the temple to see to his responsibilities there. At noon, he returned for a midday meal, and was gone again until after sunset. Each day, Caiaphas breathed a sigh of relief as he heard his father enter the courtyard at dusk, remove his outer cloak, and make his way to the chamber where Caiaphas's mother had set out their supper.

IT WAS three weeks after the visit from Joazar and Annas, and they had just sat down to their evening meal. The dried fish his mother purchased from the merchants at the market the previous day had been rehydrated and prepared alongside lentils, which she seasoned with thyme and mint leaves, and the remaining bread from the midday meal. Caiaphas watched his father hungrily mop up the food with his bread, then take a long swig of the pomegranate wine they stored in large casks along one wall of their storeroom. Abel leaned back from the table, and sighed heavily.

Caiaphas was about to ask his father if he would like him to recite a passage from his day's practice. Despite not being able to provide Caiaphas with a proper education at the temple, Abel was adamant that his son learn to read and write. Caiaphas knew it gave his father great pleasure to see him working hard to master those skills. Already Caiaphas had committed large portions of Scripture to memory, and he sometimes recited these passages to his parents after the evening meal.

But just as Caiaphas was about to speak, there was a shout from the street. A young man Caiaphas did not know burst into the chamber.

He was dressed in the garments of a newly appointed priest, and he was out of breath. He bowed quickly, murmured a greeting, and then launched into his message. "Master Abel, the revolt has begun. The Roman legions from Syria entered the city at sunset through the

Tower Gate, and stationed themselves along the northern wall of the temple. The zealots engaged first, and the fighting has broken into the Women's Court. You must come."

Caiaphas's father rose quickly. Hadassah, who had been collecting the remnants of the meal, took a step back and faltered a little before catching herself. Within minutes, Abel had gathered his things. With a quick kiss on his wife's forehead, he was gone.

The following night and day were longer than any Caiaphas had known. He and his mother put away the remains of the evening meal together. Then they sat, he in silence, she repeating her prayers over and over again as the air grew cool and the stars emerged. As evening turned to night, she turned to him and said, "We must sleep. Your father will not return until all is settled. It will do him no good if we are not rested. We must be prepared to welcome him home when he comes."

But the night came and went, and still there was no word. As Caiaphas's mother prepared the midday meal, he felt he had to break the unnatural silence that had settled over them. "Mother?" he asked.

"Yes, my son?" Her words were tender, even as he could hear her struggling to keep the fear out of her voice.

"Do you think the Roman soldiers will bring peace?"

Hadassah sighed. "If they do, it will be at a bloody cost, my son. They have no patience for these conflicts. They want us to behave, and to honor the emperor above all else. They tolerate our worship only when it does not interfere with their rule. I fear they will be harsh not only with the zealots but with any who try to intervene." She smiled gently, trying to pacify him even as she herself could not be pacified. "But do not worry. What will be, will be, and God will provide, whatever the outcome."

Caiaphas nodded, and asked no more questions.

IT WAS LATE AFTERNOON, and the shadows were growing long across the courtyard. His mother sat, her hands busy with her spinning. Her fingers flew as she pulled the woolen thread off of the distaff and wound it around the spindle. A woven basket of wool sat by her side. She hummed softly to herself as she worked. Caiaphas sat across from her, his wooden writing tablet in his hand, his mind wandering. He was attempting to copy the verses he had recently committed to memory. But he could not concentrate. As he looked up once again toward the door that led to the street, he was surprised, and then alarmed, to see the figure of Annas, entering the courtyard with his head bowed, his face pinched with sorrow.

"Hadassah." Annas croaked, and Caiaphas's mother lifted her gaze. The distaff fell to the ground as she rose, and a low wail escaped her lips. Annas and Caiaphas both rushed to her, and together they caught her before she fell. Still wailing, she lay her head on Annas's shoulder, and collapsed into his broad frame. Annas stood silently, his arm encircling her. Caiaphas stood next to him, still as a statue, as he watched his mother in the arms of the priest comforting her.

"Hadassah." Annas cleared his throat. When he spoke it was clear he was trying to regain his composure for her sake. "I am so sorry." He looked over at Caiaphas, and included him in his next words, aware that for the boy's sake as well as the mother's he must share all he could. "Abel served our God and the temple with honor. By the time he arrived last evening, the fighting was already underway. The Roman soldiers had pushed the zealots back from the temple gate. The soldiers were fierce and mighty, and they overpowered Judas and his forces immediately. But a small band of zealots broke through, entering the temple courts, and attempted to go through Nicanor's Gate to the Court of the Israelites. Abel and his guards held them off. When the Roman soldiers came after the zealots, following Quirinius's order to destroy all of the troublemakers, Abel and those with him found themselves caught in the middle."

He looked down at Caiaphas with sadness in his eyes. "We do not know whether it was a Roman blade or a zealot's dagger that inflicted the fatal blow. But when our men were able to drag his body to safety, it was already too late. The damage was done."

Caiaphas's mother lifted her head to look at him, and his tone grew even more gentle. "Hadassah, the conflict is over. We must cleanse the temple of these terrible deeds, and purify the holy places so that we can return it to a place of worship rather than one of death and destruction. Abel's body remains at the temple. We will bring it to you for burial once it has been prepared."

"As for you and Joseph," he glanced at the boy and then returned his gaze to her, "you already know your husband's request." Hadassah nodded, still hanging onto his shoulder as if she could not yet maintain her own weight. "When all of this has been settled, it would be my great honor if you and your son would leave this place and join my household. You know my wife, Tova, and I know she will welcome you into our home as a sister."

"My boy," he nodded to Caiaphas and his eyes were filled with sympathy and fire. "I have heard much of your eager mind. Your father had long hoped for a chance for you to receive more formal education. In my home, you will no longer do the work of the household, but will be sent to the temple with the other boys to learn the things of God. We will make sure you grow into a man of whom Abel would be proud."

Caiaphas's head was reeling. It was too much for him to take in at once. He found himself short of breath, struggling to understand. His father, dead. Murdered in the service of God. By Roman or zealot hand, it mattered not. He was gone. And now he and his mother were to live in the house of Annas, in the Upper City, among the elite families of Jerusalem. He would live in the same household as Eleazar, as Jonathan. He would live in the same household as Rivkah. He could hardly believe his ears.

And he would receive his education, a dream he had long held but thought impossible. He felt sick with guilt at the excitement that filled him. The prospect of learning from the great teachers at the temple was something he had wished for since he could first read his letters. Perhaps one day.... But how could he be thinking of himself at a time like this, while his father lay dead and his mother mourned? He felt as if he were being torn in two, with sorrow and joy pulling at him like ravenous animals, each eager to feed. He hung his head.

Annas settled Hadassah gently down on a nearby cask and turned to the boy. He knelt, and put his hands on Caiaphas's thin shoulders, turning him toward him. "I know there is much you must be thinking, my boy. In due time we will be able to talk more fully. Now I must return to the temple and see to my responsibilities there. I am sending a young priest named Simon to help you and your mother during this time. Simon is the younger brother of Joazar. He will be able to attend to your needs and to help with the preparations for the burial and for your move to my home."

Annas looked at the boy with tenderness, and Caiaphas was struck with how familiar this man who was no relation to him at all felt, how like a father his touch and gaze seemed. This too, made his stomach twist with a mixture of pleasure and guilt. Eager to break the exchange, he opened his mouth. He tried his best to mimic the ways he had heard his father speak to other priests at the temple, both in solemnity and courtesy. "We thank you, Master Annas, for your generosity and your kindness. My mother and I will await Simon and will prepare ourselves to join your household. We thank you for bringing the news of my father's death…" Here he choked on the word, and had to clear his throat. "Praise God that peace has been restored to the temple."

Annas looked surprised. Then he laughed, a soft chuckle that should have sounded out of place in a house of mourning but only felt kind. "Ah, Joseph, I can already tell that you are your father's son. Be strong for your mother, and know that God will make a way for you in this world. Let the pain you feel now teach you, so that you grow stronger and bolder."

Caiaphas nodded. Annas turned back to his mother, speaking with the authority of one who knew his listener needed clear direction. "Hadassah, put away your spinning now. Prepare an evening meal for yourself and the boy. Simon will be with you by nightfall. I will come again as soon as I can."

THE NEXT SEVERAL days were a blur. The body, which was brought to them on the second day, had been prepared and wrapped in linen. It was indistinguishable from the other bodies being buried by their neighbors, of men who had also lost their lives in the conflict. A handful of priests from the temple carried the body to their family tomb, a modest burial spot on the outskirts of the city. The tomb already held Hadassah's parents, and Abel's mother. His father had died in battle and the body was never recovered. Abel's corpse joined theirs.

The funeral procession was small and sedate. Their party slowly made its way through the dusty streets of the city. Exiting through one of the eastern gates, it wound through olive groves and climbed out of the valley onto a rise that housed a number of tombs including the one awaiting Abel's body. Unlike some processions, full of clanging musicians and wailing relatives, the string of mourners that made up their small group held only a handful of the surviving palace guards who served alongside Abel, his wife, and his son. Hadassah walked behind the body, small and pale, but silent. Caiaphas stayed close to her, both to make sure she did not lose her footing and for his own comfort. He and his mother watched as the men lay Abel's body in the tomb, and said prayers over him. As they returned to their home to wait out the seven days of mourning, Caiaphas found himself relieved. He was grateful that he and his mother could now turn their attention to the preparations for their move, and dwell on death no more.

Simon, who, as Annas promised, had arrived the first evening, was an eager and willing helper. He was kind to Hadassah as she struggled to delegate tasks to him that she felt were beneath his stature as a priest of the temple. At twenty years old, Simon was one of the newest priests to be dedicated. His youth made him less solemn than he rightly should have been with a grieving widow and her child. But his boyish charm was exactly what Caiaphas and Hadassah needed during that first week, as they sorted through provisions in their storeroom, and took inventory of their livestock so that Simon could negotiate a fair price at the marketplace. Hadassah was loath to give up these animals, goats and sheep she had raised since infancy and that had provided milk and clothing for their family. But Simon was able to convince her that Annas's household could more than support the addition of two more mouths to feed without the necessity of bringing livestock as well.

Almost before it had begun, the week was over. Most of their possessions were sold, and the little they owned was packed into large woven sacks, ready for the trip across the city. Simon would return the next morning with two mules to carry their belongings and to guide them to Annas's estate. At dusk, Caiaphas and his mother sat for their final meal in the home where Caiaphas had been born. His mother was thoughtful as she watched her son scrape the last remnants of their meal from the stone bowl he held.

Before Simon left, he had pulled her aside with news from the temple. In the aftermath of the conflict with the zealots, it had emerged that yet again Joazar was finding himself at odds with the Romans in power. Cyrenius was greatly displeased with the way that Joazar had handled the revolt. Decisions of who held the role of high priest, which had once been entirely the responsibility of the Jewish leadership, had become highly volatile since the Romans had tightened their control over Jerusalem. Given Cyrenius's irritation, it was considered very likely that he would order another change in the high priest as a result of the events at the temple. If this happened, the likely successor was Annas.

A valued member of the priesthood, well respected among his fellow priests, Annas would be able to maintain control during a transition without too much trouble. But since he was of a different family line than Joazar and Simon, it was a clear way for Cyrenius to exert power and to demonstrate Rome's authority over the destiny of the high priesthood. Hadassah wondered what this change would mean for her and her son. It was one thing to be taken into the home of a well-respected priest, but quite another to become part of the household of the high priest. She was so engrossed in these thoughts that she did not realize that Caiaphas was staring at her until several minutes of silence had passed.

"Mother? What troubles you?"

She paused, unsure of how much to say to her son. She could already tell that he was taken with Annas, that he was excited about the prospect of learning under him. She had a feeling his influence over her son would be great whether Annas became high priest or not. She wondered what it would mean for her son's future.

"Annas is a great man. It is an honor to be joining his household."

"Yes, Mother." Caiaphas knew his mother respected Annas. Her words said as much. But there was a hesitation in her voice that he did not understand.

"Joseph." Suddenly Hadassah spoke with urgency, clearly having made up her mind. "There is something I must tell you, something you should know."

"It is the story of events that happened many years ago, on the night you were born. You know that I was not well as I carried you. The labor came unexpectedly, before I was at term. During the labor pains, your father feared for both your life and for mine. The midwives who guided my labor were afraid I would not live through it. They cautioned your father to prepare for the worst."

"I know this, Mother."

Hadassah pressed on as if he had not spoken. "At that time, there was great unrest in the city. Herod had just died, and Joazar was serving as high priest. Herod's son Archelaus took control of our city, and his legions filled the streets. It was during the Feast of Unleavened Bread. Many pilgrims had come to the temple to worship, flocking from the hills and local towns so that the city was full of commotion and flurry. Archelaus took great pains to show that he was worthy of taking his father's place, and he did so with an expression of power and might that angered many. Joazar did his best to appease Archelaus and assure him that all would be peaceful during the celebration."

"But as with the recent incident at the temple, it was not so simple." Here she paused, and Caiaphas knew she was thinking of his father. A look of pain crossed her face. But she shook her head and continued. "During the feast, a skirmish began between the worshippers and the soldiers, and the crowd lost control. Some of Archelaus's men were stoned to death."

Caiaphas's eyes grew wide. He knew that killing a Roman soldier was a capital offense. No amount of negotiation would be able to appease the Roman authorities after that.

"Archelaus's forces were swift and deadly. They were given orders to destroy anyone in their path." Hadassah looked down at her son, her eyes wet with the memory. "They had no respect for the temple, and for those worshipping there. Your father was on guard when the soldiers descended. His mind was on me, at home, laboring, and he prayed for us as he made his rounds. But still he was committed to his duty to protect the temple, especially during this holiest of days. It was hours past sunset, and Joazar and Annas and their fellow priests were in the place of slaughtering, readying the sacrifices for the following day. They were all so young. Annas had been initiated to the priesthood only two years before. It was Joazar's first time overseeing the holiday as high priest. Your father was a bit older, and more knowledgeable in the ways of the Romans. It was he who first recognized that something was terribly wrong."

Caiaphas sat upright, listening intently to his mother's story. His father had never spoken of the night he was born. While he knew that there had been a battle that night, he had never been told more than that.

"Archelaus's soldiers surrounded the temple, blocking every gate and ensuring that those inside were trapped. Your father acted quickly, summoning all of the temple guards and instructing them to protect Joazar and the rest of the priests at all cost. Most of the priests were taken to the Chamber of Hewn Stone, where the council meets to determine affairs of the community. The guards set up sentries at the two doors, and your father charged them to defend the entrances with their lives, if need be.

"But your father knew that Joazar had to be protected in a different way. If the Roman soldiers broke through the guards' defenses, he knew that no mercy would be given to the high priest. It was your father who smuggled Joazar across the temple courtyard into the Chamber of the Hearth, and led him to the underground ritual bathing chamber that lay beyond the far wall. Annas and Joazar had been close since childhood, and Annas's love for his friend and respect for the office of the high priesthood meant that he would not leave Joazar alone. So the two men barricaded themselves within the small chamber, while your father stood guard outside.

"The fighting was fierce and deadly. Archelaus's legions killed three thousand of our people that day. Men, women, children... everyone who had come to worship God at the temple. Many of the priests and the palace guard died defending the temple from the assault. But your father stood firm against any who tried to pass him. As the fighting was dying down, and he could see that the way was clear, he led Joazar and Annas out of the temple through the Offering Gate, their cloaks over their heads just in case anyone might recognize them, their priestly robes left behind in case they were apprehended."

Hadassah smiled softly. "My labor was progressing as the fighting in the temple was ending. Just as you emerged from my womb, whole and perfect, your father arrived at our home with these two men, planning to conceal them there until it was safe for them to make their way back to the Upper City. The three of them were greeted by the midwives attending me, and they learned of your birth. Your father's tears of joy mingled with the blood and sweat that covered his face from the fighting, and both Joazar and Annas rejoiced with him at the birth of his long-hoped-for son. They declared that they would always be in his debt, and pledged to protect our young family, whatever the future held. To this vow they have remained faithful. Even after Joazar was deposed by Archaelaus, and spent years advising rather than leading the council before being reappointed to the high priesthood, he never forgot your father's loyalty and bravery. And Annas has always been good to us, thoughtful and kind."

Hadassah took her son's hands in hers and looked deeply into his eyes. "Your father saved the lives of both Joazar and Annas that day.

They have been able to achieve greatness in the eyes of our people and in the eyes of God because of your father's courage and sacrifice. And they are also in his debt for the way he gave his life for the temple in this latest conflict, defending it yet again against those who would seek to defile it. Never forget that they care for you, not out of pity or charity, but out of gratitude and duty. You are worthy of their attention and their consideration. You are the son of a great man, Joseph. You have greatness in you."

Now Caiaphas was the one whose eyes were wet with tears. He withdrew his hands from his mother's in order to wipe them. "I understand, Mother. Thank you for telling me."

Hadassah sighed. "I do not know what the future holds, my son. But whatever God has in store, we will face it together. Tomorrow is the start of a new life for us." With that, she rose and began to gather the remains of the meal for the last time in their home, as Caiaphas sat, his mind full of all she had said.

CHAPTER 3

"Joseph. Joseph!" Rivkah's cheeks were flushed and she was out of breath as she turned the corner and ran down the stone stairs that led to the lower courtyard of Annas's majestic home. She ducked her head into the storeroom and glanced around, almost missing where Caiaphas was hiding behind the wine casks and below the dried herbs hanging from the vaulted ceiling in large bunches. She had nearly turned to go when she caught sight of the corner of his garment, peeking out from behind one of the larger casks. "Aha!" she shouted. "I found you!" And with that, she turned and fled, leaving him to disentangle himself from his hiding place and rejoin the game. Upstairs, the other children overheard Rivkah's discovery, and squealed as she raced back to them.

Life at Annas's house had settled into an easy rhythm almost immediately. As Annas predicted, Hadassah and her young son had been welcomed into the household with warmth and care. Tova, Annas's wife, was a striking woman, her dark eyes laughing like her daughter's, her raven hair always coming loose from its modest braid and curling at her temples and at the nape of her neck. She was younger than Hadassah, and lively despite having already given birth to five children. It was clear that Annas was captivated by his bride of more than a dozen years. Their mutual admiration filled the entire household with a satisfaction that permeated even down to the household servants.

When Caiaphas and his mother first arrived, he had found it tremendously discomforting to be served by adults. The first several times that Lydia, a servant woman with a kind smile, had brought him his evening meal, he had risen to help her. "Sit, my boy," she said with a laugh, as she piled his plate high with roast lamb, cucumbers and onions seasoned with cumin and coriander. "You must allow me to do my job." She and her husband, Silas, were the primary servants of the household, and had been with the family of Annas for many years. Silas was the house steward and supervised the other servants, while Lydia ran the kitchen and the storerooms and made sure the house was always well-stocked and prepared for any guests who might come to call. As an influential member of the priest's council, Annas was often consulted on matters of importance to the community. While much of this discussion took place at the temple, it was not unexpected for his fellow priests to join the family for a midday or evening meal before retiring to discuss temple matters. Lydia took pride in making sure there was always plenty of food to go around. She especially delighted in seeing the young men clean the plates she set before them.

Joazar and his younger brother Simon were frequent evening guests. Though different in both age and temperament, the two clearly shared a love of good food and good wine. Annas's household provided both. Tova was a great addition to the meals as well, her joyful laugh ringing out often as she teased young Simon for his voracious appetite and chided her husband for bringing him home. "Simon, careful or there will be nothing left for the rest of us! But look how happy you make Lydia, to see you enjoying her fine cooking." Tova was gracious and magnanimous, fully comfortable in her role as the lady of this grand household. She made everyone from the humblest servant to the high priest himself feel welcome. Hadassah she treated with earnest respect and gentle care, encouraging her to rest more and worry less. Caiaphas could tell that his mother was grateful to see that they were not a burden to their hosts. Relieved of her household chores, Hadassah spent the majority of her days spinning and weaving, producing handsome fabric that she would present to Tova with shy gratitude. Tova's exclamations of delight over the tightly woven, even stitches were more than enough to make Hadassah feel that her small contribution was of value to the household.

Their new home was grander than any structure Caiaphas had seen other than the temple itself. Set on the eastern slope of the Upper City, it was two stories tall. From the rooftop the temple itself was visible, with its golden facade and white marble columns glimmering in the sun. In the morning light it shone like a beacon, calling all to marvel at the grandeur and magnificence of the God worshipped there. The house also boasted an expansive view of the Upper City and of their neighbors' homes, impressive in their own right. But the parts of Annas's home that most captivated Caiaphas were the interior rooms, from the fresco chamber with its red and yellow plastered panels, to the vestibule with its elaborate mosaic tile. Mosaics covered many of the floors, and the children had devised numerous games involving the detailed geometric patterns and floral designs. Coming from a home where the floors were beaten clay, and no amount of sweeping could ever rid them of the reddish dust that settled on everything, Caiaphas was fascinated by the clean, cold tiles that stayed cool to the touch no matter how hot a day it was outside.

The home also boasted no fewer than four ritual bathing chambers, important for a priest who had to maintain spiritual cleanliness in order to serve at the temple. The baths, which were filled by underground springs that flowed beneath the house, were a peaceful respite from the busy household above, the stillness punctuated only by the slow swish of water flowing between chambers. Whenever he could get away, Caiaphas would creep down to the baths to sit in the silence and allow himself to be lulled by the cool darkness of the water, ebbing and flowing through the underground stone tunnels.

In the afternoons, he and the other children would eat their midday meal in the main courtyard of the house, basking in the open air and devouring the food Lydia had prepared for them. When they were finished, they would entertain themselves playing games like the one he had just lost to Rivkah. Often they were joined by the two youngest children of the household. Theo, who was five, was forever trying to keep up with his older siblings. Often, he would find himself frustrated by something Eleazar had challenged him to do that was just beyond his abilities. But he was game for anything, and wanted nothing more than to be a part of their play. Matthias, who was barely walking, would squeal with disappointment anytime he was left too far behind. He would eventually give up on this pursuit and go in search of his mother. Tova would soothe him with a date or a bit of honey before returning him to the group and chastising the older children for excluding him. Eleazar would apologize to his mother, and then wait until she was out of sight before proposing some newer, more ambitious game.

But the biggest change for Caiaphas was that he now rose before daylight with Eleazar, Jonathan, and Annas, and joined them as they made their way to the temple. When they arrived, Annas would hand the boys over to Simon, who would lead them to a group of other boys, all between six and twelve years old, gathered in the southwest corner of the Women's Court under the eaves. Over the course of the morning, they would be instructed by two young priests in their letters, in Scripture memorization, and in arithmetic. Jonathan was studious and deliberate, if reticent to recite aloud. Eleazar seemed to see his schooling primarily as an opportunity to incite laughter in the boys around him. The priests, who urged him to take his lessons seriously, sometimes struggled to keep from laughter themselves. They remembered all too well what it was like to be a boy, sitting for hours on a hard, stone bench, listening, repeating, and reciting in an ever-increasing loop as the passages to memorize grew longer and more complex.

Caiaphas's thirst for learning was nearly insatiable. By the time he had been in Annas's home for a month, he had already committed to memory all of the required passages for a boy his age. It was thrilling to raise his voice among the other boys, reciting aloud within the temple walls passages from the Hallel: "The Lord has remembered us; he will bless us; he will bless the house of Israel; he will bless the house of Aaron; he will bless those who fear the Lord, both the small and the great." Caiaphas indeed felt blessed, and at times could scarcely believe his good fortune.

But his favorite part of the morning was when the students were ushered into the closed chamber where the high priest and his council gathered. The priests filled one side of the large room, but the boys were allowed to stand at the other end of the chamber and silently observe the proceedings. As the priests evaluated cases, debated issues of morality and meditated on the Scriptural underpinnings of their decisions, their solemn voices rose and fell with passion and power. Their priestly garments added a level of gravitas and authority to their words. Here even Eleazar fell silent. Caiaphas felt he would nearly burst with the pleasure of witnessing these great men seeking truth and wielding their influence as they sought to honor God and the temple with every word and deed. The memory of his father loomed large in these moments. He imagined Abel proudly looking on, gratified to see his son finally among his peers in this holy place.

Annas and Joazar were both nearly always present on these occasions, and Caiaphas took great pains to pay attention to any word either of them spoke. He was always fascinated by the way Annas maneuvered the proceedings, encouraging discussion among those he knew shared his opinions, but never letting those he disagreed with feel as if they were not being heard. Annas was nimble in his approach to the Scriptures, always able to defend his position with a passage that left others shaking their heads in respectful awe of his verbal dexterity. Joazar was less demonstrative in his leadership, holding back and allowing Annas to do the hard work of convincing the council, and only then stepping in to make a pronouncement or to ask for consensus. They were an impressive pair. Caiaphas felt sure that even the thorniest spiritual or political matter would not be beyond their ability to resolve together.

CAIAPHAS AND HADASSAH had been a part of Annas's household for just over eight weeks when the discussions regarding the succession of the high priesthood took a dramatic turn. As Simon had confided in Hadassah on the evening before their move, the relationship between the Roman governor Cyrenius and Joazar had soured considerably in the aftermath of the revolt at the temple. Caiaphas knew from the meetings of the council that pressure was mounting to replace Joazar. Annas had gone to meet with Cyrenius multiple times in the hopes of dissuading him from forcing a change. Now those conversations appeared to have come to an irreconcilable end.

On this morning, Joazar paced the floor of the council chamber as the other members sat alongside the two walls that flanked his seat. While the rest of the council sat on long wooden benches, the high priest was normally seated in an ornately carved chair mounted with crimson curtains on either side, giving it the appearance of a throne. But today Joazar could not sit still. Annas, who stood directly to his right and matched his friend's energy and intensity, was doing his best to strike a tone of measured practicality.

"Joazar, the order has already been given. I am afraid we must comply. Believe me when I say that I take little pleasure in it. But you of all people know that we operate as a body. Whether it is you or I who sit in the high priest's seat, it is our collective wisdom that guides the temple and leads our people. Remember the Proverbs... 'by wise guidance you can wage your war, and in abundance of counselors there is victory.'"

Joazar sighed. When he turned to Annas, his tone was bitter if resigned. "Old friend, these are the words of a man about to take power, speaking to one about to lose it. I have no doubt that you will guide us well. There is no one else I would rather see appointed in my stead. But to lose this high seat twice due to pressure from our Roman conquerors is hard to stomach. I do not understand God's plan in this."

Several of the council murmured their assent, and one priest spoke, saying, "Are we sure that there is nothing more that can be done?"

Annas silenced them with a wave of his hand. "When I first met with Cyrenius, the talk was of deposing and banishing our high priest from Judea." He looked quickly at Joazar. "I persuaded him that Joazar was a necessary member of our body, and that a change in the high priesthood would more than demonstrate Roman power over us." He grimaced as he appeared to be remembering the disrespectful words spoken to him by the Roman governor, irreverent toward the high office being so casually manipulated by outsiders.

Then his voice quickened as he strode across the room to where the boys were standing, straight-backed and riveted by the proceedings. "And we must think beyond ourselves, Joazar. Your time as high priest may be over, but a new generation is before us. If we are prudent in the way we manage these Romans, we can secure a better future for our sons." He looked meaningfully at Eleazar and Jonathan, and even glanced briefly at Caiaphas, whose pulse quickened at being included. "Given the fickle way these Romans assert themselves into the management of our priests, I have no illusions about how long I might hold this office. But your brother Simon will be ready for the high priesthood before too long. If it is in my power to return the title back to the house of Boethus when my time is up, it will be my honor to do so." Simon, who had been standing against the far wall away from the proceedings, raised his head at the sound of his name, then lowered it sheepishly.

Now the murmuring among the council was approving. Even Joazar had to smile, though it was a wry one. "Annas, save your charm and your flattery for your wife. It will do no good here." But despite his protestation, Joazar seemed less agitated than before. Sighing, he settled himself into the high priest's chair, relishing the position one final time. Then he gestured to Simon, who came quickly.

"Bring me a blank scroll before Annas plans out the entire lineage of the high priesthood for the next generation. I will write to Cyrenius and confirm my support of this transition. We will submit to this change for the good of the temple." Here his tone grew even more formal, and he spoke in his full capacity and role as high priest, making his final pronouncement. "Annas, son of Seth, I acknowledge your appointment as high priest by order of Cyrenius, governor of Syria and Judea. I submit myself to your priestly authority, and pledge to serve alongside you as you have need of me. May God grant you favor and longevity, and may this transition bring about a new chapter of peace and prosperity for our people."

Annas stepped forward as Joazar rose, and the two men embraced. Caiaphas watched with wonder as Joazar removed the breastplate encrusted with twelve precious stones representing the twelve tribes of Israel, and lowered it over Annas's head. Annas bowed, and when he stood, the council breathed a collective sigh. Caiaphas glanced over at Eleazar, who stared open-mouthed at his father, for once appearing to appreciate the solemnity of the moment.

ON THE WALK home for the midday meal, Annas was in a generous mood, clearly relieved that the transition of power had gone so smoothly. He physically appeared no different than he had been that morning, since the breastplate and other tokens of the office had been removed and were being safely stored at the temple until his official announcement to the people the following day. But it was evident that a weight had been lifted from his shoulders. As he strode along the short bridge from the temple that led almost directly back to their home, he surveyed the townspeople on the narrow streets below them. Women with empty satchels made their way to market, their heads bent under the heat of the midday sun. Pilgrims hurried along in the direction of the temple, bleating sheep in tow. Smiling broadly, Annas turned back to his companions and looked down at his eldest son.

"And so Eleazar, you are now the son of the high priest. Do you think this will finally encourage you to listen to your teachers? The reports I receive of you are not those befitting a priestly family. Watch out, or your younger brother will usurp you before you know it." He ruffled Jonathan's hair. "Or Joseph here." He looked fondly at the boy walking just behind him. "Ha!" His laugh reverberated along the steps they took to enter the vestibule. "Before the year is out, he will have overtaken the rest of you in both learning and holiness. And then what will you do? Will you take up a trade while this young man takes up the priesthood in your place?" Caiaphas stopped short, alarmed at the implication being made, even in jest. While he wanted nothing more than to join the ranks of the priesthood, he had no desire to make an enemy of his closest friend in the process.

He was relieved when Eleazar chuckled alongside his father, clearly unconcerned. "Yes, father, I will leave my studies and tend goats for my trade. Or become a carpenter and build wooden benches for other priests to inhabit." He grinned. "Or I will become a priest alongside Jonathan and Joseph and serve the temple as is my familial duty. The son of the high priest should have many options open to him, no?"

"Then I shall call you goatherder from now on, brother."

Rivkah's small face peeked out from the reception room where she had been waiting for them, eavesdropping on their conversation. She was always anxious for them to return from the temple. The mornings were dull for her, stuck at home with Tova, Hadassah, and the servants. She had been educated as much as was required for a woman. While she had been quicker at her studies than either of her brothers, she was also expected to acquire the skills needed to manage a household of her own one day. These lessons she learned alongside the servants, watching Tova manage the affairs of their home and following Lydia around the house as she executed the tasks that each day required. Sometimes she was allowed to join Lydia when she went to the market to purchase spices, dried fish, and other items. But most of the time she stayed at home. Hadassah, who keenly felt her boredom, had taken her under her wing and was teaching her to spin, a practice that Rivkah found enjoyable if a bit tedious. But it was better than being shuffled amongst the servants. Hadassah encouraged her in her memorization of Scripture and her letters as they worked, so there were times when she felt that the spinning lessons were more like school than anything else she might otherwise experience.

Annas burst into a smile at his daughter's impudence. While he was sometimes firm with his sons, he was never able to keep himself from being charmed by Rivkah, so much the picture of his wife but with more fire and an even sharper wit. "Yes, my dear, you must call your brother goatherder. Or you may call him son of the high priest, for that he is now as well."

"Oh, Father!" Rivkah ran to Annas and threw her arms around his waist. "What an honor! I am so pleased. I must go tell Mother." And with that she was off, braid swinging, determined to be the first to spread the good news throughout the household.

CHAPTER 4

The early years of Annas's high priesthood were some of the most peaceful that Judea had seen in generations. Joazar had been reluctant to get involved in the politics of the region, and would have been content dealing only with the affairs of the temple and its methodic structure of ritual, sacrifice, and cleansing. But Annas was deeply concerned with what went on outside the temple walls. He had watched his friend lose his grip on the high priesthood twice, and understood all too well that the management of the temple was only one aspect of his role as high priest.

Although his official duties and obligations kept him occupied the majority of each day, Annas quickly developed a broad network of scribes and tradesmen who served as his eyes and ears throughout the city, keeping track of everything from the largest conflicts between prominent families to the smallest disagreements among the merchants in the marketplace. True to his nature, Annas's appetite for information was voracious. His ability to remember the details of even the most minute circumstances and events made him a limitless source of knowledge. Caiaphas was constantly amazed at his ability to recall even a rural worshiper, in town only for one of the festivals. He marveled at the way Annas would inquire after the man's family by name.

Annas's desire to remain involved in matters of state stretched beyond the walls, not just of the temple, but of the city itself. He spent a portion of each day sending and receiving correspondence, and kept Simon and his fellow priests busy transcribing letters to those Annas believed to be allies in his quest to maintain peace and order. He was vigilant in his respect for the laws of the Scriptures, and maintained them without exception. But he had no qualms about reaching out beyond the priesthood to build relationships with Romans and other outsiders who might prove useful.

Caiaphas, who at this point had mastered not only Hebrew but Greek as well, and had excelled far beyond his thirteen years, was occasionally enlisted to transcribe and deliver letters to messengers who would carry them to their final destinations, whether via land or sea. Annas found Caiaphas to be both bright and trustworthy. Unlike other boys his age, Caiaphas never seemed to feel the need to brag to others about his participation in temple affairs. Simon, now a well-respected member of the priest's inner circle, had taken Caiaphas under his wing. He had taught him much, not only about the different personalities on the council and the ways Annas worked to keep the peace, but about the long-held tensions and disagreements that occasionally flared even among the most pious of priests.

The handoff of the high priesthood from Joazar to Annas had been graciously done, and the two continued to work in concert on many of the daily concerns of the temple. But the differences in the way they viewed the Romans occasionally led to impassioned conversations that echoed across the council chamber into the courtyard beyond. While many members of the council agreed with Annas that the Romans were powerful allies and worth keeping close, a faction of those who had been Joazar's ardent admirers were skeptical of Annas's methods. His constant correspondence with Roman authorities especially drew the ire of some of the older priests, many of whom had served in the years when Herod reigned in Judea. These priests remembered all too well a time when the man with the most power in the region cared more for Roman pleasures and esteem than he did for the people or the temple.

Herod the Great, whose rule had stretched over three decades and ended just before Caiaphas was born, had not had an easy relationship with the priesthood from the beginning. Although he claimed to be loyal to the God of the Jews, and was himself the son of a convert, Herod had been appointed as king of Judea by the Roman senate. His taste for opulence and his love of Roman art and architecture did nothing to endear him to the priests. Despite considerable contributions to the architecture of the region, and to the temple itself, he was always seen as a foreigner by the leadership in Jerusalem. A jealous and volatile man, especially in his later years, Herod left in his wake a legacy of bitterness and violence. Few wept when his death brought an end to his reign. In his efforts to cater to both Roman and Jewish interest, many felt Herod had lost his way, and failed both.

Caiaphas, who listened to Simon's explanation of these matters in disbelief, lost no time in expressing his ardent opinion that Annas was nothing like Herod. Annas was a priest first, faithful and pure. His dedication to God and to the temple was absolute. His dealings with Rome were merely pragmatic, not to mention shrewd. Simon chuckled at the boy's fervor, but did not disagree.

CAIAPHAS'S CONVICTION as to the value of Annas's approach was confirmed one afternoon as he sat in a corner of the council chamber, his reed pen at the ready to transcribe Annas's response to a letter he had just received. As Annas paced the length of the chamber, Simon read aloud from the parchment that lay in his hands, delivered that morning from the Roman governor Coponius. While many members of the council still held Coponius responsible for the revolt in the temple that had led to Abel's death, Annas had seen fit to make peace with the man. They had established a relationship of mutual if wary respect. Now it seemed that the time of Coponius's service was coming to an unexpected end.

"My dear Annas," the letter began. "You of all people know that my term in Judea has not been without its difficulties." Here Annas snorted, then gathered himself and gestured for Simon to continue. "I have just received word that my appearance has been requested by my superiors in Rome. From the whispering amongst those I trust in the capital, I believe it is likely I will be relieved of my responsibilities in this region when I arrive." This was news. Annas looked up from his pacing, surprised. "I have reason to believe that my replacement is a young man named Marcus, a cavalry solider who has risen in the ranks quickly and has made himself indispensable to several important generals. He is ambitious, and will surely begin his term eager to prove himself."

Annas had stopped pacing entirely now, and leaned against one of the columns in the chamber. Simon took a breath, and read on. "Moreover, if my suspicions are correct, I do not believe Marcus's term will be of length. He is far too attracted to power to remain at an outpost, far from Rome, without exposure to those who have so far aided in his aspirations. I anticipate that this post of mine may go through a number of hands quickly. I confess I do not know what this will mean for you or your people in the years to come."

Here Simon paused again before continuing. "You have been fair and reasonable in your dealings with me, noble Annas, and I wish to aid you if I can. As I depart for Rome, unsure where my path will lead, there is a man whose acquaintance I would urge you to make. His name is Gratus. He, like Marcus, is a young soldier in the Roman service. A man of thoughtful temper, Gratus is politic in his speech and insightful in the ways of diplomacy. He is a favorite of the emperor's step-son Tiberius, and it is likely that his star will rise along with his patron's. It would do well for you to number him among your friends, and to impress upon him your willingness to work alongside the governor in charge of Judea to maintain the peace and prosperity of the empire."

Annas's eyes brightened, and he continued his pacing as Simon read, his robe barely sweeping the floor as he swiftly made his way around the room. "When I am in Rome, I will speak to Gratus on your behalf, and will recommend that he travel to Jerusalem before too long so that you may meet and discuss these matters in person. A letter of welcome from you would help to reinforce your willingness to receive him. If we do not meet again before I leave, please remember me to the council. I bid you good health and good fortune."

Simon lowered the parchment and looked at Annas, who had turned back toward them. Annas smiled, and looked at the two young men. Caiaphas was leaning forward in anticipation of his response. Simon stood stiffly, clearly uncertain as to the proper reaction to the missive. Annas spread his arms wide, and his smile broadened.

"And just when we thought things had become a little too staid in our fair city. The merchants all getting along, the council bickering less than ever... but here is Coponius, making sure that our lives are not too dull."

Simon looked apprehensive at Annas's lighthearted tone. "I mean no offense, teacher. But is this not concerning news? This Marcus sounds like he will be a challenging force, and I do not understand how making the acquaintance of a young Roman soldier with neither title nor position is a worthy use of your precious time."

"Ah, but my boy," Annas said gently, as if explaining something to one of his younger children, "do you not understand? Coponius must be careful, as one can never know into whose hands a letter might make its way. But you must listen to what he did not say as well as to what he did. Coponius is reassuring us that Marcus can be easily manipulated. I know his kind. As long as Marcus believes that he is the one in charge, the lord of his post, he will be satisfied. He will want only to be able to send back a glowing report to the ones he is keen to impress. All we need to do is to provide him with sufficient fodder for his correspondence, something to brag about at his suppers when visitors come to call. Remember that the lofty pride of men will be humbled, and our God alone exalted. No, I do not think he will be a problem for us."

Annas bent down to where Caiaphas sat, and looked thoughtful.

"The most interesting part of this letter is the introduction to Gratus. Coponius clearly knows more than he says. This Gratus will have a hand to play in our region yet, we can be sure. And Coponius will pave the way for us to show this young man that we are no threat to Roman rule, that we will work with him rather than against him." Annas rose, and turned toward the doorway that led to the Court of the Israelites. "I am intrigued by this news, and not at all troubled. We will weather this transition as we have weathered others, with God's help and with our wits about us."

He turned back to where Caiaphas still sat, considering Annas's words. "Return with me to the temple after the midday meal, Joseph. We will write a response to Coponius, thanking him for this information and reassuring him that we will welcome Gratus whenever he determines to visit us. For now, gather the others and let us return home. Tova will wonder what has happened to us, and Lydia will scold us if the food has grown cold in our absence." He nodded to Simon, who rolled the parchment and returned it to the cylindrical scroll jar that held Annas's daily correspondence.

THE PARTY that made its way back to Annas's house was larger now, as both Theo and Matthias were old enough for proper schooling. While the younger boys ran ahead, Caiaphas hung back with Jonathan, who had grown in stature but not in boldness in the years since Caiaphas and Hadassah had joined the household. Jonathan could tell that Caiaphas had something on his mind, but saw no need to question his friend. If Caiaphas had something to share, he would share it. In the meantime, Jonathan was content to walk in silence.

Their reverie was broken by Eleazar, who noisily ran to catch up with them and slapped Caiaphas on the back as he approached. At fifteen, Eleazar had finally begun to take his responsibilities at the temple more seriously, much to his father's relief. But he remained boisterous and jovial when not on temple grounds. Like Annas,

Eleazar could charm nearly anyone. He was already able to make any of the servant girls of their household blush when he praised their cooking or admired their weaving. But he lacked the discipline and self-control of his father. Annas was forever reminding him of his duty, although the warning often fell on deaf ears.

Once, when Caiaphas and Jonathan had gone up to the roof to get some fresh air on a hot summer afternoon, Jonathan had asked Caiaphas if he thought Eleazar would be high priest one day. It was an unexpected question from the usually-reserved Jonathan. Caiaphas thought for a long time before he answered.

"Your brother is the oldest child, and it seems likely that he will someday wear your father's robes at the temple. But I wonder whether he is not better suited to a different role within the priesthood. Think about what he could do if he were in charge of the sacrifices, or managed the temple donations. Half the city would be charmed out of their firstborn lambs before every festival, and the temple storehouses would fill with trinkets given to him by the women of the city." Jonathan grinned at his friend, and nodded his agreement with this assessment of his brother.

"And what about you?" Caiaphas was curious. "Do you not one day hope to become high priest as well? You are studious enough, and no one would ever accuse you of being rash or easily swayed. You would do honor to your father's name."

"I disagree." Jonathan clasped his knees to his chest and looked out over the rooftops as he continued, for a moment appearing far younger than his eleven years. "I am not meant for leadership, Joseph. I have no need of power, and I enjoy silence far too much to enjoy the bustle of the temple, especially on the days of the festivals." He shifted his gaze toward Caiaphas, and looked at him thoughtfully. "You will make a far better priest than either of us. I know my father already sees you as another son. I would not be surprised to see you take his place one day."

Caiaphas squirmed. He knew that Annas valued him highly. Simon had shared with him Annas's dissatisfaction with the other boys and young priests at the temple vying for the favor and attention of those in charge. "They are all fawning, insincere creatures," Annas had told Simon. "There is not one of them I would trust with a delicate errand, save young Joseph. Oh, they know the Scriptures well enough, and they appear pious when it suits them. But the role of a priest is one of perseverance and devotion. Joseph demonstrates both in all he does." Simon had sworn Caiaphas to secrecy, and there was no way that Jonathan had overheard the conversation. Still Caiaphas felt embarrassed, even as he swelled with pride to think that Annas had spoken so highly of him.

The boys' conversation was interrupted by Rivkah, who had been looking for them for some time. "There you are!" She reached the part of the rooftop where they sat, pushed the stray curls back from her forehead, settled her skirts, and sat down next to Caiaphas. "What are we discussing? The gossip in the marketplace? The most recent declaration of the council? Or whether one of these days Matthias will actually learn to recite his letters? Tell me, brother," and here she arched her neck around Caiaphas to look at Jonathan, "how can it be that Annas's youngest son is already five and still prattles on like a babe in arms? Those temple priests of yours are having no success with him. Perhaps it is time I take charge of his education and tutor him myself!" She laughed. Caiaphas could not fully hide the smile that crept onto his face as he looked at her, though he tried to look disapproving at her suggestion.

Rivkah had grown even more beautiful. At eleven, she was the picture of her mother, with a touch of her father's impish grin and powerful presence. Like Eleazar, she had learned her way around the household, and could charm Silas into giving her just about anything she wanted. But she was thoughtful too, and could be gentle when she chose to be. Caiaphas was fascinated by her. Often he found himself unsure of his words when she was around. She was always teasing him, asking him questions with a sideways glance so that he could not tell if she was serious or in jest, and laughing when he fumbled over an earnest response.

But the thing that endeared her most to him was the way she treated Hadassah, who had grown even more frail in the last few years. Rivkah was forever tending to her, convincing Lydia to save her the choicest bits of lamb and sweetest dates, and sitting with her, talking quietly as they wove together. Caiaphas knew that his mother loved Rivkah. She had more than once expressed her hope that they might one day be family. Caiaphas had blushed a deep red the first time his mother suggested it, knowing that the son of a temple guard was an unlikely suitor for Annas's only daughter. Still, when he lay awake at night after the household was quiet, he sometimes allowed his mind to wander in that direction. Imagining Rivkah's laughing eyes locked on his own, he entertained the hope that perhaps it was not beyond the realm of possibility.

As Annas and the boys entered the vestibule, they were greeted by Lydia, who was beaming at them. "Master Annas, you are wanted in the reception room." She looked down at the boys. "You should all go. There is great news to be shared."

They made their way to the large hall to their left, where Tova, Hadassah, and many of the servants of the household were waiting. Rivkah had taken her place next to Hadassah, and Caiaphas caught her eye before quickly looking down at his feet.

Annas was clearly tired from the long morning at the temple. He greeted his wife with a hint of frustration in his voice. "What is it, love? We are weary and eager to eat. Can this not wait until after we have filled our stomachs?"

"Patience, husband." Tova's voice was warm but firm. "You will be glad of the delay. Silas and Lydia will be here in a moment."

As she spoke, the household steward and his wife entered carrying large trays piled high with the finest delicacies that money could buy. Behind them, two servants carried large pitchers of wine, and set them down on a round stone table near the middle of the room. Tova moved slowly over to the table, and poured a glass of the rich, red liquid. Raising it above her head, she turned to her husband and said, "My dearest Annas, our home is rich in many things. Our children especially have been a blessing from God. It has been my delight to provide you with so many fine sons and a beautiful daughter." She looked at each of her children in turn, and then returned her gaze to

Annas. "It is my joy to tell you that our home will once again be granted this gift. I am with child. Already I have felt the little one moving within me, healthy and strong, eager to join our family." Putting a hand on her swollen belly, Tova raised her eyes to her husband, who exclaimed and crossed the distance between them in an instant.

"Praise God!" Annas wrapped his arms around his wife, and then immediately let them go, remembering her condition. "This is good news indeed. And you are well, my love?"

It was Hadassah who answered. "She has been examined by the midwives, who believe the child will be here before the next festival. Tova is in good hands, and God has blessed her with a hearty constitution made for this very task." Hadassah's smile was tinged with sorrow, remembering her own struggles, but her gladness was genuine. "Congratulations, Annas. May this child increase your joy, and may God bless your household through this birth."

"Thank you, Hadassah." Annas took her hand. "I pray that our households will continue to experience blessing together." He gestured to all in the room, with the generous air of one who had just been given a great prize. "Now let us feast!"

The merriment continued for the rest of the afternoon, and the letter to Coponius was forgotten for the moment. There would be plenty of time to compose a response, and to craft a letter of introduction to Gratus. For now, the house of Annas was full of rejoicing and celebration.

CHAPTER 5

As the midwives predicted, Ben was born just before the Feast of Booths began. Annas's joy at having another healthy son was evident in the way he went about the next eight days of the festival. If possible, he was even more gregarious and welcoming to the worshipers who flocked to the temple than before. As the priests lit the large lamps in the temple courts each night as part of the celebration, it seemed that the entire community was rejoicing at the birth of the youngest son of Annas. During the day, priests carried large stone urns filled with water from the Pool of Siloam up to the temple to be poured over the altar amidst praises and prayers to God. Annas gathered his daily council and was gratified to hear the reports of another successful and peaceful festival. Even with the departure of Coponius, nothing could rob the priesthood of the feeling that all was well, and would be for some time.

Over the next three years, just as Annas expected, Marcus proved to be a relatively easy governor to influence and appease. He arrived shortly after Coponius's departure, and Annas made sure to welcome him immediately. Lydia was given the order to prepare a sumptuous feast for the new governor. Tova, recently returned to her regular duties after the rigors of childbirth, summoned every bit of charm and grace for the occasion. Marcus was duly impressed. From then on, he consulted with Annas on every matter affecting the people or the temple.

Predictably, it was to Annas he came when he was ready to announce his decision to hand over his post. Annas tried not to smile as the young man explained that he was wanted back in Rome, that there were those who had promised him opportunity if he would leave Judea and return to the capital. Annas did not mention that he had already received this information via correspondence with Gratus, who had proven to be as useful as Coponius had suggested he might be. The man replacing Marcus would be another Roman officer, a man named Rufus. He and Rufus had served together, Marcus told Annas, and he was sure that Rufus would govern the territory with the same care and attention he had given it. Annas expressed appropriate regret at the departure of the young governor. He left the meeting satisfied that this change in command would have little impact on current conditions, beyond having to host another feast and impress another eager young Roman soldier, determined to prove himself.

All this he confided to Caiaphas as they walked home from the temple the following day, grateful to have a young man by his side who was eager to listen and quick to understand the intricacies of any situation. He had all but given up trying to have this type of conversation with Eleazar. His oldest son was too hasty in his interpretation, always quick with an opinion or suggestion before he had fully thought through the implications. Eleazar regularly balked at being told what to do, determined to find his own way rather than taking advantage of the wisdom of those who had come before him. At eighteen, Eleazar was expected to join the priesthood within two years. But Annas was not convinced that the boy was ready for the responsibilities of being a temple priest, let alone prepared to take on any substantial role within the temple system. It pained Annas to admit it. But he felt it was necessary to be honest with himself about his offspring, whatever the cost.

His second son Jonathan, while thoughtful and thorough, was

mild-mannered to a fault, and his shyness was an obstacle that Annas worried he might never overcome. A priest needed to be bold, willing to fight when necessary, whether behind closed doors or in public. Jonathan avoided disagreements at all cost, and was inclined to quietly acquiesce even when he disagreed. A leader, it seemed, he was not. It was still too early to tell whether his other sons would have the constitution or mind for the priesthood, although Annas hoped they would prove themselves as they grew. At times, he found himself wishing that Rivkah had been born a boy. His daughter's intellect, wit, and sharp ability to cut through a complicated problem was unmatched among her siblings. She was feisty and self-assured, willing and able to state her mind and stand her ground.

But Caiaphas's talents were prodigious, and the fact that they were not kin meant that his allegiance to Annas was based on more than just familial ties. The boy loved and trusted him. Annas found himself turning to Caiaphas more and more as an integral part of his day, relying on him to talk through pressing matters and thorny situations. While Annas had an entire council of priests available to him, and Joazar remained one of his closest advisors at the temple, Caiaphas was unique, a young man who was not quite his son, but who held all the qualities of a successor and an heir.

As they walked, Caiaphas listened in silence to all that Annas had to share about the transition from Marcus to Rufus. He nodded as Annas finished speaking. "I think your perspective is sound, and that Rufus will be much the same as Marcus has been to us. But what does Gratus tell you of the strategy behind these transitions in the governorship? Do we know anything more from him?"

Annas smiled at his young charge. At sixteen, Caiaphas had grown taller. He now matched Annas in height, although Annas was still far broader and more muscular. But Caiaphas had developed in his own way and had grown handsome, his sandy brown curls cropped close to his head as was the fashion. His face was still mostly bare, with just a hint of growth beginning at his chin. His eyes were inquisitive and wide, similar to a cat's. Their color changed depending on the environment, from a mossy green to a yellowish brown. He held himself with a poise that belied his age, and maintained a balance of respectful deference and quiet self-confidence that reminded Annas of Caiaphas's father, Abel. The only time Annas ever saw Caiaphas uncomfortable was around his daughter Rivkah, and he couldn't fault the boy for that. If anything, it showed his good taste and discernment.

In addition to being bright and loyal, Caiaphas had a quality that Annas had not found either in his sons or in any of the other young men who gathered around him at the temple, a desire to understand the larger picture and a foresight more nuanced than his years suggested. Caiaphas was still young, and prone to believe the best of those around him. But this optimism suited Annas's purposes. He was convinced that with the right training and guidance, Caiaphas had the potential to become a man worthy of the highest levels the priesthood had to offer. Annas was determined to mold Caiaphas into a leader of his own design, one that would allow Annas's reach and influence to stretch beyond his own term and far into the next generation.

Annas sighed. "This is the right question to be asking, my boy. We know that the Romans become uneasy when anyone in the territories is in power for too long. It is only thanks to God's grace that they have not interfered with my own position thus far." Caiaphas nodded, knowing that while God was surely the one at the helm, Annas's seven years as high priest were in large part due to his political savvy and ability to flatter those who might choose to replace him. But he stayed silent and let the high priest continue.

"As long as Caesar remains emperor, Gratus believes we will see these types of transitions in the Roman governorship of Judea. He has led me to believe that Caesar, despite his power, does not trust those under him. One way he guards against rebellion is by making sure that no one stays in one place long enough to stir up trouble. But with Caesar ailing, things may soon change, in both Rome and Judea. Already Tiberius has been granted equal status in governing with Caesar by the Roman consuls. It is likely he will ascend to the throne himself before too much time has passed."

"And what does that mean for Gratus, and for us?" Caiaphas knew that Gratus was a favorite of Tiberius. The rumor was that Gratus, some twenty-five years younger, had become like a second son to Tiberius, and had fought alongside him in his most recent campaign in the service of the emperor. It seemed likely that Gratus would have his pick of positions once Tiberius was in charge.

"For Gratus, I believe it means he will ask to take over the governorship of Judea from Rufus when the time is right."

"Then this is good news indeed for us, is it not?"

Annas sighed, and slowly shook his head. "It may be. I have known Gratus now for some time, and I am still not sure what to make of him." As promised, upon Coponius's dismissal from the governorship, Annas had sent a letter of invitation to Gratus. They had been in correspondence ever since, and Gratus had traveled to Jerusalem twice. Both times he had joined them for a meal at Annas's home. He had even visited the temple, remaining in the Court of the Gentiles out of deference to the temple laws regarding where non-Jews were allowed to go. He seemed to be a pleasant and intelligent young man, obviously fascinated by the customs and practices of those worshipping. He had been kind to the children of Annas's household, praising the looks of the baby Tova held in her arms and entertaining Theo and Matthias with a small spinning top he had brought from the capital.

But Annas couldn't get over the notion that Gratus was sizing up the territory the way a shepherd evaluates a young lamb, looking it over to determine its merits and blemishes, to see whether it would prove a worthy addition to his flock. Gratus was clearly not someone who would be easily manipulated. When the time came, he would not be content to sit back and let Annas dictate the course of events as Marcus had done.

"We will have to pay close attention to these circumstances as they unfold, Joseph. For now, we will handle Rufus as we did Marcus, and pray that he will be of a similar temperament and disposition. The rest we will leave to God as our ultimate refuge and strength." They were nearing the house now, and Annas could see Rivkah waiting for them in the vestibule. "In the meantime, do not concern yourself too much with all of this. You have much better things to occupy your mind." He gestured to his daughter standing in the doorway, and laughed as Caiaphas blushed.

THE EVENING MEAL was a lively one that night. They were joined by Simon and his young bride Julia, who was much loved by the women and children of the household. Julia had been a part of the group of women who had come to attend Ben's birth, and she had endeared herself to Tova with her kind and compassionate bedside manner. She was a sweet girl from a worthy household, and Simon was clearly proud of the way Annas's family had welcomed her into their inner circle. Although they did not yet have children of their own, Julia clearly had a way with little ones. She patiently attended to Ben as he toddled back and forth between her and Tova, begging morsels of food from their plates and lifting up his arms to be held for a moment before squirming to be put down again.

As the bread and meat were passed, Eleazar entertained them all by impersonating some of the older members of the high priest's council. Pulling at his nonexistent beard and wrinkling his forehead, he mumbled his deep concerns as to the amount of grain offerings coming in that week, and whether or not the Gate of Kindling might soon be in need of repairs. Simon and Annas both chuckled, despite themselves, at the all-too-accurate impressions of the elderly priests. Tova chided her son for his impudence, but couldn't help but laugh herself at his antics. As Caiaphas looked down the table at them, and across at Jonathan, Rivkah, and the other children, he was filled with gratitude, struck by the starkness of the contrast between this boisterous company and the life he had known before his father died. He glanced over at his mother, wrapped in a thick woolen shawl despite the warm summer night. As he caught her eye, she smiled weakly at him. Despite her frailty, she always forced herself to join the evening meal. It gave her great pleasure to see her son sitting at the table alongside Annas's other children, included as one of the family.

After the meal was over, Simon and Julia departed, and Caiaphas helped his mother up the stairs to her sleeping chamber. Leaning heavily on his shoulder, she remarked at his stature, as she often did these days. "How like your father you have grown, my son. Strong and sturdy. He would be so pleased to see the young man you have become."

"Hush, Mother." Caiaphas knew that when Hadassah's thoughts turned to Abel, she grew sad and drew inward. It was better for both her spirits and her health if she focused on the present. "Let us not spend our time dwelling on the past. It was you who taught me the wise words of the Scriptures, that for everything there is a season, and a time for every matter under heaven."

"Ah, my child," Hadassah stopped and put her hand on his cheek. "You are wise beyond your years. Yes, you are right. I will do my best to look ahead rather than behind. There is much to anticipate. In just four years you will be ready for your dedication to the temple. And I hope that before then we will have something else to celebrate." She smiled tenderly. "I see the way you and Rivkah look at one another, and Tova and I have discussed the merits of such a union between our two families."

Caiaphas helped his mother gently onto her sleeping mat, and stood up, looking down at her with no small uneasiness. He forced himself to say the next words, much as it pained him to do so. "Mother, I do not know if it is a wise match, as much as I would desire it. Surely the daughter of Annas could find a worthier companion than myself. I have no gifts to give Annas, and we make our home with Rivkah's family. It would be a sorry procession on the wedding day if we leave this house only to return to it again."

Hadassah looked tenderly at her son, in so many ways a man but still a boy. "All the more reason for the two of you to be joined in marriage, Joseph. You are greatly loved by the entire household. Surely you must know that Annas has no objection to the match." Her voice rose in intensity, and she struggled to sit up, holding his hand in hers. "Your father paid a steep brideprice for you long ago. You have no reason to be ashamed of who you are. Rivkah will be the fortunate one to be joined with you." She let go of his hand, and sighed. "Now, I will rest. Thank you, my son, for your attention and care. It is well appreciated."

Feeling restless, Caiaphas returned to the courtyard where the remaining members of the household were still gathered, each occupied with their tasks or recreation for the evening. As Lydia and Silas and the other servants gathered the remains of the meal, Eleazar and Jonathan sat in a corner playing a game made of a thirty-square board and carved stone pieces, while Theo and Matthias watched and cheered them on. Annas and Tova sat in a corner, talking quietly together. Ben sat at Tova's feet, playing with the folds of her robe as she absentmindedly stroked his hair.

Climbing the outer staircase that led to the roof, Caiaphas took a deep breath as he looked out over the Upper City. On warm nights like these, he often brought his sleeping mat up here to make his bed under the stars. He liked the feeling of the evening breeze on his face, especially when he was awakened in the middle of the night by his visions. In the years since he had first begun to have them, they had not ceased, although he was now better able to control himself when they did come. But every time he thought that perhaps they were gone for good, he would wake up in the dark, his palms sweating, his breath rough, and his eyes wide.

He was only a little startled to see that he was not alone on the roof. Rivkah sat with her back to him, near the far edge, looking out across the rooftops. He hesitated for a moment before walking toward her, taking pains to make enough noise so that she would not be startled by his approach.

"Hello, Joseph." She did not turn her head, but gestured at the place beside her. "Come join me." He obliged, taking a seat next to her and surreptitiously admiring the curve of her neck, smooth and white in the encroaching darkness.

They sat in silence, side by side, until Caiaphas felt he should say something. "It is always a good night when Simon and Julia are with us in the evening, is it not? They add a liveliness to our table."

"Yes, and bring out the jester in my brother." Rivkah smirked. "Not that it takes much for Eleazar to put on a show."

Caiaphas laughed. "He does like an audience."

Now it was Rivkah's turn to laugh. "Indeed he does." She paused, and chose her next words more carefully. "Julia has been such a help to my mother with Ben, and I have enjoyed getting to know her. She and Simon seem very happy together."

Caiaphas nodded. "They are a good match."

"Yes. They are fortunate. The other day I went with Lydia to the marketplace and one of the merchants couldn't stop talking about a girl who had just been betrothed to a man three times her age, with an evil temper and a tendency to drink. I am glad for Julia that she has Simon."

Caiaphas swallowed and cleared his throat. "And you, Rivkah? What do you hope for in a husband?"

She smiled and turned to look at him now, her dark eyes overwhelming him with their soft glow. "My dear Joseph," she said, and the words made Caiaphas's stomach drop. "I know exactly what I hope for in a husband. I have known for many years, from when I first saw a young boy across a courtyard, looking so stern and forlorn. My husband will be brave, and strong, and he will become a great priest one day. And you? What do you hope for in a wife?"

Caiaphas found he could not look at her, and he dropped his gaze, letting it rest on her pale hands, folded gently in her lap. "I have little to offer the woman I would have. But I long for a wife who will challenge my mind as well as my heart, who will fill my house with laughter and wit, and who will be my partner in all things."

"Ah," said Rivkah. "Then I have reason to believe we may both be well satisfied when the time comes." With that, she reached out one of her hands, interlacing her fingers with his until they were entwined. They remained there in the dark, Caiaphas's heart gently pounding, until the household lamps were extinguished, and it was time for all to retire for the night.

CHAPTER 6

The morning of the wedding dawned clear and bright. Caiaphas, who had been staying at Joazar's house in the final days of the preparations, was unable to sit still. He paced the courtyard of Joazar's stately home as Simon, Eleazar, and Jonathan looked on, amused. Theo, now fourteen and gangly, had been included in the group of young men who would accompany him in the procession to Annas's house, although Matthias had been deemed too young and remained at home, despite his protests. Caiaphas had already bathed and dressed, and he was wearing an inner garment made of fine linen that Hadassah had woven just for the occasion. Despite her failing health, she was still able to weave beautifully. She had insisted on making all of the wedding clothes for both Caiaphas and his bride. Over this garment, he wore a woolen tunic, dyed a deep blue. His belt was a newly tanned band of leather, still stiff and smelling faintly of cedar. On his head sat a simple crown of beaten gold, a gift from Simon and Julia that Simon had also worn on his wedding day.

It seemed hard to believe that three years had passed since the night he and Rivkah sat on the rooftop of Annas's home, and even harder to believe that they had already been betrothed for nearly a year. It was shortly after his eighteenth birthday when Annas had asked him during one of their daily walks if he was ready for a wife. Caiaphas stumbled over an answer before looking up to see Annas grinning at him. Quickly collecting himself, Caiaphas cleared his throat, aware of the opportunity being presented to him and eager to capitalize on it. "Most honorable Annas, I have no father to negotiate with you the particulars of the contract. All that I own is already yours. But if you will have me, I would like nothing more than to marry your daughter."

Annas chided Caiaphas gently. "Ah, it is not I that will have you, but Rivkah. Fortunately for you, she has already expressed her wishes for the union as well. It pleases me very much to see you joined to my family and to her. I fear she will not be an easy wife, Joseph. She is far too opinionated and bold. There will be times when you will wish your bride had a lesser mind and a slower tongue. But she will love you well, and your home will be one of lively conversation and deep passion."

Caiaphas smiled. "I have had the advantage of living in your home for many years, Annas. Rivkah's temperament and character are well-known to me. The very qualities you caution me against are the ones I most treasure."

Annas nodded. "Excellent. Then it is settled. Let us not waste any more time."

The betrothal ceremony took place two weeks later. Caiaphas and Rivkah readied themselves for the occasion by bathing in one of the chambers in the lower quarters of Annas's house. As Caiaphas sat alone in the cool water, reciting the prayers of cleansing and preparation, he marveled at the prospect of becoming Rivkah's husband. He was no longer as tongue-tied around her. As he had become more comfortable, they had settled into an easy camaraderie punctuated by gentle banter and thoughtful conversations. But she could still electrify him with a look or a touch. He could scarcely believe that soon she would belong to him.

His head full of thought, Caiaphas emerged from the bath, clothed himself in clean robes, and returned to the fresco room with its brilliant panels. Seeing Rivkah, her dark hair wet and shining, plaited down her back, with a pensive look on her own face, he felt suddenly shy. Annas took charge, leading the young couple through the document containing the marriage contract, which lay on a small table next to him. He poured a glass of wine for them to share. After they had each drunk, he smiled heartily and congratulated them.

"You are now betrothed, my children. A year will pass quickly, and before you know it, we will be celebrating your marriage feast. This is a time of preparation. Rivkah, now more than before you must glean from your mother all there is to know about being a wife. I would venture to say she is an able teacher after being married to me all of this time." Annas smiled warmly at his daughter and then turned to his intended son-in-law. "Joseph, you are nearly ready to join the priesthood. Make sure that you continue to pursue your studies zealously. Our God has much still to teach you, not just about being a husband."

How right Annas had been, thought Caiaphas, as he continued to pace, his steps marking time until the marriage procession would begin. The last year had passed as if in a moment. Some of his most treasured times were the evenings when he and Rivkah were able to steal away and sit together on the roof, discussing the particulars of the day and cautiously beginning to share with one another their hopes for the future. But the bulk of his energy was occupied with temple business. He continued to learn the ways of the priesthood in preparation for his dedication, and to become more entwined in the daily proceedings of the council. As Annas's future son-in-law, Caiaphas was rightly perceived by the priests and scribes at the temple as a member of the high priest's family. While it had always been apparent that he was a favorite of Annas, the betrothal solidified his position as an important figure in the next generation of priests. Eleazar, who had already been a member of the priesthood for nearly a year, and had married Meira, the eldest daughter of another well-respected priest, a year before that, teased Caiaphas that the council must have breathed a sigh of relief when the news of the arrangement was shared. "Now they can rest easy that Annas finally has a worthy heir," he said, his dark eyes flashing with mirth at his own joke, enjoying Caiaphas's obvious discomfort. If anything, Eleazar seemed relieved that the burden of carrying his father's legacy forward had been shifted to another, leaving him unfettered from the responsibility.

It was clear even to the least observant members of the council that Annas treated Caiaphas differently than any of the other young men, including his own sons. Although not yet dedicated, Caiaphas was a regular attendee at the daily meeting of the council. While he was not permitted to sit on the council itself, he was never far from the proceedings. It was Caiaphas who first learned of the death of the emperor, shortly after Caiaphas and Rivkah's betrothal, via a messenger from Rome who carried a letter to Annas from Gratus. The news was expected, as Caesar had been ill for some time. Even so, its impact was felt throughout the temple and the city, as merchants and priests alike wondered what it would mean for them. In Annas's response, which he dictated to Caiaphas immediately upon receiving the correspondence, he thanked Gratus profusely for the information, and requested that he keep him abreast of any additional developments. So far, there had been no response.

As the months wore on, some of the priests speculated that the new emperor Tiberius was disinterested in the region of Judea. They hoped that this might mean they would be left to govern themselves with little interference. As predicted, Rufus had proven to be as malleable as Marcus. He seemed content to govern by proxy, as long as he was occasionally briefed with the kind of news he could embellish and share with those whose good opinion he sought. Others expressed concerns that Tiberius was simply biding his time, and worried that at any moment soldiers might descend on the city to instigate a new era of more assertive Roman rule.

But even these uncertainties and fears could not dampen the preparations for the marriage of the high priest's only daughter. The anticipation for the wedding festivities had been building steadily for weeks. Annas's household was in a constant flurry of activity. Silas and Lydia had their hands full making sure that everything was in place for the celebration, which was expected to span several days and include multiple large feasts and gatherings. Tova was in her element. She and Julia spent many mornings sitting together, reviewing all of the details and exclaiming with pleasure when one of them had a new idea for a dish to serve or an accessory to complete Rivkah's bridal attire. Julia was a mother now as well, her baby Eli just a few months old. More than once Tova and Julia's delighted exclamations startled the baby swaddled to her out of sleep and caused him to cry out in surprise.

Rivkah was both excited and amused by all of the fuss being made. She confided to Caiaphas that she was anxious for the day to arrive. "All this commotion, and then it will be over. In less than a week, the last scraps of food will be consumed and the wedding clothes put away, and you and I will be joined together at last." Her smile was dazzling, and he felt the familiar warmth in his chest as she looked at him. At seventeen, there was little trace of the girl he had first encountered in his father's courtyard. She had been replaced by a graceful young woman, still full of life and fire, but tempered by a maturity that made her even more appealing.

Caiaphas's meditation was interrupted by Simon, who approached him now, signaling that it was time to begin the procession. As a respected priest and Caiaphas's close friend, Simon had been chosen to lead the bridegroom to his father-in-law's house, an honor he did not take lightly. Flanked by Eleazar, Jonathan, and Theo, Caiaphas took a last look around Joazar's courtyard and made his way to the street. As they walked the short distance to Annas's home, spectators and well-wishers gathered, their oil lamps lit to symbolically show Caiaphas the way to his bride. Several blew triumphant notes on instruments made from the horns of a ram, while others sang songs of praise. Caiaphas recognized the ancient words from Scripture about the great king's marriage procession. "Go out, O daughters of Zion, and look upon King Solomon, with the crown with which his mother crowned him on the day of his wedding, on the day of the gladness of his heart." Taking a deep breath, Caiaphas reached the vestibule of Annas's house, and entered.

A canopy had been set up in the center of the courtyard. Rivkah sat beneath it, waiting expectantly. Four posts had been erected, and above them stretched a linen prayer shawl, its edges embroidered with royal blue thread. Lilies adorned the tops of the posts where the canopy began, and cascaded down, releasing a sweet aroma that filled the air. These same flowers graced Rivkah's head and entwined in her dark curls and around a delicate golden crown, the partner of the one Caiaphas wore and another gift from Simon and Julia. Her tunic was fine and white, shimmering in the late afternoon light, and thin golden bands encircled both her wrists. Although her face was entirely covered by a gossamer veil, Caiaphas could see that her cheeks were flushed with excitement and anticipation. Behind her stood Tova, glowing with pride as she gazed at her daughter. Hadassah sat just behind them. As the rest of the procession dispersed and joined the other guests, Caiaphas walked toward Rivkah, joining her under the canopy.

Annas stepped forward and stood before the two of them. The marriage scroll from their betrothal had been laid out, along with the wine. As silence settled over the wedding guests, Annas began to pray, reciting the traditional blessings for the couple and praising God for their union. When he had finished, he gestured for them both to rise. Holding the cup high, he turned slightly so that all could hear his words. "My children, may the life you share together be as sweet as the wine you now drink. May God bless you with long life and many children, and may you serve our God and his temple all the days of your life together." He handed the cup to Caiaphas, who drank from it and then gave it to Rivkah. As her lips touched its rim, the guests exploded in a shout of celebration. Annas, his face beaming, raised his hand, and his voice rose above the shouts of the others as he quoted from the Song of Songs, "Eat, friends, drink, and be drunk with love!"

The guests moved boisterously from the courtyard to the majestic reception room where the remainder of the celebration would be held. Thanks to Silas and Lydia, the long table that lined one wall was already filled with large platters of roasted meat piled high and enormous bowls of apples, nuts, and figs. Casks of wine were set in the corner of the room, and the household servants stood ready to serve. A small party of musicians was gathered, their instruments in hand, waiting for the signal from Tova to begin playing. There would be feasting and dancing well into the night, and more the following day.

Meanwhile, Simon led Caiaphas and Rivkah up the stairs to one of the sleeping chambers above. He smiled reassuringly as he left them, and returned downstairs, leaving them alone. Caiaphas turned nervously to his bride. He knew what was expected of them, and thanks to Eleazar, he already knew far too many details about the mechanics of the task at hand. But listening to Eleazar's bawdy chatter was one thing. Standing here before Rivkah, he felt he could not move. He blushed and looked down at their feet, just inches apart from one another.

"Joseph?" Rivkah's voice was soft. She reached for his hand, and as she did, she took a small step toward him so that they were nearly touching. "My husband. Help me with my veil." Her voice released him from his paralysis. Taking up the edges of the garment, he lifted it gently over her head. As her face came into view, he saw that her eyes were shining. Her smile was shy but determined. "Hello." Her smile grew as she gently put a hand on his cheek, and her touch was soft and warm. Caiaphas drew a deep breath, and put his hand over hers.

"Hello, my beautiful bride."

She sighed at his touch, and Caiaphas felt his nervousness melting away. This was Rivkah, the girl from the rooftops, his betrothed, and now his wife. He had nothing to fear.

Rivkah's eyes twinkled as one side of her mouth curved up in a teasing grin. She arched an eyebrow at him as she quoted Scripture, "I am my beloved's, and his desire is for me." Keeping her eyes locked on his, she undid the linen belt that was looped around her wedding garments, and stepped out of her outer robe, leaving only the inner tunic. Caiaphas could see the outline of her body through the fabric, which clung gently to her torso and stopped just below her knees. She smiled. "Well? Is it true, my love?" She paused. "Will you show me?"

Without hesitation, Caiaphas drew her to himself, and pressed his lips to hers, breathless and eager. The festivities downstairs continued with joyful abandon and lively singing and dancing. But Caiaphas and Rivkah heard none of it, captivated by one another and happily oblivious to the celebration below.

CHAPTER 7

Caiaphas and Rivkah had been married for only a few weeks
when a letter finally arrived from Gratus. He was in Caesarea,
where the current governor of Judea made his home, and would be
staying with Rufus briefly before making the three-day journey to
Jerusalem. The news took Annas by surprise, and there was a long
discussion at the council that day full of speculation as to Gratus's
motives and plans. The messenger who delivered the letter was a talk-
ative man. He shared that the visit was also a surprise to the current
governor, which did nothing to assuage the suspicions of those who
felt sure that Gratus was there to take Rufus's place. That evening,
after everyone else had retired for the night, Caiaphas sat awake,
thinking about all he had heard. As he contemplated, he gazed down
at Rivkah, asleep next to him, her curls loose and cascading across her
shoulders in the bed they now shared.

At first, Caiaphas had felt ashamed that he had no residence of his
own to offer his new bride. But as the days passed, he grew increasingly grateful for Annas's generosity and for the opportunity to
remain in the home they both knew so well. Annas was more than
happy to keep his daughter close rather than losing her to another
household. The abundance of his estate meant that Caiaphas could

continue to focus on his duties at the temple, which increased daily in anticipation of his dedication. Rivkah, too, was pleased with the arrangement. Her responsibilities shifted only slightly as Tova encouraged her to take on a greater role in managing the household servants. With her new status as a married woman, Rivkah slipped into her place as a supervisor with ease. Even Lydia, who had known her from birth, accepted her as Tova's surrogate on household matters. Rivkah was a generous but firm mistress. Her competency allowed Tova to focus more on her younger children, and on Caiaphas's mother, who required more care as the days wore on.

Hadassah had been overjoyed to see her son and Rivkah joined as husband and wife. But her health took a turn as soon as the wedding celebrations were over. She now spent most of her time upstairs, and only descended to soak in the sunlight during the warmest hours of the day. It was as if she had mustered up the last of her reserves to weave the wedding clothes and participate in the festivities, and her body was now protesting the expenditure of energy. She grew thinner and paler, and was often unable to stomach the food that Tova lovingly brought to her bedside. Caiaphas worried about her, and prayed that God would grant her a respite from her pain. He feared that the only way she might find relief would be in her final rest.

But the reason he now lay awake was not his mother, but his father-in-law. He could tell that Annas was anxious about Gratus's impending visit. Caiaphas had watched Annas closely ever since Gratus's letter had been read aloud. "I will be there within the week, as we have much to discuss." While he put on a brave face at the temple, there was a clear difference in Annas's demeanor once he was safe in the confines of his own home, or when he and Caiaphas were alone together. In his early forties, Annas remained a commanding figure. Although his beard now contained enough gray hairs that Tova had begun to gently tease him by calling him "old man," he showed no loss of virility or power. But there was something in this development that had shaken him.

For as long as Caiaphas had known him, Annas had been a man in total control, of his household, the council, and his own destiny. From the time he had taken over the high priesthood from Joazar, Annas had led the priesthood with unequivocal strength, his leadership absolute. Even those who grumbled about him or disagreed with his methods had to admit that he had done what many thought impossible, bending the Roman governors to his will with diplomacy and skill. Gratus's arrival in Caesarea felt like a threat to the equilibrium that Annas had so carefully created. As one whose desire for both knowledge and stability was ferocious, Annas seemed unnerved by the uncertainty in the air.

Equally unsettling were the new dreams that Caiaphas had begun to have, temporarily replacing his recurring vision of the temple in flames. This new vision was different, although no less disturbing. In the dream, Caiaphas sat alone in the Chamber of Hewn Stone where the council met. He was clothed in the robes of a priest, and he sat near the seat of honor at the end of the chamber. Although he was alone, he could hear raised voices outside the chamber door. As he strained to hear, he could tell that they were cries of anguish. But try as he might, he could not understand the words they were saying, or to whom they belonged. Somehow he could not make himself rise and see for himself what was going on outside. He was trapped, alone in the room, weighed down by his robes. He woke up gasping, waking Rivkah in his desperate attempt to catch his breath.

"My love? What is it? What is the matter?" Rivkah was confused, torn from sleep herself, and afraid that something had happened.

Caiaphas hushed her, and struggled to sit up. "It is nothing. Just a dream. Go back to sleep."

Rivkah sat up next to him, fully awake now, her concerned eyes fixed on his face. "I can see it is not nothing, Joseph. Tell me what you saw."

Despite his trepidation, he could see the loving worry in her eyes. In an instant he knew he could not continue to hide it from her. So he told her everything. About his visions as a boy and his father's admonition never to speak of them again. About his fear of what they might mean, and his fervent prayer for them to go away, which had not yet been answered.

Rivkah sat in silence as he spoke. When he was finished, she wrapped her arms around him and nestled her cheek against his chest. "Thank you for telling me, my love. But I do not agree with your father. I do not fear your visions. They are a gift from God, even if we do not yet know why. He would not give you this ability without a reason. Sleep now, and worry not." Placated, he did just that, lulled into a more peaceful slumber by her words. He felt relief at being able to at last share his dreams, at having to bear the burden alone no more. For several minutes after he had fallen asleep, Rivkah lay awake, watching his breath gently rise and fall, contemplating the visions he had relayed, and wondering at their meaning. Then she too allowed sleep to overtake her.

ON SCHEDULE, Gratus appeared late in the afternoon, a day after the Sabbath ended. Annas received him at his home. In between festivals, and with his primary responsibilities for the day remitted, Annas was able to leave the regular management of the temple to proceed in his absence. He clearly felt that whatever Gratus had to say, it would be better to entertain a more private audience before including the entire council. Only Caiaphas and Simon were with Annas as Gratus arrived, making his way up the stairs into the vestibule. Annas had been restless all morning, although his greeting was magnanimous and charming as always. Rivkah had asked Lydia to prepare food for the meeting, which was set up in the fresco room. After Gratus thanked Rivkah profusely for her hospitality, and congratulated her and Caiaphas on their recent nuptials, she left them to their discussions.

Gratus looked around the room with admiration. "Annas, your home would be worthy of any Roman citizen." He smiled, looking at the colorful panels that graced the walls. "If I did not know any better, I would think that I had not left Caesarea at all, and had merely entered a room I did not know in the residence there." This was high praise indeed, as the governor's palace in Caesarea had been built by Herod the Great, and was a grand edifice constructed in the Roman style.

Annas smiled. "I thank you, Gratus. We are taught by our God to be humble in spirit, for all riches and honor come from above. But I am gratified that my home is pleasing to you. It has served my family well for many years."

Gratus laughed. "Oh, Annas, I had forgotten how pious you are. Yes, indeed, give the credit to your god as you see fit. I will not stop you." He chuckled as he sat easily down at the table before them and took a sip of the pomegranate wine that had been set out.

Taking his cue, the other men sat down. There was a moment of silence as they helped themselves to the bread that had been prepared, and dipped it into small bowls of olive oil that glistened in the light from the lamps that had already been lit. Caiaphas looked at their Roman visitor, this man who carried himself with such confidence and ease, and wondered at him. In his mid-thirties, Gratus had been a soldier for more than a decade, hardened by battle and buoyed by success. As one favored by the man who was now the Roman emperor, he was content with his lot and secure in his status. Compared to Simon, who was a few years older than him and who, as part of Annas's inner circle, was also a favorite of a powerful man, Gratus seemed somehow grander, surer of himself, and more formidable. Caiaphas had never met anyone like him. He was both fascinated and more than a little wary.

Annas cleared his throat. "Now, Gratus, you have kept us in suspense long enough. Tell us the reason for your visit, and what it might mean for us. We are anxious to know."

Again, Gratus laughed. He looked around the room at the three men before him. "My friend, it is true that I have news to share, although I am sure that some of what I have to say you can guess. I arrived in Caesarea with papers from the emperor, releasing Rufus from his responsibilities. I am to take his place as governor of Judea, a role you know I have long coveted. Rufus is currently making his preparations to return to Rome. I will be setting up my residence in Caesarea after his departure."

Annas allowed himself a small smile. "Yes, I am not surprised by this news. We are gratified to know that after our long acquaintance we will finally be in a position to work together." He chose his next words carefully. "I pray that the days we have had of peace and prosperity under Marcus and Rufus will only continue under your governorship. I trust that this transition will be a smooth one, almost imperceptible to our people and to the priesthood."

Gratus's smile was wry, and he carefully set down his wine before he spoke. "Ah, Annas. It is here I fear we may find ourselves in disagreement. As you know, our new emperor and I have a long history. I have been fortunate enough to become well acquainted with his character. He is a great man, full of wisdom and majesty. But he is not convinced that all who live under his dominion share this good opinion of him. While Caesar was often paranoid in his concerns, Tiberius is cautious and shrewd. You have been high priest over your temple for a decade now. While it has been a time of relative calm in your region, he worries at a man so much in control. He is looking for me to make a change here, and to do so quickly."

Annas rose, and Caiaphas could see that he was working to keep himself calm as he spoke, his jaw clenching and unclenching beneath his beard. "My dear Gratus, what more can I do to show the emperor our allegiance to him and our shared desire for the success of his reign? We have worked well with your two predecessors. We pay our taxes promptly and without complaining."

Gratus rose as well, and although he still smiled his tone was firm as he spoke. "Annas, what you say is true. But Tiberius knows as well as I do that Marcus and Rufus were no more in control of your domain than a child is in control of his tutor. Let us not pretend otherwise. No, I must depose you. There is no choice. Not only that, but the next high priest must not come from your household, nor from the household of Boethus. It must be clear that neither you nor Joazar have orchestrated the change." Here he looked at Simon, who lowered his eyes to the ground at the reference to his older brother, unsure of how to respond. "I must follow the direction of my emperor, who is adamant that I begin my time in Judea demonstrating the power and might of his rule above all others."

Before Annas could speak, Gratus continued. "But let me be clear. I am coming to you not as an adversary, but as a friend. I have hope that we can find a way to work together in spite of this necessary action. I have learned that in the province of Asia the priests in their temples are assigned annually. This is the model I plan to implement here."

Startled, Annas took a step back and his voice rose. "Gratus, this is unreasonable, and near blasphemous. The high priesthood of our God is a sacred office, one that has been passed down since the days of our forefathers. It is not meant to be subject to the whims of a conquering ruler, nor to be passed around from priest to priest without any reverence for legacy or tradition. It is one thing to depose me. It is another thing to allow a Roman governor to command the high priesthood itself, and to rotate priests in and out like a farmer planting and sowing in season. You must know I cannot agree to this."

Gratus looked sympathetically at Annas. "My friend, I am afraid the choice is not yours to make. But listen well before you dismiss my plan. For now, I must choose a high priest with no connections to the families that have held the office before. I had hoped that you might propose a suitable candidate, one upon whom you could continue to exert your influence with ease. And what is a year or two in the grand sweep of your people's history? Before you know it, a year will pass, and it will be time to replace the man."

He looked at Caiaphas, and then back at Annas. "What of your sons? Your household is prodigious, and full of young men who might one day hold your office. Even the house of Boethus," and here he gestured to Simon, "has men who could ascend to the high priesthood if all goes smoothly. A few years might be all that are needed for Tiberius to feel more secure. In the meantime, you have the opportunity to demonstrate your loyalty and fealty by complying with these annual appointments."

Annas sat down heavily, but Caiaphas could tell that he was

thinking hard. "And you believe you will remain the governor of Judea for some time, Gratus? It would not do well for us to devise this plan and then to find you replaced with another governor who might not share your intentions."

Gratus smiled. "It is my aim to remain in Caesarea for as long as my emperor allows me. The sea air is a balm to me after my years of service in the Roman legion. I am more than happy to settle there and leave the daily management of this city to you and your priests."

Annas sighed and looked resigned. "Well then, I see that we must submit to this arrangement, and pray that God's hand is in it. I will meditate on a proper replacement. We will make preparations for my removal soon."

"Before your next festival, my friend."

Annas nodded. "It will be done."

By the time Gratus departed, night had fallen in earnest. The rest of the household was gathered in the courtyard enjoying the evening breeze. As Caiaphas returned to the fresco room after seeing Gratus out, he pondered this development with some alarm. How quickly things had changed. In many ways, Caiaphas still saw Annas as his rescuer, the man who had provided for him and his mother when they had nowhere else to go. But now Annas was the one with no options, forced to make an impossible choice to keep the peace. As he stepped into the room, he could see that Annas and Simon had been engaged in vigorous conversation without him. Annas, who had carefully maintained an attitude of serenity while Gratus was still with them, was no longer so self-contained. He paced like a caged animal, his robes whipping behind him as he traveled the length of the room and back again.

"I knew I could not trust this Roman snake," he exclaimed, his voice full of bitterness. "He seeks to undermine our authority, and with the emperor behind him, he has the power to do it. In one stroke, he will dismantle all we have worked a decade to build. And he calls himself a friend. Ha!" Annas stopped short before Simon. Even from the doorway, Caiaphas could see in his eyes a cold anger that he did not recognize.

Simon hesitated, and then spoke carefully. "Annas, perhaps this is not as bad as it seems? I know you have already been contemplating your successor. While obviously not something we thought would come to pass for many years, there is no need to despair that you may not still see your chosen one take your place. We need make only a few minor adjustments to accommodate Gratus. Assuming he keeps his word, the house of Annas will remain in control of the priesthood, in practice if not in name, for many years to come. You would do well to learn from my brother, that sometimes being deposed is less a final chapter and more a welcome transition to a different kind of responsibility."

Annas looked at the younger priest in surprise and then chuckled ruefully. "You have learned much from Joazar, Simon. And you are right that his example is the one I must look to now for inspiration. Joazar was gracious in releasing his position into my hands. God knows that we have been able to work together for the good of the priesthood in spite of his soured relationship with Rome. Assuming Gratus does not prove duplicitous, my situation is actually far more promising." Annas looked pensive, and his brow slowly relaxed as he considered Simon's words. "My plans will require shifting, it is true. But the house of Annas may yet emerge like Job's tree, cut down but able to sprout again, with shoots that will not cease."

Simon nodded, and then looked up sharply as for the first time both men noticed that Caiaphas had returned.

Annas gestured for him to move closer. When he spoke, his voice held an unexpected warmth that felt incongruous with both the afternoon's proceedings and with the tenor of the conversation Caiaphas had just interrupted. "My boy, how go your studies at the temple? I hope to see you dedicated before I appoint the next high priest. I will need you all the more in the years to come, if Gratus's plan is to proceed."

Caiaphas bit his lip. "Annas, with all respect, my dedication is the last thing you should be thinking about now. What does it matter when I take my place in the ranks of the priesthood now that you will be stepping down? I will of course perform my duty with all the reverence and honor that is owed our God, but I cannot help but fear for the future. How can we trust that Gratus will do as he says?"

Annas looked thoughtful. He paused, and his eyes swept across his son-in-law carefully, as if evaluating a lamb being considered for sacrifice. The expression on his face was one of focused calm, his eyes inscrutable. Another moment passed, and then he let out a breath abruptly as if coming to a decision. "That is exactly what we must do, and what we will do. Simon is right. Our strategy has not changed."

Caiaphas looked surprised. Even Simon seemed taken aback by Annas's declaration. "What do you mean? How can you say that?"

Annas rubbed at the space between his eyes, and rested his fingers on his chin. "Gratus is a different kind of Roman than Marcus or Rufus, it is true. But ultimately they are all the same. He wants to rule over us, to show his strength. He fancies himself the mastermind of a plan that demonstrates Roman force. But we will find a way to use it to our advantage. We will prevail." Straightening his back, Annas gathered up his robes, looking determined. "I will not let a Roman soldier determine how I lead my people, or how I serve my God."

With this, Annas rose and crossed the room, walking through the open doorway to the courtyard and out into the evening air, leaving Simon and Caiaphas looking at one another in wonder.

CHAPTER 8

Once the plan was put in motion, there was little resistance amongst the council members. Annas had made his peace with the decision, and became determined to see it through without delay. The morning after his meeting with Gratus, Annas went to Joazar and shared with him the details of the arrangement. By the time they reached the temple, they had already chosen a viable successor. Ishmael was a young priest from the family of Phiabi. His great uncle had been high priest in the days when Annas was a young boy. Members of his family continued to serve the temple, primarily as managers of the treasury. Several years earlier, there had been some trouble with one of his father's brothers, who was caught stealing from the temple donations and was expelled from the priesthood. Over the protestations of some members of the council, Ishmael was allowed to remain in the service of the temple despite the association. His gratitude toward Joazar and Annas for their support meant that he was all too eager to serve in whatever capacity they desired, despite his discomfort at taking Annas's title from him.

Ishmael's dedication took place within a month of Gratus's visit, and the council settled into a new rhythm of dual management. While high priest in name, Ishmael deferred to Annas on every decision, and the rest of the council maintained a delicate dance of deference between the two men. Eleazar, who had been close to Ishmael since they were boys, watched with a critical but bemused eye as his friend and his father effectively shared the role of high priest, his friend splendid in the priest's garments while his father worked behind the scenes, orchestrating the matters of the day. If Eleazar found his father's treatment of Ishmael patronizing, or his friend's behavior obsequious, he mostly kept his opinions to himself, although once or twice Caiaphas caught Eleazar smirking or shaking his head as he watched the two interact. Annas was kind to Ishmael, but kept a firm hold on all of the proceedings. His network of scribes and tradesmen grew rather than shrank in the year after he was deposed. He approached his new role with relish, and seemed to enjoy the freedom he was allowed by serving, not as the high priest, but as the power behind the one ostensibly in charge. Over time, a balance was struck so that each man knew his part to play, and played it well. Gratus appeared to be pleased with the way the transition had been handled, and all was quiet from Rome.

ON THE DAY his dedication to the priesthood was to begin, Caiaphas rose early. Rivkah could see that he was nervous. She considered him with affection as she lay in bed and watched him gather his belongings. He, along with the twenty other young men being dedicated, would be sleeping at the temple for the entire seven-day ritual. They would return to their homes only when the cycle of bathing, ritual cleansing, and sacrifice was complete.

Rivkah broke the silence. "My love." Caiaphas turned to look at her, slightly distracted. "You are ready. This day has been planned for you since you were a boy. You have only to follow the path before you."

Caiaphas smiled down at her. "Yes, Rivkah. I know. But still I do not take it lightly." He leaned over her, taking a tendril of her hair in his fingers and playing with it absentmindedly as he spoke. "This day I join my father, and yours, in a noble service. I pray that I will be worthy of it, today and in the future."

Rivkah nodded. "And you will. I know it." She sat up, and swatted away his hand playfully. "Now go and say goodbye to your mother before you leave. I will never hear the end of it if you go without giving her an opportunity to give you her blessing."

Caiaphas made his way down the corridor from the room where he and Rivkah slept to the chamber where Hadassah now spent her days. As he expected, she was already awake. When he entered the room, she smiled softly at him, the lines around her eyes creasing like fine parchment. She made a move to rise, but stopped herself, and gestured for him to come to her where she lay, seated upright on her bed.

"My son." Hadassah's hair had grown thinner, and the way she had it pulled back made the dark circles under her eyes more pronounced. It pained Caiaphas to see her this way. But he forced himself to smile as he sat gently next to her and allowed her to take one of his hands in hers.

"If only your father could see you today!" Hadassah sighed. "He would be so proud, Joseph."

Caiaphas nodded as he thought about his father. He remembered as a small boy watching Abel put on the priestly garments, donning the tunic and cap and wrapping the sash around and across his chest, tying it and letting the ends hang loose at the back. He thought of Annas, and of the many times he had watched his father-in-law dressed in the high priest's robes, officiating the annual initiation of those joining the priesthood. Now he would wear the same clothes and be anointed with the same oils, and would partake in the same sacrifices made by his father as he took his place among the ranks of the priests.

He looked down and saw that tears now hung in the corners of his mother's eyes. "I am proud of you as well, my son. You have accomplished much, and this is just the beginning. Since you were a boy, I prayed that God would use you to fulfill his purposes in this world and, like your father, to protect all we hold dear. How glad I am that God has allowed me to live to see this day."

"Hush, Mother." Caiaphas squeezed Hadassah's hand as he knelt beside her bed. "Don't talk like that. You will live for many years to come, to see your grandchildren, and to teach them their letters as you taught me mine. Now, give me your blessing so that I may depart. It would not be good for the son-in-law of Annas to be late to his own dedication."

Hadassah smiled and pulled her prayer shawl from where it lay tucked by her side. Covering herself, she bowed her head and rested a hand on her son's shoulder. Silently, she bent her head in prayer, rocking slightly back and forth as she did so. After a few minutes, she was still. Caiaphas wondered for a moment if she had fallen asleep. But then she took back her hand and removed the prayer shawl, folding it gently and resting it beside her. He rose, and was beginning to turn away when she raised her eyes to look at him and uttered the words she had taught him so many years before, from the priestly blessing of Aaron. "The Lord bless you and keep you, Joseph."

"Thank you, Mother. I will do my best to be worthy of your good wishes." Without turning back, for fear that she might see the tears threatening to well up in his eyes as well, Caiaphas left Hadassah's bedside and made his way downstairs to await the others heading to the temple.

When they reached the eastern gate, Caiaphas parted ways with Annas and the other men of his household, and joined his fellow priest-elects where they gathered in the Court of the Israelites. One by one, they were led back to the Chamber of the Hearth, where they descended a staircase to bathe themselves in the ritual bath hidden beneath the chamber. This would be the first of many times during the course of the week that they would purify themselves with water, although the only time they would submerge entirely. The rest of the week, they would bathe their hands and feet in the copper wash basin that was refilled each day with fresh water and sat in the temple courtyard beside the altar.

As Caiaphas sat in the cool dark water, he couldn't help but remember the part this chamber had played in his own history, how his father had saved Joazar and Annas by hiding them away as the Romans attacked above. At the time, Annas would have been just a few years older than Caiaphas was now, a young priest still proving himself. Caiaphas thought of his father, brave and strong with years of experience already behind him, holding back the enemy, as the other men sat huddled in the darkness, afraid for their lives. He shuddered to think how he might have felt in a similar situation, and found himself more than a little eager to ascend and return to the sun-soaked main courtyard. Shaking the water off his body, he clothed himself in the linen tunic of a temple priest for the first time. Once he was dressed, he returned to the other young men who waited, their hair still wet, for the next step of their induction to begin.

Ishmael stood, flanked by Annas and Joazar, on the steps of the Priests' Court. When all were assembled, he glanced at Annas before signaling to a group of priests who stood waiting with jars of olive oil heavily perfumed with spices. At his signal, the priests stepped forward and began pouring the oil on the heads of the young men, who knelt to receive it. As Caiaphas bowed, he felt the oil seep into his scalp, running down his neck and descending in small rivulets onto his tunic. At another nod from Ishmael, a second group of priests stepped forward carrying the sashes and headpieces that made up the rest of the priests' uniform. Carefully unfolding the sashes, they wrapped them around each young man's chest several times before tying them. Then, they placed the linen caps on their heads, still glistening from the oil, and stepped back.

Ishmael cleared his throat. When he spoke it sounded as if he were reciting words he had been carefully practicing for some time. "In the tradition of Aaron and his sons, we have clothed and anointed you as priests of our holy temple. Each day for the next seven, we will make sacrifices on your behalf. The bull and rams we slaughter here will honor our God with their sacrifice. We will partake of the offering together as a means of binding you to our brotherhood. Welcome, and may God bless you in your service to the temple."

As Ishmael finished his speech, Caiaphas glanced up at Annas. He saw that the older man was staring straight at him with an odd mixture of pride and determination. Self-conscious, Caiaphas shifted his gaze, and caught the eye of Eleazar, who was several feet to the left with another group of priests. Eleazar was also looking at him, but his expression was very different than that of his father. Eleazar was scowling. His eyes shifted from Ishmael to Caiaphas in a way that suggested he was disappointed by what he was seeing. Confused, Caiaphas looked away, but he found himself unable to shake the feeling the look had given him.

That evening, after the sacrifices had been made, the newly dedicated priests gathered in the Chamber of Hewn Stone along with members of the council to eat their portion of the meat and to take some of the wine offering that had also been dedicated on their behalf. When the food and drink had been consumed, and they began to disperse so that those priests not in the middle of the dedication period could return home for the night, Caiaphas saw that Simon still lingered at the entrance to the chamber. Approaching quickly, Caiaphas was relieved that Simon looked glad to see him, and that when he spoke, his tone was warm.

"Joseph. And so you are finally one of us. I offer my congratulations. The house of Annas can now boast of another priest following in our former high priest's footsteps. Now Eleazar will not have to carry that mantle alone."

Caiaphas sighed. "Thank you, Simon. I am honored to join the priesthood, and to represent Annas's household." Here he paused. When he spoke, his words came out in a rush.

"But Eleazar does not appear to share your pleasure at my dedication. Have I done something to upset him? Please give me counsel, Simon, as I do not wish to cause him distress."

Simon looked amused, and he shook his head as he spoke. "Caiaphas, you are a mystery. You may be wise in matters requiring intricate and detailed understanding. But there are moments where I fear you do not see the most obvious things." He leaned in and spoke more quietly. "You must know by now that Annas has chosen you as the one who will take up the role of high priest once we are finished catering to the Roman governor's whims." Caiaphas looked startled, but remained silent. "Ishmael will be replaced soon, and Annas and Gratus have determined together that Eleazar will be the next one to wear the high priest's robes."

Unsure of how to respond to the notion that his father-in-law was grooming him as high priest, Caiaphas focused on the news about Eleazar. "But then, this is wonderful. I did not think that Eleazar was interested in becoming high priest. But if he is, then why would he not be delighted?" He paused. "And still I do not understand. What does this have to do with me?"

Simon smiled. "It has everything to do with you, Joseph. Eleazar will fill the role of high priest for one year, according to the terms set forth by Gratus. With Eleazar as high priest, Annas will be able to remain in charge, and it gives you a year of preparation as you adjust to your new role as priest. If we find that Gratus needs another year to become comfortable with ending this annual charade, I will be appointed as high priest next, with the understanding that I will work closely with Annas on all matters. If all goes as planned, Annas's oldest son will have come and gone as high priest by the time you are ready to wear the robes. There will be no objection to my appointing Annas's worthy son-in-law to replace me when the time comes."

Caiaphas stared, amazed, as he took in all of what Simon had said. He knew that Annas valued him highly. There had even been times when he imagined that Annas was grooming him for a high position within the priesthood. But to serve as high priest, especially if the annual restriction was lifted, was an honor he could not fathom. Yet he had no reason to believe that Simon was not telling him the truth.

Simon continued, more gently. "Eleazar has many good qualities, Caiaphas. The role that Annas has set forth for him could be highly beneficial both to him and to the priesthood. But Eleazar has always chafed at a plan not of his own making, and resents being used as a part of his father's scheme." Simon smiled slightly, his face thoughtful. "I do not believe he begrudges you your position, nor does he desire it for himself. If anything, he pities those whom Annas has decided to utilize most." Simon sighed. "I believe it is to his detriment."

Caiaphas thought back to Eleazar's expression. Suddenly he understood that the look on his brother-in-law's face had been more disapproval than scorn. Eleazar, his childhood friend, the boy who had always been the first to initiate a game, or to devise an adventure, was being forced to serve in someone else's war, and he resented it. He balked at seeing Caiaphas dutifully taking his place as a soldier within the ranks, by contrast ready and eager to perform his duty.

Caiaphas sighed. "Thank you, Simon, for sharing all of this with me." He didn't trust himself to say any more. Bowing slightly, he left the chamber and made his way to one of the upper rooftops, where sleeping mats had been laid out for all of the new priests. From here he could look out over the rooftops of the Lower City. He stood apart from the others, deep in thought, as the evening sky began to darken.

ON THE MORNING of the third day, Caiaphas and his fellow priest-elects were waiting in the temple courtyard, ready to be assigned their afternoon tasks. The priests had completed the sacrifices of the bull and rams, and the air was still heavy with the aroma of roasted meat. Suddenly, Jonathan appeared in the door of Nicanor's Gate. He looked solemn. After speaking quietly with one of the priests standing at the entrance, he looked across the courtyard at Caiaphas and gestured for him to approach.

As Caiaphas made his way to greet his brother-in-law, he noticed a woman behind Jonathan, standing at the base of the steps in the Women's Court. Her head was covered. It wasn't until Caiaphas drew close that he recognized his wife. His heart pounded as he reached the two of them, stopping at the top of the stairs so as to remain separate from them as his time of dedication required. Jonathan, not yet a priest, retreated down the steps to stand beside his sister, and the two of them stood waiting for Caiaphas.

"Rivkah." Caiaphas looked at his bride. His alarm grew when she did not immediately meet his gaze. "What is it?"

It was Jonathan who spoke. "It is Hadassah. She did not wake up this morning, Joseph. She is gone."

Caiaphas felt as if someone had punched him in the chest. He gripped the folds of his tunic as he struggled not to tear the fabric beneath his fingers. The garments he now wore were sacred, and he must not damage them, even in mourning. He drew in a ragged breath, and forced himself to let it out slowly. Rivkah finally looked up at him, and her tear-stained face reflected the pain and grief in his own heart.

"Husband." Rivkah's voice quivered. She reached for Jonathan's hand as she spoke. "We will do everything we can so that her burial will be worthy of your family, and ours. She was like a second mother to me. I will personally see to all of the details in your absence."

Caiaphas was confused for a moment. Then suddenly he realized what she was saying. He was midway through his dedication. The laws of cleanliness and purity would not allow for him to leave the temple until the week was complete. More than that, to be near a dead body would immediately render him unclean. He would be disqualified from taking his place as a priest in the temple until the following year. He could not bury his mother. He could not leave the temple.

He looked desperately at Jonathan, and then at Rivkah, and understood that the sorrow in both of their faces was as much for him as it was for his mother. He could tell that Rivkah wanted nothing more than to reach for him. But she stood firm and maintained her distance. They stood there like that in silence, Caiaphas at the top of the steps, still clenching his tunic, and Rivkah and Jonathan, hand in hand, at the foot of the steps. When he felt he could speak, Caiaphas turned to Jonathan.

"Thank you for bringing me the news. I have every faith that you and your family will carry out my mother's funeral with care and dedication. Please see that she is buried with her prayer shawl. And if Tova can arrange for a musician to join the mourners, I would be grateful."

Jonathan nodded. "It will be done, my friend."

Suddenly Caiaphas was desperate to be alone. "I must return to my responsibilities." He turned from them and made his way past several groups of priests to the council chamber, which was unexpectedly empty. Seating himself at one corner of the room, he put his head in his hands, and wept. Several minutes went by in silence. Caiaphas began to feel his heart slowing, his breath returning to normal.

"'The Lord gives and the Lord has taken away.'" Caiaphas looked up sharply to see Annas standing at the entrance of the chamber. Annas strode forward, his face grave and his voice low. "I see the news has reached you as well, my boy. I am so sorry. Hadassah was a remarkable woman. Her love for you has been a great blessing. You could not have asked for a better mother, Joseph."

Caiaphas nodded, unable to speak. Annas smiled sadly. "And I cannot pretend to know why God would allow her to die now, when you are unable to participate in her burial. But I have faith that he has his reasons." Annas was close to him now. Caiaphas could not help but remember the last time this man had been his comforter, ten years prior, when it was not his mother but his father whom he mourned.

Clearly Annas was also remembering the moment. "When your father was killed, I told you that God would make a way for you in this world. I believe he has done so. Your mother believed that too."

There were so many thoughts rushing through Caiaphas's mind, but he did not know what to say. Annas registered the silence, and nodded. "I will leave you to your prayers, my boy. When you are finished, you may rejoin the others and we will put you to work. The temple will still be here when you are ready." And he strode out of the chamber, leaving Caiaphas alone again.

As Annas left, Caiaphas looked around the chamber, which seemed oddly quiet without priests milling around and engaged in discussion. Suddenly, Caiaphas gasped as he remembered the recurring dream that had been haunting his nights of late. Here he was, in priestly robes, alone in the Chamber of Hewn Stone. His mother was dead and the family of Annas mourned. But he was unable to go to her, trapped within the temple by his own choice to serve. Although it was broad daylight outside, he shuddered as if he had just been hit with a powerful gust of cold wind. His dream had come true. What did it mean? And what of his other dreams? Were they in fact omens as his father had warned so long ago? Shaking his head, Caiaphas quickly gathered up his tunic and hurried to join his fellow priests, no longer wanting to be alone with his thoughts.

CHAPTER 9

By the time Caiaphas's week of dedication was over and he returned to the house in the Upper City, his mother had been buried and the time of mourning was nearly at an end. Rivkah was especially solicitous of him in the days that followed. More than once she found herself soothing her young husband in his sleep as he tossed and turned, muttering under his breath, beads of sweat clinging to his brow. Although his sleep was fitful, his visions of the chamber at the temple had vanished with his mother's death. He did not remember his dreams when he awoke. It was as if his mind were providing a reprieve, temporarily shrouding his nights with a veil that could not be lifted. He was grateful.

The rest of the family was saddened by Hadassah's passing. But life in the bustling household continued, and there was always much to do. Ben was now six years old, and had joined his brothers at the temple. Already he was showing signs of a quick wit. Annas swelled with pride as his youngest boy recited his memorized Scriptures as they walked through the dusty streets. With all of her sons away during the mornings, and Hadassah no longer in her care, Tova found herself with more time. She and Rivkah embarked on several projects including a reorganization of the household servants and a thorough inventory of all of the contents of their massive storeroom. At night, Rivkah would share with Caiaphas all that she and her mother had accomplished that day. Caiaphas found comfort in the mundane details of her stories, as she enumerated the challenges of finding a new wine steward when the old one had fallen ill after many years of service, or wondered at her mother's obsession with the new crop of lambs that had just been born and appeared to be more robust than the previous year's group.

Rivkah was cognizant that these stories were less than riveting. But she saw that Caiaphas enjoyed listening to her talk, and so she stored up small details and amusing moments throughout her day to share with him at night.

"Really, Joseph, you should see her." She laughed as she pulled her knees up under her chin and turned to face him. "It is as if when Ben got too old to pamper, she replaced him with the lambs, the way she pets and coddles them." Her grin was infectious. Caiaphas couldn't help but smile as she demonstrated her mother's soft look and tender caress using his hand as a substitute.

While his time with Rivkah provided relief, Caiaphas felt less at ease at the temple, mostly because the work he had been assigned after his dedication put him regularly in the path of Eleazar. Eleazar had become sullen and withdrawn, especially around Annas. With Caiaphas, he was short and dismissive. Rivkah, who had become closer with Eleazar's wife Meira in the years since she had joined the household, shared with him that the couple was having troubles of their own. Meira, a soft-spoken girl, confided in Rivkah that Eleazar had grown increasingly mercurial since his father's removal as high priest, and she was unsure how to manage his moods. Her own health had suffered a blow after a pregnancy resulted in miscarriage. She felt ill-equipped to care for a husband who was often agitated and distant, and who drank more wine at meals than she deemed prudent.

At Annas's estate, Eleazar continued to play the role of boisterous older brother. While Matthias sat quietly studying alongside Jonathan, or questioning Caiaphas about the work going on at the temple, Eleazar and Theo were perpetually engaged in some type of physical contest. The two could often be found wrestling in the courtyard, or challenging one another to ever-increasing feats of strength. At fifteen and already the same height as Eleazar, Theo was especially enamored with his oldest brother. Although Eleazar was still more than a match for him at anything they undertook, Theo found ways to hold his own, often by cheating. But no matter how much Tova admonished her oldest son to know his place and set a better example for his sibling, Eleazar did not seem moved. In fact, the more his mother interceded, the more he seemed determined to defy her.

As the days of Ishmael's high priesthood continued, and the one-year deadline for a transition approached, Eleazar's volatility at home began to manifest itself at the temple as well, and his quiet brooding shifted to more active hostility. He began to assert himself in the meetings of the council, his voice carrying across the courtyard as he argued with his father and the other elders on the most mundane matters. Caiaphas had long since learned that the best way to make oneself heard was to confer with members of the council away from their meetings, gathering support ahead of time. He was concerned by his brother-in-law's methods, and could see that he was not alone in his worry. The looks exchanged by Annas and Joazar told him all too clearly that they were displeased with Eleazar's behavior.

It was the matter of the copper coins that finally caused things to erupt. In the past, the governors of Judea had made a practice of minting small copper coins, worth about an eighth of a shekel. These coins were used throughout Jerusalem by merchants and pilgrims alike. The council had long ago determined that they were acceptable to be traded in as payment for temple sacrifices, especially because both Marcus and Rufus had been willing to adhere to the Jewish laws regarding what could appear on a coin without dishonoring God. Continuing in a tradition begun by Herod the Great, and unlike other Roman coins and those used in pagan territories, these coins featured palms, or dates, or barley, rather than the image of an emperor or pagan god.

One morning, a letter arrived from Gratus, directed to Ishmael and the council. In it, he detailed his desire to mint a new coin for the region. He formally requested that a delegation of priests be sent to him in Caesarea to consult on the design of the new coin. This request was met with mostly positive response by the council, who felt that this concern over their opinion demonstrated a respect for the priesthood and the temple. Eleazar, whose face had grown steadily stonier as the letter was read aloud, listened to the others murmuring their appreciation for this gesture, and rose in furious objection.

"Who does he think we are? Are we his servants that we will be summoned when he calls?"

Ishmael spoke. "Eleazar, these coins are used by our people. We allow them to be traded for our offerings. Why should we not be consulted as to their design?"

Eleazar sneered at the young high priest. "It is insulting, Ishmael. Why should this Roman governor get to decide when a new coin is needed, or how it is produced?" His voice rose further until he was almost shouting. "And why should we respect the value of these coins at all, minted by foreign artisans and foisted on us like so much else?"

Joazar and Simon both stood, and Simon's eyes darkened as he looked at his young friend. But it was Annas who spoke, quietly, from where he sat at Ishmael's side.

"Eleazar. That is enough. You are my son. While you are old enough to know better, I take full responsibility for your behavior among these righteous and holy men. A wise son brings gladness, as the Proverbs say, but your words and attitude here bring me nothing but shame."

Eleazar looked at his father, and for a moment, it seemed as if he might respond in anger. Simon and Caiaphas each took a step forward, unsure of what might happen next. But then, Eleazar's shoulders sank as if he had been deflated. He hung his head.

Annas nodded. "It would be best for you to leave this council now, my son, and ask God for guidance as you seek His forgiveness."

Eleazar bowed stiffly. With one last look behind him, he fled the room.

The rest of the meeting proceeded without incident, and it was decided that a delegation would be sent to Caesarea within a few days.

Simon would lead the group, and Caiaphas would join as a representative of Annas's family, along with several other young priests. Ishmael drafted a response to Gratus's request, which the priests would carry with them on the journey as a letter of introduction when they reached the foreign city.

Caiaphas, who had never traveled more than a day's journey from Jerusalem, was eager at the prospect of being able to see Caesarea and to spend more time in the company of Gratus. He had seen from Annas the wisdom in cultivating a relationship with the Roman governor. He was grateful for the opportunity to do so as Annas's representative. He knew that his inclusion in this delegation was yet another example of Annas's faith and trust in him, and an indication of the plans his father-in-law had for his future. But he could not stop thinking about Eleazar. He was grateful when he reached home to see Rivkah waiting for him in the vestibule just before the courtyard entrance.

As the others entered the courtyard and gathered around the table, where Lydia and Silas had already laid out the afternoon meal, Caiaphas pulled his wife into an adjoining room and shared the events of the morning with her.

"You should have seen him, Rivkah." Caiaphas was now able to speak freely, away from both his father-in-law and the other priests. "He looked so angry, and then so sad. It was like watching a wounded dog who has been caught trying to steal scraps from the master's table." Without knowing he was doing it, Caiaphas paced the small room the same way Annas always did when he was troubled. Rivkah stifled a smile as she watched her husband inadvertently mimic her father's mannerisms.

"My love, you are right that he is angry, and sad. We have seen it for months now. He drinks too much wine at meals, and in the morning he looks pained. I do not know if it is his anger at losing a child, his frustration with the priesthood and my father, or something else. But my brother does not appear to be well."

Caiaphas stopped in front of Rivkah, looking surprised. "Not well?

From the way that he and Theo wrestle, it would be hard to question his virility and strength."

"Perhaps not ill, husband. But troubled." Rivkah put her hand on his arm. "I do not think Eleazar knows what he wants, beyond the ability to control his own destiny. When we were children, he always balked at being told what to do, no matter if it was for his own good or not. Do you not remember the time he burnt the roof of his mouth because he insisted on eating the lamb that had just come off the fire? No amount of warning from Lydia or our mother could persuade him to wait until it had cooled. He couldn't eat without pain for days after."

She smiled. "My brother would have been a great warrior. Give him a sword and let him prove his worth against an enemy. He is not meant for priestly negotiation or subtle politics. And he does not do well with either expectations or disappointment."

Caiaphas sighed. "There I agree with you, my love. But these are the times in which we find ourselves. Your father has been most savvy with our current governor, and I fear for the time when Eleazar takes the high priesthood. One wrong move and he could cause trouble for us all."

Rivkah looked thoughtful. "Perhaps I am naïve, Joseph. But I do not think it will come to that. Eleazar may be angry, but he loves our family and our people. He is wrestling with the part he is to play, there is no doubt. But in the end I think he will serve as he should. And Meira will be there by his side, to temper his more impulsive tendencies."

Caiaphas sighed. "I hope you are right, love."

That night, Caiaphas's dream of the burning temple returned. When he awoke in the dead of night, stifling a cry, he was not surprised. There was something oddly comforting about it, even amidst the terror, because it was familiar. He had fallen asleep worrying about his brother-in-law, and wondering about the trip to Caesarea. But all of that had been swallowed up by the vision, which did not leave space for any other thoughts. Caiaphas drew several deep breaths, and shook his head. Then, turning over, he curled his body up against Rivkah's, and returned to sleep.

CHAPTER 10

The road to Caesarea was one of many the Romans had constructed across the region. Unlike the dirt roads in the outskirts of Jerusalem that were familiar to Caiaphas, this one was lined with intricately placed blocks of stone that stretched far ahead of their party into the distance. Despite the relative ease of the journey, the road was long. By the end of the first day, Caiaphas was grateful to stop and rest.

That night, they took their lodging in the town of Lydda. They were welcomed with great fanfare by the leaders of the synagogue, and treated to a meal that had clearly been provided at great cost by the local congregants. As they sat and ate the tender stew and spiced lentils, Caiaphas marveled at the way these men, many of them far older than he, treated him and the others in their party with such deference. Priests from the temple in Jerusalem seldom traveled the countryside. Suddenly Caiaphas was very aware of his own position as the son-in-law of a former high priest. He sat a little straighter, despite the aching muscles in his back, determined to represent Annas and the rest of the Jerusalem priesthood well.

The following morning dawned clear and cool. Before the noonday meal they had reached Apollonia, where they stopped to rest. It was here that Caiaphas caught his first glimpse of the Great Sea, stretched out before them as they came up over the rise and began to descend into the valley where the town lay. Simon, who had made the journey before, smiled as he watched Caiaphas taking in the enormous expanse of water before them.

"It is beautiful, isn't it?" Simon asked. "Beautiful and fierce and beyond reckoning. Truly our God who made these waters and can subdue them is mighty."

Caiaphas nodded, and then lifted his head, his nose catching the scent of the sea, as he heard for the first time the smooth crash of waves upon rock where the water met the land. It felt like something out of a dream, like the sea itself was breathing in and out, and he looked at Simon, his eyes wide. "Indeed you are right, my friend."

The final day and a half of the journey passed quickly as they travelled north along the coast. At dusk on the third day, they reached the outer gate of the city of Caesarea. From the road, they had been able to see the outline of the palace where Gratus made his home, as it jutted out into the water atop a rocky cliff. Beyond that they could just barely make out the port where ships sailed to and from Rome. Trudging past the enormous amphitheater that stood just outside the city walls, the tired priests finally reached their destination. After a quick examination of their papers by the sentry, they were admitted into the city.

Caiaphas looked around in amazement as Simon guided their party through the streets that led to the palace. While he had of course known that Jerusalem was not the only city in the world, this was the first time he had encountered another that matched its architecture and energy. Women, children, tradesmen, and soldiers all crowded the streets. As he walked he heard both Greek and Hebrew being spoken around him. The smells of the nearby marketplace wafted toward them as they passed. His nostrils quivered as he took in the scent of roasted fish and rich spices that permeated the air. Along the largest streets, tall white columns rose up on either side, forming a kind of corridor through which they passed.

Within a few blocks, the city streets faded, and the road that lay before them was instead flanked by carefully manicured trees and shrubs. Passing through a large stone entryway, the priests made their way through a magnificent garden to the front steps of the palace. They were immediately escorted into a wide open courtyard. Even in the dusk, Caiaphas could see that the mosaics that covered the floor were extensive and intricate. He understood why Gratus had once compared Annas's home to this place. It had indeed been a generous compliment. Caiaphas again felt the weight of representing the house of Annas on this errand.

From the other end of the courtyard, Gratus emerged with several of his men behind him. In a moment he had crossed the distance that separated them. He was beaming broadly, and spread his arms wide as he approached. "Welcome, noble priests of Jerusalem. I trust your journey has been without incident. I hope you will forgive my coming to greet you now before you have had a chance to refresh yourselves. But I was informed of your approach by one of my household, and I wanted to be the first to welcome you to Caesarea. It is my honor to be your host. I am grateful for your willingness to make the journey."

As always, Caiaphas was struck by the man's confidence and the ease with which he spoke. Compared to the priests in Lydda, who treated Simon and his party like religious royalty, Gratus seemed to speak to them no differently than he would approach a merchant in the marketplace or the son of a Roman officer. And yet there was nothing in his demeanor that suggested disrespect or contempt. It merely appeared that he did not follow the same rules as others.

Simon stepped forward, and reached out the hand that contained the letter from Ishmael. He bowed slightly as he spoke. "Noble Gratus, thank you for your warm welcome. We are gratified to know that our arrival is pleasing to you. We look forward to the task of consulting with you on the minting of a new coin. We are grateful for the opportunity to do so."

Gratus laughed, and took the scroll from Simon, handing it to one of his men without looking at it. "Yes, yes, we will get to all that. In the meantime, Lucas here will escort you to your chambers, and then we will provide you with some refreshments. Let us not stand on ceremony with one another, my friend. You are my guests here." A slight young man of no more than twenty stepped forward. With a nod, he moved quickly back from where Gratus had come. Simon and the others followed, and Caiaphas took another long look around the impressive courtyard before joining them.

THE NEXT DAY it became clear that Gratus's intentions in calling for a delegation of priests were not as straightforward as he had made them out to be. The method of selecting a design for the coin was a relatively simple business. Before noon on that first morning, it was decided that the coin would feature an emblem of three lilies, a symbol that would do nothing to dishonor either the temple or the God of the Jews. In fact, since patterns of lilies graced both the lampstand and the copper wash basin in the temple in Jerusalem, and were interwoven into the architecture of the temple itself, Caiaphas felt sure that the decision would be met with hearty approval by those who had sent them.

But Gratus seemed disinterested in the discussions regarding the coin. As soon as he had agreed to the design, he rose and sighed deeply. "Now that is settled. I will have our craftsmen get to work on it immediately. In the meantime, let us retire to the lower level of the palace, and take refreshments in the open air."

Following Gratus down the stairs that led to the lower level, Caiaphas exchanged a puzzled glance with Simon, who smiled slightly and shrugged. If Gratus had asked them to travel all the way to Caesarea only to immediately agree to a favorable design, that was fine. They could stay a day longer to rest themselves, and then immediately return to Jerusalem, where their shortened absence would be well appreciated.

The staircase that led to the lower level of the palace opened up, and Caiaphas immediately felt the mist of sea air on his cheeks. The lower level was open to the elements. In the center of the large courtyard was an enormous pool, larger than the Pool of Siloam in Jerusalem. It was surrounded on all sides by great columns, and the sea itself was visible on three sides. At the far end, a table had been set up with wine, nuts, and figs. Gratus walked toward it, gesturing for the others to follow.

The men clustered around the table and admired the surroundings as Lucas poured the wine. Simon and the other priests who had traveled with them moved a few steps away to circle the pool and further examine its features. Gratus, who stood at the end of the pool looking out at the sea, gestured for Caiaphas to come closer. Smiling, he took a sip of his wine, and turned to the young man beside him.

"Caiaphas. I am glad you were able to make the journey to Caesarea."

Caiaphas nodded respectfully. "It is my honor to be here, Gratus. Your hospitality is much appreciated by us all."

Gratus continued. "And how are you finding your service at your temple thus far? It seems your friend Ishmael has played his part well, has he not?"

Caiaphas looked startled and tried to compose himself. Gratus laughed at his discomfort. "I am sorry, Caiaphas. I always forget how reverent you priests can be." Despite his apologetic tone, Gratus appeared more amused that anything else. "But you must know that while I do not share your beliefs, I mean no disrespect. Your father-in-law has done everything he agreed to do since I began my term as governor. I am grateful for his allegiance. In the end our purpose is the same: to maintain the stability and security of the region, to satisfy and serve the emperor, and to do so with the least amount of disruption possible."

Caiaphas thought for a moment, and chose his words carefully. "Our current high priest is a credit to the temple, and my father-in-law has been of great service to him as an advisor and a support. I am gratified to hear that you share a good opinion of them both. And it has been my privilege to join them in the priesthood, serving our God and working with you to ensure peace in our city."

Gratus grinned broadly. "You are a diplomat like your father-in-law, I see. I am glad to know it. My understanding is that Annas wishes to see you succeed him in the years to come. For some time now, I have been eager to learn more of the young man who has so captured Annas's esteem. I hoped that by getting you out of the temple I might be able to gain a bit more insight into your character. I see that the reports that have reached me are reliable. You may be young, but your intelligence is undeniable. You think before you speak, and speak well when you open your mouth." Gratus laughed again, but his tone was approving. "We will make good partners when the time comes, my pious friend."

Caiaphas did not know how to react. Part of him was pleased to learn that Gratus thought well of him, flattered that the governor had taken an interest in him, even to the point of manufacturing a reason for him to travel all the way to Caesarea. But another part of him felt conflicted. His allegiance was to the temple, to Annas, and to the priesthood. His God was his master, and the Romans were at best tolerant of this dedication to a deity they did not follow. He couldn't help but feel that Gratus's good opinion grew out of a sense that he would be loyal to the Romans, an ally who could be manipulated to suit the governor's will if necessary. He wondered how that opinion might change if they found themselves on opposing ends of an argument. It was an unsettling thought.

Fortunately at this moment, the conversation was interrupted by the other priests, who had finished their walk around the pool and rejoined Gratus and Caiaphas. If Simon wondered what the two men had been speaking about in private, he gave no indication. Fleetingly, Caiaphas wondered whether Simon had been privy to Gratus's true reasons for summoning them to his palace. It seemed unlikely.

The next day passed quickly. Gratus clearly enjoyed his role as host to the priests. By the time they were to return to Jerusalem, he had shown them every inch of the palace, from the lookout at the far end where the waves dashed with fury against the rocks below, to the inner rooms in which only small thin windows high above eye level gave any indication that the palace was surrounded by the sea, and then only because the smell of sea air could not be suppressed.

Outside the palace, Gratus took them to see the majestic stadium Herod the Great had built between the palace and the port. He expressed great sorrow that they would not be there to witness the annual horse and chariot races that took place therein.

Caiaphas was impressed by everything Gratus showed them. But he continued to feel uncomfortable around the governor, and was grateful when the time came for them to depart. Gratus expressed much regret that they needed to leave so soon, and loaded them up with plentiful provisions for the journey home. As they exited the main gate of Caesarea and reached the open road, Caiaphas felt himself relax, and his shoulders loosened. He was grateful to be returning home, and looked forward to rejoining the life he knew.

UPON THEIR RETURN, Caiaphas was pleased to see that all appeared to be going smoothly in Jerusalem. The priests were already preparing for the upcoming Feast of Weeks, which would be the last festival before Ishmael's term as high priest was expected to end. Eleazar, who had returned to the council meetings after several days' absence, appeared to be behaving himself, both in the temple and at home. In fact, it seemed that something in Eleazar had changed for the better since they had been gone. He was more solemn, and quieter. When he spoke to his father it was with deference. He still seemed distant at times, and appeared to lose focus occasionally. But for the most part he was a changed man. He even treated Ishmael with more respect than before. With Caiaphas in particular, a shift seemed to have taken place. There were times when Caiaphas even felt a spark of their old friendship had returned. He was relieved even if he did not understand the transformation.

He shared these feelings with Rivkah one night as they prepared for bed, shaking his head as he gently folded his outer garment and laid it aside. "I do not understand, my love. It is as if he has just remembered that we are family, and not enemies. I cannot think what has changed."

Rivkah smiled gently. Taking his hands, she led him to the bed. "My husband, you are not the only one who went on a journey in these past few weeks." She sat and patted the bed next to her. Caiaphas sat down and looked at her, puzzled.

"You are right that my brother has been restored to good judgment because he has remembered his family, Joseph. And I can shed some light on the reason. I am sorry that you will not be the first to hear it. But I thought it was necessary that my brother be reminded of the importance of family, above whatever notions he has about his own rights or ambitions."

She placed her hands on her abdomen, and looked at him with her dark eyes glowing. "I am with child, my love. The next generation of the house of Annas lives in me. While you were away, I shared the news with Eleazar and Meira. I told my brother to remember his duty, not just to our father, but to my child. That is the difference."

Caiaphas was momentarily stunned into silence. Then he regained his voice and caught up his wife's hands in joy, pressing them to his chest and looking into her eyes. "Rivkah! This is a great blessing indeed. Who else have you told?"

Julia knew, because Rivkah had gone to her when she had ceased her monthly bleeding and was concerned, and Tova, who had been sworn to secrecy. But Eleazar and his wife were the only other members of the household in whom she had confided. It was still early. Caiaphas could barely make out the soft curve of his wife's belly that suggested there might be a child within. At Rivkah's request, Caiaphas continued to keep the secret, although he longed to share the good news with Annas, whom he knew would be thrilled. He began to pray for the child, and took special pains to make sure Rivkah was not overexerting herself whenever he could. Otherwise, he tried to put it out of his head until she was ready to announce the impending arrival to the rest of the family.

Eleazar was so changed in his demeanor that any concerns Annas had about proceeding with the original plan of transition all but disappeared. As soon as the Feast of Weeks ended, the priests began the preparations for the deposing of Ishmael and the dedication of Eleazar as high priest. As a matter of formality, a letter from Gratus arrived calling for the change. The council made their recommendation without any resistance. Caiaphas had been concerned that some members of the council might not go along with the selection of Eleazar after his recent behavior, and it was true that Joazar and some of the more senior priests were not enthusiastic in their endorsement. But the old Eleazar had returned, the one who could charm even the most stubborn individuals. He dedicated himself to demonstrating just how willing and eager he was to take on the high priesthood. He flattered the members of the council who were most skeptical, seeking their advice on matters of the temple, and maintaining an air of deference beyond anything he had previously shown. By the time of his dedication, he had won over even his most reluctant critics.

The few days before the dedication, Eleazar remained in the temple overnight, in order to ensure his purity for the upcoming transition. He could not risk accidentally becoming defiled and causing any kind of delay in the proceedings. Ishmael, who had always been aware that his term would be short, seemed more than happy to be handing over the mantle of leadership to his old friend. The two young men spent the last several days of Ishmael's high priesthood together, praying and meditating as well as discussing the particulars of pending temple business. At times their voices were low and hushed and solemn. But at other moments, their laughter rang out before being quickly stifled. Caiaphas was reminded of when they were all boys together and Eleazar would impersonate the older priests and their serious concerns. It was hard to believe that Eleazar was now taking on the mantle of the very priests he had been so quick to mock when they were children.

THE MORNING of Eleazar's dedication, Caiaphas and those in the household of Annas rose before dawn and approached the temple just as the early morning light began to creep up the walls of the outer gate. Simon and Joazar met them there, and together they made their way toward the Priests' Court where Eleazar and Ishmael were already waiting. The priests took turns reciting the purification prayers over Eleazar as he bathed his hands and feet in the copper wash basin that had just been filled with fresh water. As the day broke, the other priests of the temple began to gather for the official ceremony of transition. This would take place within the Priests' Court, so that citizens of the city could gather in the Women's Court beyond and watch through the enormous Nicanor Gate that stood between the two courts.

Caiaphas's mind was distracted as he watched his brother-in-law going through the rituals of purification and dedication. He barely heard Annas as his father-in-law talked about the importance of the role Eleazar was taking on. As the priestly garments were removed from Ishmael and placed onto Eleazar, the people cheered and the temple musicians burst into a song of celebration. But Caiaphas felt as if he were watching and listening through a fog. Hours earlier, when it was still dark, Rivkah had awoken hunched over in pain, the muscles in her abdomen clenching and causing her to whimper softly. She had tried to reassure him that she was fine. But her pale face and sudden sharp intakes of breath as she tried to calm herself said otherwise.

As soon as the morning began to break, Caiaphas called for Tova, and sent a messenger to Julia to join them as soon as she could. He knew that by now both women would be with her. There was nothing he could do but pray and wait. Still, he could not help but long to be by her side. Any pleasure he might have taken in seeing the dedication of Eleazar realized melted as he thought of his young bride, at home and in pain.

It was several hours before they were able to return to Annas's house. Caiaphas went on ahead of the other men, who were still rejoicing and congratulating Eleazar. Caiaphas flew down the steps into the vestibule and up the stairs toward the bedchamber he and

Rivkah shared. Julia met him just outside the door, her arms laden with linens that appeared twisted and soiled. When she saw him, she stopped short, and sighed deeply. Placing the linens on a stool that sat outside the room, she tucked her arm gently around his and led him to an adjoining chamber. When she spoke, the words were gentle but clear.

"Joseph, let me speak plainly, for I know you are aware of your wife's condition. Rivkah has been bleeding since this morning. There is nothing more to be done. The baby is not going to survive."

Tears sprang into Caiaphas's eyes. "But my wife? How is Rivkah?"

Julia smiled softly, glad to be able to share good news. "She will be fine. She has lost much blood, and will need to rest to restore her strength. Tova and I have been doing everything we can to make sure she is comfortable and nourished. It will take time, but I do not see any reason why she will not recover. I am hopeful she will be able to bear you many children in the years to come. You are both still young, and have years left to produce children to delight you in your old age."

Caiaphas smiled gratefully through his tears, and squeezed Julia's hand. "You have my thanks, Julia, for your attention to and care of my wife. I am sad to lose a child. But I do not know what I would do if I lost her. Please accept my most heartfelt gratitude."

Julia waved aside his thanks. "Rivkah is like a sister to me, Joseph. It was my honor to come to her aid. I hope to do so as a midwife before too much time has passed."

Caiaphas took a breath. "May I see her?"

Julia shook her head. "She needs to be left alone. She will not be able to submerge herself to bathe for another day or two, until we are sure the bleeding has passed. You will need to wait until then."

Caiaphas nodded. He knew all too well that the laws of purification could not be bent, even for a man who longed to see his wife. But the knowledge that, even with the loss of the child, Rivkah remained healthy and whole, was enough to satisfy him for the time being.

Leaving Julia to continue with the work of cleaning and tending to Rivkah, Caiaphas walked down the corridor and climbed the stairs to the roof, where he stood gazing out across the rooftops, his thoughts a muddle.

So the thing that had brought his brother-in-law to his senses was no more, just as Eleazar was taking up the high priesthood and needed more than ever to remain devoted to his duty. Caiaphas wondered at God's purpose in this timing. He felt sure that his wife would have found a way to get through to her brother even without the baby. But he remained nervous that Eleazar's newfound devotion to the temple might not last the length of his term. Still, there was nothing he could do now but fulfill his own responsibilities with honor, and pray that his brother-in-law would do the same. His wife would recover, and there would be another baby. In the meantime he was a priest of Jerusalem, ready and willing to serve.

CHAPTER 11

Afterward, the council regarded the year of Eleazar's high priesthood as one of trial and testing. Within the first few weeks of his term, it became clear that Eleazar would not be as easily managed as Ishmael. While Ishmael served as high priest, everyone knew that Ishmael and Annas were working in concert with one another, and that Annas was the real authority behind the priesthood. But with Eleazar, it quickly became clear that to keep the peace, everyone needed to behave as if he were operating as a high priest with ultimate authority and autonomy, regardless of the reality of the situation.

Annas's leadership took a decidedly more covert turn as the months wore on. More and more, the daily meeting of the council was a pageant more than anything else. The true business of temple management happened in small gatherings in side chambers, or outside the temple walls themselves. Joazar and Annas took to summoning small groups of priests to Joazar's home early in the morning or late in the evening to discuss the best way to proceed on matters of importance to the temple. Great pains were taken to make sure that Eleazar was unaware of these gatherings.

At the council meetings themselves, Eleazar's mood could change in a moment. While he was magnanimous and charming when he chose to be, a perceived slight or challenge to his authority could make him turn quickly cold and harsh. His affection for wine, which had lessened in the months before his appointment, had returned with force. It was difficult not to notice how often his breath smelled of sour grapes, the edges of his mouth tinged with a deep garnet stain, or how often he stayed awake after the rest of the household had gone to sleep, continuing to drink long after the evening meal had been put away. Many times Theo or Matthias had to be called upon to wake Eleazar in the morning so that he would not be late for his responsibilities at the temple. The rest of the family learned to stay out of his way during those early hours of the day. Meira shared with Rivkah her distress at the situation, but said that Eleazar would not listen to her, brushing her concern aside as a wife's nagging.

Rivkah, who had recovered well from the loss of the baby, was the only one Eleazar never treated with scorn. Although he knew that she was no longer with child, his respect for her former condition persisted. When Rivkah and Eleazar spoke to one another, it was with a levity and a banter that reminded Caiaphas of their childhood. He saw his old friend clearly in those moments. When Rivkah gently chided her brother and Eleazar came back with a clever quip that caused Rivkah to throw her head back with laughter, Caiaphas could almost feel the old affection for his brother-in-law returning. But most of the time Caiaphas found himself disgusted by Eleazar's conduct, angry at his abuse of the high priesthood and ashamed at the way it reflected on the house of Annas.

Annas's behavior while at the temple changed significantly with Eleazar's appointment. While he never missed a council meeting, he stayed silent more often than not. Whenever a matter of any importance arose, it was usually something that had been discussed ahead of time with a smaller group. Either Simon or Caiaphas became Annas's mouthpiece, voicing the conclusions that had been reached ahead of time as if they were new ideas coming to them in the moment. Simon was particularly good at this. If Caiaphas had not been privy to the original conversations, he would have been completely taken in by the sincere and spontaneous tone Simon adopted when speaking to Eleazar and the rest of the council.

In addition to the regular oversight and management of the temple itself, the council served as judge and jury for disagreements that arose among the people of Jerusalem, especially when there was an element of Biblical law to be analyzed and applied. These disputes involved everything from theft and property ownership to inheritance and divorce, or to problems regarding spiritual purity. The most challenging cases usually centered around financial matters. As citizens of a Roman-occupied city, all inhabitants of Jerusalem were required to pay taxes to Rome. Rather than sending Roman emissaries to collect the taxes, the Romans had outsourced this responsibility to local tax collectors, Jews who were more than happy to work with the Romans in exchange for taking a hefty commission for their pains.

One such man was named Joel. His father had been a manservant in the household of Joazar when the two men were children. Joel had learned the Scriptures alongside Joazar, whose mother had treated him like one of the family when he was young. As he grew, it became clear that there were very few vocational avenues open to him beyond following in his father's footsteps. Undaunted and ambitious, Joel had chosen to pursue tax collection as a way to make his living. Despite his father's disapproval, he had amassed a small fortune, enough to support a large residence on the edge of the Upper City. His wife and children always appeared well-appointed and comfortable when they were seen in the marketplace or on their way to worship.

Despite his questionable living, Joel was a reverent man, and frequently gave sizable gifts to the temple, especially during the festivals. When Joazar had been high priest, Joel was particularly generous in his annual offering. He continued to be a significant donor to the temple's coffers. But several of the council members had begun to question whether the priesthood should be accepting gifts from one who made his living on the backs of his fellow Jews. These concerns were brought to Eleazar's attention in the days leading up to the Festival of Unleavened Bread. Eleazar immediately called the council to evaluate the case the following morning, and Joel was asked to appear the next day to answer any remaining questions and to hear the council's ruling.

That night, Annas and Caiaphas slipped out of their residence, careful that Eleazar would not see them leave. In silence, the two men made their way to Joazar's estate. Simon was there to greet them, and led them to an inner chamber where Joazar was waiting. The lamps were already lit. In the dim light, Caiaphas watched the shadows flicker on Joazar's face, lined with worry and anger. He wasted no time.

"Annas, your boy is out of line in calling Joel before the council. We all know that tax collectors as a whole are snakes and traitors. But this man has been a faithful member of our community for decades. There is no reason for the case to go forward. It cannot end well, for him or for us."

Annas sighed, and when he spoke he sounded resigned. "Yes, my friend, I know you are right. But now that the case has been brought, I see no way around it. We cannot make an exception for Joel. As much as we may be able to vouch for his character and devotion to the temple, the ways of his profession go against our written law. Does it not say in Deuteronomy that a man may not charge interest against his brother? We have overlooked this indiscretion for many years. But I fear we can no longer do so. The people will be looking to us for wisdom in this matter. We must not be made to look duplicitous in our dealings. I am truly sorry it has come to this."

Joazar pulled at his beard and sighed. Caiaphas, who had been deep in thought the entire way to Joazar's house, stepped forward and looked at the two older men. "Noble Annas and Joazar, I hope I am not being too forward in this proposal. But I have an idea that may resolve this matter in a way pleasing to all parties."

Annas smiled at him, looking pleasantly surprised and pleased. "Speak, Joseph. We are eager to hear your counsel."

Caiaphas took a breath, and began. "There is nothing in our law that specifically denounces the collection of taxes. What is our tithe but a collection for the temple? It is the other elements of Joel's business that are problematic for us. We know full well that he also makes his living as a money lender, and that the amounts he charges our people in taxes often far exceed those he is turning over to the Romans."

He looked to Joazar, who nodded for him to continue. "But Joel's oldest boy Daniel has chosen to pursue a different course than his father. With Joel's blessing, he has been apprenticed to one of the most prosperous spice merchants in the city. Daniel is building for himself a business that will likely flourish apart from his father's wealth in the years to come. Perhaps we can propose to Joel that, instead of giving to the temple going forward, he bestow gifts upon his son. Should Daniel choose in turn to give those resources to the temple, they will not have the stench of money lending, but will instead be the generous gifts of a young merchant, committed to God and to our leadership."

Annas threw his head back and laughed heartily. "Ah, God has indeed blessed me with a son-in-law. Joseph, this is a shrewd notion, one that does you credit. I have no doubt that Joel will be more than satisfied with this strategy, and I cannot imagine how anyone on the council could object. Joazar, what say you? Simon?"

Simon nodded. "I agree that this proposal has merit. The only problem is that we will have no way of controlling whether or not Daniel follows the wishes of his father with regard to the resources. It would be a great shame if he found other uses for the money given to him."

Annas scowled. "It would be a great shame indeed, and would reflect very badly on both the son and the father." Caiaphas wondered if Annas was thinking of his own challenges with Eleazar, and again felt the sting of his brother-in-law's defiance. "But we have known Daniel since he was a boy. I have no doubt that he will follow through on his father's designs for the gifts."

Joazar smiled. "Yes, Daniel is a good son. There will be no problem there." He rose from where he was seated, looking relieved. "Good. Then when the council meets tomorrow, we will bring forth this idea and hope that Eleazar finds it to his liking. As long as there is no objection, I think Simon should be the one to put it forward, and then the rest of us can come alongside with our endorsement. I do not want to give Eleazar any reason to object." He looked meaningfully at Caiaphas.

Caiaphas nodded uncomfortably. His brother-in-law remained antagonistic toward him at times, despite his best efforts to demonstrate his loyalty and respect. Any idea he put forth would be scrutinized with a greater degree of severity than others. As much as it frustrated him, he knew the most important thing was to reach the right conclusion. A proposal coming from Simon would be viewed with less suspicion. Even though Simon was next in line for the priesthood, Eleazar seemed to find no fault in him. In fact, Simon was one of the only members of the council who could consistently get Eleazar to agree with him.

The men spent a few more moments discussing the logistics of the next day's meeting, and then disbanded. As Annas and Caiaphas walked home through the quiet streets, under the cover of night, Annas let out a long sigh.

"I will be grateful when this year is over, and Simon has succeeded Eleazar. Simon is trustworthy and loyal, and I am confident that he will serve his role with honor." He looked at Caiaphas. "And then there will be nothing standing in the way of your path to the high priesthood. Ah, my boy, I look forward to that day."

Caiaphas thought for a moment about how seamlessly Simon was able to manipulate Eleazar, and wondered at Annas's characterization of him as trustworthy. He thought back again to his trip to Caesarea to visit Gratus, and remembered how he had questioned how much Simon knew about the true reasons for the journey at the time. Simon often seemed to know more than he let on, and his ability to deceive might have been a concern were he not also faithful and well-intentioned. But it was also true that Simon was fiercely loyal to Annas, and Caiaphas knew how much his father-in-law valued fidelity. He still could not believe his good fortune in having been identified by Annas as a successor. It gave him great joy to know that Annas continued to have this same kind of confidence in him.

"And I am grateful for your good opinion, Annas. I am humbled by your faith in me. I will do everything in my power to remain worthy of it."

As they reached the threshold, Annas clapped him powerfully on the back. "Continue with the kind of ideas you devised tonight, my boy, and I will be more than proud." Annas smiled. "You are learning to be both godly and cunning. For the role of high priest, you will need to be both." Caiaphas nodded, and followed his father-in-law into the house, creeping carefully past Eleazar, who had fallen asleep in the courtyard and was snoring gently.

CHAPTER 12

The months passed, and to everyone's relief it was soon time for the change of the high priest yet again. Despite Annas's initial reluctance to agree to the annual transition of power, the challenges with Eleazar suddenly made it seem like wisdom that the high priesthood should change hands rather than remaining in one man's control. Eleazar, for his part, appeared increasingly anxious himself to relinquish the role. He began to lose interest in the proceedings at the daily council meeting. Often Simon or Caiaphas had to gently direct his attention to the matter at hand when a decision needed to be made. At home, he regularly withdrew to his chamber alone, leaving Meira to spend her evenings with Rivkah and the other women of the household. Once or twice Caiaphas unexpectedly happened upon Eleazar alone, hunched over, his head in his hands. His only pleasure seemed to come when he allowed his youngest brother Ben to come to him and recite the newest Scripture he was learning, or when the two sat poring over a game in the corner of the courtyard, Eleazar coaxing Ben as he learned how to manipulate the game pieces to lead him to victory.

One morning, after the lots were cast for the daily duties of the priesthood, Caiaphas headed to the Chamber of the Hearth. The day was a cool one, and the chamber was one of the warmest places in the temple. Priests who were not on duty sometimes congregated there to warm themselves. Those who spent the night at the temple even made their beds near the hearth when it was too cold to sleep in the outside air. As Caiaphas entered the room with its domed roof, he realized that he was not alone. Eleazar lay in a far corner, curled up on a mat. Caiaphas could see immediately that he was in pain. Crossing the room swiftly, Caiaphas bent down, speaking cautiously as he approached.

"Eleazar? Are you all right? Do you need something?"

Eleazar moved as if to raise himself. But it was clear from his posture that he could not easily do so. He groaned.

Caiaphas became alarmed. "Shall I go and fetch someone?" He began to rise.

"No." Eleazar croaked as he pulled himself up with difficulty, and raised his eyes to look weakly at Caiaphas. "Please."

Caiaphas stopped, and looked back at his brother-in-law, whose face was pale and drawn. After a moment's hesitation, he sat down gently next to him and drew his knees up to his chest. "My brother." Caiaphas could see that Eleazar was struggling to remain composed. He waited. Their breath rose and fell in unison as the two men sat in silence. Eventually, Eleazar's breathing grew less ragged. His shoulders, which had been tightly pinched, began to relax. The warmth of the room enfolded them like a blanket.

When Eleazar spoke, his voice was small. "The pain is always there, Joseph. I cannot make it stop."

Caiaphas looked at Eleazar, confused. "What pain, brother? What are you talking about?"

Eleazar sighed, resigned. "My head. It has been aching for months now, Joseph. And it is getting worse."

Caiaphas looked alarmed. "Eleazar, why have you not gone to the temple healers with this pain? Or if you preferred, to your mother or Julia? Both are skilled healers and could be of use to you."

Eleazar shook his head and drew himself up as much as he could. When he spoke, there was a bitterness in his voice. "I am high priest, not a child complaining to his mother of headache. I have been sacrificing offerings daily for weeks, praying for God to remove the cause of this affliction. Nothing will help. I only need to remain strong until Simon replaces me, and then I can rest."

Caiaphas looked helplessly at his brother-in-law. "But have you told no one? Meira? Your father..."

"My father cannot know." Eleazar's voice was fierce, and he looked pleadingly at Caiaphas. "No one can know."

Caiaphas reluctantly nodded, uncomfortable. "But what can I do? What do you need? How can I serve you as my high priest? As my brother?"

Eleazar smiled weakly. "Old friend. You have always been committed to your duty. When Rivkah married you, I told her she was marrying a man who, whatever his shortcomings, would never shirk his responsibilities. I understand why my father values you so highly. You would rather die than disappoint those who have authority over you."

Caiaphas was both flattered and offended at the assertion. "Eleazar, I am committed to serve the temple. As my high priest, you are indeed my authority. But right now I am also concerned for my friend, for my dear wife's brother. Is there really nothing that can be done for you?"

Eleazar looked resigned. "There is nothing to do but wait. Simon's appointment will take place in a few weeks' time. Already the letter is on its way from Gratus making the official proclamation of transition. I will remain in my role until Simon has been instated. Then nothing else will matter. Here, help me to rise."

Caiaphas took Eleazar's arm. Eleazar leaned on him, and together the two men stood to face the entrance of the room. Eleazar drew in a deep breath, and let it out slowly, the sound echoing in the otherwise empty room. He looked at Caiaphas and smiled softly. "I am sorry, Joseph. I know I have been difficult with you, and that you do not deserve my wrath. You are a good man. You will be a worthy high priest."

He breathed deeply again, and looked more serious. "But listen to me. You must not be afraid to take control. My father is strong. He will always think he knows what is best, for our people and for the priesthood, whether he wears the high priest's robes or not. Do you think I don't know about the secret meetings and conferences that happen outside of these walls?"

Caiaphas tried his best not to look surprised. Eleazar flashed him a wry smile and continued. "Annas is mighty, and having him as your mentor will be a great benefit to you, Joseph. The years have diminished neither his influence nor his abilities. But there may come a time when you and he will not agree on what is right for our people, and then you will have to make a choice. My efforts to stand up to him have been clumsy and coarse, I'm afraid. I worry that the priesthood has suffered as a result. I would not wish the same fate for you."

Caiaphas began to respond, to deny Eleazar's assertion and defend Annas. But suddenly Eleazar bent over again and a low groan escaped his lips. Gripping Caiaphas's shoulder, he took several deep breaths to steady himself, and looked up into Caiaphas's eyes.

"I am sorry you had to see me like this, brother. But I must beg you to keep my confidence now that you are aware of my condition. Pray that God will give me the energy to fulfill my duty until the time has come for me to step down. And we will both pray for the future of our priesthood and our people, that God will grant you and Simon courage and strength."

Eleazar squeezed Caiaphas's shoulder, pulled himself up, and stepped away, his gait stiff but determined. As he crossed the courtyard and made his way toward the Priests' Court to check on the sacrifices happening there, he did not look back. Caiaphas watched Eleazar walk away, and took a moment to compose himself before following him.

THE LETTER from Gratus arrived two days later, and the process to begin Simon's appointment was immediately initiated. Caiaphas did everything he could think of to lighten the load of Eleazar's responsibilities without drawing too much attention to what he was doing. Several times he nearly found himself confiding in Rivkah or Simon. But he resisted the urge. As a boy who had lived with a sickly mother for years, Caiaphas knew all too well the signs of a body being pushed too far for its own good. He was often able to anticipate Eleazar's needs before anyone else could see there was a problem. He rose early and gathered both his belongings and Eleazar's before anyone else was awake, making this one less task that was required of his brother-in-law. If anyone suspected that something was wrong, they kept their suspicions to themselves.

On the final day of Simon's dedication, Eleazar's relief was palpable. Caiaphas stayed by his side the entire day, watching carefully lest he require any additional support. When Eleazar at last handed over the high priest's garments to Simon for the last time and said the final prayers over his replacement, Caiaphas could see he was both grateful and wholly spent. As the other priests gathered around Simon to share their congratulations and to celebrate together, no one noticed as Caiaphas and Eleazar instead made their way through Nicanor's Gate, down the stairs and through the Women's Court, Caiaphas leading Eleazar gently by the arm. Anyone who saw them from afar would have thought they were having some intimate conversation that required them to remain close. Caiaphas took care so that no one could tell how heavily Eleazar rested his weight on him as they walked.

They slowly made their way out of the temple and through the city back to the house of Annas, resting several times as they went. They met no one in the street who might stop their progress. But their luck ran out as they reached the front door of Annas's estate and began to make their way down the steps into the vestibule. Despite Caiaphas's best efforts, Eleazar stumbled clumsily on the last stair. Caiaphas grunted heavily at the sudden weight of his brother-in-law against him, and the two men faltered. They looked up to see Rivkah and Meira, with Tova and Julia just behind, coming toward them from the courtyard. The women had obviously been sitting together weaving.

Tova still held the spindle in her hand as she came forward quickly, looking concerned. Her beauty had not faded in the years since Caiaphas and his mother had first come to live in her household, although streaks of gray now shot through her black curls. But the wrinkles that surrounded her eyes and spread across her forehead looked particularly pronounced as she bent anxiously over her son.

"What are you both doing here? Has something happened with Simon's dedication? What is the matter?"

Eleazar groaned. With the help of the women, Caiaphas helped him into the courtyard, where they laid him down in one of the seats they had just vacated. Meira sat down beside her husband, resting her hand on his. Over her head, Caiaphas and Rivkah exchanged a quick glance. Her piercing eyes told him immediately that she had not been blind to his efforts over the last several weeks. He was not surprised.

Tova looked at Caiaphas searchingly. He sighed. "Everything is fine at the temple, Tova. Simon is now high priest. The rest of our brotherhood are there with him, rejoicing and partaking in the meal offering together." He looked at Julia, who sighed with obvious relief, and then turned his attention back to Tova. "But your son is not well, and has not been for some time. I have done all I can for him, and I am sorry I cannot do more. He would do well to let you and Julia examine him and determine if you might be able to give him some relief."

Immediately, Tova leaned over her son, handing the spindle still in her hand to Meira, who remained beside Eleazar, her eyes wide with fear and concern. Resting her palm on her son's forehead, Tova closed her eyes briefly as if assessing his condition. Sighing, she rose and looked at the others. "Julia," she said, her voice strong and unwavering despite the worried look in her eyes. "Go to my chamber and bring me my supplies. You know where they are."

She looked at her daughter. "Rivkah, find Lydia and ask her to prepare a stew with some of the lamb from last night's meal. Eleazar will need something to build up his strength." Her voice softened as she turned to her son's wife. "Meira, please bring some extra blankets from the storehouse. We will have need of them."

As Rivkah left the courtyard after a long look at Caiaphas, Tova turned to him. "I wish you had come to me sooner, Joseph. I can see that he has been suffering for some time. We will do what we can for him now. Please find Silas and ask him to have one of the household servants build up the fire."

Caiaphas nodded and immediately went in search of Silas, grateful that his mother-in-law was now taking charge. By the time he returned, Eleazar had been propped up by the fire in the center of the courtyard, and was weakly sipping from a stone mug that Julia held to his lips. The scents of cinnamon and myrrh rose from the steaming mug, and Eleazar's face flushed as he bent over the bitter drink. Rivkah and Meira had returned as well, and were tucking one blanket beneath him and spreading the other across his torso. Tova was by his side, rummaging through a leather satchel that contained strips of clean linen and small bottles and jars. Just as Caiaphas came into the courtyard she pulled out a small container triumphantly. "I knew I still had some," she muttered under her breath, and opened the jar to reveal a thick balm, sticky and smelling of hyssop and fennel. Dipping her fingers into the salve, she moved to her son and began to spread it on his temples and across his forehead.

Eleazar had not said a word since they entered the home. It was clear that he had resigned himself to the care of the women who now surrounded him. Caiaphas could see that he was taking deep, labored breaths, his chest rising and falling slowly, as he continued to sip the drink Julia offered him.

By the time the other men returned from the temple, Eleazar had been moved upstairs to his bedchamber at Tova's direction. This was done with some difficulty, as he was very weak. By the end of the evening he had slipped into a feverish state that had Tova and Julia scuttling up and down the stairs, barking orders and directing the household servants to bring more blankets and other necessary supplies. Annas and Simon, who had returned to the household with an air of festive celebration, immediately became serious when Tova informed them of Eleazar's condition. After Julia quietly congratulated her husband on his appointment to high priest, the men made their way to the fresco room where they would be out of the way.

Silas brought Annas and Simon their evening meal quickly, and then withdrew. Overhead, they could hear Tova's sharp voice as it rose in frustration at porridge that had not been prepared to her liking, and heard her anxiously conferring with Julia as to the next steps of treatment.

After Eleazar had been moved upstairs and Caiaphas saw that there was nothing more he could do to help, he crossed the courtyard and silently retreated downstairs to the largest of the ritual baths that sat below the house. In the cool darkness, he leaned against the cold tile that lined the small entryway room that led to the bath itself, and let himself sink to the floor. Wrapping his outer cloak around himself, he bowed his head and prayed fervently. He thought of his brother-in-law and smiled as he recalled him at ten, boyish and brash, always with a joke and ever the instigator of mischief. Eleazar had been his first real friend, and Caiaphas remembered being in awe of his confidence and swagger. The man who now tossed and turned two stories above his head was a grim shadow of that boy. Caiaphas shook his head in sorrow at the memory.

He had been there for quite some time when a slight noise made him turn his head to the entrance of the bath. He saw the slim figure of his wife gracing the entryway. He was never able to hide from Rivkah for long, he thought ruefully as he looked up at her face, lit by the lamps that stood flickering in the corners of the small room. Her expression was a mix of sadness and resignation, though her eyes still held a hint of anger as she spoke quietly.

"And so Eleazar is indeed ill."

Caiaphas nodded. She did not move closer. "You should have told me, Joseph. You should have told my mother."

Caiaphas sighed. "You know your brother, Rivkah. He was insistent that no one know until the transition to Simon was complete. I did not know what else to do."

Rivkah took a step toward him now, and he could see that she was more sad than angry. "I know." She smiled slightly as she looked down at her husband. "When will you learn that sometimes it is necessary to disobey, my love?"

Caiaphas looked up at her, his heart suddenly breaking with sorrow and pain. He felt the emotion rising in his throat as he tried to keep his voice level. "I am so sorry, Rivkah. I am afraid for him. He is very sick."

"He will die." The words came out flatly. Rivkah was not one to shy away from the truth, however difficult. He could tell that though it pained her, she had to say it. "I can see it in my mother's eyes, Joseph. He will not recover from this."

She came to him now, and sank down beside him on the hard mosaic tile that covered the floor. Leaning on his shoulder, she gathered his hands in hers. She sighed softly. "It is not your fault, Joseph. I do not think they would have been able to save him, even if they had known from the beginning."

He looked at her, his eyes filled with gratitude, as she continued. "But from now on, there can be no more secrets between us, husband. Just as you trusted me with your visions, you must trust me with anything that plagues you. Whatever you know, whatever challenges you face, let me help you, as God intended me to do. Do not try to make your way alone."

He nodded, and they sat together in the dark room, the water from the bath casting undulating shadows on the ceiling of the chamber, so that it seemed to Caiaphas as if they were beneath the water, looking up from a deep, watery grave.

By morning, Eleazar was gone.

CHAPTER 13

After Eleazar was buried and Meira, heartbroken but resigned at the death of her husband, returned to her father's home, Annas threw himself back into the business of the temple with a fervor that startled everyone. It was true that, without Eleazar, Simon's transition would be more challenging. Caiaphas knew that Simon was grateful to have Annas's help in navigating the more difficult members of the council and learning how best to transition from a supporting role to one of leadership. But Simon already had a capable mentor in his brother Joazar, who was well respected among the council members, some of whom were even more comfortable with Joazar's leadership style than with Annas's. The entire priesthood was laboring to rebound from the unanticipated vacancy within their ranks, and Annas's continual presence served more as a reminder of the suddenness of Eleazar's death than anything else. A letter from Gratus arrived within days of Eleazar's passing, sharing his condolences and offering his services for whatever Simon needed during the early days of his priesthood. Despite the hardship, Caiaphas had no doubt that the temple leadership would endure, and that Simon would prove to be a capable and shrewd leader. He worried that his father-in-law, a

127

man uncomfortable with change and loss outside his control, might take longer to recover.

Annas had taken to rising even earlier than normal, arriving at the temple before the first light had reached its tallest columns. After confirming that the water basin was filled with fresh water, and that the priests in charge of the morning sacrifices had begun to stoke the fire for the first offerings, he would climb the stairs that led to the southern tower and make his way around the outer wall of the temple, watching the sun rise over the eastern wall as he paced alone up and down the perimeter.

It had been almost a month since Eleazar's death when he asked Caiaphas to join him. Caiaphas was silent as he shadowed his father-in-law through the morning's duties. It wasn't until they were standing at the edge of the eastern wall that Annas spoke to him directly.

"And so, you are now my oldest son, Joseph."

Caiaphas looked up at Annas, surprised. "Annas, as much as I am honored by that distinction, I cannot claim it. Jonathan deserves that name more than I do. Truly, it is a blessing to be a member of the house of Annas as your son-in-law. The plans you have for my role in the priesthood are an inheritance greater than any I deserve. I would not take the title of heir as well."

Annas smiled gently as he looked approvingly at Caiaphas. "So many times when you speak, I hear your father, Joseph. These words are his. Always striving, never feeling worthy of his place in our priesthood. But Abel was every inch a priest, and more deserving than most. So are you, my boy. You must know that I have always seen you as one of my own children, ever since you and your mother came to live with us."

Annas looked pensive, and shifted his gaze from Caiaphas to the city that lay before them, spread out under the sun that now shone with the clean intensity of the early morning. As he spoke, he walked slowly west along the length of the wall. Caiaphas followed just behind. "But if it is difficult for you to receive this title for your own sake, think of my daughter, and of the job you will soon hold. The council has been more than patient with the annual transition of high priest from man to man, and Ishmael and Eleazar both fulfilled their roles according to plan." Caiaphas thought he saw Annas blanch slightly as he said his son's name, though he continued as if nothing had happened.

"But I have reason to believe from my most recent correspondence with Gratus that we are nearly at the end of this charade." He looked at Caiaphas sharply, his face clearly reflecting his resentment at the Romans for their interference in the high priesthood appointments. "Tiberius appears to be pleased with the way we have worked with Gratus over the last several years. Gratus feels confident that the next appointment for high priest will be the one to break the cycle. Simon is a good man, and I have no doubt that for the next year he will serve our people well. In a few weeks, he will appoint you as captain of the temple. Then we will begin to prepare the priesthood, our people, and the Romans for the next chapter in our history, with you at the helm and me by your side."

Annas's face shone, and he looked at Caiaphas with a triumphant gleam in his eyes. Caiaphas felt slightly uncomfortable as he returned the older man's gaze, so determined and certain, like an ox singularly focused on the plow, unswerving and allowing nothing to disrupt its progress. He tried to look confident. Captain of the temple was an important position. The only person in the temple with more power was the high priest himself. Simon had served in this capacity under Eleazar. It came as no surprise that, as the next man being groomed for the position of high priest, he would be given the job. But Caiaphas felt he still had much to learn. He wondered if he would feel ready when the time came.

If Annas noticed Caiaphas's reticence, he did not acknowledge it. Instead he continued, taking a step away from Caiaphas and gesturing to the city below. They had now reached the southwest tower, and the Upper City spread out before them. In between buildings they could see dozens of people already starting their day, weaving in and out of entryways and along dusty corridors, headed to the temple or the marketplace. From this vantage point, everyone from the wealthiest merchant to the humblest manservant looked the same. Caiaphas wondered fleetingly how different his life might have been had he not found himself a part of his father-in-law's household.

Annas was still speaking. "This year we must do everything we can to ready you for the high priesthood. I believe it is now time for you to have a residence of your own. I had hoped that by this time your household would be a bit larger. But it has not yet been God's will to bless you and Rivkah with children." It was the first time Annas had mentioned this fact. Caiaphas's brow wrinkled slightly as he thought of Rivkah. Since the first child they had lost, there had been another pregnancy that had not resulted in a child. He had begun to worry that they would be doomed to suffer the same pain his father and mother had experienced, as pregnancy after pregnancy failed before his own birth.

Julia's experience had been a great comfort to him and to Rivkah. Simon had confessed to him that Julia too had experienced a number of unsuccessful pregnancies, both before and after the birth of her son, Eli, who was now two years old. Eli was a vibrant and healthy child, and Julia, who was an accomplished midwife, saw nothing to suggest that Caiaphas and Rivkah would not also be blessed with viable offspring in time. Both Caiaphas and Rivkah had been praying diligently for a child, and Rivkah had sent additional grain offerings to the temple with specific prayers for fertility and health. However, there was so far no indication that these had been answered. He knew it was a source of great pain and anxiety for her.

Suddenly Caiaphas realized that Annas had been looking at him for several moments in silence. He was stirred from his reverie by something else Annas had said. "A residence? What do you mean?"

Annas smiled. "My father Seth owned several properties in the Upper City. The home in which we live is the smaller of the two that our family still controls. As much as it pains me to lose you and Rivkah, I think it is time for you to take over our other residence." He pointed now across the rooftops, and Caiaphas could clearly see the roof of Annas's estate, where he had spent so many evenings as a boy.

Annas gestured further to the left, and pointed to a home that lay several streets beyond the one Caiaphas knew so well.

The first thing that struck Caiaphas were the multiple entryways that flanked the front of the huge edifice. Although he was too far away to make out many details, he could see three distinct entrances, each capped with its own pointed roof. The main part of the estate was bordered by no fewer than four courtyards. The outer walls appeared to have been recently plastered, gleaming with new lime mortar, which gave them a bright, white appearance. These walls, contrasted with the ruddy red of the clay roof tiles, gave the entire estate the impression of having been newly constructed, although it was clear that the building had stood for many generations.

Caiaphas was astonished. The look on his face must have reflected his feelings, because Annas laughed out loud. It was the first time Caiaphas had heard his father-in-law laugh since before Eleazar had died. "My boy, you did not expect that you and Rivkah would live with us forever, did you? My sons are quite comfortable remaining at our estate. But it would not seem right for our next high priest to make his home with his father-in-law. I have no doubt you will be able to make good use of the space before long."

He clapped Caiaphas on the back, looking very pleased. "The repairs on it are almost finished. You and Rivkah should be able to make the move within a few months. Silas and Lydia will remain with us, but their son Nathan and his wife Rebecca will be joining you. I trust that they are fully capable of running the household led by Rivkah's able hand." Caiaphas thought about the couple, who currently worked alongside Silas and Lydia at Annas's estate. Nathan was a hardworking and stoic man, and his wife Rebecca was pleasant and good-natured, even if she did sometimes engage in gossip with the other household servants. He had no doubt that Rivkah, trained by Tova's excellent example, would be able to manage them well.

He took a deep breath. "Annas, I am humbled with gratitude by this blessing. I do not know what to say."

Annas smiled. "There is no need to say anything, my boy. I am pleased to be able to provide for you and Rivkah in this way. I know you will make good use of the gift. My only sorrow is that I will no longer have you on hand for ready counsel. But it is time."

Caiaphas looked at his father-in-law, overwhelmed. Annas smiled again, looking satisfied, and clapped him effusively on the shoulder. "Now, let us return to the Priests' Court. Simon and Joazar will be wondering what has become of us." With that, he turned and strode off toward the nearest stairway. After a last lingering glance across the rooftops of the city, now glimmering in the full light of the morning, Caiaphas followed him.

THE NEXT SEVERAL months were a flurry of preparation. Rivkah and Tova were busy from morning until night preparing for the move. If Rivkah was feeling at all apprehensive or mournful about leaving her childhood home, she showed no indication. On the contrary, her delighted laugh could often be heard echoing across the courtyard as she and Tova sorted through linens and pottery and made lists of household items that would need to be ordered from local merchants for the new residence. She seemed tired at the end of every day, and was often asleep by the time Caiaphas reached their bedchamber. But otherwise she seemed altogether pleased by recent developments.

Caiaphas, who had been a bit concerned as to how Jonathan would react to this shift in the normal order of inheritance, was gratified when Rivkah's brother quietly took him aside and congratulated him. Jonathan was now nineteen years old and actively involved in preparations for his own dedication at the temple, which was set to take place in the same season as Caiaphas's promotion to high priest. Betrothed to a sweet girl named Sera who was a distant relative of Tova's, Jonathan had already made somewhat of a name for himself for his precision and facility with numbers. Caiaphas suspected that he was being groomed for a place in the temple treasury.

This role suited the young man well. He was still quiet, his dark eyes often lowered as if he were hoping not to be noticed. But his mind was quick, and Caiaphas knew that he observed much more than he let on. On nights when the entire family was gathered, Tova's three youngest sons were often to be found hunched over a game of dice in a corner of the courtyard, their boisterous play resulting in shouts of triumph or outrage depending on the outcome of a particular roll. But Jonathan never joined in, preferring instead to remain in the company of his father, Caiaphas, and whatever guests had joined them for the evening. He almost never spoke unless he was directly questioned. But Caiaphas could tell that he was always listening, always silently engaged in the conversation at hand. As twins, Jonathan and Rivkah had a unique connection. It was Rivkah who could draw Jonathan out the most, triggering a shy smile that made him look quite handsome. But these days she rose early and was usually in bed before the sun had receded below the horizon, and was therefore not often part of their evening assembly.

A week before the move was scheduled, Caiaphas awoke to his wife stirring, her body gently shifting as she eased herself over to the side of their bed, obviously trying not to wake him. He lay in silence as he listened to her softly rise, and watched her surreptitiously as she carefully pulled her fingers through her tangled hair and then expertly plaited it so that the resulting braid fell across her right shoulder and down to her waist. Resting a hand on her side, she walked a few feet over to a window and looked out across the courtyard, then turned back slightly in his direction. The light streamed across her body, highlighting her silhouette through the thin fabric of her garment.

Caiaphas sat up suddenly, staring at his wife. They had been so busy over the last few weeks that the two had spent barely any time together. When he was not at the temple or otherwise occupied with temple business, he had tried to stay out of her and Tova's way as they made the final preparations for the move. Many afternoons Julia joined them to help with the final details. More than once Caiaphas had happened upon the three women engaged in deep conversation, which had turned to charged silence when they realized he was within earshot.

Suddenly, he knew why, and was more than a little abashed that he had not realized it before. In a moment, he was out of bed and crossing the room to Rivkah, who smiled tenderly as she saw the look on his face. "And so, my love, I can hide it from you no longer, I see." Taking his nearest hand, she pressed it carefully to her abdomen. He could immediately feel the soft rounding of her belly under his fingertips. Taking a step back, he examined her carefully, his eyes tracing the curve of her breasts where her garment was straining against her growing bosom, and following the fabric down as it spread tightly across her stomach. There was no hiding it now that he knew the truth. The grin that spread across his face was matched by hers as his eyes came back to her face.

"How long have you been with child, my love?" Caiaphas could feel his heart beating powerfully in his chest. When her answer came, it was all he could do to keep from shouting for joy.

"Several months now, Joseph. Already I can feel our little one within me, moving with strength. There is nothing to indicate that the birth will not proceed well. My mother and Julia have both been watching me closely. They are confident that this baby will survive."

She led him back to the bed and sat beside him. "And there is more good news to share, now that it can be hidden no longer. Julia, too, is with child. It seems that we will both be welcoming children into this world before many months have passed. So the priesthood will be doubly blessed, as the households of Joazar and Annas both welcome new life within the same year." There was a flicker of pain across her face, and Caiaphas knew she was thinking of Eleazar. But then she shook her head softly and rested her cheek on his shoulder, sighing.

"We will welcome our new baby into our new home, my husband. And before another year has passed, you will be made high priest. God is indeed blessing us richly."

Caiaphas nodded. "And we must do all we can to be worthy of the blessings, Rivkah." He inclined his head so that it lay on top of hers, and they fell silent apart from their shared breath, which rose and fell in the cool night air.

CHAPTER 14

Rivkah's belly grew hard and round as the months passed. Caiaphas urged her not to work herself too hard. Still, her commitment to her responsibilities never waned. Buoyed by the move to the new property, which had gone smoothly, Rivkah was busy establishing herself as the lady of the estate. She could not afford to be seen as anything other than meticulous and exacting as she set expectations for the household staff. She knew that once the baby was born, she would by necessity be absent or otherwise occupied at times. She wanted to make sure that there was no doubt as to her ultimate authority. At twenty, she did not have the benefit of long experience. But her keen intuition and sharp wit made up for what she lacked in years. Nothing escaped her notice. Caiaphas couldn't help but chuckle as she berated Rebecca, several years her elder, for being over-friendly with the young man who delivered the spices they had ordered from the marketplace one afternoon.

"Really, Rivkah," he asked her later when they were alone. "What is the harm in her talking to the man?" But her stony stare made him forego this line of questioning. He left her to manage the household in peace after that.

Julia, while not related to them by blood, had become a sort of adopted sister to Rivkah. Although ten years separated the two, their friendship was one of mutual trust and respect. The differences between Rivkah's passionate nature and Julia's gentle one might have led to misunderstanding and discord, but instead the two women complemented one another perfectly. While Julia's presence always contributed a sense of tranquility to any room she inhabited, Rivkah brought out a liveliness in Julia that did her good. And Julia's wise counsel had more than once pulled Rivkah back from following her first instincts toward confrontation, helping her to seek a more measured and often more successful outcome.

Now that both women were expecting, they spent even more time together, weaving swaddling clothes and comparing aches and pains as afternoons turned to evenings and they waited for Caiaphas and Simon to return from the temple. Julia had been tremendously helpful in the move from Annas's house. She and Simon still lived in Joazar's estate, which was more than able to support their growing family. They would likely remain there for many years to come. So it was with a degree of vicarious pleasure that Julia helped Rivkah establish a household of her own. She and Simon spent many nights dining with them, while their son Eli followed the household steward Nathan around like a tiny shadow. Julia and Rivkah tried not to laugh as the little boy inadvertently imitated the man's distinctive gait and manner. Nathan was not amused, but took it well enough. Caiaphas was pleased at the notion that his household already contained some of the merriment he remembered from his days as a child in Annas's home.

Jonathan also dined with them often. While his presence did not lend the same frivolity to the table, he was welcomed with warmth. His sister, especially, was happy to have him near, and Caiaphas enjoyed watching the two of them together. Jonathan was all too willing to listen quietly as he and Simon discussed matters of temple business over dinner. There was much to review in the months leading up to Caiaphas's appointment and Simon's deposition. Jonathan's occasional input was thoughtful and succinct, even if it sometimes suggested he was not critical enough of those on the council, his respect for their position clouding his otherwise clear intellect. He did not like confrontation, and when he did put forth an opinion, it was almost always one that urged compromise over conflict.

Fortunately for everyone, Simon's term as high priest had been a relatively stable one, once the shock of Eleazar's death had worn off. Annas, who had taken the news of Rivkah's pregnancy as a sign that God's favor was once again upon his household, had settled back into his role as an elder statesman, albeit one with tremendous influence and authority. Annas trusted Simon, and his belief in the younger man permeated the entire council. Caiaphas watched with fascination as Simon deftly maneuvered between Annas and Joazar. Somehow Simon managed to make each man feel as if he were the sole and indispensable advisor to the high priest, a feat that Caiaphas envied. He was not at all sure his own talents in that area would be up to the task when the time came.

JULIA'S LABOR began just after the Festival of Weeks had ended. Both Rivkah and Tova spent several days at Joazar's estate, sending regular messengers back and forth to the houses of Annas and Caiaphas and to the temple with updates. Simon and Julia's second child, a girl, was born very early in the morning on the third day. News of the birth reached Simon at the temple just as he had finished overseeing the morning sacrifices. Caiaphas, who was with him when the message was delivered, smiled and offered his friend hearty congratulations.

"She will be beautiful like her mother, Simon. No doubt she will have many suitors among the great families of Jerusalem. This is a sweet blessing, indeed."

Simon smiled as Caiaphas spoke. "Yes, Joseph. A healthy child is truly a gift from God, a heritage from the Lord. Julia suspected she carried a girl. While I would have wished for a second son, you are right that this child may do more for our family in marriage than any boy might have done. She will be called Martha."

It was only weeks later when Rivkah began to feel the first pangs of childbirth herself. Julia, who was unable to attend the birth due to her own confinement, recommended several of the most well-regarded midwives in the city to care for Rivkah during her labor. Tova never left her daughter's side throughout the ordeal, which progressed rapidly and painfully. Caiaphas, who had just returned to the estate after his morning responsibilities at the temple, found his home taken over by Tova and her helpers. Both Nathan and Rebecca were scuttling about, gathering linens, stoking fires, and preparing stone jars of hot water that were carried carefully upstairs to the room where Rivkah labored. Her moans echoed across one of the upper courtyards where Caiaphas paced, punctuated by long silences and occasional wailing. He could hear the low murmur of Tova's comforting voice as she calmed her daughter and urged her to continue.

After what seemed like hours, Caiaphas heard Rivkah whimpering softly. Then suddenly she released a guttural noise that sounded like it had come from a wounded animal. In the silence that followed, he could make out the thin, anemic cry of a baby, and the low whisper of congratulations and praise from the women attending the birth. He fell heavily to his knees, looking up at the open sky and murmuring prayers of thanksgiving.

By the time Tova came and found him, he had collected himself and was back to pacing the length of the courtyard, anxious for news as to the state of his wife and child. Tova smiled as she approached, and reached out her hands, which he clasped. "All is well, Joseph. You are the father of a son, small but strong. He fought hard for breath when he first emerged, though he is breathing clearly now. Rivkah did a mighty job delivering him. She is spent, but the women are tending to her. She will recover from the ordeal."

Caiaphas squeezed her hands with perhaps more pressure than he intended. Tears flickered in the corners of his eyes. "Thank you, dear Tova, for all that you have done for us." He swallowed hard. "I pray that our son will be a credit to the family of Annas. I am overjoyed at this news." Releasing her hands, he took a step away. "I will go now and draft letters to be sent to both your estate and to the temple, announcing the birth of my son Judah, named after my mother's father."

He and Rivkah had long ago determined that if they had a son, it would be an occasion for tremendous joy and gratitude. In the Scriptures, it was Leah who had chosen the name Judah, a name of reverent praise. It was a family name, and one that would honor Hadassah, who would have cherished this day beyond measure. Caiaphas was eager to see the child. But he knew that this meeting would have to wait until the evening before the circumcision, when guests would gather at their home to recite psalms and prayers in preparation for the ritual and subsequent celebration.

BY THE TIME Judah had been circumcised and officially welcomed into the community, and the requisite burnt offerings had been made at the temple in recognition of the birth, the time was fast approaching for the changing of the high priest. Rivkah's confinement was over, and she had begun making preparations for the many feasts and dinners they would be hosting as part of the celebration, often with Judah swaddled tightly and slung across her chest.

Simon received word from Gratus that he planned to travel from Caesarea for the ceremonial transition, the first time he had attended in person since he had taken the role of governor. While in Jerusalem, Gratus would be staying at the palace that Herod the Great had originally built for his own use. A massive edifice some distance north of Annas's home, the palace stood against the western wall of the city, and was easily four times the size of Caiaphas's estate. Caiaphas had never been inside the palace, although during the time of Annas's tenure as high priest he had several times carried messages from his father-in-law to the Roman governors who had stayed there during festivals. Waiting in the large and well-manicured garden for a reply, Caiaphas had been taken with the striking architecture of the place, complete with three enormous towers that rose up into the sky. They had been constructed with such precision that it almost appeared as if they were etched from a single piece of hard, solid rock.

Caiaphas was not sure what to expect from his next meeting with Gratus. Their time in Caesarea had shown him all too clearly that the man saw him primarily as a pawn in the Roman governor's partnership with Annas to maintain control of the region. For Caiaphas to have any chance of working effectively with Gratus, he knew he would have to prove himself to the man, to show that he was more than just his father-in-law's instrument. He did not relish the task before him.

As the time grew near for Caiaphas's appointment, he began to see that it was not just Gratus to whom he needed to prove himself. He knew the other priests on the council respected his intellect and passion for study. His dexterity with language and his extensive memorization of the Scriptures was well-known. He was a valuable resource among the council members when they were mulling over a particularly intricate portion of the law or needed assistance in translating a letter written in Aramaic sent from one of the rural synagogues that littered the landscape of Judea. But even within the temple, Caiaphas knew he was seen primarily as Annas's representative. Now that the plan to elevate him to the highest office had been revealed, he knew that most council members and other priests assumed that Annas, not Caiaphas, would be the one leading them in the years ahead.

Caiaphas sighed as he thought about his father-in-law. Annas was a great man. The gratitude that Caiaphas felt for all that Annas had done for him could not be overstated, especially as he looked at his wife, holding their newborn child, in the home Annas had provided. The death of Eleazar and the challenges with the Romans had curbed a bit of Annas's good humor and levity. Still, there was no one whom Caiaphas admired more. And yet, Caiaphas could not help remembering the warning Eleazar had given him in the last weeks of his life. He did not like to think about what would happen if he and Annas ever found themselves on opposite ends of an argument. Annas was magnanimous to a fault, but there were very few who had ever contradicted him. Caiaphas was loath to be one of the first.

Caiaphas looked again at Rivkah as she cradled their son, her head bent down toward him so that her curls partially obstructed her face and lay in tangled ringlets across her cheek. Judah had not taken well to suckling. Caiaphas listened to Rivkah's soft voice as she chided her son to take in the milk that was waiting for him. The baby nuzzled his small head against her, his mouth working to find its mark. Caiaphas heard Rivkah sigh as the child latched and began to feed. He could not help but think of his father as he looked down at his son, now nestled against his wife's breast. He felt a pang of sorrow that Abel had not lived to see his grandson. There were so many things Abel had missed, even if it was his death that had served as the catalyst for much of it.

Caiaphas thought back to the time he and his father had walked the perimeter of the Pool of Siloam, the day after he had his first nightmare of the temple burning. His father had been so stern and resolute, so determined to protect Caiaphas from anything that might harm him. Caiaphas could remember the look in his father's eyes as he had cautioned against revealing the dreams to anyone, and the advice he had bestowed: "You must be strong, you must be unshakeable, and you must be prepared to serve God and the temple above all else." On the cusp of becoming high priest, Caiaphas felt the weight of his father's words clearly. He was determined to take his father's counsel, whatever the cost.

THE MORNING after Gratus arrived in Jerusalem, a delegation from the temple was sent to welcome him to the city. Caiaphas, along with Annas and Joazar, strode through the crowded streets to Herod's Palace. Jonathan, who had been dedicated just days before along with a dozen other young men, rounded out their party. He and Caiaphas walked a few paces behind Annas and Joazar. As usual, his dark eyes took in the scene around him with a quiet intensity that made Caiaphas smile.

"And so, Jonathan, you are now one of us." Jonathan nodded as they walked, their steps raising small dust clouds as they passed.

Caiaphas continued, looking over at his brother-in-law with gratitude. "I will be very glad to have you by my side as I begin my service as high priest."

Jonathan looked pleased, and the edges of his eyes crinkled. "I will be glad to be there." He hesitated, and then continued. "The last several years have been challenging ones for our family."

Caiaphas knew he was thinking of Eleazar, and then he suddenly remembered that Jonathan had also been the one to bring him the news of his mother's death. As much as he had felt trapped within the temple, he wondered whether Jonathan had ever felt trapped outside, unable to enter the innermost circle of priests during the events of the last several years since his father's deposition and especially during his brother's term as high priest. Caiaphas was very glad that they were both now of age, and would be able to share whatever was to come together, as brothers and fellow priests.

Annas's other sons still felt like children to Caiaphas, although at seventeen, Theo clearly thought of himself as a man already. He was taller than Jonathan, and took after his father in both height and girth. Theo was boisterous and energetic, and Tova was forever having to remind him to show proper respect when temple priests came to call for Annas. Matthias, at fourteen, was more like Jonathan, content to remain in the background and eager to keep the peace. At eight, Ben was the scholar of the family, demonstrating proficiency far beyond his years. Often when Caiaphas came to call, it was Ben who would approach him first, eager to show him some piece of parchment on which calculations were scrawled, or to recite some section of Scripture that he had just mastered.

These musings kept Caiaphas's mind busy the rest of the way to the exterior gate of the palace, where Annas and Joazar stood waiting for him and Jonathan. Together, the four men entered the grounds and wound their way through an elaborate garden to the left of two main buildings, where they were ushered into a large hall. The decorations that covered the walls and columns were grand and ornate. The lamps and other ornaments that graced the room glittered with both gold and silver accents. When Gratus joined them a moment later, he was wearing a sumptuous robe with a large jeweled clasp at the neck. He grinned as both Annas and Joazar bowed at his arrival. Caiaphas and Jonathan followed suit.

"Please, gentlemen, rise. I am gratified to see you, and look forward to our time together. Come and join me for some refreshments."

It was Joazar who spoke, his tone formal and measured as always. "Noble Gratus, we are very pleased to welcome you to our fair city. But we pray you will forgive us if we do not tarry long. We have much still to do in preparation for Simon's deposition and young Caiaphas's ordination." He glanced back at Caiaphas, who felt self-conscious as all eyes turned to him.

Gratus's smile remained, although he looked slightly disappointed. "Joazar, I understand there is much to be done. I had hoped to hear more from you about how the preparations have been going thus far, and how the mood of the people has been these past few months. It is some time since I have received a letter with news regarding the state of the city. I trust that all is well?"

Now Annas stepped toward Gratus, and instinctively Joazar took a step back as Annas began to speak. "Gratus, we are fortunate in that there has been no news to report." He smiled broadly. "Joazar's son Simon has been a faithful and strong high priest for the last year, and the people are more than satisfied with his leadership. You know that I hear much of what goes on in the marketplace and throughout the city." Gratus nodded, his full attention on Annas now, who spoke with both authority and assurance. "Any who would seek to make trouble have been identified and addressed. All is quiet in the streets of Jerusalem. Everyone is looking forward in anticipation to the ceremony and celebration ahead. Our people are more than ready for a high priest whose term will extend beyond a single year."

Here Gratus laughed, and clapped his hand on Annas's shoulder.

"Ha! And now we have reached the crux of our discussion." The unspoken question lingered in the air for a moment, the silence heavy with anticipation. "Yes, Annas, I believe we have reached the end of this chapter in your people's history. I have been corresponding with Tiberius, who is satisfied that the region is secure. He has granted approval to remove the requirement of annual transition. My congratulations to you." He nodded toward Caiaphas, but Caiaphas couldn't help but feel that he was still speaking to Annas.

Caiaphas returned the nod but remained silent. Gratus looked at him a moment longer, then turned back to Annas.

"Now, Annas, before you leave me, I did want to speak with you about a curious matter of which I have recently been apprised." He rummaged through his robe and pulled out a piece of parchment, which he unrolled and smoothed out. "Last week I received a letter from a friend of mine in Sepphoris." Jonathan and Caiaphas exchanged a puzzled look. Annas's face was impossible to read as he waited in silence for Gratus to continue. Sepphoris, the capital city of Galilee, was a five-day journey from Jerusalem, and lay to the north. As far as Caiaphas knew, it was a Jewish city loyal to Rome. To his knowledge there had been no news from that region for some time. He leaned forward, curious as to what Gratus might be about to share.

Gratus took a breath, and then read from the parchment in front of him. "My dear Gratus, I hope this letter finds you in good health. I am writing to you, as promised, with any news of disturbances or unrest that might reach into your territory, so that you can be apprised of any conflict before it becomes problematic. You may recall that our fair city was the unfortunate location of significant difficulty during your time in the Roman legion. We remain ever grateful for your service to us during that time."

Here Gratus lowered the parchment and looked over it at Annas. "They are referring, of course, to the trouble with Judas of Gamala, of which I know you are all too familiar." Annas nodded, and looked gravely at Caiaphas. Caiaphas realized with a start that they were speaking of the zealot whose revolutionary actions had cost him his father.

The surprise on his face must have been apparent, for Gratus put down the parchment and turned toward him, the jewel at the nape of his neck glinting as he did so. "Yes, Caiaphas. Perhaps you did not know that I served as part of the Roman legion that was sent to quell the disturbance in Jerusalem when you were a boy? It was my first campaign. We were ordered to Sepphoris, which Judas and his men had attacked and plundered for weapons and other supplies. After securing the city, we followed the rebels down to Jerusalem, where we engaged them in combat. I know that your father was one of the casualties. From what Annas has told me, his death was a great loss. It was a nasty business." He shook his head as if to clear it of the memories of that day.

Caiaphas looked at him in amazement. How had he never known that Gratus had been among the Roman soldiers that day? Had Annas intentionally kept this information from him? He looked searchingly at Annas, who seemed to be avoiding his eye. Over his shoulder, he saw Jonathan's face, and he could tell by his expression that he too was surprised.

It was Joazar who broke the silence, his voice low. "Yes, Gratus. We need no reminding. What news is there from Sepphoris? What does your friend say?"

"Of course." Gratus returned to his parchment, and continued to read. "While all is quiet for now, a rumor has reached us of a boy from Judea, some fifteen years old, the son of a priest they call Zechariah. When he was born, his father apparently pronounced that he would be a prophet, although to date no one has seen anything to indicate that the child has any special gifts." The tone in Gratus's voice made it clear that he did not see any reason to believe it would be otherwise. "Recently, though, we have learned that the boy has disappeared. Some say they saw him travel south. Recently we received word that he has been seen east of Hebron, in the wilderness there."

Gratus looked around at them all, and then continued to read. "You may recall that Judas of Gamala displayed similar tendencies, retreating to the wilderness and setting up a remote location from which to amass followers and foment talk of revolt. For too long we kept silent, thinking that Judas was merely a defiant youth operating out of reckless anger, and that his movement would die out long before it threatened anyone. We do not want to make that mistake again."

Gratus lowered the parchment and looked at Annas inquisitively. "I ask you, Annas, what do you think of this rumor? I know you too well to think that you have not also heard about this boy. If my sources are correct, he has been seen most recently within a two-day journey from Jerusalem. If there is anything to be concerned about, I want to know of it, especially on the cusp of the high priest ordination. We cannot afford for any disturbance to interfere with the peaceful transition of power, especially now that Tiberius has lifted the restrictions on that office."

Annas smiled. But as he spoke, Caiaphas thought he heard an undercurrent of gruff hostility in his father-in-law's voice. "Gratus, you say you know me well. In that case you must know that there is nothing I want more than for this transition to go smoothly, and nothing I will not do in order to make sure it occurs as planned." He paused. "I have heard the same rumor as you, and likely from the same source." He smiled wanly. "We have seen no indication that this boy is anywhere near our city, and I do not believe there is any reason for concern. If there is any hint of him in Jerusalem in the days to come, I will hear of it immediately, and we will take necessary action." There was a finality in his tone that suggested that this put an end to the discussion.

Gratus appeared unruffled by Annas's demeanor, and smiled magnanimously. "This is why I prize you so much as an ally, Annas. I knew you would have the matter under control." He looked around at each of them in turn, and then nodded curtly. "Very well. Thank you for your warm welcome and assurances. I will not keep you any longer. Go back to your temple and continue the preparations. I will send a messenger if anything arises between now and the day of ordination."

He turned, and without a backward glance, strode across the hall and left them.

CHAPTER 15

As the time of Caiaphas's appointment approached, his dreams grew more vivid. There were nights when, as he was wrenched out of sleep, his nostrils quivered with what he was sure was the smell of wood burning, and his ears rang with the screams of terrified people as they fled the encroaching flames. While he was still at home, he could comfort himself by drawing Rivkah to him, taking care not to disturb the child who now lay at her side. His wife's warm, still-sleeping body soothed him and chased away the images that continued to flash across his troubled mind. But in the final days leading up to the transition, he was required to remain in the temple overnight, to ensure his purity for the ceremonies ahead. Those nights the dreams were particularly intense. When he awoke, there was nothing he could do but stifle a cry, wrap himself more tightly in his garments, and pray for dreamless sleep.

The morning that was set for the beginning of the transition dawned cold and clear. Caiaphas awoke long before the sun began to rise, and quickly dressed in his regular garments, knowing that this would be the last time he would wear them. He left the warmth of the Chamber of the Hearth, and strode toward the Priests' Court, where a small group of priests who had been on overnight duty were beginning to gather. These priests, who had risen even earlier than Caiaphas, had already bathed and opened the main doors of the temple. They were just completing the process of casting lots to determine their daily morning responsibilities when Caiaphas approached. In silence, he watched them divide into two groups. Armed with several lit torches to help them see more clearly in the still dusky morning air, they went their separate ways to two different staircases that led to the outer wall of the temple. Caiaphas knew that each group would patrol a section of the wall, looking for any danger or anything amiss, before returning to give a report, at which point they would scatter to perform the necessary tasks before the rest of the priests arrived. There was bread to prepare for the morning meal offering, and several priests would be given the responsibility of clearing the altar of the ashes from the previous day's sacrifices.

Caiaphas stood alone near the copper wash basin that sat on the southern side of the court, lost in thought. He could not count the number of mornings it had been he who had risen early with his fellow priests, climbing the cold stone steps as part of the morning patrol. It was all so familiar to him. In many ways the temple felt more like home to him than his current residence, where he still occasionally felt like a visitor, albeit a welcome one. More than once he had turned the wrong way down a corridor of his estate, and had to double back to find his way. Rivkah had laughed at him when he sheepishly confessed this to her one morning, her dark eyes shining with affectionate amusement. But here at the temple, Caiaphas knew every column, every doorway, and every chamber.

Almost every chamber. With a flash of recognition, Caiaphas realized that the one chamber he had never entered in all of his time at the temple was one that would now be opened to him, at least once a year. The Holy of Holies, the most sacred place at the very center of the sanctuary, could be inhabited by none but the high priest himself, and then only on the Day of Atonement. On that holiest of days, he would be responsible for seeking forgiveness for all of the Jewish people, including the entire priesthood. Clothed in white robes, he would shed the traditional vestments of the high priest and stand alone, without Annas or any other priest beside him. On that day, he would serve as a priesthood of one, performing rituals dating back to the time of Moses, the future peace and prosperity that only God could grant resting entirely on his shoulders. It was a heady notion.

These thoughts occupied his mind so heavily that Caiaphas did not notice the priests returning from their patrol until the priest leading the group to his left called loudly, "Is all well?" He jumped slightly, but recovered himself before the prescribed answer came from his right, "All is well." At this, the priests began to disperse. Four young men from the second group moved to the basin in front of Caiaphas. Rolling up the sleeves of their robes, they washed their hands and forearms in the cool, clear water that filled it. Moving over to the altar, two of the priests cleared the piles of dark grey ash, while the other two gathered any offerings that had not been consumed by the fire from the previous day's contributions. These pieces would be returned once the altar was cleared and new fires built with fresh wood.

As Caiaphas continued to observe, two additional priests came from behind him, carrying bundles of wood from the Gate of Kindling that lay further back along the southern wall. He moved quickly to get out of their way, and watched as they neatly built two new pyres on the altar, one for animal sacrifices and one for incense offerings. Once these were in place, the priests worked together to replace the older offerings from where they had been removed. Then all but one of the priests stepped back. The one who remained lowered his torch to the wood at the base of each pyre, which quickly began to smoke. By the time Caiaphas turned away, flames were licking the edges of the logs and igniting the offering remains.

More priests arrived at the temple now, and gathered around the copper basin to wash before participating in the next round of lots. These assignments would determine who would take on the remaining daily tasks of slaughter, cleansing, and prayer. This morning there was a particular hint of anticipation in the air, and everyone was going about their responsibilities with an extra sense of urgency. The transition from Simon to Caiaphas would be officially ratified with a ceremony that morning. There was much to be accomplished before it could begin.

The sun rose overhead and Caiaphas made his way back to the Chamber of the Hearth, where Simon was already waiting for him. As the current high priest, Simon would be an integral part of the proceedings. Caiaphas entered the room and Simon looked at him and smiled warmly. Simon had always been a friendly face, one for which Caiaphas was forever grateful. He would never forget the way Simon had helped him and his mother prepare to move to Annas's home in the days after his father's death, giving Hadassah comfort and showing him kindness. At the time, the ten years that separated them felt like a vast gap. A decade later, Simon felt more like an older brother than anything else, especially in Eleazar's absence. Whatever Caiaphas thought of his friend's methods of persuasion, and whatever doubts he occasionally had about his authenticity, Simon was nonetheless an ally he was grateful to have by his side. Not for the first time, Caiaphas was struck by his own good fortune. As an orphan and only child, he could have been abandoned and alone, forced to rely on the kindness of strangers for food and shelter. Instead, he found himself part of one of the most prestigious families in Jerusalem, a father and a husband, surrounded by powerful friends and family, and about to take on the esteemed title of high priest.

This was the beginning of his true service to the temple. Everything he had done to this point had been preparation for this moment. Although he was terrified at the prospect of letting down those who were relying on him, he felt an odd peace as well. He knew that Annas, Joazar, and the other priests would be there alongside him, to guide and advise him. He knew that Rivkah also was ready to share in his trials and challenges, her sharp mind able to cut through the thorniest matters, and to offer counsel when he brought home his concerns. More than anything, he felt that God was with him. That morning, as he entered the Chamber of the Hearth, he heard the priests beginning to recite the twenty-fourth psalm, and the words reverberated in his mind as he and Simon descended into the ritual bath to cleanse themselves. "Who shall ascend the hill of the Lord?

And who shall stand in his holy place? He who has clean hands and a pure heart." He was ready.

After bathing, Simon and Caiaphas returned to the chamber, where several younger priests had prepared the garments that Caiaphas and Simon would both wear prior to the ceremony itself. The linen undergarments came first, over which Caiaphas pulled a light linen robe and a wide cloth belt that was wrapped around his body several times before being tied at his back. The linen was smooth and soft, the stitching so tight and fine that even Hadassah would have been impressed by the workmanship. While the undergarments were plain, the robe was embroidered with delicate flowers in deep purple, scarlet, and blue. Once these garments were in place, Simon and Caiaphas knelt, side by side, and the younger priests anointed their heads with the heavily perfumed oil that was used only for special ceremonies. Caiaphas felt the weight of the oil as it slid down his temples. His nose caught the scent of frankincense, which had a crisp, woody aroma. As the priests murmured prayers, they wrapped clean linen around the two men's heads, and finished them with a knot at the nape of the neck. Across the top of Caiaphas's head lay a flat, smooth section of white linen over which a crown would later be placed.

For the last time, Simon was dressed in the remaining high priest's garments as Caiaphas stood watching in silence. Once this was finished, the two men rose and walked slowly from the chamber across the Priests' Court, and up the set of stairs that led to the temple porch, just in front of the sanctuary itself. From this perch, Caiaphas could see across the courtyard to Nicanor's Gate, where a large gathering of worshipers and others eagerly waited to witness the transition of power. The rest of the priests had already gathered at the base of the stairs. The members of the council, including Annas and Joazar, regal in their finest robes, were standing on the steps themselves, forming a sort of corridor for Simon and Caiaphas to walk through to reach their destination.

Following Simon, Caiaphas mounted the steps, his eyes lowered. When they reached the top of the stairs, Simon gestured to Caiaphas to take his place to his left. Tradition dictated that when a high priest was dedicated, the man standing to his right would be his second, in case for any reason he was not able to fulfill the duties of high priest. In this case, since Simon was still more than capable of serving, and was not being replaced due to age or infirmity, the council had determined that he might continue to serve as Caiaphas's second even after his term ended. Caiaphas had seen no reason to object to this plan, and Annas confirmed that Gratus also was in agreement.

Once Simon and Caiaphas were both in place, Annas, who had been chosen by Simon to officiate the ceremony, cleared his throat and stepped forward. His voice echoed across the courtyard as he spoke. A hush fell over the crowd. "People of Israel, we gather today to witness the transition of power from Simon, son of Boethus, to Joseph Caiaphas, son of Abel and of the house of Annas. Simon has been a worthy high priest. He will be inscribed in our history as one who served his people well." Annas nodded to Simon, who bowed slightly in response. "On this day, we witness the appointment of a new high priest, one we trust will continue the good example set by his predecessor."

Annas gestured to Caiaphas to take a step forward, which he did. Annas spoke again, his voice loud and commanding. "Great council of the priesthood, do you approve this young man as our next high priest?" Around him, priests were bowing and murmuring assent. Annas paused as he looked up and down the rows of priests that filled the stairs. Nodding approvingly, he stepped toward Caiaphas, positioning himself so that he was in front of him with his back to the rest of the priests.

Standing before Caiaphas, Annas clasped him firmly, his strong hands solidly gripping the younger man's shoulders. His voice low, he spoke only for Caiaphas. "My boy, I am so proud. This is truly a day of triumph for us." The words hit Caiaphas like an arrow finding its mark. His chest swelled with pride and wonder. Still amazed that his father-in-law had seen fit to help him rise to such a position, Caiaphas felt like David of old, chosen by the great prophet Samuel from among his brothers and anointed for service.

Stepping back, Annas took his place among the council, and nodded to Simon.

Simon stepped forward, and two other young priests joined him. Together they removed the ceremonial garments that Simon wore until he was left in only the linen robe and undergarments. Turning to Caiaphas, the priests slowly lowered the tunic of deep blue over his head. Sleeveless, this tunic was heavier than the other robes, its fabric thicker and coarser, and its edges were embroidered with dark blue diamonds. Tassels of scarlet and purple interspersed with small golden bells lined the bottom edge, which tinkled as the tunic was tied at the sides. On top of this tunic, a heavily embroidered vest was placed over Caiaphas's shoulders and around his torso, with golden cords holding it in place. In the center, a breastplate was fitted into the open space and secured with more golden cords. This breastplate was decorated with twelve large gemstones, set in four rows of three each. These stones of reminder, Caiaphas knew, stood for the twelve tribes of Israel, and were there to symbolize that the high priest represented all of the Jews and their descendants.

Finally, the other priests stepped back, leaving Simon with one last item to bestow. Raising his arms high, and positioning himself so that his action was visible to the watching crowd, Simon placed a gold crown across Caiaphas's forehead, so that it sat just below the linen turban already in place on his head. This crown was made of thin hammered gold. Across its front were inscribed the words, "Holy unto the Lord." Once he had done this, Simon took a step back, lowered his hands, and smiled at Caiaphas. Turning forward to face the others, he cleared his throat and announced, "We will repeat this robing each day from now until the next Sabbath. But from now on high priest Caiaphas will be taking over the responsibilities of the office. The transition is complete."

Immediately, there were shouts from across the courtyard, and the temple musicians began to play a triumphant song of celebration. The cacophony of noise was in stark contrast to the silence of a moment before, and Caiaphas had to restrain himself from shouting aloud for joy. He felt it was important for him to maintain a sense of decorum during his first moments as high priest, although inside he was bursting.

THE NEXT WEEK PASSED QUICKLY, as each morning he and Simon carried out the ritual of transitioning the ceremonial garments from one to another, followed by official meetings with various members of the council to receive reports on the current status of each aspect of temple business. First came reports on the treasury and the temple guard. Then those who managed the storehouses for animal, grain, and incense offerings were called forth to provide information and an accounting of the lambs, doves, jars of incense, and sheaves of wheat available for sacrifice. Gamaliel, a small man the same age as Simon, with a dark beard and a thoughtful manner, was responsible for the education of those still too young to be priests. He provided Caiaphas with a thorough update on the boys who gathered daily at the temple to be taught their letters, Scripture, and mathematics. Simon informed Caiaphas that Gamaliel's son, who was six years old and had just begun to join his father at the temple for lessons, had already surpassed all of his peers. The boy, named Joshua, was devouring Scripture at a rate familiar to those priests old enough to remember Caiaphas when he had begun his own studies. Gamaliel appeared especially gratified when Caiaphas expressed interest in meeting Joshua and examining him personally. He left the chamber promising to bring the boy to their next meeting.

Caiaphas was pleased to see that all was in good order, and he listened carefully as each man gave his report. He questioned the priests thoroughly during the meetings, both to glean a better understanding of their areas of responsibility and to demonstrate his interest and care in all temple matters. He could sense Annas and Joazar standing behind him throughout, nodding approvingly as he went about this exercise. Simon, too, appeared to be satisfied with the way he was beginning to establish himself as high priest.

By the time the week was over and he was able to return home, Caiaphas felt drained of energy, his mind teeming with all he had learned. Despite months of preparation ahead of his appointment, and the years he had watched both his father-in-law and others in the role of high priest, he had not understood the full complexity of temple management before now. He thought with greater appreciation of Rivkah, who was charged with a small household and a handful of servants. In many ways, the temple was its own kind of estate, but significantly larger and more complex, with many more people, animals, and possessions to oversee and control.

He told her as much when they were finally able to steal away for a moment. She laughed heartily, her eyes flashing. "Only you, my love, would compare my small responsibilities to the running of the entire temple." But he could tell she was pleased at the compliment. She smiled up at him, and then sighed as she leaned against the wall in the upper corridor where they stood together, raising a hand to his face as she did so.

When she spoke, her voice was light and teasing. "And so, Joseph, I suppose I must say goodbye to this cheek, which has already begun to hide itself from me." Now that Caiaphas was high priest, he would no longer take a blade to his beard or hair. Already there was growth across his face that felt rough to the touch as Rivkah cupped her hand on his chin.

Caiaphas looked down at his wife, and suddenly all of the tension and anticipation he had been holding over the last week released. He groaned slightly and pulled her closer, curving his arm firmly around her waist. She leaned into him, and together they stood there in silence, their breath rising and falling as one. Below their guests were already arriving. Caiaphas could just make out Nathan's low murmur as he welcomed them and led them to the central courtyard of the estate. People greeted one another with boisterous excitement. Caiaphas could hear the clanging of platters and the clinking of goblets as Rebecca and her staff arranged the food and drink that had been prepared in anticipation of the gathering.

Caiaphas knew that the next several nights would be spent in celebration. He would be the center of attention at lavish parties held at both his home and at the house of Annas. The wine would be flowing, the plates of roasted lamb and grilled fish piled high. Many priests and other respected members of the community and their families would be joining them for jubilant singing, dancing, and feasting. The festivities would begin early and stretch late into the night. Everyone seemed to feel that Caiaphas's appointment was ushering in a new era, with Rome content to leave Jerusalem in peace, and the management of the temple secure and stable. From Annas and Joazar to the marketplace merchants, and even to Gratus, whose messenger had delivered his congratulations earlier that afternoon to the temple, all appeared to be in the mood for rejoicing. While Caiaphas's dearest wish was merely to spend time in peaceful quiet at home with his family, he understood that rest would have to wait. His responsibilities were just beginning, and only God knew what lay in store for him in the years ahead.

PART II

CHAPTER 16

When Caiaphas awoke, the first thing he remembered was the heavy warmth of the chamber. As he lay in bed, breathing deeply, he was conscious of his bedclothes, which had shifted off of him in his sleep. The cool air that played on his bare legs served as a stark contrast to the heat of the room in which he had just imagined himself. He lay in the darkness, listening to Rivkah's soft inhale and exhale beside him, and contemplated what he had just seen.

He had been in the Chamber of Hewn Stone at the temple. The walls appeared dirtier than he knew them to be, and the furnishings of the place were different. But there was no mistaking the room where he had spent so many hours, where he gathered the council of priests daily to settle disputes, to review matters of doctrine, and to receive reports on all aspects of the temple. In this vision, Caiaphas was not in his usual place, seated in the center of the proceedings. Instead, he watched from the back of the room, able from that vantage point to see all those gathered.

There was clearly some sort of trial taking place in the chamber, a normal if not common occurrence during a regular council gathering. While the priesthood was limited in its ability to pronounce judgments on the people of Jerusalem, there were still many offenses that fell under the priests' jurisdiction. On these matters, their authority was honored by Jews and Romans alike.

In the center of the room stood the three young men on trial. Their clothes were rough and soiled, their wrists clapped in iron chains that trailed onto the floor of the chamber. Just behind them, a man stood, his broad chest making him seem larger than all of the others gathered. Something about his bearing made it clear that he was in charge of the prisoners. Despite his gray hair and beard, there was no question in Caiaphas's mind that the men in chains would be no match for him should they choose to revolt against their shackles. Still, the prisoners seemed unruffled, their heads held high, their shoulders gently sloping and relaxed, facing the council.

By contrast, the priests of the council appeared agitated, incensed at the men who stood before them. Their brows knit, they gestured amongst themselves, their frantic whispering and the anger on their faces standing in direct contrast to the peaceful demeanor of the men on trial. As Caiaphas took several steps closer, one of the priests raised his head. Caiaphas saw with great surprise the face of his brother-in-law Matthias, the lines on his face and the gray at his temples suggesting that this vision was taking place in a far distant future. Then the large man overseeing the prisoners turned, and Caiaphas saw plainly the face of Matthias's older brother Theo, also aged far beyond his current years.

Looking around, Caiaphas caught glimpses of others he recognized. Eli, the son of Simon and Julia, was there, looking serious and calm in the midst of the anger that surrounded him. Next to him was Joshua, Gamaliel's boy, still handsome despite the furrows that age had etched onto his forehead. As Caiaphas watched, Joshua leaned over and spoke quietly to the high priest, who sat in his place of honor at the center of the room. The man in the high priest's robes was unrecognizable at first, but raised his head slightly as Caiaphas drew closer. Caiaphas realized with a start that it was Ben, Annas's youngest son, now at least as old as his father. Ben looked so much like Annas during his time as high priest that Caiaphas had to blink to reassure himself that it was not in fact his father-in-law before him.

Although Caiaphas could see everyone plainly, and could move about the chamber himself, the sound of the proceedings was muted, so that he could only make out mutterings and whispers. As Ben rose to his feet, drawing himself up majestically before the prisoners, Caiaphas could see that he was about to pronounce judgment on those who stood before him. Ben's eyes flashed dangerously, and his lip curled into a pitiless smile as he surveyed the scene. Caiaphas was reminded for a moment of Eleazar, and the look that used to come onto his face just before he pinned Theo down in a wrestling match.

As Caiaphas watched, unable to look away, Ben pointed at the prisoners and spoke. His words broke through the veil of the dream in which Caiaphas knew he was immersed. "For blasphemy, and continuing to stir up division among our people, you are hereby sentenced to death by stoning. Your sentence will be carried out immediately. Take them away." Ben's voice, though measured and even, was filled with a quiet rage that made his words cut through the air like a blade. As soon as he finished speaking, he nodded to Theo, who took the chains that bound the men and roughly led them out of the room. As the rest of the priests murmured their assent, Caiaphas saw on Joshua's face a look of grim satisfaction. Looking back at the prisoners, Caiaphas was again struck by their lack of emotion, their seeming willingness to accept their fate without resistance. The one in the center's hair was the wildest and most tangled, and his injured face bore the signs of a recent struggle. Caiaphas couldn't help but wonder if the wounds he saw there, still fresh and angry, had been inflicted by the temple guards. But the man's eyes were clear and serene. As he passed by, Caiaphas shuddered as he wondered what his story might be, and what he had done to incur such wrath from the council.

And then, before he could see anything else, Caiaphas found himself awake, his lungs filling with the cool air of the night as he shook his head to clear it. His dreams, which always seemed to return just as he thought he might be free of them, had been particularly vivid of late. He had no doubt that this dream in particular had been brought on by the stresses that currently faced him at the temple.

MORE THAN A DECADE into his service as high priest, Caiaphas had experienced periods of calm and periods of turmoil. It had been three years since the most challenging moment of his high priesthood had come and gone, and he thought with satisfaction on how he had handled the conflict. When Gratus sent word that they must meet, that he had news that Caiaphas needed to hear in person, Caiaphas was immediately concerned. The relationship between himself and Gratus up until that point had been smooth, in part due to the fact that Annas continued to play a role in managing the information being shared with the Roman governor. Caiaphas sometimes resented the fact that both Annas and Simon still treated him less like a high priest and more like the eager young pupil he had once been. Nonetheless, he was grateful for their continued participation in the management of both the temple and the city.

Annas, already halfway through his sixth decade, showed no decrease in either vigor or determination. More than ever, he remained immersed in the daily operations of the temple, even as Tova chided him to allow the next generation of priests to make their own way. "You are worse than a mother sparrow, fretting over her young ones instead of letting them fly free." Tova laughed as she looked at her husband over her weaving, glancing at Jonathan and Matthias, who sat at the table with them. "Our sons have become men themselves, with families of their own, or have you not noticed?" Jonathan, reserved as ever at thirty-two, grinned at his mother, but did not respond. Next to him, his wife Sera held their youngest child, a girl, who lay asleep against her mother's chest. Matthias, who at twenty-six had become very like Jonathan in manner and personality, did not look up from his food, but allowed himself a small smile as he continued to pick at his stew. Although Matthias had no children, he too had been married for several years. His wife Hannah, who sat directly across from him, chuckled softly at Tova's question.

Tova leaned away from the table toward her other two sons, Theo and Ben, who sat in another corner of the courtyard, deep in conversation. Theo, whose broad shoulders and torso made him the largest and most imposing of his brothers, had more than enough energy to spare. When he did remain seated for any length of time, it was usually because he was engaged in some kind of strategic planning or plot. Ben, who at twenty had just become a priest in his own right, greatly admired Theo, nine years his elder, and was always eager to show him that he could hold his own, despite being slighter and less physically imposing.

Tova called to them to get their attention, and when they both looked up, she laughed. "What are the two of you scheming now?" She smiled benevolently as she ran her hand along the fabric she had been weaving, looking for snags or loose edges. "The look on your faces… you look just as you did when I used to catch you stealing figs from the storehouse." She turned back to Annas, who was watching her with growing amusement. "Never mind, love. I see that these boys of ours may be grown, but they are still in need of a father's strong hand."

This scene had been shared with Caiaphas by Jonathan, who told him the story as they stood side by side preparing to enter the ritual bath at the temple, just before the preparations for the Day of Atonement were to begin. Caiaphas smiled as Jonathan relayed the conversation, which he could picture exactly as if he had been there. Although amused, he couldn't help but wish that his mother-in-law's admonition had been taken a bit more seriously by everyone involved. There were many on the council who still went to his father-in-law first with their concerns. It did not help that all four of Annas's remaining sons had become influential figures within the temple. Jonathan had begun his service in the treasury as anticipated, but had been given more responsibilities as time went on and he proved himself capable. He now worked closely with Simon in overseeing multiple areas of temple management, while Matthias, who shared his aptitude and love for facts and figures, happily took over his former role. Theo was second in command of the palace guard, and the father of three strapping boys of his own, the eldest of whom had already begun his lessons at the temple. Even Ben, as a new priest, was treated with a respect that belied his youth and sometimes brash manner, and his talent as a scholar was rightly admired by all.

Caiaphas reflected on the memory as he shook himself free of the remaining bedclothes that clung to him, and slipped out of his bedchamber into the corridor beyond. Quietly, he made his way into the nearest open courtyard. As he stood in silence, the chill of the night air ruffling his garments, he thought again about his last meeting with Gratus, three years earlier.

The message had come through Simon, who had been sent to welcome the governor upon his arrival to Jerusalem. Temple preparations were just starting for the Feast of Unleavened Bread, and Caiaphas was not anticipating having to entertain or receive visitors until the feast had begun. But Simon's message made it clear that an adjustment would need to be made. The fact that Gratus would give Simon no more information regarding his news made it clear that urgency was of the essence. The following night, Caiaphas sent word to the governor that he would be able to receive Gratus at his home just after dusk. Rivkah was tasked with preparing a meal with the help of Rebecca, who had become an accomplished cook under Rivkah's tutelage. The entire household was filled with an air of anticipation as they waited for the Roman governor to arrive.

When Gratus at last entered Caiaphas's estate, the look on his face gave Caiaphas some peace. The older man seemed comfortable, with his usual air of someone accustomed to his own authority. As he settled into a seat of honor in one of the larger banquet halls that had been hastily set for his visit, he looked around approvingly. "You and your father-in-law have such handsome property, Caiaphas. It is a great pleasure to visit with you when I am in Jerusalem." He gazed admiringly up at the columns that lined the room in which they dined, their smooth white rounded shafts narrowing slightly where they met with the square capital at the top of each one. In between every column, the rounded archways that led to the inner courtyard were evenly set and perfectly built, reflecting a precision that had clearly required enormous skill and labor to achieve.

Caiaphas was pleased by his guest's compliment, although he shrugged it away as he called Nathan forward to pour the wine. He hated to admit that this man's opinion still meant something to him. From the first time they had met, nearly twenty years before, when he was still a boy in Annas's house, Caiaphas had been impressed, though intimidated, by Gratus. There was a part of him that longed for more of the confidence that seemed to come so naturally to the Roman, who never appeared to question his own intuition or judgment.

The wine poured, Nathan and Rebecca quietly removed themselves, and Caiaphas and Gratus were left alone. Gratus watched them leave. When their steps had finished echoing through the stone hall outside the chamber, he turned to Caiaphas. "And so, my friend, our partnership draws to its inevitable close."

Caiaphas looked at him, surprised. Gratus had been governor of the territory for eleven years. From everything Caiaphas knew, the emperor had been pleased with his service. As Gratus was a favorite of Tiberius, it was understood that he would continue to have his own say as to whether he remained or not. Caiaphas had always assumed that the governor was more than content with his post. His home in Caesarea was extremely comfortable, and the region had remained in relative peace, especially since Caiaphas had become high priest. Yes, there were always rumors of those who traveled the countryside, talking of revolt against the Romans, but very few of these rabble-rousers ever made it to Jerusalem. Those who did were quickly identified by Annas's network of spies, and just as quickly silenced by the temple guard.

Caiaphas could think of no reason why Gratus himself would have requested to be recalled to Rome. This change must be coming from the emperor himself, or from those he trusted to manage his affairs. Caiaphas knit his brow and looked at Gratus, genuinely concerned. "Are you not satisfied with your post in Caesarea? Or are there other reasons for this change?"

Gratus smiled, and Caiaphas thought he saw the smallest hint of bitterness in the Roman's eyes as he spoke. "I would be happy to live out the rest of my days in Caesarea, Caiaphas. Your father-in-law made a powerful ally, and you have proven to be a worthy successor. No, it is not my choice that takes me back to Rome. It appears that in my years away from the emperor, another has taken my place as his advisor and confidant." His eyes now definitely held an air of bitterness, and for the first time Caiaphas had a sense that this man who always appeared so impervious had a weak spot. "The commander of the guard, a man named Sejanus, has become highly influential in Rome. He has suggested to Tiberius that it is time for a change in Jerusalem. Apparently Sejanus has put forth a young general named Pilate for the position, and Tiberius has been convinced. I received word less than a week ago to ready myself for the arrival of Pilate. I have no doubt that he carries with him papers for my removal and his assignment."

Gratus leaned back and looked around the room before speaking again. "I wish there was more I could tell you about this new governor. But I have only the reports that have reached me since I first heard rumors of Sejanus's endorsement. He is a younger man than you, though he has been battle-tested. If Sejanus has put his confidence in him, he is also someone who knows how to flatter those in power." Gratus's lip curled slightly. "He will arrive determined to show strength. I have been made to understand that he knows very little of your people and customs. He will need to be taught, but carefully." Gratus smiled. "I have no doubt that there are those among your council who could do the job nicely."

Caiaphas returned the smile, although he sighed as he did so. He had taken for granted that Gratus was immoveable. He had grown used to the man, even fond of him. As Caiaphas became more comfortable in the role of high priest, he had felt Gratus's respect for him grow, despite his father-in-law's continued participation in matters involving the governor. The mutual admiration between the two of them was a key factor in his success, and in the stability they had created together. Although Gratus did not worship the God of the Jews, he had never done anything to undermine the council's authority. While Caiaphas always had the suspicion that Gratus found their ways more quaint than worthy of honor, he was content to leave them to it.

Caiaphas remembered all too well how his father-in-law had worked with previous governors. This first characterization of Pilate made him sound suspiciously like Marcus and Rufus, the two previous governors Annas had so expertly managed. Caiaphas could picture the look on Annas's face when he learned Gratus's news, how Annas would eagerly look forward to the challenge of bending yet another impressionable Roman governor to his will. But Caiaphas couldn't help but think that this new man might not be as malleable as those who had come before. He allowed this sentiment to release in another sigh as Gratus looked at him in silence, waiting for his response.

"As always, Gratus, I am grateful for your willingness to keep us informed of Rome's plans. I am sorry for this news. You have been an ally and friend to my family, to my father-in-law before me and to myself. You will be missed."

Gratus smiled, and raised his glass to Caiaphas. "I wish you luck, old friend. I will be watching from Rome. This Pilate does not know what awaits him."

Indeed, Caiaphas thought, Gratus's words had been prophetic. Pilate's arrival in Jerusalem had been a disaster from the beginning. He had traveled first to Caesarea and, as Gratus had anticipated, delivered papers announcing his appointment as governor. As soon as Gratus returned to Rome, Pilate set out to visit Jerusalem. Under cover of night, he traveled into the city and arrived at Herod's Palace with his guard. But as morning light began filtering through the streets, even before the first sacrifices had been made at the temple, angry citizens began converging there to share with the priests what Pilate had done.

The new governor had brought with him a legion of armed soldiers, who had stationed themselves outside the entrance to the palace, just within the gardens that surrounded it. These soldiers carried standards, large wooden poles with huge gilded shields at their pinnacle. But unlike previous governors, who had respected the Jewish laws regarding idols and figures, Pilate's men carried standards topped with enormous eagles crowned in laurel wreaths and bearing both the name and likeness of the emperor on platforms beneath their talons. It was everything the priests could do to reassure the angry mob that they would act immediately, and it was with some consternation that the council hastily gathered to determine how best to proceed.

Joazar, who had become less active within the priesthood since a fall left him partially disabled, was at the temple that morning being seen by one of the temple healers. He slowly made his way into the council chamber, helped along by Simon's teenaged son Eli, and took his seat at one of the wooden benches, his pale face a mixture of pain and fury. The priests began to congregate, young and old murmuring together as they discussed the matter at hand. As Caiaphas strode into the chamber, his robes trailing behind him, a hush fell over those gathered.

Simon called the council to order, and his voice echoed as he spoke. "Noble members of the council, we gather this morning to discuss the matter of the governor's standards, which he has brought into our city. They are an outrage and an affront to our God. We must address the offense immediately. High priest, what would you propose we do?"

Caiaphas looked around at his council. So many men he respected were gathered. He knew this moment was a crucial one in his priesthood. How he dealt with this new governor would determine, not only his relationship with the man, but also the way he was seen by those whose good opinion he still sought. Although he had already been high priest for eight years, the lack of any major conflict up until this point meant that he had been able to rest on his father-in-law's good reputation without too much effort. That time was over.

The next several days were tumultuous at best. At Caiaphas's command, the council sent a small delegation to Pilate to request that the governor remove his standards. Simon, who led the group, told Caiaphas of his reception with Pilate, which was brief and awkward. Pilate, affronted, not only rejected the request but immediately left the city with a small party, leaving behind his armed guard and the standards, which glittered mockingly as the soldiers stood guard at the palace entrance. As soon as the people of Jerusalem realized that Pilate had retreated to Caesarea without removing the offending effigies, they flocked to the temple again, demanding further action.

Ultimately, the council had little choice but to send a group of priests to Caesarea to attempt to negotiate with Pilate. This party, which included Theo and Jonathan, embarked on their journey only to find themselves joined by hundreds of angry citizens of Jerusalem, carrying sacks hastily packed and leading mules along the dusty road. By the time they reached Caesarea several days later, the mob had swelled to nearly a thousand men. The Jews were allowed into the city and led by armed guard to the stadium where previous Roman governors had hosted chariot races and physical competitions of strength and agility. The Jews set up camp within the walls of the stadium to await Pilate's next move.

Jonathan and Theo attempted to arrange for a private audience with Pilate, knowing that it was their best chance at reaching a conclusion that would allow both the Jewish leadership and the Roman governor to appear in control. Jonathan, reserved and respectful, might have been able to explain to Pilate why the people were so agitated by his actions, and to negotiate a way to settle the matter quietly. But Pilate refused. Instead, he insisted on meeting them at the stadium, in the heat of the day, his forehead shining and his temples damp as he ascended to the podium to address the crowd gathered. As he began to speak, his guards emerged from their hiding spots throughout the stadium. It became clear that he was prepared to bend those congregated to his will by brute force if necessary.

But Pilate had not bargained on the passion of the people. When the Jews gathered saw the soldiers' spears glistening in the heavy air, they fell to their knees as one. The men toward the front of the crowd opened their garments at the throat and chest, revealing their bare skin to the governor in a gesture of quiet defiance. They would not be cowed, not even by the threat of death. When Jonathan was finally able to report to Caiaphas after he had returned to Jerusalem, the awe in his voice was palpable as he relayed the scene.

"You should have seen our people, Caiaphas. They were resolute and immoveable. The guards were unsure how to proceed. They kept glancing at one another across the heads of those kneeling before them, frozen." He shook his head as he remembered. "The look on the governor's face was one of shock, and you could see the fear in his eyes. I do not think Pilate understood until that moment how ill-prepared he was to serve in our territory." Jonathan laughed, but there was no mirth in it. "I believe he must be questioning his mentor Sejanus's kindness in putting him forth for the position."

Caiaphas allowed himself a smile in response to Jonathan's story, which he had heard rumors of in the two days before Jonathan and Theo finally returned to Jerusalem. By then it had been more than a day since a small band of Pilate's soldiers had arrived, and had quietly released the armed guard still stationed at Herod's Palace from their duty. The standards were taken down, and must have been either stored within the palace or smuggled out of the city by night. They had not made an appearance since.

The throngs of people that poured back into Jerusalem in the days before and after the standards were removed were giddy with triumph and success. At all hours of the day and night celebrations could be heard emanating from houses in both the affluent and humble sections of the city. Sacrifices at the temple were coming in droves, as people brought extra offerings of thanksgiving and praise to God for delivering them from the heavy hand of Rome.

But the council that gathered each morning tried to maintain a more measured tone and attitude about the matter. Annas and Simon were particularly concerned that Caiaphas understand the gravity of the situation, and the ways it might influence their future relationship with the governor.

"It is not an auspicious beginning," said Simon, as the three men remained in the Chamber of Hewn Stone after the council meeting disbanded for the day and most of the priests returned to their temple responsibilities. He was rubbing his forehead as he paced back and forth, while Annas sat several feet away and Caiaphas stood in the center of the room. "Pilate has been humiliated in a most public way, and I fear he still does not understand why the offense was problematic in the first place. How could they have sent a man to us who is so unfamiliar with our ways? How could Gratus have allowed it to happen?"

Annas watched him, sighing. "Simon, since when have the Romans been worthy of our trust, or generous in their understanding? Gratus was his own man. But for all his bluster, he respected us. This Pilate is a much more dangerous ally, if we can even call him that. He is an ignorant fool."

Caiaphas tried to suppress the frustration he felt as he looked at the two older men, both of whom spoke as if the weight of the problem fell on their shoulders rather than on his. As high priest, this was his burden, his responsibility, and he knew it even if they did not. He understood all too well the dilemma before him, and he was determined to take action to do what he could to find a remedy. Clearing his throat, he stepped forward. Both men stopped what they were doing and looked at him.

"Annas. Simon. Believe me when I say that I know the position is a challenging one. But if Pilate is to be governor here, we must find a way to work with him." He took another breath. "I believe we must make him feel welcome, must show him that we are willing to be ruled." Annas looked angry, and Simon blanched. But Caiaphas continued, trying to fill his words with gravitas and authority even as they tumbled out of him.

"We serve our God, not the Romans. But Annas, it was you who taught me how important it is for them to feel as if they are in control. The only way Pilate will be of any use to us is if we can convince him that he is the one in charge of our territory. I believe I must be the one to do it. I must go to Caesarea."

If Annas had appeared angry before, it was nothing compared to the look that now spread across his face. He leaned forward as if to stand, but Simon put a hand on his shoulder. After a moment's hesitation, he remained where he was. It was Simon who eventually spoke.

"Go to Caesarea? Caiaphas, you cannot be serious. As high priest, your responsibility is here. The temple cannot bear your absence."

Caiaphas shook his head. "It can and it will, my friend. My responsibility is to the temple, you are right. And my allegiance insists that I make this man our ally, for the good of our people and our future." He inclined his head toward Simon. "Surely you can execute my responsibilities while I am away, Simon? You were my teacher in the high priesthood, and I know there is nothing that will escape your notice."

He turned to Annas, his voice rising slightly, although he tried to keep his tone deferential. "And noble Annas, how can you think that the temple will lack anything while you and your sons remain? There is no one else in whose hands I would trust the responsibility of oversight in my absence. It was, after all, your temple long before it was mine." He held back a wry smile as he saw his father-in-law soften slightly. He knew that he had achieved his objective, that Annas would support the endeavor despite his disapproval. He cleared his throat. "It will be but a handful of days, and the preparations for the Feast of Unleavened Bread will still be underway when I return." He looked at them both, and allowed a brief moment of silence before he continued. "Then it is settled."

AFTER CAIAPHAS HAD COME and gone from Caesarea, he marveled at how smooth the journey had been from beginning to end. As he and Rivkah sat at their evening meal, their son Judah sitting quietly between them, he shared with her how Pilate had received him with a graciousness that stood in stark contrast to the Roman's initial behavior, greatly mollified by the gifts and tokens that Caiaphas had sent ahead, finely woven linen, vessels of gold and silver, and delicacies including ruby pomegranates and rich oil pressed from olives. Pilate was obviously impressed by Caiaphas's party, which although small included both Gamaliel and his son Joshua, who served as their manservant. The priests had taken great pains to dress in their most elaborate and ornate garments. Caiaphas had consulted with Matthias before the journey, combing through the treasury for the most impressive tokens that he could both bestow as gifts and wear himself before Pilate. If his goal had been to impress upon the new governor both the weight of his own position, and the great value he saw in Pilate, he could not have been more satisfied with the result.

Caiaphas saw almost immediately that, yet again, Gratus had proven to be a wealth of knowledge, even as Gratus himself had doubted the value of his information. Even more so than the governors who had come before him, Pilate was a man taken with power and privilege. If he had been horrified that his first appearance in Jerusalem had been greeted with derision and scorn by the poorest of her citizens, he was equally flattered and placated by the idea that the most important member of the community had now come to pay him a personal visit. Several times during the course of their brief stay in Caesarea, Gamaliel reiterated to Pilate what an honor it was for Caiaphas to have traveled to meet him, and how he had made the journey against the recommendation of his most learned advisors. "But our noble Caiaphas knew that a man like you must be greeted properly," Gamaliel would finish, stroking his beard and nodding sagely as Pilate murmured his appreciation.

Indeed, the trip to Caesarea had been a defining moment in Caiaphas's priesthood, one that three years later he looked back on with great satisfaction. The relationship with Pilate continued to be challenging. The man was not sophisticated in his intellect or understanding. More than once Caiaphas marveled at how someone with so little sense of nuance could have risen to such a position. But Pilate liked the way he was treated by Caiaphas and by the other priests to whom he eventually granted audiences in both Caesarea and Jerusalem. They had settled into an understanding that, for the time being, was operating well. More than that, the incident with the standards allowed Caiaphas to take action for the first time in opposition to his advisors. He had emerged with a victory that gave him greater confidence in his own ability to lead. The last three years had brought with them more moments when he knew that Annas or Simon disagreed with him. There were even times when he found himself wondering what types of conversations or meetings were going on without his knowledge. But, from the start of Pilate's term, there had been a shift within the priesthood. Caiaphas felt himself being taken more seriously as high priest and ultimately as the one in charge.

It was this pleasing thought that stayed with Caiaphas as he took a last look around the courtyard before returning to his bedchamber, where Rivkah still lay, peacefully asleep. Taking care not to disturb her as he climbed back into bed, he gently untangled the bedclothes and covered himself. Within minutes he fell into a dreamless sleep from which he did not awake until daybreak.

CHAPTER 17

The Day of Atonement was one of the longest days of the year from the perspective of the priesthood. For Caiaphas in particular, it was a day full of import and responsibility. The climax of forty days leading up to the festival itself, days in which the priesthood prepared the people for the annual cycle of repentance, fasting, and celebration, it represented the final day of offering and sacrifice that closed the season. On that day, the fate of the people would be sealed for another year. It was on the shoulders of the high priest that this fate lay.

Throughout the days of preparation, the priests set aside the finest livestock and grain offerings for the sacrifices ahead. Simon commissioned an inventory of all the storehouses of the temple to ensure the quality of their contents. Matthias was kept busy procuring the necessary oils and spices that would be required for the offerings, and flour that had been carefully milled by hand was purchased from local merchants and delivered to the temple. At Caiaphas's estate, Rivkah too was occupied in preparation for the feasting that would follow the festival. She and Rebecca spent hours reviewing the dishes planned for the feast. Nathan was constantly going to and from the marketplace to obtain various ingredients and items for the celebration.

For the household, it was especially important that all of the work be finished ahead of time, because the Day of Atonement itself would be spent in prayer and fasting. No work could be done until sundown that night. Unlike some of the other festivals, where people would flock to the temple to observe the sacrifices of the priests and to bring their own offerings, the Day of Atonement was spent at home by those not intimately involved in the temple rituals. Because Caiaphas was high priest, his household would be the final destination for many celebrating the end of the festival. Tova and Julia both planned to spend the day with Rivkah at Caiaphas's estate. As soon as night fell, the three women would spring into action alongside the household staff to make the final preparations for their guests, who would arrive famished from a day of fasting and ready to feast.

For Caiaphas, it was the day itself that held the most significance. As a boy, he remembered Annas readying himself for the Day of Atonement for weeks beforehand, and the hours his father-in-law spent in quiet meditation in his bedchamber while Tova admonished the children to leave him in peace. Caiaphas knew all too well that this was the day when the high priest performed his most important role, as the sole representative of the people before God. When he entered the chamber of the Holy of Holies to sprinkle the blood of the bull that had been sacrificed, he was continuing a tradition that had upheld his people since the days of Moses. Although the ark of the covenant no longer sat within the sacred space, having been lost before the destruction of the first temple, the spot where it once stood was holy ground. The area was raised to show its importance, and the blood that was spilled over the spot would mingle with the incense, filling the room with thick, heady smoke that blurred his vision and caused his nostrils to burn.

For three days beforehand, Caiaphas slept at the temple in order to prevent any potential defilement that would make him unable to participate. Each morning he descended the stairs from the Chamber of the Hearth and cleansed himself in the bath below, ensuring his purity for the rituals ahead. On the morning of the Day of Atonement, he rose early and strode past the Offering Gate to where the animals were being readied for the day's sacrifices. In addition to the regular offerings, a single bull and two goats would be required. As he approached, the priests who managed the livestock brought forth the animals for one last inspection. The goats' hair had been brushed clean until it shone in the early morning light. Their plaintive bleating traveled across the courtyard as the other priests began to gather. The bull's coat was a ruddy red, and he stood as high as Caiaphas's shoulder, gently pawing the ground and snorting so that clouds of dust emanated from around his hooves and below his nostrils.

Caiaphas appraised the animals carefully. It was crucial that there be no blemish or imperfection in any of the livestock sacrificed today. Pleased with what he saw, he nodded to Simon, who in turn gave the order to a handful of young priests standing by, their white robes pristine, waiting for his signal. The men approached the bull and led it up a ramp onto the slaughtering block. One priest took a linen cloth that had been soaked in frankincense and oil, and held it close to the bull's nose, which quivered as it took in the calming scent. The animal's eyes closed, and it did not resist as it was carefully positioned on its side, its hind feet tethered and its neck exposed. Two priests knelt beneath the head, holding a copper vessel in which they would catch the blood as it fell, while another brought forth the blade that would be used for the sacrifice. Satisfied that all was proceeding as it should, Caiaphas left the slaughtering block and climbed the steps that led to the sanctuary itself, stopping just in front of the gate. There he turned and waited as the young priest in charge of the two goats followed, leading the animals until they stopped on either side of him.

As Caiaphas stood, silent, feeling the weight of the breastplate and crown he wore over his ceremonial linen garments, Simon came toward him carrying a small wooden box. Inside were the two smooth stones hammered from pure gold that he would use to cast lots for the animals before him. The goats were identical. But these stones would allow the priests to determine which would serve as a sacrifice, and which would be led into the wilderness, symbolically carrying on its head the sins of the people, away from the city to its destruction on the cliffs that lay beyond its walls. Clearing his throat, Caiaphas spoke, his voice carrying across to the Priests' Court where the rest of the priesthood now stood waiting.

"On this day, we serve as representatives of our people, taking the wrath of our God's supreme justice upon ourselves, atoning for the indiscretions of our citizens along with our own. These animals will share in our burden, one becoming a sacrifice to our God and the other taking away our transgressions as it leaves our presence. In a ritual that goes back to our forefather Aaron, we now determine their fate."

Opening the box, Caiaphas thrust his hands into its cavity and drew out the stones, taking care not to look at them as he did so. He clasped one in each hand, and these he raised outstretched so that all could see. He spread his arms wide, each hand hovering over one of the goats. After pausing a moment, he turned his palms up and opened them both toward the sky. Looking into his right hand, he immediately saw the etched markings that meant this goat was destined for the altar. Closing his hand tightly around the stone and feeling the cool weight of it, he raised that hand high while lowering the other one. "To God we give our offering! It is determined."

THE REST of the day passed in a haze of blood and perfume. Once the goat to his left had been prayed over and led away, and the remaining bull and goat were both slaughtered, it was time for Caiaphas to prepare himself to approach the Holy of Holies. Four times he would enter the small, sacred room, bringing with him the blood and incense that he would sprinkle and spread on the altar. Between each offering, he would return to the Chamber of the Hearth to bathe and change his garments, caked and heavy with soot and dried blood. There he would kneel and pray, praising God for bringing him through the ritual unscathed. Caiaphas had been taught from the time he was a boy the risks the high priest faced in entering the chamber, and how only one who was pleasing to God would be able to live through the experience. He emerged from each session spent and filled with gratitude to see the light piercing through the outer gate.

By the end of the day, his hands were blistered from carrying the incense pan in and out of the sanctuary. His back ached from spending hours prostrate, unwilling to raise his eyes any higher than was necessary to make his way in and out past the heavy curtain that covered the entrance to the room. As he bathed for the final time, Caiaphas allowed his body to sink beneath the surface of the bath, his ears filling with water and drowning out the evening prayers and songs that drifted down from above, the priests marking the day's end as the sun set. The water was cool, untouched by the warmth of the sun. The stone bottom of the basin felt cold and solid beneath his sore feet. The tendrils of his beard and hair curled in the water like grape vines just before the harvest, twisting on themselves and clinging to his temples and neck as he raised himself up out of the water. He felt satisfied and relieved, and the knot of muscle that had been resting between his shoulder blades for weeks began to loosen.

THE PRIESTS who walked through the streets toward Caiaphas's estate an hour later made up a large and handsome party. Caiaphas led the group, his hair still glistening and his white linen tunic shining in the twilight air, the ceremonial garments put away until the next time they would be needed. Behind him were Annas and his sons, along with Joazar, who was helped along by Simon and Eli. At fourteen, Eli was the youngest of their party, and his main responsibility was to ensure that his uncle had everything he needed. Bringing up the rear were Gamaliel and his son Joshua, the other teenager of the group, accompanied by another young man named Saul who had become a favorite of Gamaliel's during Caiaphas's term as high priest. Together, these men and boys represented some of the most influential families in all of Jerusalem. But it would have been hard to know it from the levity and good humor that permeated the group as they walked. Ben had slowed his steps to keep pace with Joshua. The two were snickering at something, their cheeks bulging as they tried not to laugh out loud. Jonathan, just behind Annas, kept looking back at them sternly. But even he could not bring himself to admonish the two young men on such a magnificent evening. As the group walked on, their quiet conversation was interrupted only by the stray guffaw emanating from Ben and Joshua. Their footsteps echoed softly on the dusty streets of Jerusalem, as they passed household after household just about to begin their own celebrations.

By contrast, Caiaphas's home was a flurry of sounds and smells. Nearly every corner of the estate had been taken over by the celebration about to burst from within its walls. All of the torches were lit, and Rivkah raced from room to room, her cheeks flushed as she shouted orders to Nathan and called out to Rebecca to check on the progress of the meal in its final stages of preparation. Tova and Julia laughed as they watched her scurry through the main banquet hall, her tunic barely touching the ground as she went. Now in her thirties, Rivkah had grown accustomed to her role as the wife of the high priest. She carried herself with a command that made everyone within earshot jump at her directives, even as her eyes still twinkled with the wit and charm that had first impressed Caiaphas so many years before.

The only people not caught up in the commotion were the two children who sat in a side courtyard, warming themselves together by the fire. The girl's hair glowed in the flickering light, its golden waves framing her young face and gathering softly at her shoulders. There could be no looking at Martha without recognizing her as the child of Julia and Simon, her almond-shaped eyes bearing witness to her parentage as much as her golden hair. She had Julia's sweetness, although there was an impishness and intensity in her that sometimes took her more even-tempered mother by surprise. A folded swath of linen lay in her lap. The needle and thread that sat there untouched suggested that her intention had been to embroider the garment. Instead, however, her attention was fixed on the boy to her right, who sat with his shoulders drawn close together, a woolen blanket covering him as he stared into the fire.

Judah's curls were exactly like his father's. Caiaphas's influence was also evident in the shape of his face and chin, and in the way he studied his surroundings, careful and curious. But his eyes were dark like Rivkah's, and the skin that stretched across his cheeks was sallow and pale. Judah had been sick for as long as he could remember, his body weak even as his mind had developed far beyond his eleven years. It was clear that, even with the blanket and the fire, he was not warm enough. Martha looked at him, concerned, as she lay aside her embroidery.

"Judah, what is it you need? Shall I fetch another blanket?" Her look of gentle concern seemed out of place on her young face, her knit brow more like that of a new mother than of the child she still was.

Judah looked up at her and smiled, and his eyes crinkled at the corners as he did so. "Ah, Martha, my caretaker." He looked back at the fire, the smile still playing across his face. "How often must I remind you that, just because you were born weeks before me, you are not responsible for my wellbeing?"

Martha rose, and when she spoke it was with a hint of frustration. "Judah, that is nonsense. I will be gone but a moment, and will return with something to warm us both." She crossed the courtyard before he could answer her, and returned carrying two stone mugs of steaming liquid. She smiled conspiratorially at Judah as she sat next to him, taking care not to spill the drinks as she did so.

"Nathan is just putting out the vessels of stew and drink. I convinced him to give us some of the honey wine before the feast." Gently, she placed one of the mugs in Judah's outstretched hands, and adjusted the blanket that had slipped from his shoulders. Settling herself next to him, she held up her own mug, and smiled. "Drink, Judah. It will warm you."

Judah obediently took a sip, and the sweet liquid slid down his throat like a soft caress. He sighed. "Thank you, Martha. Already you are a healer like your mother. What would I do without you to take care of me?" Mollified and pleased, she leaned her head on his shoulder. The two children sat in silence, watching the flames, as the rest of the household bustled around them.

By the time Caiaphas and his party reached the main gate of the estate, everything was ready. Rivkah hurried to meet them, her smile warm. She greeted her husband first, and then welcomed each of them in turn. When she reached Jonathan, she searched his eyes, and was satisfied by the look therein that all had gone well at the temple that day. As twins, Rivkah and Jonathan shared a unique ability to communicate without words. Caiaphas often teased his wife that he wished Jonathan could teach him the trick. "Ah, my love, but then we would have no need to speak, and I do so love your voice," Rivkah would say, as she gently rested a hand on his bearded cheek, stroking the hair that had long since covered his face and crept down his chin. He could not argue with her when she put it that way.

Within hours of their arrival, the house was full of guests, bellies bursting with the sumptuous feast that had been prepared and eaten, and hearts warmed by the wine that was flowing freely. Clusters of people congregated in each of the main courtyards, warming themselves around the fires, all of which were lit and crackling merrily in the evening air. The main banquet hall, in which the food had been laid out on wide wooden tables, was filled with the sound of music, as a small band of musicians played in one corner. The horn blared triumphantly as the melodies played by the lute and harp mingled with one another. The musicians' voices rose in boisterous celebration above them all.

Judah and Martha had long since abandoned their place by the fire. As the night air grew colder, Tova encouraged her grandson to join her upstairs, away from the chill of the evening. Martha, on the other hand, was pleased to participate in the festivities. She enjoyed sampling all of the delicacies that had been prepared, returning again and again to the banquet hall to taste one more morsel or to refill her mug with more of the honey wine. The musicians also captured her fancy. She laughed with delight as she watched them play, her eyes bright as she tried to follow the quick movements of the lute player's fingers as they danced across the strings. And then she was dancing herself, swaying with the music and twirling so that her robes lifted from the ground and encircled her like an embrace, her golden hair streaming behind her as she did so.

From a far corner of the banquet hall, Joshua stood and watched her. Although he was engaged in a rousing game of dice with Ben and Eli, whose laughter and cries punctuated the musicians' melodies like uneven drums, he found his eyes drifting again and again to the girl as she danced, laughing to herself as she dipped and bowed, her face rosy and her eyes shining in the torchlight. Eli, wondering what was distracting his friend, looked up and followed Joshua's gaze to where his sister danced. He frowned.

"That girl! What is she doing? Sometimes I think she forgets she is no longer a babe in arms, toddling around with no care as to who might be watching. If our mother saw her, she would not be pleased."

Ben, whose attention was now also drawn to Martha, laughed as Eli looked at him in surprise. "Eli, you are too serious. This is a celebration, and your sister is celebrating. We could all stand to rejoice a bit tonight."

Eli, disgruntled but not willing to argue with Ben, who was six years his senior and already a priest, turned back to the dice after another hard look at Martha. The girl had stopped dancing and was seated on a wine cask near the musicians, trying to catch her breath. As she scanned the room, she caught Joshua's eye, where he stood, still watching her, his expression inscrutable. Their eyes met, and her face flushed a deep red. She immediately looked away. Rising from her seat, she ran from the room, fleeing the hall for the coolness of the open courtyard just beyond it. She did not look back.

As she fled, Joshua's face broke into a grin. He too lowered his head, returning his eyes to the dice that Ben and Eli were taking turns scattering across the stone floor. Still, the smile lingered long after Martha was gone, and it took several moments before he found himself able to refocus on the game being played at his feet.

<h1 style="text-align:center">CHAPTER 18</h1>

Often in the mornings, if the air was clear and the hour early enough, Caiaphas and Rivkah would begin their day with a walk. Climbing one of the four staircases located at the corners of the property, they would quietly retreat to the upper level, careful not to disturb Judah or the household staff, some of whom were just beginning to stir. Around the perimeter of the estate, a limestone walkway made a path wide enough for at least three grown men to walk shoulder to shoulder. The walkway cut across the estate as well, encircling the main building and wrapping around it like a crown. At a leisurely pace, it took the two of them about twenty minutes to stroll the entire length of the perimeter and around the inner circle twice. It was during these walks that they discussed many of the pressing issues weighing on them, from Rivkah's concerns about Judah's health and education, to Caiaphas's most recent frustrations with the council or with the Roman governor.

As they walked, Caiaphas couldn't help remembering the many hours they had spent on the roof of Annas's house side by side, deep in conversation, seeking to study one another like particularly intriguing scrolls that warranted further scholarship. Fifteen years into their marriage, Caiaphas still felt there was much he did not understand about the woman who walked beside him, her gait purposeful but light, her eyes fixed on the horizon. But he did know with certainty that he had come to prize her intellect and good sense more and more with every passing season. Since the death of Eleazar, when she had made him promise to keep no more secrets from her, he had been true to his word, and had been richly rewarded by the wisdom and foresight she brought to any issue he lay before her.

It was Rivkah who proposed that he send to Gratus for information as to how Rome was taking the news of the death of the Jewish upstart named John, and more importantly, how the Romans were viewing the subsequent unrest that was occurring in Jerusalem as a result.

The man John had been known to the priesthood by reputation since his boyhood, the son of the priest Zachariah whom Gratus had questioned them about in the days before Caiaphas's appointment as high priest. Annas had reassured the governor at the time that there was no cause for alarm, and had assured Caiaphas of the same when he questioned his father-in-law about it later. Indeed, for many years after, nothing was heard from the young man.

But for several years before his death, John had been making trouble in the region, performing mass rituals where he bathed people on the east bank of the river near the town of Bethany, a two-day walk from the city and the temple. John claimed to have authority from God for his actions. While Caiaphas and the other priests knew this to be a hoax at best and blasphemy at worst, many people had been persuaded by John's call to repent and be cleansed in the rushing waters of the Jordan. Despite their mounting concern, the council was wary of interfering due to the people's fervor. They decided their best option was to remain silent and keep a watchful eye on the situation. Eventually, the upstart had drawn the ire of King Antipas, who ruled the regions of Galilee and Perea under the authority of the Roman emperor, and he was unceremoniously thrown into prison for his outrageous statements and disruptive behavior.

Those who followed John were distraught when he was imprisoned by Antipas. Rather than taking it as a sign that he might not be a prophet after all, as Caiaphas had hoped might be the reaction, they became convinced that he was being persecuted for his fervency and holiness. For the priesthood, however, this development was not unwelcome. Antipas's actions meant that the man had been silenced without them having to involve themselves in the matter. Annas had put it most plainly when he and Caiaphas met to discuss the development. "Let the people deluded enough to think him anything but a lunatic blame the Romans for persecuting their hero. Our hands will be clean of it, and John will waste away in a prison cell, silenced and alone."

But then Antipas, impulsive and taken to dramatic gestures, had beheaded the man after a particularly raucous celebration at his palace, leaving his body to his followers as a symbol of his disregard for the supposed prophet. And the anger that had been quietly simmering among John's followers exploded into public outrage. After they buried the body and mourned, a few threatened to retaliate against the Galilean king. Determined to keep John's memory alive and his message intact, they began congregating in the marketplace in Jerusalem and outside the gates of the temple, proclaiming the things John had taught them. The council, which had hoped the death of John would be the end of the matter, soon realized that the problem had increased, not decreased, with the troublemaker's death.

With encouragement from Annas and Simon and other members of the council, Caiaphas took action. He sent Theo and a faction of the temple guard to gather the most militant and outspoken of John's followers. After holding the men for several days, just until their tempers had cooled and they might listen to reason, Caiaphas brought them forth at one of the council meetings, planning to publicly admonish them for their behavior in the hopes of persuading them to give up their foolishness. As he looked at their faces, dirty and rough from too many nights spent out of doors, and gaunt from lack of proper food and drink, he felt both anger and pity for them.

When he spoke, it was with the tone of a stern yet loving father reprimanding his wayward children. "Surely, brothers, you can see now that this John you followed was nothing more than a blasphemer, who sought to take you away from the traditions of our fathers and the commands given to us by our God from the time of Moses. We are your leaders, and the temple is the only place in which you should seek repentance. You must heed our warnings and abandon this madness. Only then will you find mercy at the feet of our God, who pardons all who come in earnest supplication." He sighed. "If you persist in this way, you will do nothing but bring the might of Rome down on all of our heads, and where will we be then?"

The men who stood before him were silent, but Caiaphas could see immediately that they were neither cowed nor swayed by his reproach. Blinking, he realized that they reminded him of the vision he had seen of similar young men, also dirty and disheveled, also seemingly unperturbed to be standing before the council, facing the judgment of priests to whom they should have felt both allegiance and reverence. His anger, which had up until that point been mingled with compassion, flared as he stared incredulously at the eldest of the young men.

"Andrew." The youth, no more than twenty, looked up at him. "You are known to us. Your father has brought you to the temple for the festivals since the days when you could barely recite the prayers. I am ashamed on his behalf that you now count yourself among this pack of rebels. And I see that not only have you decided to go down this path, but you have encouraged your younger brother to join you." Caiaphas nodded at the boy who stood just behind Andrew, a head shorter than his brother, looking abashed at being called out even as he held his head high.

Andrew looked up at Caiaphas, and when he spoke his eyes were sad and solemn. "Noble Caiaphas, I mean no disrespect by my actions. But I cannot unknow the truth I now know. John is gone, but his message lives on. Nothing will ever be the same."

Annas, who stood behind Caiaphas, suddenly snorted loudly. All eyes turned to him. "Young man. We have seen upstarts like your precious John come and go. It is the temple that remains, and our priesthood within it, standing for our people against the tyranny of the Romans and against those who would seek to destroy the peace we have fought so hard to maintain. Not only that, but we have God on our side, making our path straight and standing as our rock and our fortress. You know nothing of truth, boy."

There were murmurs of assent behind Caiaphas. Andrew's brother looked down at his dust-covered feet, his toenails chipped and ragged where they hung over the edge of his too-small sandals. Andrew took a deep breath, his jaw set and one fist clenched by his side, but he did not reply. Caiaphas could see now that there would be no easy resolution to the matter. Suddenly eager to bring the audience to a close, he nodded to Theo, who came forward and untied the chains that bound the men's wrists. As he stepped away, Caiaphas put out his hands to silence the priests, who were still murmuring amongst themselves, and raised his voice.

"It is my determination that these young men have rebelled against their families, and must return to the houses of their fathers immediately. Our guard will escort them from the temple to their homes. We will pray that those who share their blood may be able to gain more of an advantage in their understanding, and will succeed in turning their hearts from this folly."

Rising swiftly amid the renewed murmuring of the council members, Caiaphas strode from the chamber, making his way across the courtyard without turning back. He did not slow his pace until he found himself in the Chamber of the Hearth. There he allowed the warmth of the room to envelop him as he sank down on one of the stone benches that lined the walls. He felt a mix of emotions, and relished the opportunity to be alone with his thoughts for a moment. He did not like the fact that Annas had spoken out against the rebels. While he did not disagree, Caiaphas couldn't help but feel that Annas's actions undermined his own authority. Not for the first time, he felt a mix of hostility and resentment toward his father-in-law. He wished that the man who had been so instrumental in affording him his position as high priest would give him the space to inhabit the role for himself.

This was at least part of the reason that Caiaphas did not inform either Annas or Simon of his message to Gratus in the days following

John's death until after he had received a response. Gratus, ever a friend to the priesthood, was quick with his answer, and thankfully he was able to report to Caiaphas that the emperor was relatively indifferent to the events unfolding in Galilee and Jerusalem. After his return to Rome, Gratus had renewed his close relationship with Tiberius despite the best efforts of Sejanus to thwart him. His information came directly from conversations with the emperor.

"You have no need for concern, friend." The letter, which had been delivered by Gratus's personal messenger, was both frank and reassuring. "The emperor does not think very highly of Antipas. The man's impetuous decision to execute John only served to solidify the emperor's poor opinion of him. As for John, the rumors that reached Rome were of a wild man working alone. I have been able to share with the emperor your council's actions in admonishing his followers after his death. The emperor has asked Pilate to keep him informed of any other disturbances in Judea, and has made it clear that he expects Pilate to maintain order. But you and I both know that this responsibility falls more to the priesthood than to the governor. I have no doubt that your temple guard is more than up to the task."

Caiaphas smiled when he read the letter, grateful for the information and pleased that Gratus continued to be a resource and friend, despite his change in circumstances. In many ways, having an ally in Rome was even more valuable than having a governor on whom he could rely. Pilate might be only a few days journey away, but there was no doubt that his presence so far had caused more aggravation than aid for Caiaphas. Fortunately, the governor seemed content to remain primarily in Caesarea, traveling to Jerusalem only for the festivals. As long as Caiaphas sent regular messengers to Pilate, laden with both gifts and information designed to reassure the governor that everything was being handled by the priesthood, he left them in relative peace.

Caiaphas was especially gratified to be able to share the news from Gratus with the council. It was a moment of triumph for him. The impressed looks from the older members of the priesthood, along with Annas's approving if surprised gaze, went a long way toward reassuring him that his position as the leader of the priesthood remained intact. Jonathan had congratulated him afterward in private. Rivkah too was delighted to hear that her suggestion had yielded such rich and encouraging results. Her praise for the way her husband had handled the situation was especially sweet.

"And now, love, the man is dead and buried, and his followers have scattered. Rebecca was telling me only yesterday that she was speaking with another household servant. The woman told her that young Andrew and his brother have been sent by their father to live with their uncle in Bethsaida, to work the sea for fish and to be reminded of their responsibility to their family. She said her master is confident that a few months of sweat shed on behalf of their uncle will be just the thing to rid them of their foolish notions." Rivkah smiled, and rested her hand on his arm as they walked, her fingers soft against the fabric of his tunic.

It was a great relief when the reports from the marketplace came that the gossip about John was beginning to die down, that people were again concerning themselves with which merchant was charging too much for spices, and how robust this year's crop of wheat might be based on last year's rainfall. Caiaphas was grateful for the brief respite, even as he knew that it was only that. Always there was the nagging feeling that the older members of his council were not entirely trustworthy. He worried too that some of the younger priests were not sufficiently devoted. More than once he had to reprimand Ben and Joshua for the way they spoke to him and other members of the priesthood. Even at home there were troubles. Rivkah was constantly fretting over Judah's health, and Tova and Julia were forever trying some new remedy or tincture designed to strengthen him. Although not even the most skilled healers could find anything the matter with the boy, Judah remained weak and sickly no matter what they did, susceptible to any illness that struck their household. There was always something to occupy his mind, to distract him from his responsibilities, to keep him awake at night.

AND THEN THERE was the one they called Jesus. Like many who lived in the smaller towns and villages surrounding Jerusalem, Jesus journeyed from his home in Galilee to the city several times a year for feasts and festivals. Annas thought he remembered Jesus as a young boy coming to the temple and, unbeknownst to his parents, remaining after they departed for home. Annas recalled the boy's family coming to look for him days after the festival ended and finding him immersed in study, seated among the other students. When Annas questioned the teachers, they shared their astonishment that a young peasant boy with no formal training seemed to know so much about God and the Scriptures. Now in his thirties, Jesus had amassed a small group of followers, and rumors of miracles and bizarre stories about him began to circulate throughout the countryside. The priesthood took notice.

When Annas first learned that Jesus and John were cousins, he was surprised that this bright young Galilean, who asked insightful questions and was respectful to the priests during his temple visits, could possibly be related to the unkempt man who had taken the countryside by storm with his ranting. "But John was a troublemaker from the start," Simon reminded him, as Annas, Caiaphas, and Simon discussed the matter together just after the annual Feast of Dedication. "Remember, we had rumors of John when he was still a boy, wandering the wilderness and sustaining himself on bugs and berries. What an embarrassment he must be to his parents. No, we must not hold Jesus's relations against him. He appears to be quite different from his wayward cousin, despite his humble beginnings." At the time, Annas wholeheartedly agreed, and Caiaphas shared his father-in-law's opinion. But it soon became clear that Jesus was more of a problem than he first appeared.

It was the matter of the temple disturbance that marked a change in the way the priesthood viewed the man. It was just before the Feast of Unleavened Bread. For weeks the temple had been bustling with activity, preparing for the thousands of pilgrims about to descend on the city. The lambs that the priests would be using for the Passover sacrifice had been selected. Simon and Jonathan were working tirelessly to make sure that the priesthood had everything at their disposal in anticipation of the holy day. As usual, local merchants had been chosen to sell these and other sacrificial animals to accommodate the travelers who had journeyed to Jerusalem without animals of their own. The merchants traditionally set up their stalls in the long, low building at the southern wall of the temple area, just past the Court of the Gentiles. This edifice, which had been constructed by Herod the Great when Annas was only a boy, stretched the length of the court and was more than large enough to accommodate the sellers.

The merchants, among them the tax collector Joel's son Daniel, who was there to sell spices and perfume for the incense offering, were loud and boisterous. The air was filled with their haggling and punctuated by the sounds and smells of their animals and their wares. For several weeks, it was as if the marketplace had moved from its usual spot in the Upper City to the temple grounds. Oxen, sheep, and doves spilled out of the building into the Court of the Gentiles. The bleating of sheep and the cooing of doves could be heard from morning until night, even from within the Chamber of Hewn Stone where the council met.

In addition to the merchants, there were the money changers. Because the temple did not accept currency other than the temple coin, pilgrims were required to trade in their shekels and the copper coins minted by the Romans in order to pay the annual temple tax and to purchase the goods they needed for their worship. Matthias worked closely with the money changers to determine the rates of exchange, and was able to provide a thorough report to the council that suggested they would be blessed with handsome profits, providing the priesthood with more than adequate funds for the upcoming year.

With each passing festival, the merchants and money changers set up their stalls ever closer to the temple itself, until they sat just outside the southern gate that led to the Women's Court. Jonathan had quietly raised a question about it several weeks before, just as the preparations had begun. He wondered aloud whether it might be more appropriate to move the merchants back across the courtyard, further away from the holy ground on which the temple stood. Others on the council responded, arguing that it was actually a benefit to have the animals closer to the slaughtering block, and to allow the priests to more closely monitor the money changers. Annas was particularly adamant that it was necessary for the priests to have oversight into the merchant's dealings. "After all, the animals and money that flow from these stalls are ultimately entering the temple with the pilgrims," he argued, looking perplexed that anyone would find this a problem. "What use is it to make worshippers leave the temple grounds only to return with their sacrifices and taxes?"

In the end, Caiaphas agreed with his father-in-law, and Jonathan was quick to let the matter rest. Caiaphas put it out of his mind, and had completely forgotten the conversation until the shouting from the courtyard began. Occupied with his responsibilities within the Priests' Court, Caiaphas did not immediately know that there was anything amiss beyond the usual scuffles and quarrels that occasionally broke out between the merchants and their customers. He was not informed as to what had happened until it was all over.

By multiple reports, Jesus, along with a group of his followers, entered the temple through the eastern gate. As they crossed the Women's Court and saw the merchants and money changers to the south, Jesus apparently became agitated. Striding across to the southern gate, he made his way out into the Court of the Gentiles. Theo, who was standing above the scene on the southern wall of the temple with several other members of the guard, was stunned to see the man suddenly rush at one of the stalls and knock it over, scattering coins and parchment everywhere. The doves from the stall next to the one that had been overturned were startled, and began to coo anxiously and flap their wings from within their cages. The money changer whose stall had been disrupted began angrily shouting at Jesus, who completely ignored him.

Continuing his rampage, Jesus overturned several more tables. Pulling out a whip made of knotted twine, he walked purposefully toward the oxen and sheep that stood waiting to be sold, untied them from their posts, and began striking them so that they fled across the courtyard away from the temple. When he was finished, he returned to the center of the Court of the Gentiles, his face flushed and the hair at his temples wet with sweat, and stood still, looking around. There were still flurries of feathers from the doves that continued to flutter with agitation. The money changers whose tables had been upset were on their knees, frantically trying to gather the coins that had rolled over the uneven pavement, settling in crevices and scuttling across the dusty ground. From above, Theo could barely make out the man's expression, but he thought he looked satisfied and spent as he surveyed the damage.

At this point, Theo and his men left their post and sped down the stairs, hurrying to the courtyard just in time to see Jesus, flanked by several of his followers, leaving the temple through the same gate from which he had entered. Unsure as to whether or not to pursue the man beyond the temple grounds, Theo questioned several of the merchants as to what had happened and what Jesus had said to them. All of this he then reported to Caiaphas, who had just completed the day's sacrifices and was washing himself in the copper wash basin in the Priests' Court.

"Noble Caiaphas, I cannot tell you what it was that provoked him." Theo shook his head, and his broad shoulders sagged as he detailed everything he had seen and the reports he had gathered from witnesses. "I have never seen the man so much as raise his voice before. He has been nothing but respectful of the priesthood and the temple during his previous visits. But with my own eyes I saw him today, zealous and wild, more like his cousin than himself. It was as if he were possessed."

Caiaphas sat down heavily on the steps of the temple, and rubbed his forehead with his still-damp fingers as Theo continued.

"His words, too, suggest that his mind may have been made weak by some kind of illness or delusion. I questioned Daniel, who told me that he heard Jesus call this place his father's house. Unless I am mistaken, Jesus comes from Galilee, the son of a common tradesman. Even if he were from Jerusalem, the temple belongs to no man, not even to the priesthood. And one of the money changers said that he spoke of destroying the temple and building it again. These are dangerous words, Caiaphas. I fear there is more trouble to come."

Caiaphas sighed deeply as he thought over what Theo had shared. The news was not good. There had been troublemakers among the people for as long as he could remember, of course, individuals who amassed groups of followers and threatened either Rome or the priesthood with rebellious talk and secret plots. Some of these people proved to be more of a threat than others, and the Romans had been swift and brutal in their punishment of any they saw as dangerous to the stability of the region. Several hills not far beyond the city walls revealed the remains of some of the most gruesome chastisement. Against a stark sky, beams of wood reached toward the heavens, the sweat and blood from those who had been nailed there still visible, dark and mottled.

But the typical zealot had at the heart of his cause the destruction of Rome, and in this the priesthood was at least sympathetic if not supportive. By rights the high priest should have been the supreme authority in the region, second only to the God he served, supported by a council of holy and powerful men. The priesthood had long suffered the indignity of having to share power with a rotating roster of Roman governors and kings. In Jerusalem, merchant and zealot alike longed for a return to an earlier age when the council's word was law, and the priests answered to no one but God. For a man to come along and threaten their authority, and to attack those coming to worship at the temple that had been consecrated for that purpose for nearly a thousand years, was a strange new form of rebellion, one that Caiaphas could not understand. He lay awake long into the night, mulling over the incident, unable to put it from his mind.

By the time the council gathered the next morning, the news had reached them that Jesus and his followers had left Jerusalem, heading north toward Jericho. There was vigorous debate among the priests as to whether or not he should be followed and apprehended, whether any action needed to be taken against him. Annas was furious, and he paced as he spoke, urging the council to seize the moment to make an example of Jesus.

"We cannot allow this kind of disrespectful violence to go unpunished, Joseph." Annas turned to his son-in-law and looked at him reprovingly. "Whether the man is truly dangerous or merely disturbed, think about how it will look to the people if we allow him to desecrate the temple grounds and then walk away, unscathed. Think of how it will seem to Pilate when he hears of it."

Caiaphas lifted his head sharply as Annas continued. "Do you think he will not receive some kind of report of this? Perhaps if he were in Caesarea, it might have escaped his notice. But you know he arrived several days ago for the feast. I do not think we will be able to shield him from it." Simon and several of the other older priests nodded vigorously, murmuring their assent.

Jonathan, who had been silently observing the proceedings, rose, and addressed Annas firmly but with deference. "Father, I agree that from now on we must be on guard against this man and those who follow him. But I believe the less we make of this incident, the better. The animals have all been returned to the merchants, and peace has been restored. No goods were stolen and no creatures harmed. If we let it pass, in two days all will be focused on the slaughter of the lambs, and this will be merely an amusing incident of a strange man. Pilate will only be concerned if we seem concerned."

Caiaphas scanned the members of the council. He could see the younger priests, including Matthias and Ben, looking approvingly at Jonathan. Aware of the rift in the priesthood, and uneasy about the fact that he would be disappointing someone regardless of what he decided, he sighed. "I agree with Jonathan." Avoiding his father-in-law's eye, he continued. "The man is a peasant, known for telling stories and little else. He is a troublemaker, there is no doubt, and more like his cousin than we previously thought. But for now we must appear to find him less than important, and no reason for alarm."

Before his father-in-law could respond, Caiaphas turned and addressed Annas directly. "I know you have ways of monitoring that extend far beyond our city walls. If you and your spies choose to keep an eye on this man going forward, I will not stand in your way. I only ask that they use discretion. The last thing we need is for Pilate or worse, Rome, to be alerted to our fears."

Annas did not look happy, but when he replied it was with begrudging agreement. "It will be done as you say. If there is anything to report, we will make sure to bring it to your attention." Caiaphas nodded, and they moved on to other matters concerning the upcoming festival. They did not speak of the man again for almost three years.

CHAPTER 19

Two years had passed since the incident at the temple. While there were no major disruptions during that time, there had been changes, both among the priesthood and within Caiaphas's own household. Despite Rivkah and Caiaphas's most fervent hopes, there had been no more pregnancies after Judah's birth. However, Judah had at last begun to show some improvement, thanks to their prayers and offerings, and Tova's skillful application of treatments including anise and cinnamon, the latter of which was procured at a steep price from the spice merchant. He had grown taller, helped by the robust portions of Rebecca's cooking that Rivkah urged on him at mealtimes, and was usually well enough to attend lessons at the temple with the other boys in the mornings. His mind was sharp like his father's, and showed no signs of weakness or deficiency, much to Caiaphas's relief. Simon's son Eli, only three years older, would arrive early at the door of Caiaphas's estate to walk with Judah each morning. Together the boys would slowly head to the temple, stopping as necessary along the way, as Judah tired easily. Upon returning to the estate, he spent most of his afternoons by the fire or resting in his bedchamber, continuing his studies or simply meditating on the things he had learned that morning.

Julia was particularly solicitous of Judah's health. Whenever she came to call, which was often, she would bring some new balm or tea for him to sample, complete with an explanation of the good it would do him. It was with her encouragement that he began to take his own stroll in the mornings before he left for the temple, following a shorter route along the same path his parents took. She enlisted Ben, for whom she had held a special affection since his days as an infant, to assist Judah with additional stretches and exercises just before the evening meal, after which Ben would return to his father's house for the night. As the youngest of Annas's sons, Ben was accustomed to being the one fussed over and spoiled. Tova still treated him like the baby of the family, although he was already twenty and engaged to be married. Even Annas was more indulgent with him than with his older brothers. Julia thought that, in addition to the physical activity being good for Judah, it was beneficial for Ben to be given the responsibility of a mentor and helper. Rivkah especially enjoyed watching her youngest brother, by nature arrogant and bold, dutifully guiding her son through the exercises Julia prescribed.

Julia had been convinced that Judah's strength would only grow as time went on, and she was delighted to see the small hints of progress she observed. She remarked as much to Rivkah as they sat in the main courtyard of Caiaphas's estate, preparing the bitter greens that would be used at the Passover meal that would mark the beginning of the Festival of Unleavened Bread. As the two women sat peeling the leaves off the stalks and placing them in a woven basket that sat between them, Julia watched Judah, who was engaged in a lively board game with Martha across the courtyard from them, his face flushed from the warmth of the spring day and from the pleasure of the activity.

"He looks well, Rivkah." She smiled her sweet smile, the wrinkles around her eyes soft as she gazed tenderly at the two of them. Now in her forties, Julia had lived through much sadness in the years since her daughter had been born, including the deaths of two more children, each of whom had lived only days after their births. The last year had also brought the death of Joazar, who had finally succumbed after having been ill and frail for some time. As he was Simon's older brother and the head of their household in addition to being a fixture at the temple and in the community, his passing was difficult for them all. Simon, who inherited his brother's property, and with it the responsibilities of a large household complete with livestock and over a dozen servants, was hit particularly hard by the loss. Julia had been expending much of her energy in supporting her husband as they sought to establish themselves as the new proprietors of the estate. Although Simon had grown up in the home, and Julia had lived there since their marriage, it was a significant transition to make. Rivkah often wondered if Julia's frequent visits were as much for her sake as a chance for Julia to take a break from being the mistress of a grand household, to revert to an easier time when her responsibilities were far less complex.

But Julia's two living children, Eli and Martha, brought her much joy, and she and Simon shared a sameness of attitude and perspective that allowed them to face their increasing obligations together with positivity and gratitude. As the second son, it had not been guaranteed that Simon would ever own either a home or land. Both Julia and Simon recognized the blessing for what it was. No matter what happened to them, their children would be well provided for, especially as it seemed that Julia was unlikely to bear any more children.

At fifteen, Eli was a handsome boy, serious and shy. He reminded Rivkah of her brother Jonathan, always quiet and observing, eager to please and thoughtful to a fault. Jonathan must also have sensed the similarity, and had taken the boy under his wing, enlisting his help at the temple in translating scrolls and running errands, among other things. Like Caiaphas before him, Eli was occasionally tasked with taking dictation for some of the priests at the temple. He quickly gained a reputation for being both thorough and swift. Martha, at twelve, was as vivacious and lively as her brother was reserved. More than once, Caiaphas had remarked to Rivkah that the girl seemed to take after her more than Julia. "If she did not have Julia's golden hair, I might have wondered if Martha and Judah had been somehow switched at birth," he would tease her as they walked the perimeter of their estate.

"Ah, but there is no mistaking that Judah belongs to you, love," Rivkah would respond, laughing. Indeed, there were times when the resemblance took her breath away, especially now that Judah's skin was not quite so pale. When she looked into the eyes of her son, dark hazel orbs that shifted their color depending on the light, Rivkah could not help remembering the boy who had stolen her heart so many years before. His hair, too, reminded her of her husband's boyhood curls, the sandy brown waves soft to the touch and high-lighted in the summer with golden edges.

Rivkah was lifted from her reverie by Judah's bright laugh, brought on by some tease or jest from Martha, which echoed across the court-yard and made both women smile to hear it. "Yes, Julia." Rivkah reached for another handful of leaves as the pile in their basket continued to grow. "He is stronger than he has ever been, thanks be to God and to your tender care. I am most grateful."

Julia sighed contentedly as she watched the boy with her daughter, now bent together over the game and contemplating their next moves. "It has been my pleasure to do it, Rivkah. You and Caiaphas are like family to me. There is nothing I would not do to ensure the happiness of both our households. As you know, it is still my hope that one day we may find our two families merged into one."

Rivkah smiled a little sadly, looking away from her friend as she did so. Ever since they had been with child at the same time, she and Julia had talked about the possibility that their children might one day marry and form a union between their families. The house of Boethus and the house of Annas were two of the most prestigious in Jerusalem. A marriage between the child of Simon and the child of Caiaphas would be an enormous sign of strength and solidarity, one of which all Judea would approve. But Rivkah was not confident that her son was healthy enough to marry, even with the improvement he had recently shown. Although Martha and Judah clearly shared a deep affection for one another and would make a good match, she worried that at any point his health might take a turn and leave the girl a widow before her time.

Eager to change the subject, Rivkah looked down at the leaves in her hands and was reminded of the weeks of preparation that had led up to this final task. "Is your household ready for the celebration, friend?"

The distraction was effective. Julia sighed and turned her attention back to her work. "Yes, we are nearly ready. This morning I received word that my relatives from the west, those that live near the Valley of Elah, will be with us by nightfall. Simon is especially anxious that things go smoothly, as this will be our first year serving as hosts since Joazar's passing." She rubbed the palms of her hands with her thumbs and grimaced. "I spent the morning preparing the bed chambers for all of our kin, and my hands still ache from the washing. But I want everything to be perfect."

Unlike other holy days, where the sacrifices and rituals took place at the temple from beginning to end, Passover included the ceremonial slaughtering of a lamb for each household, which would then be taken home and eaten as part of a meal among family and friends. The dinner, which was festive and often lively, especially once the wine was consumed and the singing began, commemorated the exodus from Egypt by the Jews that had taken place generations before, and led into a week of celebrating freedom and deliverance. For the next seven days, people from the city and far beyond would flock to the temple to praise God and to offer more sacrifices there. Every household in Jerusalem would be filled to the rafters with out-of-town guests and visitors during the week, and the energy in the streets around the temple would be palpable.

It was a time of particular anxiety for both the priesthood and for Pilate. Always in Jerusalem there was an unspoken tension between Roman rule and the leadership of the priesthood and the temple. Even in years when there had been no recent uprisings or skirmishes, the Romans were wary of too many Jews gathering together at one time. The crowds that flocked to the city at Passover exacerbated this concern, and the fact that the Jews were celebrating their victory over an oppressive conquering people was not lost on those who advised the Roman governor. Although Pilate kept a low profile during the holiday, remaining at Herod's Palace with only a small guard, Caiaphas knew he was there to observe and to ensure that everything went smoothly. Pilate had never fully recovered from his first experience with the Jewish people over the standards. He knew all too well that their tenacity and might was a force with which to be reckoned. He was prepared, if necessary, to take steps to remind the Jewish people of his existence and of their place within the Roman empire.

The priests, too, had much on their minds as the day grew closer. For weeks they had been preparing the temple for the influx of pilgrims, performing repairs and cleaning every chamber and corridor. The altar was washed and prayed over daily, and all of the priests' robes were fastidiously mended and purified in anticipation of heavy usage during the week. Caiaphas dictated letters to the heads of local synagogues, urging them to encourage their congregants to approach the holiday with joyful celebration and a peaceful spirit. He knew that Annas and Simon were also engaged in conversations with local leaders, and were on the alert for any potential trouble that might be brewing among those planning to descend upon the city. In addition to sending a letter of welcome, Caiaphas himself visited Pilate just after the governor arrived in Jerusalem, bringing him several expensive vials of perfumed oil and reiterating how grateful they were to have him in attendance for the festival.

By the time Caiaphas reached home on the day before the Passover sacrifices were to be made, he was spent. Julia and Martha had already returned to Simon's estate. Rivkah was busy reviewing final details with Nathan and Rebecca. After sitting quietly with Judah and listening to him recite the Scripture he had learned most recently, Caiaphas retired early. By the time Rivkah joined him, he was fast asleep. That night, no dreams disturbed his slumber.

CHAPTER 20

The morning of the slaughter was cloudy and brisk. Caiaphas reached the temple before dawn, and it was some time before the air warmed enough for him to go about his work without shivering, despite the layers of linen and wool that covered his torso and reached down to his ankles. After greeting Simon and Jonathan, who had also just arrived, the three men joined in a morning prayer of thanksgiving before proceeding to the copper basin to wash their hands and feet in preparation for the day. The lambs to be offered on behalf of the priesthood would not be sacrificed until later that afternoon, just as the sun began making its journey toward the horizon. Those lambs, already lined up near the altar, would be joined by the ones brought by the first wave of pilgrims. All would be slaughtered before the sun had fully set, so that the carcasses could be roasted and eaten that same evening, according to tradition.

By twilight the temple was heavy with the sweet thick smell of the sacrifices, as if the blood that had been spilled and then sprinkled on the altar permeated the air itself. As the final lambs were butchered and readied for transport, and the portions divided among those worshiping, the scent began to change with the evening incense offering, adding myrrh and clove to the mix of pungent odors filling the place. By the time the third group of pilgrims departed with their lambs ready for roasting, Caiaphas was grateful for the final ritual bath of the evening, from which he emerged quickly and headed toward home.

Gamaliel, Saul and Joshua, who would be joining his family for the meal, had gone on ahead with the lamb carried between them, skinned, disemboweled, and tied to a branch of pomegranate wood, ready to be roasted. Already the fire at home would be lit and stoked, and Nathan would be waiting to tend to the animal, which would roast while the rest of the meal was consumed and the prayers said over the various elements of the feast.

As Caiaphas entered the main doorway of the estate, he strode through the central corridor that led to the main banquet hall in the center of the property. To his left, one of the household's younger manservants bowed and took his tunic. The boy knelt before him and dipped a linen cloth into a large stone basin of cool water that sat at his side. Removing his sandals one by one, the young man wiped the dirt and grime that had settled on Caiaphas's ankles and feet during the walk from the temple. Although the water was already the color of clay from the previous guests who had arrived before him, the cloth was clean enough to perform its task. Caiaphas murmured his appreciation as he replaced his sandals and entered the main hall.

The long low table had been set for the feast, and scattered pillows and blankets lay around the table to encourage an atmosphere of relaxation and ease. Caiaphas could see that already the plates had been piled high with the thin, charred bread that would make up a large portion of the meal. The casks of wine were set to the side, waiting to be poured. On the table were squat bowls full of the leaves that Rivkah and Julia had prepared, ready for the blessings that would be repeated over them. He could smell the lamb roasting in the nearby courtyard. The scent made his stomach lurch with hunger. Looking around, his eyes found Rivkah, beautiful as always, with her hair pulled tightly back in a braid that hung down her back. Her cheeks gleamed with the hard work of the day and with the salve she had just wiped across them to rid them of the soot and grime they had gathered from checking on the progress of the lamb. Judah stood by his mother, thin but otherwise looking healthy and eager for the meal. On the other side of the table, Gamaliel was deep in conversation with Saul, and had not yet noticed Caiaphas's arrival.

Toward the end of the room, Caiaphas noticed with surprise that Joshua was not alone, but was standing with Eli and Martha, showing them the small figurine of a donkey he had whittled out of olive wood. Martha was clearly taken with the toy, which was artfully made, and was clapping her hands with delight as Joshua held it out to her. Rivkah, who had by this time made her way over to Caiaphas and welcomed him with a kiss on the cheek, bent close to his ear and spoke softly.

"Julia and Simon have been overrun with guests and relatives, and asked if Eli and Martha could take the Passover meal with us and remain throughout the festival. I knew you would not object to having them here." She smiled broadly, looking over at the young people, who had now been joined by Judah. He too was charmed by Joshua's handiwork, and he and Martha bent over the figure together as Joshua looked on with satisfaction.

Caiaphas returned his wife's smile. He was fond of Simon and Julia's children, especially Martha, and he felt that Eli, with his kind-hearted and quiet spirit, was a good influence on Judah. Indeed, of all the young men in their community, Eli was the most evenly matched to Judah's disposition and temperament. Even Joshua, who had continued to rise in Caiaphas's esteem as a scholar since Gamaliel had first introduced him to the boy twelve years before, could be aggressive at times, especially when he was aiming to impress those around him. Joshua was clever and charming, and had many admirers, which gave him an elevated impression of himself despite still being two years away from entering the priesthood. Here in Caiaphas's home, his behavior was tempered by the presence of the women and by the close proximity of his father. But at the temple among the other boys he sometimes allowed his pride to prevail, especially when under the influence of Ben, who had been his partner in mischief more times than Caiaphas could count. Ben had grown more serious since becoming a priest and a husband, and Caiaphas hoped the same would be true of Joshua. But he could not help remembering the Scripture that cautioned that pride led to disgrace, while humility instead bred wisdom. If the vision he had seen in his dreams was indeed prophetic, a future existed in which Ben would be high priest and Joshua would serve as his second. Caiaphas prayed that it would be so, if only because it would suggest that both boys had grown into men worthy of those esteemed positions.

Brought back to the present by his wife's inquisitive stare, Caiaphas realized that he had not yet given her a response regarding Eli and Martha. He laughed. "I have no objection, my love. This is a time for family to be together. I am more than happy to welcome Simon's children into our own family for the celebration." Satisfied, she moved away. Caiaphas followed her, and took his place at the head of the table, ready to begin the Passover meal.

THE LAMPS HAD BEEN LIT for many hours by the time the last bits of lamb were eaten and all of the prescribed blessings and rituals had been said and done. The wine flowed freely all evening. The faces gathered around the table glowed with both the flickers of the fire-light and the warmth of the drink. Martha's head was resting heavily on Judah's shoulder, who looked ready for sleep himself. Her eyelids fluttered even as she tried to concentrate her attention on Joshua. He was telling stories of how he and his father had traveled to several villages on the outskirts of Jerusalem so that Gamaliel could instruct the local synagogue leaders on matters of Scripture. As he spoke, he grew animated. His dark hair and flashing eyes made him look more like a powerful orator than a teenaged boy telling stories about shacks with dirt floors and thin porridge, where he and his father were welcomed as honored guests.

At the other end of the table, Rivkah politely inquired after Saul's family, who lived too far away to travel to Jerusalem for the Passover.

The son of a wealthy man, Saul had been sent from Tarsus, where he was raised, to Jerusalem to learn at the temple from the time he was a small boy. He had returned to the house of his father to learn a trade before finally settling in Jerusalem as part of the priesthood. Gamaliel had taken him under his wing, and the young man had thrived under the older priest's tutelage. Rivkah smiled warmly as she asked Saul questions about his studies, eager to make him feel comfortable in her home.

Caiaphas and Gamaliel were also deep in conversation, their heads close together, oblivious to everyone else. Gamaliel was sharing with Caiaphas the latest news from Tiberias, a city on the western shore of the Sea of Galilee, which Antipas had built and named in honor of the emperor in the hopes of garnering favor by the gesture. The Roman king had also constructed a large and majestic palace there, in which he resided when not visiting Jerusalem or traveling within his own territories. Gamaliel, recently returning from a visit to Sepphoris, had stopped in the neighboring pagan city on his way back to Jerusalem to purchase supplies for the journey home and to visit the mineral hot springs, known for their therapeutic properties. As Gamaliel was going to be in the region, it provided an opportunity for him to meet with local leaders in person and to bring news of any disruptions or brewing conflicts back to the council. He had already given a full report to Caiaphas and the priesthood. But there were still pieces of information that he continued to share with Caiaphas as he recalled them in the days that followed.

"You will not believe the gossip that is being bandied about in Tiberias, Caiaphas." Gamaliel was reclining at the table, the plate before him filled with crumbs, his wine glass nearly empty. He smiled broadly. "It seems that Antipas shares our concerns about the man Jesus. Since the commotion at the temple, it is said that Jesus has been spending much of his time in the north, near Capernaum, a morning's walk from Antipas's palace. Antipas has heard of his growing followers, and the rumors about Jesus are growing wilder by the day. There is even a tale about his walking on the waters of the Sea of Galilee. The man who told me that story was particularly amused by it, but apparently Antipas is none too pleased." He paused, aware that his next sentence was an incendiary one. "The rumor is that Antipas suspects that Jesus is the man John, whom he executed, back from the dead, returned to seek revenge."

As Gamaliel expected, Caiaphas looked slightly shocked. Then both men laughed heartily, their voices rising with mirth until even the children at the other end of the table looked up from their conversation. Shaking his head, Caiaphas took a deep breath and tried to compose himself, while Gamaliel readjusted his tunic and took the last sip of his wine. Gamaliel waited a moment, and then leaned forward, his tone more serious.

"Now Caiaphas, all amusement aside, I must ask. Are we certain that John was killed and buried, and that there is no chance that he has returned? I agree that the notion that this Jesus has taken on the personhood of a dead man is utter foolishness. But I would not be so quick to dismiss the fear that John might still remain among us, especially if he was executed under suspicious circumstances. Is there any reason to take Antipas's concerns as more than guilty paranoia?"

Caiaphas sighed. One of his greatest challenges within the priesthood, about which Simon had cautioned him in the days before his appointment as high priest, came when he found himself engaged in debates with those who shared a different philosophy from his own. Members of the council, although alike in dedicating themselves to the temple and to God, in reality belonged to several different religious schools of thought, among them the Pharisees and the Sadducees. Gamaliel, by far the most respected and prominent member of the Pharisees within the council, was often the voice representing a dissenting opinion when matters of the spirit and death entered into their conversation. As a Sadducee and the son-in-law of a Sadducee, Caiaphas held a differing view on these subjects. The two groups were alike in many ways, and there were times when Caiaphas forgot that their beliefs differed at all. But despite his deep respect for Gamaliel, he could not understand how such a learned scholar could believe in stories that even his son Judah had long outgrown.

Caiaphas was careful to keep his voice light as he responded, having no desire to engage in rigorous debate on this celebratory evening. "Ah, my friend, your grandfather's influence is showing. I know Hillel was a great man, and we owe much to his teaching. But I will never understand this fear of resurrection and the dead that you and your Pharisee brothers entertain. I would sooner believe, like Antipas, that one man could turn into another, than to hold to a philosophy that believes the world to be filled with unseen spirits and life beyond the grave."

He raised a hand as Gamaliel seemed poised to interrupt him. "Yes, I know you will point to the visions of Daniel, and to the Scripture that talks of those who sleep in the dust rising again." He smiled as Gamaliel nodded, a bit sheepishly. "I know the Scriptures as well as you do, friend. I have studied its words until they are burned on my mind. I have meditated on them for many hours, seeking wisdom with a heart inclined toward truth. But nothing in my study has convinced me that a body once in the grave can return to life." He sighed, suddenly more deeply affected than he had expected to be. "Indeed, if I believed it to be possible, there are many whose return I would fervently seek." He closed his eyes. For a moment the image of his mother flickered across his vision, her eyes filled with tears and pride as they had been the last time he had seen her.

Gamaliel realized he had struck a nerve. He was suddenly very conscious of being a guest, in the home of the high priest no less. Clearing his throat, he sat upright for the first time in hours. When he spoke it was with deference and a greater degree of formality. "Noble Caiaphas, I am sorry. I did not mean to cause you distress. I only thought you would find the rumors amusing. My travels were surprisingly uneventful, as you already know. The region of Galilee seems at peace. I saw nothing on my journey to suggest that there is any insurrection developing. If your father-in-law's spies have uncovered nothing in the marketplace or in the outskirts of Jerusalem, I am certain there is no reason to be concerned."

He rose, gathering his tunic, and looked across the table to Saul, who was still engaged in conversation with Rivkah. "And now,

Caiaphas, I think it is time for me to gather my party and take my leave. If I can pull Joshua away from his dwindling audience, that is," he smiled, gazing down the table at his son, who was still happily engaged in his storytelling. Eli was the only one still paying attention. Martha and Judah had both succumbed to sleep and were leaning on one another, her golden hair mingling with his darker curls and falling down both of their backs.

Caiaphas stood. At this Rivkah broke off her conversation with Saul and they both rose as well. After saying their goodbyes, Caiaphas escorted Gamaliel, Saul, and Joshua to the front gate of the estate. By the time he returned, Rivkah had roused the sleeping children. Eli, who would be sharing Judah's room for the remainder of his stay, helped his friend out of the hall and toward their bedchamber, while Martha, who would be occupying an empty chamber next to theirs, followed behind the two boys, yawning and stretching as she went. Caiaphas and Rivkah also made their way up the stairs. By the time the lamps in the hall were extinguished by Nathan, both of them were already asleep.

THE VISION that wrenched Caiaphas awake only a few hours later was different from any he had had before. Unlike his other dreams, all of which had taken place within the temple itself or on the temple grounds, this one found him standing on rocky terrain, an uneven dirt path curving before him that led up a slope and out of sight. Although the grass and shrubbery that grew in scattered pockets across the landscape was lush and green, the general appearance of the place was dusty and remote. Caiaphas could tell immediately that he was no longer in Jerusalem.

As he looked around, he noticed a small gathering of people up ahead of him, just past the bend in the path. He walked briskly to catch up with them. As in all of his dreams, the participants took no notice of his presence, and he was able to move past them without incident. As he overtook them and had a full view of the scene before him, he stopped short. Ahead of him was the rock face of a cave in which a rectangular-shaped hole the size of a large man had been cut. Caiaphas knew immediately that this was a grave site. Inside there would be a section of rock hollowed out, large enough to lay several dead bodies out on stone benches. These type of rock-cut tombs were used by those who could afford to house multiple members of their family who had died, while individuals with fewer resources would bury their dead directly in the ground, one by one. His father's body lay in a tomb very much like this one. He remembered as a boy watching as Abel was gently placed inside and the men who had carried him slowly pushed a large stone across the entrance, to protect the body from the elements and from predatory animals and others who might seek to molest it. This tomb was still open. Caiaphas thought that perhaps they had not yet laid the body to rest.

He realized that the people behind him must be mourners, come to honor the dead. Turning to examine them, Caiaphas saw indeed that many of their faces were lined with sorrow. Near the front of the group, two women in particular, who looked alike enough to be sisters, were weeping openly, their eyes red and swollen. They leaned on one another for support. Caiaphas could see they were deeply grieved.

But as he watched them, he saw their expressions suddenly change. The woman in front stared wide-eyed, her intake of breath rapid and audible. The other woman grabbed onto the arm of her sister's garment, her hand clenched tightly. All around them, the mourners' faces were shifting. Some looked afraid, while others appeared to be astonished. The weeping had ceased, and all were staring at the same spot behind Caiaphas, near the tomb's opening.

Whipping around, Caiaphas saw two men before him. The first, whom he had not noticed before, was the man Jesus, whom he and Gamaliel had just been discussing that evening. Jesus looked slightly older than when Caiaphas had last seen him, during one of his visits to the temple. His beard was longer and a bit more tangled, his robes dusty and ragged at the edges. Caiaphas could see the streaks on his face where tears must have recently fallen, leaving sharp lines down both of his cheeks. But now he was smiling, his shoulders back and his head high, as he held out a hand in front of him.

As Caiaphas looked at the one to whom Jesus was extending his hand, he immediately understood the reaction of the mourners. This man stood no more than two paces in front of the opening in the rock, from which it appeared he had just emerged. Unlike all of the other people there, who were dressed either in mourning clothes or in their everyday garments, he was wrapped in thin pieces of linen that covered his entire body. The fabric had been wrapped around each of his limbs separately, so that his arms and legs resembled infants bound in swaddling clothes. His torso too was draped in linen. Across his face another section of fabric was wound. But this section was looser than the rest, and the top half of his face was visible over the cloth. The skin around his eyes was dark and heavy, as if he had been asleep for many days. But his eyes were alert and bright. He was gazing at Jesus with an expression of rapturous joy. As he reached out and they clasped hands, Caiaphas understood with a jolt that this man was no man at all, but the corpse who had been buried in the tomb before him, somehow no longer dead but alive.

Caiaphas sat up in bed, panting, his entire chest drenched in sweat. His breathing, which was rough and ragged, took several minutes to return to normal. He struggled to calm himself, his mind reeling. As his breath slowed and he was able to collect his thoughts, he thought back to his debate with Gamaliel over the resurrection of the dead. Could it be possible that the Pharisees were in fact correct, that there was a way for one who was no longer living to return? Or was this just his imagination run wild, fueled by their conversation and perhaps provoked by the abundance of wine and rich lamb he had consumed that evening?

Bowing his head, Caiaphas took another deep breath. His mind drifted back to the psalms that he had known since he was a child and that he had heard so many times the day before, recited during each wave of the slaughter of the lambs and again sung at the Passover table with family and friends after the meal. Forcing himself to focus on the reassuring words of the psalmist rather than on his wild thoughts, he recited them to himself, over and over again, bowing slightly back and forth as he did so. "The faithfulness of the Lord endures forever. The Lord is on my side; I will not fear. What can man do to me?" Calmed by these assurances, and becoming more and more certain that this dream, unlike his other visions, must be without greater meaning, he fell into an uneasy sleep. He did not wake again until morning.

CHAPTER 21

The rest of the spring and the summer were unseasonably hot. By wintertime, all were grateful for the cooler temperatures that meant that the courtyard fires were lit early and burned late into the night. At the temple, the priests began to wear their heavier robes and tunics. Caiaphas found himself spending more of the time between his official responsibilities in the Chamber of the Hearth, which remained warm regardless of the weather outside. The Feast of Dedication came and went, and Judah's health continued to improve, so much so that Caiaphas began to allow himself to hope that his son might one day be well enough to take his place in the priesthood alongside his father, grandfather, and uncles.

It was on a particularly cold afternoon upon leaving the chamber that Caiaphas found himself pausing as he heard muffled voices to his right, toward the northwest end of the temple building. As this was not a usual place for priests to gather unless they were retrieving salt from the Salt Chamber to be used in the sacrifices, he was surprised to hear the sonorous voice of his father-in-law, as well as that of Simon, conversing in a manner that suggested they were trying not to be overheard. Curious, Caiaphas crept closer to where they stood, and hid himself behind a column a few paces from them.

Annas sounded agitated even as he tried to keep his voice low. "The man is a nuisance, Simon, and a heretic. I am glad we were able to keep the disturbance quiet. But I am concerned that this is not the last we will hear of him. The reports are coming more frequently now."

Simon's voice was calm and measured as he replied, clearly attempting to placate the older priest. "Noble Annas, I give you my assurance that nothing more need be done at this time. The men we sent trailed him and his followers all the way to Bethany, where they appear to have settled. It has been over a fortnight and we have heard no more from them. Clearly he must realize how close he came to being apprehended this time. Perhaps it has finally given him pause. We must pray that he will show more wisdom going forward in how he chooses to approach the temple, especially during a holy celebration."

Annas sighed, but it was clear that Simon's words had served their purpose. The next time Annas spoke it was with less urgency, though no less irritation. "I agree, Simon, and I pray it will be so. But tell me again, what did Ben tell you the man said about his father? We are certain he is the son of a builder, are we not? A common man who works in wood and stone?"

Intrigued, Caiaphas took a step closer. Even so, he had to lean in to hear Simon's next words, which sounded more defeated than his last. "Yes, Annas. He is from the humblest of families, and there is nothing remarkable about his lineage. But I fear that his claims about his father point to something more troubling, as he appears at times to be claiming God himself as his father. You know, of course, that he also was here at the Feast of Tabernacles, although then he remained in the outer courts of the temple. We have been told that he claimed to be sent from God directly at that time, and he gathered quite a crowd to him. Theo sought counsel from me as to how to handle the situation, and I gave the order to arrest him if he caused any more disruption."

Simon paused, remembering. "On the final day of the feast, he returned. But instead of renewing his outrageous claims, he began quoting from Scripture and speaking of himself as someone who had water for those who might thirst, despite carrying nothing but the clothes on his back. Theo became convinced that the man was not in his right mind. As the crowds appeared to be intrigued but divided, Theo determined that the best course of action would be to ignore him entirely."

Annas sighed again, heavily. "I cannot say I agree with Theo's decision, Simon. My son is a fine priest, and I am gratified by the way he has handled his responsibilities since he was promoted to the captain of the guard. There is no one among our ranks whom I would rather have by my side in a fight than Theo. But this man's claims grow more and more wild with each incident. Anyone claiming the authority that belongs rightly to us as priests will need to be stopped eventually. I am grateful that thus far he has not called for outright revolt, and that his followers appear to be fishermen and peasants rather than warriors. But there is something deeply disturbing about him nonetheless."

Caiaphas, incredulous at what he was hearing, could picture the look of angry frustration on his father-in-law's face as Annas continued. "It is only a matter of time before his antics reach the ears of Joseph, or worse, of Rome. I fear that my son-in-law, wise though he may be, does not have the stomach for the kind of governance required here. And if Pilate catches wind of anything that looks like discord among the ranks of those who worship our God, it will give fuel to the notion that we need more of his oversight rather than less. No, we must continue to keep this to ourselves, and take care of it before it becomes a problem we cannot easily control."

Caiaphas's head jerked up at the first mention of his name, and he grew increasingly more uncomfortable as Annas continued. He bent around the column until he could see the outline of the two men, shrouded in shadow, standing against the back wall of the temple building beneath the eaves of the roof. As he watched, Simon clapped his hand on Annas's shoulder, and nodded seriously. "I am in agreement, Annas. I will speak to Theo again, and we will be on alert in case the man decides to return to Jerusalem. If we need to make an example of him, to remind our people of the might of the priesthood, and to demonstrate the severity of judgment that those who mock the temple and our God can expect, we will do what must be done."

Annas bowed his head in agreement and clasped Simon's other shoulder. The two men stood in silence for a moment before parting ways. Simon moved south around the back of the temple building, while Annas turned toward the place where Caiaphas stood, still concealed by the column. Caiaphas shrank back as Annas strode quickly past him, the older man's gait still strong and powerful. When he was sure that his father-in-law was out of sight, Caiaphas emerged into the sunlight, letting the warmth of the sun's rays fall on him even as the chilly afternoon breeze played in his beard and spread across his face.

In a daze, Caiaphas walked to the closest staircase that led to the upper level of the temple. Almost without thinking, he strode along the outer perimeter, walking east. As he reached the northern tower, he turned, gazing back across the temple grounds. He watched as the sun reflected off the golden spikes that lined the roof of the sanctuary building, and looked past the temple to the Roman fortress that lay just beyond the temple grounds. The Antonia Fortress, which had been built by Herod the Great in an effort to further fortify and protect the temple, rose far above the outer wall, its towers level with the top of the sanctuary. In contrast to the ornate white and gold decorations of the temple, the fortress was gray and unadorned, its four towers rising up, stalwart and solid, into the air.

Caiaphas heard a noise behind him. Turning, he saw that he was no longer alone. Jonathan was making his way toward him, his dark head shining in the glow of the late afternoon sun. As Jonathan reached him, Caiaphas smiled warmly at his brother-in-law, although his eyes remained troubled. He was relieved to be in the company of one who had always been a voice of reason and sanity even in the most trying times.

Jonathan greeted him with a smile equal to his own. But his dark brow furrowed as soon as he grew close enough to see the expression on Caiaphas's face. "Are you unwell, brother? You look as if you have been too long in the smoke of the sacrifices. Have you come up here to breathe some fresh air? It is a good spot for that kind of relief, no doubt."

Caiaphas shook his head, and paused for a moment, unsure how and if to share the thoughts that continued to rattle inside his mind. He grimaced as he put his hand to his forehead, and sighed as he looked at Jonathan. "Dear brother," he began slowly. "You know how I wrestle with the fear of living in the shadow of my father-in-law. It is no secret that Annas and Simon continue to wield significant power within the priesthood."

Jonathan smiled gently. "Yes, brother, and I have counseled you before that your fears are unfounded. While it is true that both Annas and Simon are revered and honored members of our priesthood, and do hold much sway, especially among the older members of the council, they swore allegiance to you when you became high priest along with the rest of us. I have no doubt that anything they do is in your service, and in the service of our God, to whom we all owe our very breath."

Caiaphas looked at his brother-in-law warily, and when he spoke his voice was unexpectedly raw with emotion. "And what would you say if I told you that Annas and Simon have been keeping secrets from me, secrets about those who would attempt to disrupt our peace? What if I told you that there have been more incidents with the man Jesus, and that I have purposely been kept in the dark about what has transpired?"

To Caiaphas's surprise, Jonathan did not appear at all startled. In fact, his face abruptly shifted from a look of bemused indulgence to one of concern. He leaned forward, his tone earnest and grave. "Joseph, you must not concern yourself with any of this. Trust that the council is working together for the good of all who profess to love and serve our God. I have some knowledge of what you speak." He smiled sheepishly. "One benefit of being quiet and reserved is that people sometimes forget I am in attendance, and I hear things not always intended for my ears."

Jonathan continued. "I would urge you not to pursue this further, nor to allow your thoughts to be clouded with worry. The less you are involved in any action taken against this man, the better. I believe that Annas is intending to spare you the indignity of dealing with the trouble, and to keep your conscience clear in the event that Roman authorities become involved. If you know nothing of it, you can honestly profess your lack of knowledge. You know that Pilate will assume that any matter that has not reached the high priesthood must be inconsequential indeed. Allow yourself to be guided here, my friend, for the sake of us all."

Caiaphas stared at his brother-in-law, incredulous. Jonathan seemed slightly uncomfortable, but he stood determined as Caiaphas surveyed him, uncertain. He had been convinced that Jonathan would be equally horrified to discover that he did not know all that was being done in the name of the priesthood. The fact that Jonathan was apparently not only aware of this, but condoned it, was both surprising and unnerving, and gave him pause. Was it possible that there was some kind of wisdom here? Could it be that there were things he would do well not to uncover, ways in which his ignorance might be a blessing? He felt ill, his stomach turning, as he remembered the manner in which Annas and Joazar had operated during the years when Ishmael and Eleazar had been named high priest. Unlike Ishmael, he was no neophyte, no pawn in a larger scheme. He was a scholar in his own right who had held the office for thirteen years, a man well-versed in the law and respected by his peers. It was he who had smoothed over the early challenges with Pilate, and maintained a relationship with Gratus that continued to serve the temple well. Unlike Eleazar, who was difficult and divisive, he had always been faithful and devoted to the priesthood and to his duty. He hated the fact that he was being shielded from information, and couldn't help but feel that by doing so, Annas and Simon were judging him unworthy to carry the full weight of his position. He felt alternately furious and dejected.

Cognizant of the turmoil his friend was experiencing, Jonathan remained silent a moment longer. When he spoke it was gentle, his voice low and soothing. "Joseph. We have known each other since we were boys. I would never knowingly encourage you down a path that would lead to either shame or guilt. For now, I urge you to let this matter rest. The time may come when you can no longer remain distant from this ugly business. But do not trouble yourself about it in the meantime. There is no need to undermine those who would seek to uphold and protect the priesthood on your behalf, especially when there are many other things that deserve your attention. Fix your mind on those, friend, and let the rest be."

Caiaphas sighed deeply, and he felt suddenly very tired. "Yes, Jonathan. You are right. This is wise counsel, my brother, and I am grateful for it. I will do as you say."

Jonathan allowed himself a small smile. Caiaphas saw in his expression the same look that Rivkah gave him at the end of a long conversation when she was satisfied that her advice had been received and would be heeded. Suddenly, he found himself longing to be in her presence, to share with her the events of the day and to see her dark eyes, so like Jonathan's, flash as she processed the information and gave her thoughts. She would likely share her brother's opinion on the matter, as usual. He was hopeful that this second perspective would provide him the peace he needed to let it go.

Indeed, by the time Caiaphas was able to provide his wife with a report of all that had transpired at the temple, he had become nearly convinced of the wisdom of Jonathan's advice. Rivkah's adamant reassurance that her father, however bombastic, would never betray the honor of the priesthood was additional fodder for the course he had already set for himself. He would remain alert against any disturbance that might come, but would endeavor to trust in the council, and especially in those who had served the priesthood for longer than he himself had been a priest.

As the weeks, and then months, passed, this strategy proved sound. No hint of any disturbance reached Caiaphas's ears despite his heightened attention to the possibility. Once or twice, he considered broaching the subject with Simon or his father-in-law. But ultimately he decided against it. The winter passed quietly. Before he knew it, the almond trees were beginning to flower, their white and pink blossoms exploding across the hills surrounding the city and filling the air with a sweet, honeyed fragrance that signaled warmer weather was coming. Soon the barley would be ready for the harvest. Before long, the time for the Passover would again be upon them.

CHAPTER 22

It was on the last day of the Fast of Esther that Tova fell ill. The messenger who arrived at Caiaphas's estate looked fearful as he relayed the message to Caiaphas that Jonathan was requesting his sister's presence. Julia too had been sent for. She and Martha were planning to be at Annas's estate before nightfall. The urgency with which Rivkah packed supplies for herself and Judah and departed suggested that she was seriously concerned for her mother's wellbeing. Her eyes were distracted as she ran from room to room, gathering clothing and linens, herbs and oils. Judah, who had become well-versed in the cultivating and preparation of medicinal remedies thanks to his own poor health, had become a valuable aid to Rivkah when such things were required. It was he who packed the large leather pouch of balms and ointments as Caiaphas looked on, unsure how best to be of assistance.

With a kiss on the cheek and a request that he add additional portions to the next day's offerings at the temple on Tova's behalf, Rivkah was gone. The estate felt suddenly quiet. As Nathan and Rebecca lit the fires and began to prepare the evening meal, Caiaphas paced the largest courtyard and prayed fervently for the health of his mother-in-law. In her mid-fifties, Tova's childbearing years were behind her. But she remained a powerful and vibrant force within the family. As the mother of five boys in addition to his own wife, Tova had always felt invincible to him, especially in contrast to his own sickly mother, whose one successful pregnancy had nearly taken her life. The wife of Annas needed to be especially strong, Caiaphas thought ruefully as he considered his father-in-law. There was no question in his mind that Tova was well-suited for the role. Despite the fact that all of her living sons now towered over her, especially Theo, Tova could still silence each of them with a stern look. Even Annas deferred to her more often than to anyone else, male or female. Her laugh, which Rivkah had inherited, could put an entire room at ease, and the way she had welcomed a scared little boy and his grieving mother into her home so many years before was something that Caiaphas could never forget nor repay.

BY THE TIME Rivkah and Judah arrived at Annas's estate, the lamps were lit and the sun had nearly completed its journey beyond the horizon. Rivkah unwound her outer cloak and handed it gently to Lydia, who was waiting for them in the vestibule near the entrance. Lydia, who had served the family since she herself was a teenager, and remembered welcoming Tova into the household as a young bride, looked relieved to see Rivkah. The older woman clasped both of Rivkah's hands tightly, bowing and murmuring to herself as she did so. Her face was lined with worry. Her silver hair, although bound tightly, was escaping in small tufts that she had clearly neglected to smooth in her eagerness to care for her mistress and for the household.

Lydia's husband Silas was also waiting for Rivkah at the entrance to the reception room where the rest of the family sat eating dinner. He greeted them warmly, and ushered them into the room, leading them to a table laden with food and drink. Annas sat at the head of the table. By his manner Rivkah could tell immediately that her mother must have made some improvement since she had been summoned. He was seated upright, a wine goblet in his hand, and he was looking around at his sons, their wives, and their children with an air of settled ease that allowed Rivkah to take the first deep breath she had allowed herself since the messenger entered her home.

Jonathan saw them first and immediately rose to greet his sister. Embracing her with one arm, he reached out his other hand and clapped Judah gently on the shoulder. Judah looked up at his uncle, grateful. Rivkah searched Jonathan's eyes, and was additionally reassured by what she saw there. Softly shaking herself from his embrace, she made her way around the table to her father, who beamed as he saw her coming toward him, and allowed himself to be greeted with a kiss on the forehead.

"Rivkah!" Annas was clearly pleased to see her, and his booming voice caused the rest of those gathered to look up from their plates. Theo and Ben, who had been singularly focused on consuming as much of the meal in front of them as possible, both grinned at her, identical but for the fact that Theo was a head taller than his younger brother, even when seated. Matthias, who was across the table next to the empty seat recently vacated by Jonathan, silently nodded his greeting as well. Looking down the table, Rivkah noticed two unoccupied places set with plates that contained remnants of the meal. She realized that Julia and Martha must have already arrived and eaten before taking their place at Tova's bedside.

Rivkah was just about to begin questioning Annas as to her mother's health when she heard Julia's voice in the courtyard outside. Julia entered the doorway of the hall, her face flushed from activity, but nonetheless looking calm and in control. When she saw Rivkah, she smiled, relieved. "Ah, Rivkah. My friend, I am so very glad you are here. Your mother will be as well."

As if she already knew the question on Rivkah's lips, Julia continued. "She is all right. A little weak, and in need of rest, but nothing that a week or two of care and extra attention will not heal."

Rivkah, who had by this time reached her friend's side, clasped Julia's hands and leaned forward. "What happened?"

Julia shook her head. "I am not certain. I think perhaps in the preparation leading up to the Feast of Lots, especially during the days of fasting, she neglected herself. Her energy is not what it once was. I think sometimes she forgets that she is as mortal as the rest of us." Julia laughed gently. "I know another woman who occasionally does the same." She looked sideways at Rivkah and tilted her head toward her friend. It was an old joke between the two of them that Rivkah did not know how to be still. Julia had more than once reminded her that God himself rested on the seventh day, and that there was no shame in it.

Rivkah smiled. Her relief flooded her with gratitude, and she could not muster even a slight defense against her friend's accusation. In truth, she was proud to be compared to her mother. And while there were those from whom she desired to learn serenity and stillness, Tova was not one of them. "Come, let us go to her, and I shall see for myself."

Together, the two women left the hall as Julia began to share with Rivkah the particulars of Tova's condition and her plan for treatment. Within moments of their departure, Martha appeared at the doorway to the hall. When she saw Judah, who had joined the rest of the family at the table and was beginning to pile his plate with the remaining stew and lentils that filled the largest bowl, she beamed at him and rushed immediately to his side. In the past year, she had grown taller, so that they were almost the same height now, and her body had begun to take on the curves of a woman. Her beauty was undeniable, and the brightness of her eyes and smile was radiant, especially when she was pleased, which was often. More than once Judah found himself thinking of her when they were not together. When she was near him, he felt a weakness that could not be explained by his lingering health troubles.

Martha, for her part, treated him exactly the way she had since they were small. Seated next to him, she fussed over him, making sure he had all of the choicest bits of the meal that remained. She called Silas to bring him a glass of goat's milk with honey that she herself had prepared and brought with her from her father's house. Judah protested, sure that this drink had been intended for Tova. But Martha would hear none of his objections. She looked so delighted when the frothy beverage was brought and set before him that Judah ceased his complaining and dutifully drank it as she watched him attentively, one hand cupped under her chin as her elbow rested on the table in front of her.

Ben, who had been watching this exchange from the other end of the table, chuckled and leaned toward his father, who despite having finished his meal was still seated, satisfied and lost in thought. "Father, it seems the marriage canopy may not be put away for long in your household. I see that Simon's daughter has become a beauty, and that her affection for Judah has not waned with age. How long do you think before Simon and Caiaphas discuss the particulars of their union?"

Annas looked at Ben, a little taken aback. Then he laughed heartily. "My son, I did not know that in addition to priest and husband you had also added matchmaker to your responsibilities." He smiled indulgently at his youngest son, and continued. "Yes, she is a beauty, a golden lark filled with the same sweet song as our ravens Tova and Rivkah. I once warned Caiaphas that Rivkah might prove too strong-willed for him. I do believe that Caiaphas may one day be required to have this same conversation with young Judah."

Annas sighed and leaned back, his shoulders wide and relaxed as he surveyed all those gathered. Indeed, like the Scriptures said, children were a blessed reward. He thought about his wife, whom he had no doubt was receiving both tender care and gentle admonishment from their daughter even now, and his sons, grown men and fathers in their own right, who were taking their place both within the priesthood and within his household. Jonathan and Matthias had each taken on distinct responsibilities in the management of the estate in the last several years. Matthias, with his mind for mathematics and his attention to detail, worked closely with Tova and Lydia to direct all matters involving the buying and selling of goods. His young wife, Hannah, had proven to be a shrewd manager and contributor to the household in her own right. It was Matthias who oversaw repairs and improvements to the home while Annas was busy at the temple. Annas had been particularly pleased by the report from the craftsman who they had engaged to repair the mosaic floor in the main hall. The man had respectfully complained to Annas that his son was a hard negotiator who knew a fair price and would not budge.

Jonathan's contribution to the estate was less concrete, but equally significant. His sensitivity and willingness to listen made him an ear for many of those who constituted Annas's household, from the aging Silas, to the youngest manservant, to Tova herself. It was Jonathan who earlier that day had gone searching for his mother when she did not answer his call, and discovered her on the cold floor of the storeroom, her face pale and damp, her limbs limp. It was he who had carried her up the stairs in search of help, and who had arranged for the messengers to be sent to Julia and Rivkah before Annas was even aware of his wife's condition.

Looking across the table, Annas's eyes fell on Theo and Ben, both still enjoying the final remnants of the meal. Despite being born nearly a decade apart, the two were extremely close. Their wives, who had been friends themselves since childhood, spent much of their time together as well, and Theo and Ben were nearly inseparable when they were at home. They were often joined by Gamaliel's son Joshua, more so now that he too was preparing to enter the priesthood. Annas knew that Ben's relationship with Joshua concerned Tova, as she saw that the two young men encouraged one another toward rash and showy behavior. But Theo, though brash in his own way, had a mature level-headedness that the other two lacked. Since taking on the role of master of the temple guard, he had shown himself to be both bold and discreet, two qualities Annas highly valued. Annas was justifiably proud of the men his line had produced. The shadow of the loss of Eleazar, though still painful, had waned as the years passed.

Annas's eyes drifted to where Martha and Judah sat, and he smiled as he watched the girl enthusiastically recounting the details of her morning to Judah, who sat listening as if in a trance. Ben was right, he thought as he observed them, that a union between these two was a most likely outcome. Despite Judah's health, which continued to be a subject of conversation and concern within the family, it appeared he would be well enough to take on both the responsibilities of the priesthood and the burden of a wife and family. Annas knew this must be a great relief to Caiaphas and Rivkah. Judah was their only child, and as the years passed it seemed more and more likely that he would remain so.

Looking at Judah, now thirteen and gangly, Annas was reminded of Caiaphas as he was when he and Hadassah had first come to their estate. It had been twenty-five years since Abel's death. Annas could hardly believe that the pale, quiet boy whom he had welcomed into his home then was now firmly ensconced in the role of high priest. Caiaphas had proven to be a valuable and worthy addition to his family, and had thus far fulfilled his responsibilities as high priest with dignity and skill. While Caiaphas did not share Annas's gifts as an orator and debater, he was fair and thoughtful. A peacemaker by nature, Caiaphas had learned to be shrewd as well. His early work with Pilate, Annas had to admit, was masterful, and his relationship with Gratus had over time usurped Annas's own.

If Annas had any reason to be disappointed in Caiaphas, it was that his son-in-law lacked the kind of ferocity needed to fully inhabit the high priesthood, to lead with unflinching determination, especially in times of challenge. Being a leader ultimately required passion beyond that of a regular man. From the beginning, Annas had hoped that losing his father would kindle Caiaphas's resolve, growing him into a person of tenacity and determination. Instead, Caiaphas had remained humble to a fault, always striving to find a way to satisfy everyone, and inclined to attempt reconciliation even in the face of immoveable forces.

As a result, Annas had learned to supplement his son-in-law's defects with his own strength, working within the confines of his established position as an influential member of the council and using the relationships he had spent decades building for that very purpose. With Ishmael, Annas's role had been explicit, with Eleazar covert. But with Caiaphas it felt organic, like a powerful ox clearing a path for the faithful farmer to follow, making the way straight and unencumbered and ready for sowing. It was a system that functioned well, as Caiaphas was for the most part willing to be guided and advised by those on the council whose beards were already gray and who had lived through many more years and experiences.

Annas frowned slightly as he considered his son-in-law's more recent behavior toward him. Caiaphas was questioning him with more regularity of late, and seemed less willing to take his advice without significant discussion and support from others on the council. He and Simon had both noticed that Caiaphas had more than once taken action without consulting them at all. Although the matters were small, and the actions themselves not inconsistent with the advice they might have given if asked, it did not sit well with him.

Annas had been a member of the priesthood for nearly four decades. He had spent his entire adult life serving God and his people from within the temple. He knew each family whose sons filled the ranks of the priesthood. Thanks to those he employed to keep him informed, he knew all that went on both inside and outside the city walls as well. The idea that Caiaphas seemed to think he could operate autonomously was ill-conceived at best, and it only made Annas more determined to make sure that nothing escaped his knowledge or oversight.

THESE CONCERNS HAD ONLY BEEN EXACERBATED by a conversation with Rivkah the last time she had visited Annas's estate. She had come to see them just after the Feast of Dedication, bearing with her a basket full of grapes and dates, dried and pressed into cakes for storage and preservation. These sweet cakes, which Lydia had taught her to make as a child, were a particular favorite of Tova's. Rivkah always made more than was necessary for her smaller household, and shared the surplus with her parents once they were prepared.

After Rivkah deposited her supply of cakes in the storeroom, she spent some time visiting with Lydia, who asked after Nathan and Rebecca and wanted to hear all about Judah's most recent accomplishments in his studies. When she had finished answering Lydia's litany of questions, she went to the fresco room, where Annas often retired after the evening meal. The shadows were long by the time she greeted her father and took a seat beside him. For a moment he was reminded of when she used to join him, her dark head barely reaching his shoulder, as he sat reviewing his correspondence and meditating on the events of the day. Although she was now a wife and a mother, the same age Tova had been when she gave birth to Ben, it did not take much for Annas to see in his only daughter the feisty young child who had always been so quick with questions, longing to know the information contained in the scrolls piled on the table, eager to share her perspective and opinions.

"And so, my dear, you are now not only the daughter of a high priest but the wife of one as well." Annas's smile was broad and warm as he contemplated his daughter. "Truly you are most blessed."

Rivkah laughed. "Oh, yes, it is a blessing indeed to be without my husband during every festival, and for days before, and to know that at any moment the priesthood may require his presence, day or night." She looked thoughtful, though her smile was playful as she spoke. "When my mother used to tease you and call the temple your Rachel, I did not understand it. But I see now that it is your treasured first love as well as my husband's, a beautiful bride whose hand requires great labor and sacrifice. My mother and I must satisfy ourselves as the Leahs of our households, fruitful and honored even if we must be content with second place in your affections."

Annas threw his head back and roared with laughter. "Ah, Rivkah, your wit has not faded with age. But, you are hard on your old father, and on your husband. You may remember that, unlike Jacob, Joseph's love for you came first, long before he wedded himself to the temple. I have no doubt you hold much sway in his mind and heart even as he has dedicated himself to God's holy place. In fact, daughter, I wonder if you might be of service to me, and to him, on a matter of some importance." His smile fading, Annas leaned forward and fixed Rivkah with a firm gaze.

He took a deep breath. "Joseph has served the temple well in his time as high priest. No one can question his loyalty or devotion."

"But?" Rivkah's voice was quiet, almost a hiss, as she took in her father's concerned look, his dark brow, and the way he was leaning toward her, like a benevolent lion preparing to pounce.

Annas smiled gently. "But you and I both know that he does not have the temperament for challenge or conflict. As a boy, he was uncomfortable when your brothers fought, and age has not increased his tolerance for disagreements. He will always look for the way of compromise if he can find it. Joseph is a great man for times of peace. But I fear he is not well suited for battle. And there is trouble brewing that he does not yet recognize."

He leaned back in his chair and smiled. "Fortunately, he is surrounded by those with more of an appetite for such things, and advisors like myself and Simon who can navigate these waters with confidence and force. He need only let us do it, and trust our instincts and direction when the time comes. I know he listens to you. I wonder if you could not encourage him to that end."

Rivkah blanched, and her eyes flashed darkly as she looked at Annas. "You underestimate him, Father." Her voice was hard and low as she continued. "If anyone has a reason to dislike conflict, it is Joseph. You of all people know too well that conflict robbed him of his father, and that he has seen more loss and death than most." She straightened up. "But he is stronger than you give him credit for, and his desire for peace is one of wisdom, not naiveté." Rising, she took a step away, and then stopped and turned back. "He understands more than you know. I do not doubt he will rise to the occasion if required." With that, she turned and left the room as Annas watched her, frustrated.

As he thought back on his conversation with Rivkah, Annas shook his head. It had been foolish of him to think that his headstrong daughter could be moved to act on his behalf, a miscalculation on his part. Of course she would stand by her husband, the man to whom she had been bonded by marriage and daily life, over the father with whom she had not shared a home for some time. He should be proud of her loyalty, her willingness to stand up to him in favor of the man she married. But as it was he could only be disappointed by her refusal. They did not speak of it again, but he felt that his daughter now viewed him with a slightly more watchful air, as if she did not fully trust him.

RIVKAH REMAINED at Annas's estate for several weeks after her mother's collapse, until Tova was feeling well enough to resume her responsibilities and Rivkah felt quite sure she had regained her strength. By the third day, Theo and Ben had been sufficiently unhelpful and in the way so that Rivkah suggested they might do well to spend the evening with Caiaphas at his estate, both to keep him company in his family's absence and to remove themselves from her presence. The two objected until Julia stepped in and suggested that perhaps they could escort her and Martha home on their way, at which point they reluctantly agreed.

When they reached the gates of Caiaphas's estate, the aroma that greeted them told them that Rebecca had not been skimping in Rivkah's absence, but had prepared a meal more than worthy of a high priest and his guests. Indeed, Caiaphas was not alone, but had been joined for the evening meal by Gamaliel, Joshua, and Saul, all of whom were already seated. Nathan quickly set two more places at the table so that Theo and Ben could join them. The men ate heartily and well. Their praise for the grilled fish on which they feasted, seasoned with salt and olive oil and served alongside lentils and bread, was generous and appreciative. Rebecca blushed as she thanked them, and retreated from the hall delighted by the compliments and empty plates.

After the meal, the talk turned to the upcoming Passover, and to the preparations that had already begun as all of the citizens readied the city and the temple for the multitude of pilgrims they knew would be descending upon them within weeks.

"Is it true, Joseph, that both Pilate and Antipas plan to be in Jerusalem for the festival this year?" Gamaliel looked thoughtful as Caiaphas nodded. "I wonder at their intentions, and whether we will have any trouble from the people because of their presence."

Caiaphas tried to look less concerned than he felt about the news that Gratus had recently confirmed via messenger. "Gamaliel, I am sure there is no cause for alarm. You know that Antipas becomes restless staying in his own territory for any length of time, and that he is always fearful of spies and others who might be plotting against him. I imagine he thinks it is a good time for him to visit with Pilate, away from the prying eyes of those in Tiberias and Caesarea. We will leave the two of them to their politics in the palace, and will go about our business at the temple as if they are far from here."

Gamaliel nodded. Theo, who had been listening as he drained his goblet of wine, chimed in. "If either they or their soldiers seeks to disturb the rituals or sacrifices, they had better think twice." He grinned. "The guard is more than prepared for the Passover celebration, and well-equipped to deal with any pilgrims who become unruly within the temple grounds. But we would be more than happy to extend that readiness to the Romans if need be."

Caiaphas smiled at his brother-in-law as Ben and Joshua boisterously voiced their approval at this declaration. He spoke deliberately, though he was careful to keep his tone light. "It will not come to that, Theo, although I appreciate your enthusiasm. But you will have your hands full enough with those who have come to the temple to worship. You know as well as I do that we have had our share of trouble with our own people without having to worry about the Roman governor or king." Caiaphas could not be sure, but he thought he detected a note of recognition in Theo's eyes, and felt certain they were both thinking of the disturbance among the money changers and merchants three years before.

Ben, who had not noticed this exchange, passionately expounded upon Theo's thoughts as if Caiaphas had not spoken. "The Roman soldiers had better not come anywhere near the temple. They have no reason to be in our city to begin with, and the temple is no place for them. I know my father would never have allowed their presence to interfere in any way with our sacred celebration. I hope you will not either, Joseph."

Caiaphas stared at him. When he spoke, his voice was cold. "Your father is not high priest, Ben. I am. And I have no plans to allow the Romans to interfere in our festival."

Ben looked taken aback. "Of course, brother. I meant no disrespect. I only wish that we were free to manage ourselves without having to maneuver around the egos and expectations of men like Pilate, who do not know or honor our God."

Caiaphas sighed heavily. "It is hard to know God's plan in this, Ben. His thoughts and ways are not ours. Yet we know his path is a level one, and we need only to walk the road set before us. I trust that you and all of those in our priesthood will remember your duty, as I do mine."

Ben nodded quickly, and Caiaphas turned away as the conversation shifted back to the particulars of the temple preparations and the need for more qualified merchants who could be trusted to give pilgrims a fair price in exchange for their animals. Caiaphas remained silent as the others discussed possible candidates, trying not to let Ben's words affect him too much as he contemplated the days that lay ahead.

CHAPTER 23

Rivkah had been away for less than two weeks when Joshua arrived at Caiaphas's estate, out of breath and asking for an audience with the high priest. It was after the evening meal. Caiaphas was taking a turn around the perimeter of his property, walking the rooftop pathway he and Rivkah often used, when Nathan called out to him from below that Joshua had arrived and was requesting to see him. Caiaphas, surprised, asked Nathan to send the boy up to him. He made his way over to the top of the stairway just in time to see Joshua emerge from below.

Joshua, at nineteen, had grown into an extremely handsome young man, an attribute overshadowed only by his fierce intelligence and ability to interpret and understand Scripture. If there was any truth to the notion that wisdom was an inherited trait, there was no question that this was the grandson of one of the greatest scholars since the days of Solomon, and the son of a man who was regarded as one of the most learned men of his time. Gamaliel had raised his only son well, and although Joshua's temperament did not always match his intellect, he was nonetheless impressive as he sat at the temple and debated with priests twice his age as to the meaning or ramifications of a particular law or precept. Caiaphas was looking forward to initiating Joshua into the priesthood officially, and hoped that the weight of that responsibility would continue to shape his character as well as his mind.

As Joshua joined him, the last rays of sunlight cast a glow over the rooftops. They stood for a moment side by side, facing north, the sun setting to their left over the western walls of the city. Barely visible in the distance across the rooftops was Herod's Palace, its towers rising high above the rest of the buildings surrounding it. Caiaphas knew that even now, Pilate and Antipas were each on their way to Jerusalem. They would meet at this location, where they would remain for the duration of the festival. In addition to the three towers, the palace contained two large wings separated by an expansive garden. When Pilate traveled to Jerusalem, he usually set up residence in the northern wing, closest to the towers. Caiaphas imagined that Antipas would likely settle in the southern wing. The two Roman leaders would find occasion to meet in the shared reception room, receiving guests, conferring on matters of local importance, and trading gossip regarding the constantly fluctuating allegiances and factions that made up Roman society. As much as Caiaphas would have liked to know the entire contents of their conversation, he was primarily concerned that it involve the Jewish leadership and the temple as little as possible. As soon as the final sacrificial fires had gone out in the temple and the last of the lambs had been roasted and consumed, he hoped they would begin to make arrangements to return to their own cities, far from Jerusalem.

Sighing as he considered this, Caiaphas turned to Joshua, who was waiting for an invitation to begin. "Welcome, Joshua. What news?"

Joshua took a deep breath before he began to speak. Then the words came spilling out as if he had been holding them back with difficulty. "Noble Caiaphas, my father asked me to come to you directly now so that you are aware of the situation before it is brought up in the council meeting tomorrow morning, as it surely will be. He hopes that it means nothing, and that there is no need for alarm. But he is shaken, to be sure. I believe he will not be alone once the rumors begin to spread."

Caiaphas knew Gamaliel to be both steady and calm. The notion that something had happened that had left the older priest troubled was indeed concerning. Putting his hand on the boy's shoulder in what he intended to be a steadying manner, he said, "Joshua, I have seen many things in my time, both as high priest and in the years before. Tell me what it is you have been sent to report."

Joshua took another breath. "Three men arrived at our house just before the evening meal, their sandals and the edges of their robes dusty and muddied by the road from Bethany, from which they had just traveled. They brought with them strange news of a man who they claim has been raised from the dead."

Caiaphas's eyes widened slightly, but he fought to keep any emotion from his face as Joshua continued.

"From what we have been told, the man lived with his two sisters near the outskirts of the town. A young man not much older than myself, he fell ill suddenly and died within the week. After much mourning he was placed in his family's tomb. Several days later, our guests, who live not far from the place, noticed a group of people heading up the path to the tomb, and they followed out of curiosity. When they reached the rock where the man had been buried, they noticed immediately that the stone that should have been blocking the entrance had been moved away. As they looked on from a distance, they saw a figure emerge from the tomb, still wrapped in burial garments. One of the men explained that he crept nearer to get a closer look just in time to see another person take the dead man's hand, and triumphantly call for the mourners to remove the linens from the body. The one who made this proclamation, and who indeed appears to have taken credit for the supposed resurrection, is all too familiar to us."

Caiaphas spoke quietly, and he did not look at Joshua as he did so. "Jesus."

Joshua looked at him, startled.

"Yes, Caiaphas. That is what the men told us. It is not unknown to us that Jesus and his followers have spent time in Bethany, although the last reports that Annas shared with the council were that he appeared to have settled across the Jordan in Perea. But how did you know this? Have you received other reports of the incident already? Have you considered how we will handle those who will undoubtedly be afraid of this rumor, who will want to know what it means and if it could possibly be true?"

Caiaphas ignored the questions, and asked one of his own. "I trust that you came directly to me and that you have no plans to visit any other household this evening?"

Joshua hesitated a moment, then raised his eyes to look directly at Caiaphas. "Gamaliel sent me to you, and he sent Saul, who was with us when the men arrived, to your father-in-law's house. I cannot say if any other priests will know of this before morning. But my father thought it important enough to inform you both before then."

Caiaphas sighed heavily. He was sure that as soon as Annas was told, he would share the information with Simon. He had no doubt that by the time they reached the temple in the morning, the two men would have devised a plan for how to handle both Jesus and the people's response, a plan they would assume Caiaphas would unquestioningly embrace and order to be implemented without delay. They would be convinced that the resurrection itself was a hoax, designed to inspire loyalty and to increase the man's perceived significance, and would be determined to quietly stamp out anything that might be seen as a threat to the temple's power and authority. While Caiaphas did not disagree, he had the unfortunate advantage of knowing more than they did about this matter. The knowledge made him feel suddenly tired, as if his shoulders were sagging under the weight of the very stone he had seen moved from the tomb's entrance in his dreams.

"Thank you, Joshua, for coming to me. You may return to your father's house and tell him that I have received the message and greatly appreciate being informed. We will speak more of this tomorrow at the temple."

Joshua looked as if he were about to say more, then thought better of it and nodded briskly before turning and disappearing out of sight as he entered the stairwell that led back to the main floor. Caiaphas waited until Joshua was gone, then made his way inside and walked slowly down the corridor to his bedchamber. With Rivkah still at her father's house, the room was empty. Caiaphas sank down on the bed, putting his head in his hands.

He had known this moment would come, no matter how many times he tried to convince himself otherwise. Each time he woke from the vision of Jesus clasping the hand of a dead man, he had tried to persuade himself that it must be an illusion, a fantasy, and nothing more. It made no sense, that a common peasant from Galilee could claim to bring a man back from the dead. Yet his dream, and now this report, told a different story.

From the days of Aaron and Moses, it was the priesthood that had been designated as the spiritual authority of the people. For generations, the pious and dedicated men who had come before him had served as judges, settling disputes and meting out justice. They had devoted themselves to the rituals of sacrifice and supplication required by God. The temple healers had been granted the ability to provide care and comfort to those who were ill, and God worked through them to heal those in need. But even the most venerated priests would never pretend to have power over life and death. A rebel who threatened revolution in an attempt to appropriate power was one thing. But from what Caiaphas understood of Jesus, the man appeared to be attempting to usurp power, not just from the priests or the Romans, but from God himself. He shuddered at the thought.

Caiaphas was sure that the morning would bring outrage and fear from those on the council. They would be afraid that this man was scheming against the priesthood and planning a revolt of some kind. He was sure that Annas, who no doubt knew more than he did regarding the man's recent movements, would arrive determined to stop Jesus in his tracks, whatever the cost. While Caiaphas appreciated his father-in-law's passion, he felt that this was a situation that required delicacy rather than brute force. With Passover approaching, it was the worst time of year for something like this to be foisted upon the leadership of the temple. If either Pilate or Antipas received word of it, they would be understandably alarmed. Antipas, with his fears about Jesus already enflamed, would not be content to let the matter rest. Pilate would feel tremendous pressure to take a stand against anyone inciting unrest among the people just before a holiday, when the eyes of Rome were particularly watchful. They had to be extremely careful.

Caiaphas found himself longing for Rivkah, who was the only living person who knew about the dreams that still haunted his nights. He wished she were there to rub the back of his neck with her soft hands, and to allay his fears, to listen to his concerns and share her perspective. But she was still tending to Tova, across the city at her father's estate. There was no way he was going to call her back for something like this. He wondered whether she had been there when Saul came with the message for Annas, and whether she had perhaps been privy to the tale. He doubted very much whether Annas would have received Saul with others present, especially at that time of day, and thought it unlikely that Rivkah would have any reason to be a part of the conversation. But still he found himself hoping he was wrong, knowing that she would at once recognize the story as the one he had shared with her from his visions, and would immediately understand the gravity of the situation.

AFTER A RESTLESS NIGHT OF SLEEP, haunted as he was by the face of a man half-covered in burial linens, and another face that shone with joy despite being tear-stained and worn, Caiaphas rose early. Taking a circuitous route north through the Upper City, he strode through streets just beginning to stir, as bleary-eyed household servants emerged from doorways, readying themselves for the marketplace. The white walls of the homes he passed gleamed in the soft morning sunlight. Ahead of him, he could hear the murmur of merchants as they began to set out their wares, the air thick with newly pressed oil and freshly baked bread. He was tempted to continue walking, to lose himself amid the burgeoning bustle in the streets, to find a quiet corner where none would think to look for him. Instead, he turned east just before he reached the marketplace itself, and strode with purpose toward the temple. He went directly to the Chamber of Hewn Stone. As soon as enough priests had gathered to represent the majority of the council, he called the meeting to order. He knew by the way the members were gathering in clusters, whispering furiously and looking anxious, that the news had traveled among them. Already tensions were high.

Caiaphas first brought forth Gamaliel, who had been seated a few feet away from him, and asked him to recount the story that had been told to him by the men from Bethany. Annas, who caught Caiaphas's eye as soon as he entered the chamber, was the first to speak once Gamaliel was finished. Annas's was a voice that commanded attention, and it carried throughout the room.

"It is clear that we have let this Jesus alone for too long. He has now resorted to a new level of blasphemous activity in order to gain influence among the people. Whether or not we believe there is any truth to these rumors, we cannot afford to sit by and do nothing while the numbers of those who follow him grow. Like other revolutionaries and troublemakers who have come before him, he grows bolder with each season. Our most recent reports tell us that his followers are calling him Teacher and Master and even Lord. It is lunacy, and it must stop."

Simon, who had been waiting for Annas to finish, stepped forward. Caiaphas had the distinct impression that he was watching a carefully orchestrated dance between the two men. He felt a pain behind his eyes begin to pulse. Simon, who did not have the same raw magnetism as his father-in-law, nonetheless spoke with conviction and authority. "It is unfortunate timing that this has occurred just as Pilate and Antipas both arrive in our city. It is unlikely we will be able to shield them from the rumors that by tonight will be whispered in every corner of the marketplace, and will no doubt reach the walls of the palace before long. We know that Antipas is fearful of any who might threaten his authority, and that Pilate will not want to demonstrate any weakness, especially in front of the Roman king. Moreover, if we let Jesus go on like this, he will soon have more followers than we have pilgrims in the temple, and then what will we do? When they arrive in Jerusalem for the Passover, Pilate will send in his soldiers, and there will be Roman legions marching in our streets, such as we have not seen in many years."

Annas spoke again, continuing as if he and Simon shared a single voice. "We must act, and quickly. Send the temple guard to Bethany to arrest the man, and keep him under our close supervision until the festival is over. Send messengers to Pilate and Antipas that the man is in our custody, and that he will remain there until the city is once again quiet. If during that time we are able to persuade him to cease this behavior, perhaps we can send him away and be done with him. If not, we will need to take more aggressive action to ensure our safety and security without arousing the Roman leaders further. But I do not think it will come to that."

Caiaphas rose, his head pounding as he stepped forward, the blood rushing in his ears. He felt sick, and when he spoke his voice was like a whip, cutting furiously through the air. "You know nothing at all." As soon as the words escaped his lips, there was a gasp among the priests. He could see the shock on his father-in-law's face as he turned to him.

"What? Joseph, are you unwell?" Annas took a step toward him, but Caiaphas put out a hand to stop him.

"I am fine, Annas. And perhaps as your high priest it is time you called me by my father's name rather than the one you used when I was a boy."

Annas stepped back quickly as if he had been slapped. He said nothing as he stared at his son-in-law, incredulous.

Caiaphas looked around. For a brief moment, he thought he saw flames licking the walls of the chamber as they did in his dreams of the temple burning, and he closed his eyes to rid himself of the sight. When he opened them again, the flames were gone. He stood still, blinking, as the priests gathered around him, silent and waiting. Then he spoke clearly and deliberately, as if reciting a solemn prayer.

"There is no greater call than the one to preserve our nation, our way of life, our people. Our God has bestowed that responsibility upon us, and we will hold firm to it. But we must not incite rebellion in the service of trying to quell it. If we go after this man now, what of those who follow him? Do you not remember the young men who were with John, and how resolute they were in their conviction about him, even after his death?"

He looked around at the faces of the priests who watched him in silence. "This man is no simple revolutionary, inciting rebellious feelings in those who long to take on the Romans. He is after the hearts and minds of our people. I fear his ways are unlike any who have come before him. I do not believe a man like Jesus will be convinced to change his course, no matter how persuasive our methods. He will need to be stopped, and stop him we must."

Caiaphas took a slow breath, and the thoughts that had caused him to toss and turn long into the night flowed like water from a deep underground well. "But we will need to destroy not only him, but the belief in him that exists among those whom he has so far deceived. If he must die, it is better that he die in disgrace, discredited and robbed of any power he might have. He must be like a sacrificial animal on the altar, slaughtered on behalf of our people to ensure them a future safe from both Roman destruction and from the worship of one who is clearly unworthy. If he dies, let him die so that an entire nation will not perish, so that our people can have peace. If need be, we will be the righteous instruments of this deed. For now, though, we must watch and wait, and seize our opportunity when the time is right, and not before."

Caiaphas looked at Annas, who had taken another step back and was staring at him. Caiaphas felt as if he were seeing things more clearly than he had ever seen them, like a new bride whose veil has been lifted seeing the one to whom she has been united for the first time. "I know there are those among our ranks who would seek to stamp out this troublemaker like a worm beneath our feet. But we must tread carefully, lest we accidentally create a martyr to be worshiped after he is gone."

At these words, Caiaphas faltered slightly. Jonathan came swiftly forward to take his arm. Caiaphas made as if to shrug him off, but allowed himself to be led back to the seat of honor reserved for the high priest. There was little conversation after that, and within minutes the priests began to leave the chamber, murmuring to one another as they did so. Annas hung back a moment, then appeared to think better of it, and strode out of the chamber without looking back. No one seemed willing to approach Caiaphas, and Jonathan remained by his side in silence until nearly all of the others had left the chamber.

When Jonathan spoke, his voice was low, and he leaned close to Caiaphas's ear as he did so. "You know, brother, that Annas and Simon will be unlikely to support a plan that does not include arresting Jesus immediately, assuming he does in fact return to Jerusalem for the Passover."

Caiaphas sighed, shaking his head. "They must be made to understand what is at stake, Jonathan. Annas and Simon have grown too used to power, too accustomed to being able to manipulate those they would seek to control." He smiled slightly. "I know all too well what they are capable of when they believe they know best." He put his hand on Jonathan's arm, imploring. "But you must be my ally here, brother, as we navigate how best to handle both the priesthood and this trouble. We are in new territory. I fear the old ways will not accomplish the results we need."

Jonathan nodded, his brow furrowed. "I am at your disposal, Joseph. We must pray that wisdom will prevail. We know from the account of Job that long life brings understanding. But I am in agreement that in this case our elders may not know what is best. And yet I hope we may yet avoid any of this. Perhaps Jesus and his followers will stay away this Passover. They must know the dangers they face if they choose to enter the city."

Caiaphas nodded, but in the pit of his stomach he knew that this was a vain hope. Somehow he had no doubt that the man whose face now haunted his dreams would not be kept away by the threat of arrest or the specter of the priesthood's potential wrath. This year the Feast of Unleavened Bread would not pass without incident, of that he was sure. Again he found himself thinking of his wife, and fervently hoping that Rivkah would be waiting for him when he returned home that evening. She had been gone too long.

CHAPTER 24

By the time Rivkah returned to her own estate, confident that her mother was now fully mended and able to run her household without help, the preparations for the Feast of Unleavened Bread were well underway. Nathan and Rebecca, along with Rebecca's younger brother Malchus, who had joined the household after his mother's death had left him and his sister orphans, were hard at work readying the house and gathering the supplies that would be needed for the feast. Rivkah was pleased to see how much work had been done in her absence. Both she and Judah were clearly relieved to be back in their own home. Rivkah confided to Caiaphas that, while she had not in fact been privy to the initial conversation between Saul and Annas, she had witnessed many priests coming and going at odd hours from her father's estate. More than once she had come upon Annas and Simon engaged in hushed conversation that ceased as soon as she entered the room. She had noticed a definite change in Annas's behavior toward her since the council meeting the morning after Saul's report, a wariness and a coolness that had not existed before. Jonathan had shared with her the particulars of that meeting, and as soon as she heard the story from Bethany, she recognized it as one of Caiaphas's visions.

"My love, I so wanted to return to you immediately. But I had to make sure that my mother was well enough to prepare the Passover without me before I left." She looked regretful as she twisted the edges of her skirt in her hands, her eyes downcast.

Caiaphas looked at her with gratitude, and gently grabbed her hands, unraveling them from the cloth and squeezing them. She glanced up at him and smiled. "You are here now, Rivkah. And I have no illusions that this matter is settled. I am afraid there will be many more opportunities for you to be my support and wise counselor in the days to come."

Indeed, it was only a few days after their reunion that the reports reached Caiaphas that Jesus had in fact entered the city. Crowds gathered around him, ranging from curious bystanders to dedicated followers. Several of the priests who arrived at the temple just before the first sacrifices shared that some of those who congregated around the man as he made his way through the eastern gate of the city greeted him as they might a king, with shouts and bows. The priests explained that they had severely rebuked these individuals and urged them to repent of their idolatrous behavior before God at the temple, then hurried away themselves so as not to be late for their own morning responsibilities. None of the priests could say for certain whether Jesus himself had entered the temple, although Theo and his guard were on the lookout all day. By nightfall the rumors were spreading that the man and his followers had returned to Bethany and would not be lodging overnight within the city walls. Annas and Simon, who had been adamant in the morning council meeting that Jesus must be apprehended, were furious that he had managed to slip in and out of the city without being caught. But Caiaphas was hopeful that the day was a good omen. If Jesus could be in the city without causing too much disruption, it meant that they might still get through the festival without arousing Pilate or Antipas to anger or concern. Both men had recently arrived and set up their respective convoys at the palace. Caiaphas felt confident that they were still ignorant of the troublemaker who was taking up so much of the priesthood's time and concern.

"My brothers, may I remind you that our primary responsibility is to our people, to prepare for the Feast of Unleavened Bread and to carry out our duties of sacrifice and honor to our God. This one man should not be a reason for alarm unless his presence inhibits our people from coming to worship or distracts us from the mandates given to us by the law to fulfill. We must treat him as simply another pilgrim, coming to worship and give thanks to God for the freedom granted our ancestors so many years ago. We will pray that the aroma of the lambs being slaughtered this Passover season will refocus our people, reminding even those who have been entranced by this man that true freedom can be given to us only by our God. Those of us who have dedicated our lives to the priesthood must be the example. Our energies must be unified, directed toward the things that matter and away from distractions."

Although Caiaphas could tell that many of the priests were not satisfied with his approach, no one dared to question his authority or argue with him openly within the Chamber of Hewn Stone. That night, however, Annas and Simon visited him at his home, and attempted to convince him to change his mind. "Caiaphas," Annas began, and the word sat heavy and awkward on his tongue. "I wonder that you do not see the wisdom in getting rid of this man before he becomes a larger threat. The heart of a man plans his way, as you well know, and the Scriptures teach us that there is wisdom in looking ahead and not merely waiting on impending disaster."

Caiaphas smiled at his father-in-law. "Ah, but Annas, how does the Scripture end? The Lord is the one who establishes a man's steps. We are in the right here, and this man is nothing more than an interloper, however savvy he might be. Our God will protect us from this menace. If and when the time is right, we will act. But I will not allow our priesthood to be defiled in the process. We are more than merely soldiers, Annas, protecting a stronghold from an enemy. You and my father both taught me that."

Annas looked taken aback at this reference to Abel, and Caiaphas could see that he thought carefully before he spoke again. "Your father was a godly man, Caiaphas, both a priest and a warrior. I do not know if he would agree with your assessment."

Caiaphas sighed. "And yet, thanks to a revolutionary not dissimilar to this man Jesus, we cannot ask him for his opinion on the matter." He paused. "My father died defending the honor of our temple and our God. There is nothing I would not do to honor that legacy. But you must abide by my judgment here, Annas."

He turned to Simon. "You as well, old friend. I know you both have the best interests of the temple at heart. But I must ask that you show solidarity with me in this. Many among our priesthood will look to you for their example. It will not do for us to appear divided or conflicted as to our course of action."

The two men left shortly thereafter. Caiaphas could tell they were dissatisfied with the way the meeting had gone. When he shared the conversation with Rivkah as they lay in bed that night, she smiled and nodded slightly. "They are both accustomed to winning every argument, Joseph. My father has been the most prominent voice among the priesthood for decades. Eleazar challenged him, but he was brash and divisive. The priests respect you, and so for the first time Annas must accept that there is another who has both the authority and the wisdom to lead, and that you are capable of doing so without his direction. It is not easy for him, I am sure."

Caiaphas sighed. "And yet I am not confident that he and Simon will comply with my instruction, my love, as much as it pains me to admit it. We know from experience that Annas's reach stretches far beyond the temple. I do not doubt that he will employ every instrument at his disposal to seek an end to this man and his followers."

Rivkah nodded. "Then you must do all you can to ensure that you are one step ahead of him, and that you and Jonathan are kept abreast of every action taken on behalf of the priesthood."

Caiaphas nodded silently, and watched as his wife settled into the bed beside him. He was still awake, mulling things over, long after she had fallen asleep. It was not that he feared his dreams, although because of them he had no relief from the worries that filled his days. But he felt as if each night drew him closer to some inevitable conclusion that he had not yet seen in his visions. He was both afraid and curious as to what new revelations his slumber might reveal.

THE FOLLOWING morning was filled with final preparations for the Passover. At daylight, Jonathan and Caiaphas met to oversee the washing of the altar. There were letters of correspondence to be sent to local synagogues, some of which required advice as to whom among their congregants would not be able to participate in the festival due to recent indiscretions or illness. Joshua had been extremely useful in parsing out some of the thornier theological questions, at which point he and Ben retreated to the Women's Court, where the younger boys were receiving their lessons beneath the eaves nearest to the Chamber of Oils.

After this was complete, Matthias occupied several additional hours with a detailed report of the financial preparations and a review of the decisions he had made regarding the newest merchants and money changers who would be allowed to peddle their wares and do their business on the temple grounds throughout the festival. All needed to be approved by the high priest. Caiaphas found himself meeting with a series of earnest and nervous tradesmen, who bowed and fumbled and expressed their appreciation at having been deemed worthy to join the stalls of those who were already actively engaged in trade and commerce just beyond the temple walls.

By the time the sun had reached its pinnacle and the stone steps that led from Nicanor's Gate down into the Women's Court were radiating a heat that made the air flicker around them, Caiaphas had grown both weary and hungry. He and Jonathan retreated to the cool of the Chamber of Hewn Stone to consume some of the leftover portion of the meat, bread, and wine that had been set aside for them. He was grateful for this moment of calm, and remarked to Jonathan that this was probably the only real rest they would have until after the Passover was over. Returning to his food, he was surprised to see

Theo striding into the chamber, with Ben and Joshua following close at his heels.

The look on Theo's face was unmistakably one of rage. His nostrils were thin and white, and Caiaphas could see a tightly clenched fist making its way in and out of the folds of his robe, his other hand fingering the curved dagger that lay in its sheath at his hip. While most of the priests were without any kind of armor or weaponry, the treasury of the temple did house its fair share of arms. As the master of the guard, Theo was one of the only priests who was never without a weapon. While it was primarily ceremonial in nature, the blade was finely crafted and more than capable of causing damage if pressed into service. Although Caiaphas had never seen Theo wield it, he had no doubt that his brother-in-law would be swift and deadly if the need arose.

Jonathan was on his feet first, brushing the crumbs from his tunic, and moving toward his younger brother in alarm. "Theo? What is it? What has happened?"

Caiaphas rose as well, glancing from the faces of Joshua and Ben, who looked somehow both sheepish and upset, to Theo, who had begun to pace the length of the hall. Theo stopped in front of Caiaphas and took a deep breath. He squared his shoulders before he began to speak.

"Noble Caiaphas, we have had a new disturbance with the man Jesus." Before Caiaphas could interrupt him, he continued. "He has escaped our grasp yet again, I am ashamed to report, no thanks to the antics of these two. They think they are clever. But their cleverness has robbed us of an opportunity to bring the man to justice without causing too much attention." He scowled. "Annas and Simon will be furious."

Caiaphas fought the strong urge to rebuke Theo. It was his judgment and opinion that should be considered, not those of his father-in-law or Simon. But his curiosity to understand what had happened overcame his pride, and he said simply, "Tell me what has happened."

Theo nodded briskly and began to relay the story. Jesus and his disciples had entered the temple grounds just after sunrise. For a second time, Jesus appeared to have caused a disturbance among the merchants' stalls as he passed, releasing animals and overturning at least one of the tables closest to the southern gate of the temple. Leaving this chaotic scene hastily before anyone could call for the temple guards, he moved to the Women's Court, where he knelt down among the boys in the middle of memorizing Scripture, and began to tell them a story about a fig tree that grew on the outskirts of the city on the road from Bethany. Those listening were entranced. The boys quickly forgot their lessons and gathered around him, clamoring to hear more.

Ben and Joshua had been leaning against the pillar nearest the boys, amusing themselves by testing one another's knowledge of the more arcane teachings of Joshua's grandfather Hillel. They found themselves drawn to the man as well, and immediately recognized him as the one who was causing so much distress among the priesthood. It was Joshua who first had the idea to question him themselves. As Jesus rose from where he knelt among the children, Joshua approached him boldly.

"Sir, you speak as one who has much authority in this place, though your robes suggest that you do not have the formal teaching of even the youngest boys in whose midst you currently find yourself. Tell me, on whose authority do you share these stories with those who should by all rights be learning their lessons from the priests of the temple?"

Jesus looked at Joshua for a moment without speaking, as Ben looked on, delighted by his friend's nerve and audacity. For a moment, Joshua was unsure whether the man had either heard or understood him. Then Jesus gave a small smile and spoke.

"You are a man with many questions, I see." His eyes peered into Joshua's, and the younger man found himself holding his breath waiting for the response. "I will also ask you one question. If you answer my question, I am happy to answer yours."

Joshua looked over at Ben, who shrugged, and then slowly nodded.

"You know the man John, my cousin, of whom I am sure you have heard many things." Joshua took a step back, surprised that Jesus would bring up the subject of John, who had been the source of so much trouble both in Jerusalem and beyond. "When he lived, he bathed many in the Jordan River. Any who came to him seeking to repent of their sins and be cleansed, he welcomed. I know that many questioned whether or not there was any power in his actions. I ask you, by what authority did John perform these rituals?"

Joshua's face went pale. He took another step back toward Ben, who came up to meet him. By now all of the boys had abandoned their lessons and were watching with deep interest. Even the young priests who were supposed to be teaching them were silent, their eyes fixed on Jesus. Others, who were at the temple to exchange money or to worship and make sacrifices, had also stopped on their way across the courts to observe the conversation. A small crowd had gathered, one that included several other priests who had come to see the cause of the break in lessons.

Ben leaned his head close to Joshua, and murmured under his breath so that no one else could hear. "Friend, this man has caught you with his question. If you denounce John as a mere peasant with no greater calling, you risk stirring up the ire of the people, many of whom still consider John to have been a prophet. But you cannot grant that John had any kind of divine authority in what he was doing. You are in a bind indeed."

Joshua nodded, his eyes still on Jesus. After a moment he stepped forward until he stood before the man again. He smiled, his handsome features arranged into a carefully bemused expression designed to indicate that he was not in any way thrown by the exchange. "This is a noble question, one that is not worthy of a simple answer. I cannot say upon whose authority John operated. That is between him and our God."

Jesus returned the smile. Although his was neither as handsome nor as polished as Joshua's, there was a quiet power in it. "Then with all respect I will not answer your question either." Bowing politely, he turned from Joshua and knelt again among the children, who stared at him with mouths gaping and eyes wide.

Joshua looked at him, incredulous, and then turned back to Ben, whose brow was knit and who was clearly deep in thought. Then, as if he had made a sudden decision, Ben stepped forward. When he spoke there was a sweetness to his tone that anyone who knew him well would recognize as dangerous. "Teacher," he began, and Jesus turned to look at him. "I see that regardless of your education or background you are wise and full of truth. I too have a question for you. You know the emperor Tiberius calls upon our people to pay a tax to Rome. For many of our citizens this is a burden that weighs heavily on their households. There are some who would argue that our people already pay a tax to the temple, and that for those who worship our God this is the rightful place for any financial gifts. What say you to this? Should our people be beholden to a foreign emperor, giving funds that might otherwise go toward sacrifices or to benefit the priesthood?"

Ben kept his tone light as he spoke, but the faces around him reflected the seriousness of the question he posed. Everyone knew that the emperor's tax was the source of much consternation among the people. It was an argument over this very tax that had led to the revolt that had robbed Caiaphas of his father. If Jesus was a revolutionary like his cousin John appeared to have been, he would likely balk at the idea that money was being diverted from the temple to pacify Roman rule. His answer to Ben's question might provide fodder to demonstrate the danger he posed to the people. It was a carefully laid trap. The crowd, which had continued to grow, held its collective breath as Jesus opened his mouth to respond.

The expression on his face was inscrutable. But there was a sadness in Jesus's voice when he spoke. "Why do you test me?" He looked around at those gathered, and saw a man at the edge of the crowd who had clearly come from delivering a sacrifice. The man's clothing suggested that he was a pilgrim, not native to Jerusalem.

Jesus called to him. "My friend, do you have a Roman coin that I might see for a moment?" The man looked startled, but obligingly dug his hand into a small pouch tied to his belt, pulled out a coin and dropped it into Jesus's hand. Jesus looked up at Ben. "Whose is this coin? Who made it, and to whom does it pay tribute?"

After a moment, Ben responded. "It is Tiberius's coin, and carries his name and inscription. It is not used here in the temple."

Jesus smiled. "Then there is no harm in its being used to pay a Roman tax. Give to the emperor the coin of his own making, and give to God the things of God. This is my answer."

Ben's eyes widened for a moment, and then narrowed as he continued to look at Jesus, his face flushing slightly. He looked for a moment as if he might speak again. Then shaking his head, he withdrew to where Joshua was waiting for him.

By this time Theo and the guards had been notified as to the presence of Jesus, and had assembled just beyond the Court of the Israelites. As they entered the Women's Court, they could see the man, surrounded by the temple youth, their wooden tablets resting in their laps, unheeded. The crowd around him was now large enough that it spilled out into the center of the courtyard. There was a hush in the air, as if everyone was waiting to see what would happen next.

THEO PAUSED in his retelling as he continued to clench and unclench his unoccupied fist. "We were at a loss, Caiaphas. The man had answered well, and with nothing that we could proclaim as blasphemy despite his impertinence in refusing to answer Joshua. Moreover, I could see in an instant that the crowds were taken with him, and that any action we might take to apprehend him would be seen as extreme and prejudicial."

Caiaphas nodded. People from the surrounding areas had already begun gathering in Jerusalem. The temple was full of pilgrims getting ready for the festival that was only two days away. The last thing the priests wanted to do was cause any kind of disturbance or scandal that might reach the ears of either Pilate or Antipas. They had to be extremely cautious.

Theo sighed deeply before continuing. "These were not the only questions posed to the man. When the other priests saw that Joshua and Ben had received no satisfactory answers, the discourse continued. Matthias, who had just come back from escorting the tradesmen from your presence, paused to ask a question regarding the greatest commandment. I believe he was hoping to catch Jesus in his lack of formal training. But the answer the man gave was in line with the law. Even Matthias had to concede it. After that, no one dared come forward. I hoped the crowd might disperse so that we could either take him into custody or escort him out of the temple. But no one moved."

Theo looked up at Caiaphas, knowing that the next part of his story would be the most inflammatory. "It was in the silence that followed that Jesus began to speak directly to the people who had gathered. He warned them, Caiaphas. He warned them about us."

Caiaphas looked alarmed. Glancing back at Ben and Joshua, he saw their expressions shift from ashamed bemusement to anger. "What?"

It was Ben who spoke. "He called us hypocrites." His eyes flashed darkly and there was an edge in his voice. "He warned that the people should not follow our example in the way we worship and honor God, and that what we do, we do for our own benefit and comfort. He warned that the priesthood was greedy and blind." He paused. "He called us vipers."

Caiaphas was stunned. He had not expected this. With everything they had experienced with Jesus, the man had never directly insulted the priesthood or spoken ill of those in authority. He now understood why Theo was concerned about how Annas and Simon would react. He himself shuddered to think how his father-in-law would respond when told of the incident.

His voice rose as he spoke. "Where is he now? Why did you not hold him?"

Theo shook his head. "The people were all around him, Caiaphas. They were everywhere. There were too many eyes, too many people who could easily be spies for Pilate or pilgrims with their own agendas. When Jesus was finished speaking, he looked around at us all one last time. Then he turned and left the temple by way of the eastern gate, heading toward Bethany. I sent some of our guard to follow, although I gave them orders merely to observe and not to engage. They returned once Jesus and those with him had passed through the olive groves and begun to climb the mountain summit. He is beyond our reach for now, unless we decide to give chase outside of the city."

Jonathan, who had been listening in thoughtful silence to all that Theo had shared, spoke quietly. His voice was grave. "Caiaphas, this is troubling news indeed. I am afraid we can no longer sit back and wait. We need a plan. The Passover is nearly upon us, and this man's antics are becoming more worrisome with each passing day. I know you are hoping to avoid any kind of confrontation, especially during the festival. But I believe we may no longer have a choice."

Caiaphas sighed heavily. "Yes, it appears that something must be done. But we must avoid bringing the entire priesthood into this matter. The fewer men who are party to our plans, the better. We will meet tonight, at my estate, to determine how to proceed." He guessed Theo's question before it was asked. "I will inform Annas and Simon of all that has transpired. For now you may proceed with your regular responsibilities."

A look of grateful relief spread across Theo's face. "Thank you, Caiaphas. I am sorry we were not able to do more. But I am confident that we will find a way forward. May God be with us."

Caiaphas nodded, and Theo left the chamber with Ben and Joshua trailing behind, leaving Jonathan and Caiaphas to consider all they had been told. The time to rest was most definitely at an end.

CHAPTER 25

The group that gathered at Caiaphas's estate that evening was somber and subdued. Even Joshua and Ben, who were usually to be found charming Rebecca into giving them items from the storehouse that Rivkah had set aside for other purposes, were keeping to themselves by one of the fires, whispering together as they looked around at the long faces of those who had congregated in Caiaphas's courtyard. Gamaliel was there, although Saul was not with him. Annas and Simon stood together. Nearby Jonathan and Matthias were watching Theo as he paced the length of the yard, stopping only to warm his hands by the fire. They were waiting for Caiaphas, who had arrived before them and retired to his chamber. He wanted to pray, to quiet his mind, and to discuss with Rivkah both the events of the day and what the night might hold. He had no desire to keep the other priests waiting. Yet he tarried, feeling certain that any decisions made would determine more than merely the actions taken by the council in the days ahead.

"The man is mad, Rivkah, if he thinks we will not act." Caiaphas looked at his wife, his face lined with frustration. "And yet he taunts us with his words, almost as if he desires to be arrested. I do not understand his plan. He must know that we have the power to crush

263

him, to scatter his followers and to punish him for his behavior. He is not safe. But still he does not seem to be afraid."

Rivkah shook her head. "Joseph, you must not dwell too long on the man's motives. Your job is to protect the people, to honor God and to quell those who would seek to dishonor the priesthood. I know your visions give you pause. You know I believe they are a gift given by God to provide perspective and knowledge beyond what others can see. But you must not let them hold you from action."

Caiaphas sighed deeply. She was right, of course. He had no way of knowing what the man's intentions might be. Ultimately, as much as he wanted to understand, it did not matter. He must fulfill his responsibilities. This would be difficult enough without wondering why Jesus had chosen to blatantly and openly challenge the priesthood. For now, Caiaphas's path was clear. He needed to convince Annas and Simon that any decisive action must wait until after the festival. The Feast of Unleavened Bread was only two days away. But the celebration that followed would stretch on for an additional seven days. In order for those among the priesthood to remain undefiled and pure throughout the festival, they would need to take special pains to limit their contact with any individuals who were either pagan by birth or tarnished by association. Any military action would immediately render those involved unclean until such time as they could be cleansed and purified. No matter what else happened, it was imperative that the priesthood remain unsullied.

When Caiaphas finally made his way down the stairs and into the courtyard, he was pleasantly surprised to see that all those gathered appeared to comprehend the gravity of the situation. He spoke first, and without interruption, and laid out his plan. Theo and the guard would remain watchful and vigilant. They would do everything in their power to keep the man Jesus from interacting too much with the people at the temple. The rest of the priests would keep their distance, engaging him no more with questions and doing nothing to provoke a reaction from either him or his followers. Here he shot a quick glance at Joshua and Ben, who both looked appropriately remorseful and cowed. They would go about the business of the temple as if Jesus were a flea, an insignificant bother not worthy of their attention. As soon as the final day of the festival was at an end, and it had been confirmed that both Antipas and Pilate had left the city, the priests would call Jesus to an 'official meeting of the council, ready to confront him and determine what action needed to be taken against him.

"We must weather this man's assault on us with the measured good humor of a father dealing with a willful child, one who is not old enough to feel the rod of discipline. He must be to us as a babe in arms, whose flailing fists are nothing but a nuisance."

Annas, whose strong objection Caiaphas assumed was forthcoming, nodded silently as his son-in-law spoke, and murmured his agreement with uncharacteristic compliance. He was stoic and stiff, and barely raised his voice above a whisper as he gave his consent. Simon too, acquiesced without opposition, and the others quickly followed suit. Theo, who was clearly still agitated by the events of the day, showed the most passion in his reaction. But even he ultimately expressed his willingness to proceed with this strategy. The meeting was surprisingly brief. Almost before it had begun, the priests were saying their goodbyes to Rivkah and departing, their murmured whispers echoing across the courtyard as they filed into the dusty street and parted ways toward their homes.

Caiaphas was unnerved. It had been too simple to convince Annas and Simon to hold back. Just a day before, they had been adamant that Jesus must be arrested without delay. Now suddenly they both appeared all too willing to wait. He shared his concerns with Rivkah, who found herself unable to reassure him. She too was perplexed by her father and Simon's reaction, and could no more explain the change of heart than he could. That night, Caiaphas's sleep was fitful and troubled. The dream of the temple burning, which had until recently been replaced by other more urgent visions, returned with full force. The screams of those trapped by the fire echoed in his ears and woke him more than once. Flames danced beneath his shut eyelids as he tossed and turned, unable to keep still.

The whole next day held an air of uneasy calm. Caiaphas, whose eyes were rimmed with dark circles from the sleepless night, went about his responsibilities at the temple in a daze, as if he were pushing his way through the thick curtain that guarded the Holy of Holies. Jonathan, whom he had tasked with keeping a watchful eye on the other priests, and who had come to give him an update at dusk, reported that nothing out of the ordinary had occurred all day. Theo and the guard were in a constant state of patrol, climbing the stairs to the upper level of the temple, marching the perimeter, and surveying each courtyard and chamber before beginning again. They made their presence known in every section of the temple grounds, including among the stalls where the merchants and money changers were hard at work buying and selling and readying themselves for the day of commerce ahead. All was quiet, or as quiet as could be expected on the eve of the sacrifices.

There was one moment when Jonathan happened upon Simon just as he was finishing a conversation with a pilgrim. The man, whose hair was dark and who bore a scar across his left cheek, looked suspiciously at Jonathan. For a brief moment Jonathan thought he saw fear in the man's eyes. As Jonathan continued to hold his gaze, the man's hand went almost unbidden to the small woven pouch he carried at his belt. Then he hurried away at once. When Jonathan questioned Simon about it, the older priest shrugged it off. He shared that the man had discovered a blemish in the lamb he was planning to bring for sacrifice, and was seeking advice as to whether he would need to substitute one purchased from the local merchants for his own. Jonathan was unconvinced that he had been told the entire story. But the man was gone and there was no way of validating Simon's report, so he let the matter rest.

That night, the evening meal at Caiaphas's estate was an intimate one. Only Jonathan joined the family as they ate their last meal before the beginning of the festival. The house had already been cleared of all leaven in preparation for the feast, a ritual that hearkened back to the exodus from Egypt, when the Jews, escaping the wrath of Pharaoh, had no time to allow their bread to rise. Rivkah and Rebecca prepared for weeks by using up the remaining stores of anything containing yeast. Immediately after sundown as was the custom, Rivkah walked slowly through the storehouse with a candle and a feather, ceremonially searching for any remaining leaven and reciting a final prayer of preparation. All was ready for the holiday to begin.

THE NEXT MORNING was a cool one, though the sky was clear. Any hint of a cloud had burned off long before the sun rose above the pinnacle of the Antonia Fortress, whose towers stretched high into the heavens. Caiaphas had no time to think of anything but the sacrifices being made. By midday, the winds had shifted. A dry, sweltering heat settled over the temple. Caiaphas's robes dripped with sweat and blood. A mixture of the two mingled in his hair and beard, making him more anxious than ever to retreat to the ritual bath beneath the Chamber of the Hearth, where he donned fresh robes and returned for the next round of sacrifices. As the last of the lambs were led to the slaughter, Caiaphas noticed for the first time that several of the priests were not in attendance. He wondered what could have kept them away. On a day like this one, there were always several priests who were unable to participate due to illness or some other familial responsibility. But none would willingly miss the final slaughter, when the lambs destined for the homes of the priests would be sacrificed. As he looked around, he could see Jonathan, Matthias, Joshua, and Ben. But he was unable to find either Annas or Simon. When he turned to where Theo would normally have been stationed, standing with the guard in the Priests' Court just in front of the steps that led to the temple porch, he realized with a start that his brother-in-law was also missing, along with several of the more senior members of the guard.

Caiaphas found himself fighting against a deep feeling of foreboding as, a short time later, he and Jonathan walked through the dusty streets from the temple to his estate. Around them, they could hear as households began to celebrate the Passover together. The scent of rich, roasted lamb drifted into the street, the smell rising with the evening breeze that had returned after the heat of the day. His face was clean and shining from the last time he had descended into the bath. But he had been so distracted by then that he barely remembered washing the blood and soot from his body and pulling on the clean, white robes that signified another year of sacrifices was complete.

From the moment he observed his father-in-law's absence, Caiaphas tried to reassure himself that there must be some reasonable explanation. Perhaps Tova had fallen ill again, and Annas was forced to go to her, so quickly that he could not stop to explain his departure. But any speculation as to what the reason might be brought a single, tear-stained face to his mind. Jonathan, who had noticed the missing priests around the same time as Caiaphas, was clearly also shaken by it. Although neither voiced their fears, Jonathan had not left Caiaphas's side since they had emerged from the Chamber of the Hearth. He remained with Caiaphas on the walk home rather than making his way toward Simon's home, where he had been planning to take the Passover meal.

As the two men approached Caiaphas's estate and drew near the entrance closest to the temple, it was Rivkah who greeted them. She was standing in the doorway, clearly awaiting their arrival with impatience. Her face was ashen, her eyes black and blazing like embers. When she saw her husband and brother approaching, she flung herself toward them. Her voice trembled as she spoke, and she spat out the words as if she could no longer keep them contained.

"They've arrested him, Joseph. They've arrested Jesus, and they've taken him to my father's house."

CHAPTER 26

It was all Caiaphas could do to keep his composure as he stared at his wife, incredulous. For a moment no one spoke. It was Jonathan who broke the silence. "How do you know?'

Rivkah shut her eyes and shook her head before answering. "A messenger came yesterday from Annas's house and requested that Rebecca's brother spend the Passover with them. Tova was anticipating a large number of guests, and thought it would be helpful to have an extra set of hands to prepare the feast. Silas and Lydia are no longer young. I have no doubt that they were more than happy to have Malchus at their disposal to fetch and carry up and down the stairs to the storeroom. Nathan and Rebecca had no objection to the plan, and Malchus was willing, so we sent him to my father's house last night after the evening meal. He was supposed to stay through tomorrow, but returned to us less than an hour ago. There was blood on his cloak, and he looked to be in shock. Rebecca sent him to me immediately."

"Where is he now?" Caiaphas had regained his voice, and spoke hastily.

"He is in the far courtyard. But Joseph, please be gentle when you question him. He fled my father's house as they were returning with

Jesus, and came here instead. I believe he fears he will be punished for abandoning his responsibilities."

Caiaphas drew a deep breath. By now they had entered the estate and were drawing near the far courtyard, passing the doorway that led to the room where Caiaphas knew the table had been set for the Passover meal. By law he was required to eat the lamb before the day was over. For now it would have to wait. He had to know what his father-in-law had done.

Malchus was standing with his back to them. A young man of no more than twenty-four, his thin shoulders were hunched and taut. There was something in his stance that made him look like a gazelle, every muscle tensed and ready to flee at the first sign of danger. As Caiaphas, Jonathan and Rivkah approached, he turned, and they saw that his eyes were wide and rimmed with tears, threatening to fall at any moment. Caiaphas appraised him quickly, and saw at his right shoulder a dark stain that might have been blood, although he did not appear injured. His body was shaking in the night air, despite the cloak he still wore over his tunic. At that moment, Rivkah reached out her hand, and took his in hers. When she spoke her voice was measured and soft.

"Malchus, do not be afraid. Tell Master Caiaphas what you told me. It is all right."

Caiaphas was taken aback by his distress. Malchus had been living with them for some time now. This was the first indication Caiaphas had ever seen of either fear or fragility, despite Malchus having recently lost his mother. A slighter and more soft-spoken version of Rebecca, Malchus had proven to be both bright and hardworking, and was a welcome addition to the household. He was fifteen years younger than his sister, and clearly admired both her and Nathan, with whom he had an easy rapport. Something had obviously shaken him deeply.

Caiaphas nodded at the young man encouragingly, and waited. In the silence, Malchus took a deep breath, and began to speak.

"Noble Caiaphas, I went to your father-in-law's estate yesterday evening, and immediately began working with the household staff to complete the preparations for the Passover. It was late when we finished. I made my bed upstairs in a chamber that had been prepared for me. Today I rose early and continued my work, stopping only to take some refreshment midday with the others. At dusk, I was told to wait in the vestibule just before the entrance to the courtyard, so that when the lamb was delivered from the temple, I could receive it and bring it directly to the fire for roasting. I had been waiting no more than a few minutes when I heard a flurry of voices in the street. I rushed to the entrance to see what was happening."

"When I stepped outside, I saw nearly two dozen men, standing in three groups. One included your father-in-law, and Master Simon, and several other priests from the temple. They were still wearing their ceremonial robes, and the white of their tunics shone bright. The second group was dressed in more humble clothing, with rough woolen tunics and cloaks. Some of their faces were obscured by hoods, and a few carried torches. They were standing in clusters, murmuring to themselves, and one man from this group was speaking with the priests. His hair was dark, and on his left cheek there was a scar that curved under his chin."

With a start, Jonathan looked at Caiaphas, concerned, as he recognized by description the man with whom Simon had been conferring at the temple. Caiaphas silently gave his brother-in-law a nod, acknowledging the reaction, and waited.

Malchus continued. "The third group looked to be made up of Roman soldiers, a small detachment from the guard stationed outside Herod's Palace. I saw them only two days before, patrolling the gardens near the front gate, when my route took me past the palace while running errands for Nathan in preparation for the Passover. Although there were only a handful of them, I was surprised to see them there. I could tell that the other men were keeping their distance from them with similar trepidation."

If Jonathan had looked concerned before, it was nothing compared to the alarm tracing his brow at these words. Caiaphas felt sick. If Pilate's soldiers were somehow involved in this plot, the likelihood of keeping it hidden from either Pilate or Antipas would be nearly impossible. More than that, it suggested the possibility that Annas had been working in concert with the Romans, behind his back. He could scarcely believe what he was hearing.

Malchus went on, unaware of the effect his words were having on them. "At that moment, Master Annas saw me standing there, and gestured for me to draw near. As he did so, the group led by the man with the scar turned and began to walk away from the house, heading north. Master Annas instructed me to leave my post and follow them, to accompany them on their errand and to return to the house only when it had been completed. I did not dare disobey, and hurried to catch up with them as they moved rapidly away through the streets."

Rivkah spoke. "You were right to obey my father, Malchus. Go on."

Malchus gave her a small, grateful smile before continuing. "We walked in silence, heading in the direction of the temple. When we reached the temple grounds, we left the city through the eastern gate, descended into the valley beyond, and began to climb the rocky face of the hill."

Caiaphas knew the place. He could picture the olive trees that dotted the hillside, their mangled and bent trunks nestled into the dry ground and their branches twisting skyward.

Malchus continued. "As we approached a clearing, the moon broke through the clouds, and fell upon a group of men, kneeling together at the base of one of the trees." He hung his head. "I must confess that I am not entirely sure what happened next. The one who had been leading us strode toward the group. Then there was a cry, and one of the men who had been kneeling leapt forward. He struck me with something, and I felt a sharp pain on the side of my head. When I put my hand to the spot, it was wet with blood. Then suddenly I was falling and everything went dark. As I lay there with my eyes shut, I felt something soft against my face. I heard a whisper of a voice above me, although I could not make out the words. In an instant the pain disappeared as quickly as it had come. When I raised my hand again to the spot, it was warm and dry." He shook his head as if it was still foggy from the memory.

"By the time I opened my eyes again, the man they call Jesus had been surrounded on all sides by our party, his hands tied roughly behind his back. Some of the men were jeering at him, although the man with the scar stood apart, silent, watching. The ones who had been with him in the grove were fleeing, but no one followed them. I could see two of Jesus's followers as they raced up the mountain, their tunics trailing behind them. I raised myself up off the ground and saw several of those with whom I had come glancing at me in disbelief and fear, their eyes fixed on the side of my head."

He looked imploringly at Rivkah. "I did not know what had happened, but I was afraid. The man Jesus was not putting up a fight. I could see his eyes shining in the moonlight, his face calm and still despite the assault. At that moment, he was pushed roughly forward, and the men began to lead him back toward the city. I followed, but remained several steps behind the rest. I felt somehow that none of them wanted to be too close to me. I knew then that I must return to this house and inform you of what had transpired. I trailed the party with their prisoner and then slipped away just after we entered the city gates."

Again he hung his head, and his voice was small and solemn. "I am sorry for leaving my post, Master Caiaphas. I hope you will forgive my disobedience, and am prepared to accept your judgment."

Caiaphas spoke, and as he did, he felt as if he were speaking to his own son. Although Malchus was more than a decade older than Judah, the expression on his face was that of a much younger boy. Caiaphas felt a strong urge to reassure him that he was not about to face the wrath of the high priest, whose eyes he was nervously avoiding as he fidgeted with the edge of his worn cloak.

"You did right by coming to me, Malchus. I am not displeased with your actions." Malchus looked up, his relief palpable. He wiped his eyes with his sleeve, and continued to look gratefully at Caiaphas, who began to pace the length of the courtyard. "These are strange times, and it is not always easy to discern the correct path. But our law teaches us that folly is a joy to him who lacks sense, while a man of understanding walks straight ahead. You have been sober-minded in this matter, and have provided me with information that I would not have apart from your report. I thank you."

Jonathan, who had been standing next to Rivkah, spoke quietly. "Malchus." The young man turned to him. "You appear to be whole and unharmed. Yet your story suggests that you were attacked. There is blood on your garments. We know there have been rumors that Jesus has the power to heal. Is it possible that the touch you felt was his?"

Malchus shook his head. "I do not know, Master Jonathan. And yet..." He trailed off, his eyes looking away as if seeing something beyond the courtyard walls. Again tears threatened to fall from his eyes, and when he spoke his voice trembled. "I cannot explain it."

Caiaphas stopped pacing and whirled around, glaring at his brother-in-law with mounting frustration. "Jonathan, this kind of questioning is futile. We already know there are rumors of the man's ability to heal. What of it? Our temple healers have the ability to cure far worse than a surface wound, as does your own mother. Moreover, there would be no reason for Jesus to waste his abilities on one of the men sent to take him captive. He is more unbalanced than we already suspect if indeed he is performing miracles on his enemies." Shaking his head, Caiaphas continued to pace, his mind racing.

Jonathan looked uncomfortable, and said no more. Malchus, who had been glancing between the two of them anxiously, lifted his hand to the side of his face, stroking it absentmindedly with his fingers. It was Rivkah who ended the interview. Without looking at Jonathan and Caiaphas, she took Malchus by the arm and walked him to the hallway, where she instructed him to go to Rebecca and Nathan, to cleanse himself and put on fresh robes. When she returned, her mouth was set and determined, and she spoke with authority.

"Husband, before anything else is done you must eat and drink. The lamb is ready and the wine is poured. My father may have lost his way, and appears willing to forego rituals that have been observed for generations, commanded by God. But I know you are not."

He began to speak, but she raised her hand and he fell silent. "My father is no fool. He must have known that Malchus would come to you. Even if he did not suspect it ahead of time, he will realize by now that he did not return with the others. I see no harm in commemorating the Passover before you take action. It will give you a moment to think and pray, to be reminded of God's provision and his wrath against those who disobey his commands." Her eyes were troubled as she continued. "I knew my father to be capable of many things. But I did not once imagine that he would go against the direct orders of the high priest. And to enlist the help of Roman soldiers is a dangerous business. I fear my father has gone astray, given himself over to his desire for control with no thought of the consequences. But his lapse in judgment will not make yours any less blameworthy. You must tread carefully, my love, to ensure that in your rightful anger you are not rash."

He sighed deeply, and felt Jonathan's answering exhale beside him. He knew she was right. Even so, it took all of his strength to nod his head, and to turn, not out into the streets toward Annas's estate, but to the room where the meal was laid. Rebecca and Nathan were both already there. Nathan was carving the lamb, while Rebecca, who must have just returned from tending to Malchus, was beginning to distribute the charred bread, made without leaven, so that each plate had a portion of its own. Judah sat at one end of the table playing with a spinning top Caiaphas recognized as one that Martha had given him, and did not immediately look up as his father entered the room. Caiaphas watched as his son twisted the stem of the top between his fingers, setting it whirling on the tabletop, where it danced in and out of the plates and cups that lay neatly set in a row. The top wobbled as its rotation slowed and grew wilder in its manner, dipping and weaving as if it had drunk too much wine, until finally it landed with a clunk on its side, spent. Caiaphas felt a kind of sympathy for the thing, as his own head felt almost as wobbly and turned around as his son's toy.

He took his seat at the head of the table, and began to say the prayers over the meal. Rivkah joined him, lighting the long, thin candles that sat in a silver candelabra nearby. Their tiny flames flickered like watchmen as the bread, wine, and lamb were distributed and eaten. The meal was strange and silent, with none of the celebratory atmosphere that usually characterized the Passover celebration. Nathan, who had disappeared as soon as the wine was poured, did not return until they were finishing the final prayer, praising God for his delivery of their ancestors from Egypt, and draining the fourth cup of wine. As Nathan stepped into the doorway, Caiaphas could see that he was not alone.

CHAPTER 27

Theo entered the room briskly, and his eyes met those of his brother-in-law with a mixture of respect and defiance, as if daring Caiaphas to reprimand him for his presence. His cloak was slightly askew, and Caiaphas could see underneath that he was still wearing the ceremonial robes of the day, along with his sheath and dagger, whose hilt was clearly visible at his side. Caiaphas suddenly realized that a part of him had been expecting this intrusion ever since the interview with Malchus. He acknowledged Theo with a small nod, and slowly rose to his feet. Jonathan quickly followed his lead as Caiaphas turned to Rivkah.

"My love, I pray that you will excuse us." He looked at his son, who was using the final scraps of his bread to mop up the remnants of lamb that still lay on his plate. "Judah, stay with your mother." Rivkah, who had moved closer to Judah as soon as Theo entered the room, put a firm hand on the boy's shoulder, causing him to look up at her in confusion. Caiaphas could see that her fingers were pressing down with more force than was strictly necessary. He felt a pang of longing as he stepped away from them and toward Theo.

As he and Jonathan followed Theo out of the room and into the hallway, he spoke quietly. "Is the prisoner here?" If Theo was at all surprised at Caiaphas's knowledge of the situation, he did not show it.

"Yes, noble Caiaphas. My guards are holding him in the interior room just off the northern courtyard. Annas and Simon are waiting for you there, along with several other members of the council and a handful of witnesses who have come forth to give testimony against him. There are others who followed in the shadows as we brought him here. But overall the city is too preoccupied with the Passover celebration to take much notice."

Caiaphas sighed heavily. This was small comfort, although he was sure that Annas and Simon were feeling victorious. His stomach, full as it was from the lamb and wine he had just consumed, lurched uncomfortably as he considered what they had done. In the midst of one of the holiest festivals, against the direct orders of the high priest and apparently with the help of Roman soldiers, his father-in-law and other respected members of the council had arrested a man who had already proven to be a cunning and slippery foe. Now they were meeting in secret, not as part of the full council at the temple, which would have given the trial legitimate authority, but under cover of darkness, while others in the city celebrated the Passover, oblivious and unconcerned.

He felt his anger rise as he continued down the hall and into the open courtyard. The fire upon which the Passover lamb had been roasted was still lit, and a gathering of men was huddled around it for warmth. He recognized several of them as tradesmen whom he knew were regularly employed by Annas as messengers and scouts. From the time he was a boy, he had been aware that Annas kept a network of people loyal to him in the city. It had always seemed a shrewd way to keep abreast of the events taking place beyond the temple walls. He had even encouraged it as high priest, grateful for the information it provided. But as he surveyed the men who congregated there, murmuring amongst themselves, their hardened faces lit up by the flickering flames, he found himself wondering not for the first time at both their methods and their allegiance.

From behind him, Nathan and Rebecca emerged, carrying

steaming mugs of spiced wine, which they distributed among those gathered in the courtyard. Caiaphas smiled ruefully as he imagined Rivkah, troubled and agitated though she must be, never failing to take seriously her role as the mistress of their household. He watched as a young man he did not immediately recognize came forward to receive a mug of wine from Rebecca, then observed his face fall as both she and Nathan questioned him. Cupping his hands around the stone mug, the youth retreated quickly into a far corner and sat with his shoulders hunched forward, his face obscured by the shadows cast across the yard.

Caiaphas stopped Nathan as he made his way back across the courtyard. "Who is the young man with whom you were just speaking, Nathan? I do not think I know him."

Nathan scowled. "Master Caiaphas, if my brother-in-law is to be believed, he was with Jesus when he was arrested. Malchus recognized him immediately. But when Rebecca asked him, he denied it, and looked offended at the suggestion."

Caiaphas looked again at the young man, who was drinking deeply from his mug. As he tilted his head backward, his eyes caught the light. Caiaphas suddenly realized that he did in fact know the youth, though it had been several years since he had laid eyes on him. This was the younger brother of Andrew, the follower of the beheaded John, who had boldly gone before the council and declared his allegiance to the discredited rebel, and whom the council had sent away to be reconciled with his family. Caiaphas recalled the way the lad had stood then, still and resolute at his brother's side, unwavering in his dedication. Though the years had added stubble to his chin and a ruddiness to his complexion, Caiaphas was sure it was the same man. He was sorry to think of the boy's father, who had watched his son follow after one disgraced revolutionary, only, it seemed, to have seen him shift his loyalty to another.

Jonathan, at Caiaphas's side, touched his arm gently. "Caiaphas, they are waiting for us." His reverie broken, Caiaphas followed Jonathan and Theo as they crossed the courtyard and entered the interior room where the others were gathered.

The chamber was small compared to the large courtyard from which they had just come, although it was grand in its own way, with imposing columns lining three of the four walls. A large mosaic covered the floor, and the intricate patterns of geometric shapes and designs were just visible in the lamplight, which danced along the floor and cast oblong shapes across the ceiling and walls. Around the perimeter of the room, oil lamps had been lit and set upon bronze stands that sat just below shoulder height. The lamps were filled with a thick, viscous oil made from olives, and contained a wick to draw the oil up to feed the flame. They gave the scene a ghostly quality. The light flickered, rising and falling with any movement, and plunging corners of the room into shadow whenever the flames wavered in intensity.

As Caiaphas entered the room, he immediately saw Jesus, who stood in the center of a group of men, his garments disheveled and his face bruised. Caiaphas could see on his right cheek a mark where he had obviously been struck with sufficient enough force as to leave evidence of the deed. Caiaphas's anger flared again as he looked around and saw the smug, satisfied faces of a handful of his fellow priests, men whom until now he had trusted and thought loyal to him. He noticed the absence of Matthias and Ben, and wondered whether his father-in-law had thought they could not be trusted to keep the matter a secret from him. Gamaliel and Joshua, too, were missing from this gathering, as was Saul.

The priests who stood with Annas and Simon were mostly older, contemporaries of his father-in-law, and men who had from the beginning questioned whether Caiaphas was ready for the position of high priest. Resentment came flooding back as he remembered those early days, when he had been so eager to prove himself worthy of their approval and respect. Nearly fourteen years later, it seemed that nothing he had done had been enough to convince them. He felt sick.

Emerging from a darkened corner of the room, Annas approached, with Simon following directly behind him. The expression on his father-in-law's face was grave, although Caiaphas could see in Annas's eyes a look with which he was all too familiar, one of deep satisfaction that Caiaphas recognized from times when Annas felt most powerful and in control. It was the same look he had given Caiaphas on the day he had been declared high priest, and when Annas had bound Caiaphas and Rivkah together in marriage. As these moments and others flashed across Caiaphas's mind, he realized suddenly that Annas must have seen himself as lord and master on each of these occasions, orchestrating events and manipulating situations in the way he thought best. The flicker of resentment that had been steadily growing within Caiaphas's chest flooded him with heat. He felt his face flush as he stood silently, waiting for his father-in-law to speak.

"Caiaphas." The word still sounded wrong coming from Annas, as if when he looked at Caiaphas he could not help but see the boy Joseph instead of the man before him. The brief hesitation in his voice only added to Caiaphas's mounting bitterness. "Before you say anything, know that what we have done, we have done in service to you and to the council. I am sure you can see the wisdom in leaving the high priest unsullied by this business. We thought it best to remove you from the arrest itself, so that your conscience could be clear before God that you did not take action against a criminal during a festival. Rest assured that Pilate has already been informed. We have told him that we have the situation under control, and that we will include him as needed to ensure that justice is served and peace is maintained. I trust that you can appreciate the value in our methods, if unconventional, and see that now we will be able to proceed as we must in order to protect our people and the temple with as little disturbance as possible."

Caiaphas gaped at his father-in-law, stunned. He could not fathom that Annas thought he would be convinced by this argument, that he would be content to go along with the plan quietly and without challenge. The fire in his chest leapt within him, and the heat spread across his shoulders and arms, making him feel as if he were wearing the heaviest of woolen cloaks. But when he finally spoke, his voice was low and steady, and he measured every word. "If this is truly how you see things, old man, then we are more at odds than I thought possible."

Annas jerked his head up abruptly, obviously taken aback by Caiaphas's reaction. Simon, too, looked shocked. Caiaphas continued, struggling to keep the scorn out of his voice. "But I do not believe it is. No, this was not done to honor the council or to protect the office of the high priest. This was done out of service to your own whims, your own desire for control. And in this desire, you have lost all perspective. It is clear that you no longer value serving God above all else." He paused, his emotions warring within him as he debated how far to take the accusation. "I wonder perhaps if you ever truly have."

As soon as the words left his lips, Caiaphas knew there was no going back. Annas's face twitched almost as if he had been struck. His eyes immediately darkened. Caiaphas could imagine the muscles in his father-in-law's back flexing, readying themselves to do battle like an athlete before a wrestling match. He continued, undeterred. "I have always been obedient to you, Annas, deferential and respectful. You have been like a father to me, and more than a father. As a boy, I would have done anything you asked. It was my honor to serve you always. I watched while Eleazar raged against you with shame, and not once have I done anything to question your role as my elder. And yet this is how you repay me, with lack of trust, operating behind my back, and going against my clear command." He shook his head. "When was it that you lost faith in me, Annas? When did you decide that you could not trust me with your schemes?" His bitterness was raw and palpable, his voice shaking even as he fought to keep it steady. "Am I your high priest or am I not?"

It was as if Caiaphas had been storing every slight, every questionable deed, and every overbearing action in a giant stone jar that had just been smashed irrevocably to pieces. The words came cascading out of him, unbridled and without restraint. "Not only that, but you have enlisted our enemies to help you in your mad quest to crush this troublemaker. How could you have called upon Roman soldiers to participate in this act? Have you forgotten your own words, that no Roman would ever determine how you serve your God? You were the one who taught me that they are our friends only so much as we need them to maintain our autonomy. Or have you forgotten to whom you ultimately owe loyalty and devotion?"

The fire in Caiaphas's chest was raging now, unquenched by the horrified look on Jonathan's face. He felt it continue to rise as he went on. "You should have known better than to enlist foreign aid to engage in this dirty business with you. But then, from the beginning, your relationships with those outside the temple have been suspect. As a boy, I watched the way you managed the transition from Joazar to yourself, admiring your ability to convince the Romans to allow you to take over in his stead. It appears that both Joazar and Eleazar were right to question your closeness with our adversaries. I wonder now whether you were working with them even then, manipulating your own friend as you once manipulated your son, and now seek to manipulate me." Breathing heavily, Caiaphas exhaled, his eyes the color of golden amber in the lamplight. He looked up at Annas, the expression on his face almost plaintive now. The fire in him had nearly burned itself out, and only embers remained, glowing hot and heavy, pressing down on his chest and making it hard to breathe. There was a catch in his voice, and he felt scalding tears blossoming just behind his eyes. "My father saved your life. Is this how you honor his sacrifice, by humiliating his son with your deception?"

The question sat heavily between the two men. Annas looked deeply shaken, more so than Caiaphas had seen him since the death of Eleazar. Behind him, Simon's face was pale, and he shook his head as he spoke, his voice small and tentative. "We tried, Caiaphas. We tried to get you to see reason, that we needed to capture this man before he caused any more trouble, before he succeeded in turning our own people against us with his lies. But you would not listen."

Caiaphas turned to Simon, the rage that had so recently filled him twisting into a deep, hollow sadness. "Simon. My friend. You have been dear to me through the years. Julia, Eli, and Martha are like family to me. But I see now that you have always been Annas's man, not mine. There have been times when I wondered at your sincerity. Even during our journey to Caesarea to see Gratus, I questioned whether you had more insight into the visit than you displayed. Your ability to flatter and influence is impressive. I know it has served the priesthood well through the years. I suppose I was naive to think that your manipulation did not extend to me as well."

Simon was silent, and Caiaphas looked back at his father-in-law, who still had not spoken. The silence grew. Caiaphas felt as if the shadows were slowly closing in on him, the walls of the chamber not unlike the temple walls of his dreams, with the flames of the lamps casting long shadows onto the columns and across the faces of those around him. Given the size of the room, there was no way that his conversation with Annas and Simon had not been overheard by the others. Yet he felt deeply isolated and alone as he looked around at the faces of those gathered. Theo in particular looked furious, and Caiaphas could tell that he was resisting coming to his father's defense. The prisoner, whose eyes had been downcast since Caiaphas entered the room, lifted his gaze. Caiaphas realized with a jolt that the man's expression was oddly sympathetic. Caiaphas shifted uncomfortably and looked away.

It was Jonathan who finally broke the silence, his voice calm and measured as always, his manner formal. "Noble Caiaphas. We cannot undo the deeds that have been committed this evening. With the Romans involved, we must see this trial through so that we can provide a report to Pilate in the morning. Whatever it is that remains unresolved with our fellow council members, it will need to wait until we are through this business. Shall we call forth the witnesses?"

Caiaphas nodded, grateful for Jonathan's level head and assistance. As the priests gathered together and the first witness took his place before those assembled, Caiaphas took a deep breath and stepped back until he stood alongside his brother-in-law, avoiding the prisoner's eyes as he did so.

CHAPTER 28

In a blur of revolving faces, men came forward one by one to share evidence against Jesus. Caiaphas barely heard the first few men who testified. The witnesses seemed to blatantly contradict one another, fumbling over their statements. They continuously looked to Annas and Simon as they answered questions posed to them by Jonathan, who had taken over the interrogation. All Caiaphas wanted to do was retreat from the room, to escape into the cool night air and return to Rivkah and Judah. But duty held him there even as he fought to concentrate on the proceedings. The fury and sadness that had so recently ripped through him had left him exhausted. A dull ache spread from the back of his head around toward his temples, accompanied by a persistent pounding that made him wince.

Then a new man stepped forward, one Caiaphas recognized as Daniel, the spice merchant whose father Joel had been a boyhood friend to Joazar. Daniel had for many years been one of the most prominent merchants present during the festivals, selling his wares just outside the temple gate. He had been brought to testify to the things Jesus had said among the money changers and merchants on the day he had been questioned by Ben and Joshua. Another man stood with Daniel, a money lender whom Caiaphas remembered had been instrumental in establishing the exchange rates with Annas during his father-in-law's time as high priest. Together the two men dutifully described how Jesus had threatened to destroy the temple. Their testimony reminded Caiaphas forcefully of times when Annas and Simon appeared to speak as one, their alternating voices carefully choreographed for the purpose of persuasion. His head throbbed as he watched them taking turns providing their evidence, reciting their lines like boys sharing the Scriptures they had memorized. Finally he could listen no more.

"Enough." Caiaphas strode forward, pulling back his shoulders. He held himself as high as possible as he surveyed the room. Annas had stepped back and was standing next to Simon, his face inscrutable and in shadow. Jonathan, who had been standing beside Caiaphas during the interrogation, remained a few paces behind him. The other priests and witnesses, including Theo and the other members of the guard, stood in a loose circle around the prisoner. Caiaphas steadied himself, and faced the man.

"What say you to these accusations, to these men who testify against you?" Caiaphas looked at Jesus, who appeared small and defenseless, his cloak torn and his sandaled feet dirty from the dry ground of the olive grove where he had been found. "Have you no answer to give? Here is your opportunity to speak, to redeem yourself, to contradict any lies you have heard with the truth."

Jesus remained silent, and lifted his face again until he and Caiaphas were staring directly at one another. The prisoner's eyes were full of sorrow, but his gaze was piercing and clear. His brow was dirty, and the mark on his cheek was still prominent, the skin red and slightly swollen, as if it might be hot to the touch. Still he said nothing.

Now the anger that Caiaphas had so recently directed toward Annas flared in a new direction as he considered the man before him. Unlike himself, this man was not required to be in this position. This was a circumstance of his own making, one he could easily have avoided. But for a few rumors, and some dangerous talk, Jesus could be asleep in his own bedchamber, somewhere far from Jerusalem. His back might be satisfyingly sore from the masonry work of the day, his belly full of some humble but nourishing meal, his dreams free from any terrors or visions. Unlike Caiaphas, this man was unfettered by responsibility, family, or allegiance. Any trouble in which he found himself was trouble he alone had initiated and enabled.

Caiaphas's fate, on the other hand, was sealed the day his father was slain and Annas determined to keep his promise to care for Hadassah and her son. From the day he entered Annas's home, he had been groomed for a role in the priesthood, one he had to admit he had fiercely desired. But at the time he had no way of knowing that he would never truly be free of Annas's control over him, never fully able to decide his own fate or determine his own destiny. It was always Annas who would be orchestrating behind the scenes, Annas using him to achieve his own ends. Even Caiaphas's marriage to Rivkah, it seemed to him now, had been a way to keep him close, to keep him in line.

He turned again to Jesus. "We have heard many tales told about you, stories of miracles and healing that have reached our ears from far beyond our city walls. Those who follow you consider you to be a man of influence and power. You operate independently from the priesthood and draw our people away from the temple. We have watched and listened as you criticize and insult our methods, and question our motives. And yet we have also heard you profess to honor God, and your knowledge and understanding of the Scriptures is impressive." Caiaphas thought ruefully of Joshua and Ben and their brash attempts to discredit the man, and how instead it was the priesthood that had appeared foolish as a result.

Caiaphas continued. "But you cannot be both servant and ruler. It is time now for you to make a choice. Will you bow to the authority given to us by God, or will you show yourself to be a rebel like your cousin, a man unwilling to submit to those called to protect him? After all, it is not you but the priesthood that stands between the people and Rome, defending our traditions and values from those who might seek to defile our holy temple. We are the ones who intercede on behalf of the people during our holiest days. While you roam the countryside telling tales and amassing followers, it is our bodies that bend over the place of slaughtering, making sacrifices to God, our hands that build the fires on which we give the offerings for both ourselves and the people. As high priest, it falls to me and no other to enter the Holy of Holies, to annually petition God for another year of blessing."

Caiaphas looked down at the ceremonial robes he still wore, shimmering white in the lamplight, unblemished and pure as they had appeared when he pulled them on at the temple after the final sacrifices of the day. Despite the aching in his head, he felt his chest rise with pride. "As a priest of the temple, I have devoted my life to God, to serving him and ensuring that his temple remains holy and strong, even as we know that greater triumph still lies ahead."

He glanced at Jonathan, who raised his head slightly in acknowledgement. "The Scriptures tell of a future that we have not yet seen, a time when our people will no longer feel the weight of foreign rule, when we will be truly free in our land, promised to us by God." He thought back to mere hours before, when he and his family had taken the Passover meal, to the prayers they had recited after the lamb and wine were consumed. "We are those who come before, working and waiting for one who will rise up from our own, a king and conqueror who will reign once and for all."

Caiaphas looked at the prisoner before him, bound and beaten as he was, and a look of pity crept across his face. "I do not think our God would have chosen one like you for such an honor." He thought about Jesus, this common tradesman who seemingly healed household servants and escorted buried men from their tombs. The man, whose lineage had long since been confirmed by Annas's spies, was of humble birth and lowly status, no more royal than the shepherds who guarded the flocks on the rolling hills beyond the city walls. Caiaphas found himself wondering what hopes and dreams Jesus's father might have had for his boy, and what a disappointment he must have become to those who raised him.

Caiaphas glanced over at Annas, who had not moved since the interrogation had begun, and whose face still appeared solemn. His eyes took in the older man's broad shoulders, his imposing presence.

As he did, Caiaphas was struck with the thought that his father-in-law resembled a king more than anyone he had ever known. Not even Gratus, who always appeared in ornate robes and extravagant adornments during his years as governor, had ever seemed as regal. A twinge of regret pulled at Caiaphas as he considered the accusations he had hurled at his father-in-law. He wondered whether he would ever be able to make things right again. The contrast between the prisoner and Annas sat heavily on his mind. Suddenly he knew what he must do.

There was still a way to redeem this wretched evening, despite the way it had been mangled by those too impatient to wait until the proper time. Almost eagerly, he turned back to Jesus. "There is a simple solution to this matter, one that will honor both God and the priesthood. Here before these witnesses, admit that you are no king, that you have no authority over either the temple or those who serve it. Declare your allegiance to us." Magnanimously, he gestured to the man's restraints. "Do this, and we will set you free."

In the silence that followed, Caiaphas took a deep breath. For the first time since he had entered the chamber, he felt a ray of hope. Jesus might be a troublemaker and a zealot, but from everything he knew, the man was not a fool. Caiaphas was confident that he had led the interrogation in the correct and necessary direction, away from the scattered bits of evidence and accusation brought forward by compromised and unreliable witnesses. Whatever Jesus had or had not said in the past, it would not matter. With these questions, Caiaphas had left him no space for evasion or misrepresentation. With Jesus's answer, he would be forced to admit his own limitations and weakness in front of those gathered, and by doing so acknowledge his submission to the authority of the priesthood. Armed with his declaration, the council would have little trouble convincing his followers to abandon him. Unlike John, who had been killed while the people still admired and revered him, Jesus would be discredited at the height of his power, forced to live out the rest of his days exposed and humbled. The priesthood would emerge, damaged but not destroyed, and ultimately more unified as a result.

Caiaphas caught Annas's eye as he stood waiting for Jesus's response. He was relieved to see that his father-in-law's expression was no longer as grave. In fact, Annas looked almost pleased. Caiaphas could only assume that, despite everything, the older priest was impressed with the approach he had taken and saw the wisdom in it. In an instant, it was as if he were a newly appointed priest once more, advising Annas on some intricate matter and basking in the glow of his father-in-law's good favor. Although remnants of anger and bitterness still festered within him, Caiaphas had to admit that he still longed for Annas's approval. At least part of the reason for his outburst had been the sinking sensation that his father-in-law no longer respected or trusted him. The look on Annas's face now served as a soothing salve that made him reconsider his previous doubts.

Caiaphas glanced around the chamber, and saw equally approving looks on a number of the priests' faces. Even Theo looked impressed, and Jonathan gave him a slight smile. The pain in Caiaphas's head began to recede. He could see the end of the interrogation fast approaching. He thought with anticipation of being able to recount to Rivkah all that had transpired. In the morning, members of the council would go to Pilate and reassure him that the threat had been removed without need of force or further Roman intervention. Within days, both Pilate and Antipas would leave Jerusalem as planned and return to their homes in Caesarea and Tiberias. In the peace that followed, Caiaphas would find a way to reconcile with his father-in-law, seeking Rivkah's wise council to heal the relationship in a manner that would both honor Annas and preserve his own reputation. As with the events surrounding Pilate and the standards, Caiaphas would emerge more in control of the temple than he had been before. Eventually, this incident would be nothing more than a distant memory, an unpleasant but effective recalibration of the power behind the priesthood, and the defeat of yet another in a long line of troublemakers and zealots.

As the silence continued to stretch, Caiaphas allowed his thoughts to drift further ahead, feeling more confident with each second that passed. All would be well. His son Judah would grow to be a man, and would take his rightful place within the priesthood. Judah, Eli, Ben and Joshua would usher in a new generation of priests, ones loyal to him as the high priest of their youth. Gratus's last letter had suggested that Tiberius continued to be satisfied with the region and with Pilate's management, flawed as Caiaphas knew it to be. This approval was in large part thanks to his relationship with Gratus, a steadfast resource embedded within the Roman court, despite his no longer holding any official office in Judea. And yet, Caiaphas thought ruefully, I have never mistaken Gratus as anything other than a foreign ally, one born out of necessity and duty rather than affection or love.

Caiaphas realized suddenly that the man Jesus was staring at him, as if he were waiting for Caiaphas to be finished with his thoughts, as if he could hear them aloud and was biding his time until they had run their course. Perplexed, Caiaphas tilted his head slightly and looked at the man before him.

Jesus was standing taller now. Although his hands remained bound behind his back, his stance suggested a man steady and unafraid. The look of compassion and sympathy had returned to his eyes. Caiaphas was frustrated to see that it remained directed toward him. When Jesus spoke, his voice was level and strong. Although it was not loud, it filled the chamber. "I cannot admit what is not true. What I am, I am. My authority is from God, not man." There was a pause, and then Jesus continued, his words landing on Caiaphas like kindling on a pyre, scorching him with their quiet intensity. "Whether the temple stands or burns to the ground, your God and I are one."

In an instant, Caiaphas felt his anger come flooding back as if it had never left. In a blink he saw the familiar vision of the temple burning, as potent as if he were deep in the darkest of nightmares. Every fear he had ever had as to the legitimacy and prophetic nature of his dreams hit him with full force. He stared at Jesus with his mouth wide. Did this man somehow know about the dream that had haunted Caiaphas since he was a boy? Was this a veiled threat that reached into a future where the temple would in fact fall? Or was Jesus just senseless enough not only to claim divinity, but to blindly threaten that which was most precious to the priesthood, sealing his own fate in the process?

With fury coursing through every nerve in his body, it was as if for a moment Caiaphas lost control of his limbs. He watched aghast as his palms rose and his fingers curled inward, clenched into mangled, open fists, reaching for the high priest's robes draped across his torso. He heard rather than felt the fabric rip under the pressure from his hands, which had taken on the appearance of an eagle's talons, rigid and formidable. Horrified, he looked down as he heard the gasps of those around him echoing through the chamber. His ceremonial robes, holiest of the clothing the high priest wore with the exception of the golden breastplate and crown, were in tatters, long slits pulled through the fabric on both sides of his chest so that it looked as if he had been mauled by a beast. His eyes wild, he looked at Jonathan, who was staring at him in horror and disbelief. He remembered another time when he and Jonathan had faced one another in a moment of pain. Yet even the news of his own mother's death had not led him to defile the uniform of his office, the mark of his righteousness as a high priest of the temple.

And then suddenly he knew it was all the fault of this man before him, this reckless madman who had provoked him thus, whose existence had caused a wedge between him and his father-in-law that might never be repaired. It was one thing to be a revolutionary, to raise up rebels to fight against the Romans. But Jesus was at war with his own people, claiming a power that could never be his to command, claiming to be equal with God. Not only that, but his very presence had caused the priesthood to become divided. It had prompted Annas to turn to the Romans for aid, an act that had the potential to turn deadly if not checked. With a sharp pang, Caiaphas remembered the circumstances of his father's murder, and the skirmish between the Romans and zealots that had led to his death. History had shown all too powerfully the peril in involving the Romans too much in the affairs of the priesthood. It was this very danger that was upon them again, thanks to Jesus.

The rage Caiaphas felt was deeper than any he had ever known.

The voice that rose out of him was guttural and raw, bouncing off the walls of the chamber and ricocheting into the night. "Blasphemy! Outrage! There is nothing more we need hear." His breath was coming fast and shallow now, but his mind felt suddenly as clear as a deep pool of water, undisturbed and serene, and strangely disconnected from his pain and fury. "The Scriptures clearly tell us the way to handle one who blasphemes the name of our God, and who does so with such audacity. Death awaits this man, as surely as in the days of Moses. There can be no other path."

He turned to Theo, who was standing at attention, ready and eager to do his bidding. "Take him away."

The members of the guard sprang into action. Following direction from Theo, they unceremoniously dragged the prisoner from view. Caiaphas sank slowly to his knees and put his head in his hands. He stayed there, rocking slightly back and forth, as he heard the other priests usher the witnesses out of the room. He waited until there was silence around him. Then he lifted his head, and saw that only Jonathan remained in the chamber. He had been joined by Rivkah, who stood uncertainly in the doorway, watching her husband with concern.

Caiaphas felt suddenly exhausted, as if he had just completed a long journey and could go no further. As he attempted to rise, he discovered to his dismay that his legs, spent from a long day of sacrifices at the temple even before his encounters with Annas and Jesus, would not carry him. And then he was weeping, the tears flowing thick and fast down his cheeks, dampening the torn and mangled robes that still covered his torso. In an instant, both Rivkah and Jonathan rushed to him, kneeling beside him on the cold, mosaic tile. They sat together as one, as Caiaphas's sobs slowly subsided. Silence again filled the chamber. In the stillness, the wicks from the lamps crackled softly from their lampstands, their flames flickering eerily across the three of them like a haunting caress.

PART III

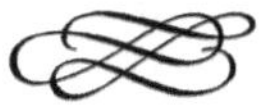

CHAPTER 29

Six years had passed since the unfortunate business with the man Jesus. Pilate had been called upon to act in the sentencing of the man, as Caiaphas had known he must be from the moment Caiaphas learned that Roman officers had assisted in the arrest. Although the thing was messy from beginning to end, the Roman governor had effectively done the job required of him. Jesus met his end as so many criminals had done before him, nailed up beyond the city walls for all to see, a cautionary tale of the results of crossing the priesthood and their God.

In leaning on Pilate for the requisite power and might needed to definitively rid themselves of the rebel, the priesthood provided the Roman with an opportunity to show himself to be in control of the region, whatever else happened behind closed doors. Afterward, Pilate seemed more in awe of the priests than before. He remained bewildered by their beliefs and passions, but was more cognizant than ever that the strength of their convictions was not something with which to be trifled. He kept his distance for a year after those events, remaining in Caesarea. Then he began again to visit Jerusalem during the festivals. Clearly he had decided that, despite his wariness, he would prefer to keep the Jewish leadership close.

In the years that followed, various factions began to emerge from the shadows in Judea. Followers of Jesus continued to gather even after his death, and strange rumors about them were always circulating. New threats emerged. Nearly every festival, it seemed, another would-be deliverer would appear in Jerusalem, speaking out against the Romans and claiming to be the one who would bring an end to foreign rule. The temple guards were vigilant in monitoring and silencing anyone who might be seen as a threat within the city walls. But the outskirts and neighboring towns were harder to control. Ultimately, it was here that Pilate met his downfall, bringing Caiaphas down with him in his bloody wake.

Three days journey from Jerusalem to the north lay a mountain that had from the days of Moses been considered a place of blessing, called Gerizim. In the nineteenth year of Caiaphas's high priesthood, rumors began to reach both Caesarea and Jerusalem of a man in that region who was claiming to be a new Moses. He was rapidly gathering a following, and the peasants and fishermen joining him were arming themselves with all manner of weaponry. If the reports were to be believed, the revolutionaries' mission was to climb the mountain and reclaim the blessing they felt was rightfully theirs. What they might do after this was uncertain. But theirs did not appear to be a movement of peace. There was no telling how much trouble they might cause if they decided to turn their eyes toward Jerusalem, or worse, Rome. Caiaphas was deeply concerned, and met with the council on multiple occasions, discussing various options and methods for dissuasion and deterrence. Ultimately it was decided that the priests would send a delegation to the man to see if he could be made to see reason. Although no one was eager to engage the troublemaker, it had become impossible to stand idly by. The memory of their last encounter with a rebel making blasphemous claims was too fresh to ignore.

But before this could be accomplished, Pilate acted. In his hubris, he decided that he would not waste time consulting with Caiaphas or seeking advice from his own advisors. He ordered a detachment of cavalry to the spot with instructions to eliminate the threat, orders that they carried out to devastating effect. Men, women and children were slaughtered on the side of the mountain. The leader of the rebellion died alongside those who had followed him so faithfully. The bodies, which piled up alongside the narrow road that cut through the mountainside, rotted in the heat of the sun, and were ravaged by wild animals before they could be retrieved and given proper burials.

Within weeks, a messenger arrived from Rome, calling for Pilate to return to the capital and defend his use of force, as complaints from family members of those killed had reached the ears of the emperor by way of the neighboring Syrian governor. The man was no fan of Pilate, and was more than happy for the opportunity to cause trouble for him. Pilate was unceremoniously removed from office and replaced by a man virtually indistinguishable from him. Before Caiaphas and the council were able to make sense of the change and determine a strategy for wooing and befriending yet another foreign governor, a second letter arrived, this one calling for the removal of Caiaphas as well.

IT WAS evening when Caiaphas received the messenger at his estate. As he read the contents, he felt his breath quicken and his chest tighten. Rivkah found him in an open courtyard, pacing in tight circles and muttering to himself in the cool of the night. One look told her that something was wrong.

"My love." She approached him quickly, her strides swift and smooth as she crossed the courtyard and stood before him. "What is it?"

He looked up at her, his face stricken. Although at forty his cheek was bearded and his forehead lined, Rivkah saw for a moment the face of the forlorn little boy she had known so many years before. When he spoke, his voice carried a note of plaintive disbelief. "I am deposed, Rivkah." Saying the words out loud seemed to make them more real. Caiaphas sank to his knees, shaking his head slightly.

"What?" Rivkah looked aghast, and knelt before her husband, putting a hand on his robed knee. "Oh, Joseph. Why?"

Caiaphas continued to shake his head. In silence, he passed his wife the parchment, which she took. Her eyes scanned the first section, which included a formal greeting from the Syrian governor. She stopped at the beginning of the next sentence, and read aloud. "Noble Caiaphas, it is said by those Romans most well-learned and wise that every new beginning comes from some other beginning's end. You know by now that Pilate has been recalled to Rome. With his departure, the emperor has with new eyes examined the region in which you have for so long been our appointed representative among your people."

Caiaphas sighed bitterly as he heard the words anew from his wife's lips. The fact that a Roman official he had never met was bold enough to address him as if he were a centurion in a foreign army was appalling. It had been like this ever since he could remember, this struggle for power between his people and the Romans. As a boy, he had seen over and over again the way the Romans had inserted themselves into the proceedings at the temple. He watched as Annas, Joazar, and others fell prey to their whims and their ways. Annas had labored with all his cunning and might to ensure Caiaphas's appointment as high priest, certain that it would give the Jewish leadership a firmer footing. Turning foe into friend for the sake of the greater good, Annas had attempted to create an environment where the high priest could govern and rule apart from Roman interference. But even Annas had found himself irrevocably intertwined with his enemies, beholden to them and conspiring with them to suppress those who challenged the priesthood's authority. It was a dangerous game, and the priesthood found itself on the losing end time and time again.

Still, Caiaphas remained grateful to Annas for preparing the way for his appointment as high priest. For nearly two decades, he had done everything in his power to serve the priesthood and the people well, striving to fulfill a destiny that his own father had barely dared to imagine for him, long before it ever seemed possible. Caiaphas had endeavored to work closely with the Romans while maintaining the integrity and autonomy of his leadership, a task that had become significantly more difficult as the years went by. Now all of it was coming to a rapid end.

Rivkah glanced at her husband briefly, then returned to the letter. "It has been decided that a fresh start is needed in Jerusalem. With the dismissal of Pilate, it seems an opportune time to begin anew within your temple as well. The task of choosing the next high priest has been given to the current governor in Caesarea. We trust that you will be able to advise him as to a suitable candidate for the position."

Rivkah looked up at her husband again. When she spoke it was with tentative but genuine hopefulness. "Joseph, I know it is painful to be removed. But all is not lost if you are able to influence the choice of your successor. There are many among the priesthood who would serve well. Your influence may still be felt for many years to come." Caiaphas remained silent. She knew he was at war within, angry and sad. Losing his position was a blow from which he would not easily recover. But she also knew that he had survived much worse. As they knelt together, she reached gently under his chin, raising his eyes to meet hers.

"My love." She smiled. "Your knowledge of the Scriptures is far more expansive than my own. But even I know that the prophets talk of God's ways being higher than ours. We cannot know the reason for this end. But perhaps, like the Romans, we can take solace that a new beginning remains ahead for us, one that we do not yet see."

Caiaphas smiled slightly, and took both of Rivkah's hands in his. Turning them over, he examined the pale, slender fingers, the cool palms made rough from weaving and grinding grain. Although he still felt raw and unsettled from the news he had received, there had always been something in Rivkah's touch and her words of thoughtful encouragement that made everything less troubling. He nodded, not yet trusting his voice. Together they sat in silence, hands clasped, each deep in their own thoughts.

THAT NIGHT, Caiaphas dreamed again of his youngest brother-in-law Ben in the role of high priest, presiding over the council and conducting the trial of rebels called before the priesthood for their crimes. He awakened briefly. When his mind melted again into slumber, a new vision arose before him, vibrant and bright in sharp contrast to the one he had just seen in the shadowy Chamber of Hewn Stone.

In this vision, the sun was shining brightly. He was walking along a rough path carved into the side of a mountain, his sandals kicking up dust as he hurried along. He felt that the body he inhabited was somehow fragile and worn. When he looked down, he was not surprised to see that his hands and feet appeared older and more withered than he knew them to be. His knuckles were scuffed and dirty, his back ached, and his legs felt as if they have been climbing for some time. Before him a few paces, a slender young woman walked, leading a bull calf like those used in the temple for sacrificial offerings. Upon the animal, several large woven sacks had been tied, including a long, narrow bundle wrapped in what looked like temple linens. The girl before him appeared to be no more than twenty, her long hair braided and shimmering golden in the sunlight. Her clothing was plain but sturdy, clearly intended for traveling. The bottom of her cloak was covered in mud that had dried in the sun, making the edges stiff and heavy. She did not turn back, but picked her way along the rocks steadily and with purpose.

Glancing around, Caiaphas tried to identify the place where he stood. He knew by the terrain that they were no longer in Jerusalem, but he did not immediately recognize his surroundings. Ahead of him, he saw the hill rising before them, the landscape shifting from dry, rocky ground to more fertile, lush land as olive and acacia trees gave way to juniper and cedar. The route they traveled was less road than trail. He watched as the girl before him stumbled slightly before righting herself again. As the path began to climb more steeply, Caiaphas turned and looked behind him. It was then that he knew where he was.

In the distance below them, he could see the gleam of sunlight bouncing off water, light reflecting across the surface of one of the large rectangular pools that lay less than a day's walk from Jerusalem, just south of Bethlehem on the road to Hebron. These pools, thought to have been constructed by King Solomon in a former age, provided water to Jerusalem and to the temple through an intricate web of aqueducts and tunnels that flowed down the hill, across the valley, and into the city. The Pool of Siloam, where Caiaphas's father had spent so many hours pacing and meditating, was one of the largest recipients of this water. Even the ritual bath beneath the temple grounds in which Caiaphas had bathed so many times was fed by this source.

As it always did, the sight of water calmed Caiaphas. He breathed deeply, hoping to catch its fresh, cool scent. They were too far away for that, however. By the position of the sun Caiaphas could tell that they were headed west, away from Jerusalem and further up into the Judean hillside. He could not understand why he was there, alone with a woman too young to be a daughter, nor why they were traveling at a pace that seemed to suggest they were fleeing something, or someone. Troubled, Caiaphas tried to catch up to the girl ahead of him, to see her face, and to determine what he could from her countenance. Just as he was about to reach her, however, the dream faded and he awoke, left with only questions, and the lingering sensation of the sun warming his face.

CHAPTER 30

After Caiaphas was deposed, his estate ceased to be the destination for council gatherings or large feasts. As a result, he and Rivkah found they no longer required the number of servants they had been maintaining. Around the same time, Nathan's parents Silas and Lydia, who had both served the house of Annas into their seventies, grew too frail to continue in their positions. A distant cousin offered the family a place in the nearby town of Jericho, a humble dwelling with land enough to support a small household. The road there was treacherous and not well suited for aging bodies. But Silas and Lydia were both still healthy enough to make the journey. Nathan came to Caiaphas and requested leave for himself, Rebecca, and Malchus to accompany his parents on the way, and to stay on until they were settled. Caiaphas dismissed them willingly, and told them to stay as long as they saw fit. He was not surprised when the letters, which at first arrived regularly, began to dwindle. When Nathan sent news that Malchus had taken a wife from among the daughters of his relative, and that Silas, who had lived to see the wedding, had gone to his rest shortly thereafter, Caiaphas knew they would not be returning to Jerusalem.

This suited him and Rivkah perfectly well. The last celebration that had required the benefit of a large staff had come a year before Caiaphas was deposed, when the wedding of their son Judah was held at their estate. Martha made a beautiful bride, and Rivkah was delighted to welcome her into their home as a daughter. Julia had made sure that Martha was not only an accomplished cook, but also knew her way around both a loom and a larder. Her contributions to the household more than made up for the loss of Nathan and his family.

Even so, it was Martha's more intangible qualities that were of most value to their home. When Judah was with her, he seemed stronger and more vigorous. His eyes shone with delight at his good fortune in acquiring such a wife. Caiaphas was charmed by Martha, whose wit and passion reminded him of his own bride in her youth. After so many years of being one woman among a slew of brothers, Rivkah relished her role as mother-in-law with great satisfaction. Indeed, the only person for whom the wedding was bittersweet was Julia, who felt the loss of her daughter deeply despite having greatly desired the union in the first place. In part to soften the blow, there were many evenings where Julia and her son Eli left their own estate to join Caiaphas and his household for the evening meal, leaving Simon to satisfy himself at the temple with his fellow priests.

Gamaliel and Joshua had also been frequent guests at Caiaphas's estate before Judah and Martha's wedding. But they came less frequently after Martha became a part of the household, and all but ceased their visits once Caiaphas was no longer high priest. At first, Caiaphas thought it had something to do with the ever shifting loyalties of the council. He wondered whether Gamaliel thought to better his son's chances of one day becoming high priest by distancing himself from his old friend. Caiaphas would not have blamed Gamaliel if he had chosen to more closely align himself with those who might enable his son to best prosper, withdrawing from one who might inhibit Joshua's opportunities.

But Rivkah was shrewder than her husband. She had noticed the way that Martha and Joshua looked at one another on the occasions she had seen them together. She saw how Martha's cheeks burned when Joshua fixed his eyes on her for more than a few moments. She was not at all surprised that the young man, who continued to show great promise at the temple and who was much admired and respected by many, had decided to remove himself from her daughter-in-law's presence, for his own sake as well as hers. Rivkah knew that Martha loved Judah with fierce and tender care, and would never do anything to hurt her son. Even so, she felt it was better for everyone if Joshua kept his distance, and told Caiaphas so.

"My love, I have no doubt there is wisdom in what you say." Caiaphas was amused by his wife's serious expression as he considered her. "I cannot pretend to understand the ways of love. There has only ever been one woman who captured my heart. I cannot conceive of being tempted by another." Rivkah smiled despite herself, and her face softened slightly. "But I am sure you are right. I will let the matter rest, and trust that Gamaliel and Joshua are operating for their own worthy reasons."

THE CHANGES WROUGHT by Caiaphas's deposition stretched far beyond his own household. Jonathan, who had been chosen by Pilate's successor to take Caiaphas's place after strong encouragement from the council, was extremely reluctant to assume the role. He served only fifty days before negotiating the transfer of the position to Theo, who seized it with keen enthusiasm. Theo's term lasted longer than that of his brother. But after five relatively peaceful years, the grandson of Herod the Great replaced Antipas as king of Judea, and sought to exert his own influence in the region, replacing Theo in the process. The yoke of Roman rule became increasingly heavy with each deposition and interference. The balance that had been so carefully maintained during Caiaphas's term felt more and more like a distant memory.

Simon, with his flattering ways, managed to ingratiate himself with the new ruler almost immediately. He was given the post of high priest a second time, with the understanding that it would be a temporary assignment. After a year he had accumulated enough esteem in the eyes of the new king, called Agrippa, to convince him to bestow the mantle upon Annas's son Matthias, who by then had risen to prominence within the temple and was well known for both his piety and his facility with finances. But Matthias's term was also shortened by Roman tensions and political maneuvering. Despite their best efforts, neither Caiaphas nor Simon were able to impact the choice of his replacement. For the next two decades the house of Annas fell out of favor with those determining who sat upon the highest seat of the council. Caiaphas was forced to take a less active role, allowing others to lead while he watched and waited.

After Jesus's trial and for the remainder of Caiaphas's term, Annas kept his distance from the temple. Whether or not he felt remorse for betraying Caiaphas's trust and bringing Roman forces to bear on the situation, he clearly thought it best to remove himself from matters of the priesthood, at least for a time. The relationship between Caiaphas and Annas remained strained, even as their wives both fervently prayed for them to find reconciliation. But as the years passed, and especially once Caiaphas no longer served as high priest, the two men settled into a peace that, while not the same as before, contained enough mutual respect and affection to satisfy both Rivkah and Tova. When they were together, Annas had taken to reminiscing about the early days of his priesthood, especially during the years when Joazar had first served as high priest. Caiaphas relished the opportunity to reflect on a time when his father Abel was a member of the priest-hood, and before the Romans had begun to intervene too heavily in determinations of temple leadership.

In the ensuing years, especially when one of his sons wore the high priest's robes, Annas continued to serve as a source of influence and expertise, though he remained ensconced within the walls of his own estate. Theo in particular sought his father's counsel on issues of theo-logical import during his term. As time went on, however, Annas began to grow increasingly disillusioned and distracted. His mind, which had always been sharp and quick, faltered. There were times when he misquoted Scripture or misremembered the name of a pilgrim coming to visit Jerusalem. Caiaphas found it painful to watch the man who had once loomed so large in his eyes grow smaller in both stature and faculty.

TWO YEARS after his wedding to Martha, while Theo still served as high priest, Judah took the vows of the priesthood, much to Caiaphas's relief and satisfaction. Judah began serving at the temple under the watchful eye of Jonathan, who made sure he was not taxed with anything that required too much physical labor. As the seasons passed and Judah and Martha's union failed to produce a child, however, Caiaphas began to worry. He feared that yet another generation of his family would suffer the challenges both his mother and wife had endured on their journey to motherhood. He and Rivkah sent many additional offerings to the temple along with prayers that their son would be blessed with offspring.

It was another decade before Martha's belly finally began to swell. The child born, a girl whom they named Miriam, was small but robust. Tova and Julia both attended the birth. They bustled around the estate as the decades appeared to melt off of them, shouting orders at Rivkah and working to make everything ready for the baby's arrival. Tova, who by this time was in her seventies and whose hair had gone completely white, was the first to come to Caiaphas and Judah with the news that the baby had been born. Her face flushed with joy and delight at the birth of her great-granddaughter.

Unfortunately, the celebration in the household was short-lived. Just after Miriam's birth, Judah's health took a turn for the worse. By the time the girl was able to toddle around the estate, her father was no longer strong enough to serve at the temple. He was forced to renounce his place in the priesthood, much to the dismay of those in both Annas and Caiaphas's households. After that, Judah spent his days at home much as he had in his youth, most often huddled under blankets near one of the courtyard fires. Caiaphas, watching him, was painfully reminded of his own mother during the last years of her life, and how she never seemed able to sufficiently warm herself. Miriam, who had inherited her mother's golden curls and lively nature, would sit at her father's feet, playing with her favorite doll, which Martha had made for her from discarded rags and cedar branches. She would lean against Judah's legs, and he would absentmindedly stroke her hair and gaze into the fire as she sang a child's tune, her voice sweet and lyrical. When Miriam was not with her father, the girl clung to Rivkah, who was more than happy to take her granddaughter under her wing, teaching her how to weave and spin as Hadassah had taught Rivkah when she herself was young.

But Judah's failing health was not the only blow that Rivkah and Caiaphas suffered during those years. By the time Miriam was eight years old, the ever shifting landscape of the high priesthood and Roman authorities had taken yet another turn. At that time, the Roman governor was a man named Felix. Jonathan, who had been sent to Rome on a different matter, found himself in the unique position of being able to make a recommendation to those in power. He suggested Felix for the appointment. The man appeared to be a good choice. His brother was prominent within the Roman court and had found favor with the emperor. Gratus, who was traveling at the time and was not in Rome to greet the delegation from Jerusalem, was not available to give his opinion. But Jonathan, whose habit of seeing the best in people had not diminished with age or experience, was impressed by Felix's bearing and his respectful treatment of those from the priesthood who had traveled to Rome. Caiaphas saw no reason to question his brother-in-law's judgment.

This positive impression soon proved to be a false and costly one. Shortly after Felix took up his residence in Caesarea, the problems began. First, there were the rumors that the new governor was eliciting bribes from tradesmen in Jerusalem in exchange for exclusive purchase of their goods. Several of the most prominent merchants in the city had come to the council with grievances against him. Jonathan felt deeply responsible for the dishonest dealings of the man he had put forth for the governorship. "This is my fault, Caiaphas. If it hadn't been for my recommendation, we would not be in this position." Caiaphas tried to assuage his brother-in-law's guilt, assuring him that it had been an honest mistake. But Jonathan would hear none of it.

Most problematic, however, was the way that Felix had determined to handle the zealots who once again began to gather across Judea, both in the outskirts of the city and within Jerusalem itself. The Romans had become more and more exacting in their annual taxes as the years passed. The more prosperous the city became, the more the Romans saw it as an opportunity to reap the benefits from the populace as well as from the temple. The people became more disgruntled with each passing season. The council continued to do their best to dissuade citizens of the city from protesting or causing any disturbances. As in the past, however, they had less control over those in the smaller villages surrounding Jerusalem.

The first reports of murders reached the council just before the Feast of Dedication was about to begin. It seemed that the most prominent and outspoken rebels were disappearing, or else were found dead in their bedchambers, wounds in their sides or back, their bedclothes bloody and twisted. One assassin was caught, dagger in hand, creeping into the open doorway of a home in the Lower City. He was brought to the temple for questioning. The man ultimately confessed that he had been sent by a messenger from the palace in Caesarea to attack the master of the house, who was known to have close ties with the zealots.

Jonathan requested to be sent to Caesarea without delay. He confronted Felix, hopeful that his initial endorsement would grant him some sway with the Roman governor. Not only did Felix not deny the accusation, he intimated that he was more than willing to continue these efforts until he had either intimidated or eliminated all of Rome's enemies in Judea. Jonathan returned from the journey shaken and deeply concerned. He spent long hours with fellow members of the council, discussing how they might be able to dissuade Felix from this approach without aggravating the governor further, and burned sacrificial offerings of petition asking God to soften Felix's heart and cause him to change his mind.

Unfortunately, it seemed that Jonathan's visit had created an unintended consequence. Felix now became convinced that Jonathan was plotting his removal as governor. Paranoid and impulsive, Felix decided to make sure that Jonathan would not have the opportunity. It was two weeks after the Feast of Dedication just before dusk, as Jonathan was setting out from the temple after his daily responsibilities, that he was set upon by a group of men. His attackers all wore cloaks with hoods, so that those who witnessed the assault from a distance were unable to identify them. But the wounds the men inflicted, from daggers hidden beneath their tunics, were swift and effective. By the time Jonathan's body had been carried to Annas's estate, there was nothing anyone could do for him.

Caiaphas, who received word by messenger and rushed there from the temple, found his brother-in-law laid in the open courtyard, the rest of the family standing around him in a circle, weeping in shocked silence. The first person he recognized was Jonathan's wife Sera, her tear-stained face rising to meet his from where she sat, bent over her husband's motionless body. Annas, ashen, stood over her, looking as if the slightest breeze might knock him over. Tova was by his side, straight-backed and rigid, her mouth set and determined. Rivkah, who had also been summoned, arrived moments after Caiaphas. He heard her footsteps as she raced through the vestibule, her breath ragged as she burst into the courtyard. Seeing Jonathan's body, she stumbled forward and fell at his feet, her raven hair covering the torn and bloody tunic he still wore. Her grief magnified Caiaphas's own sorrow as he considered Jonathan, his brother, his companion, and his friend. He could scarcely believe that Jonathan's dark eyes, always so attentive and thoughtful, had been closed for good.

CHAPTER 31

The loss of Jonathan confirmed what Caiaphas had always feared, from the first time he had witnessed his vision of Ben as high priest so many years earlier. As the years passed, he had observed each of the men in his dream grow in maturity and prominence within the temple, maneuvering the shifting popularity of the house of Annas and the ever-increasing pressure of the Roman authorities with skill and shrewdness. Caiaphas watched as Theo, after his term as high priest, returned to his previous role as captain of the guard. It suited him well. Despite his advancing years, Theo's physical presence and stature had not diminished. Matthias, too, maintained a place of respect and power within the temple even after his time as high priest came to an end, reverting to his role within the treasury. He and his wife Hannah also took on a greater role in the running of Annas's estate as the years passed.

Simon's son Eli, who had himself served a term as high priest in the years since a member of Annas's family had worn the robes, had grown into a deeply thoughtful and important priest in his own right. Calmer and more measured than either Joshua or Ben, and persuasive in a different way than his father Simon, Eli had a harmonizing effect on the proceedings whenever he was involved. More than once,

Caiaphas had been impressed by Eli's influence over the more passionate members of the council. Even Joshua and Ben, both still occasionally aggressive and overeager in their zeal for advancement and desire for power, had become men of distinction and honor within the priesthood.

But when Caiaphas thought back to his vision, he had often found himself wondering why Jonathan was not among the men who gathered to try the young rebels. Surely a person of Jonathan's stature and wisdom would have been a desirable and necessary participant. Caiaphas had found his absence troubling, and his concern was renewed each time the vision returned to him in his dreams. As he observed Ben presiding over the council and passing judgment on the prisoners, he would glance at each of the priests present in turn, hoping to catch sight of Jonathan, even though he knew beyond a doubt that he would not be there. Now he knew why, and the pain of the loss gripped him even as he endeavored to remain strong for Rivkah, and for the others left behind.

Annas was never the same after Jonathan was murdered. Tova, whose light also dimmed with the unexpected death of a second son, redoubled her efforts in caring for her husband, who took to his bed and refused any efforts to restore him. Even Rivkah was unable to bring her father much solace, though she spent many afternoons at his bedside before returning to her own household, weary from the tears she wept as she walked through the darkening streets. Caiaphas would wait for her at the threshold, and together they would eat a somber meal with Judah, Martha, and Miriam before retiring early. By now, any residual anger that Caiaphas felt toward his father-in-law had all but disappeared, replaced by a dull sadness that was only exacerbated by his wife's sorrow.

It was a mercy when Annas finally breathed his last. With Annas gone, Tova's strength and resolve weakened as well, and the family laid her to rest beside her husband only a few years later. Their remaining sons grieved their passing. Then, along with their wives and children, they set about attempting to establish a new equilibrium at the estate over which Annas and Tova had held sway for so many years.

The loss was especially difficult for Rivkah, who within four years had buried both her parents and her closest brother. Miriam, now twelve years old, was a sweet comfort to her. The girl, who had inherited Martha's nurturing spirit together with Julia's tenderness, seemed able to pull a smile from Rivkah even on her hardest days. Miriam took to joining Rivkah and Caiaphas during their morning walks, keeping a few paces behind them as her grandparents spoke quietly of the news of the day, or reflected on those they had lost.

There were two years of reprieve after Tova's burial, during which Caiaphas stayed closer to home, striving to take advantage of the respite he was afforded after over four decades of service to the temple. While he continued to attend the daily council meeting, eager to maintain a presence among those he had led for so long, he grew increasingly frustrated by the various factions that continued to divide the priesthood, escalating tensions and fracturing unity at every turn, making it harder than ever to stand firm against the Romans. At home, too, there were worries that plagued him, keeping him from his dreams late into the night, long after Rivkah had fallen asleep beside him, the lines on her face softened by sleep. Judah's health was not improving, despite attempts by both Julia and the temple healers. Caiaphas feared that it was only a matter of time before his son would succumb to the ailments that had plagued him since his infancy.

Judah lived just long enough to see Miriam grow as tall as her mother, her vitality and strength a solace to him even as his own health worsened. More than anyone else, it was Miriam who was able to convince Judah to eat when he had no appetite, or to try whatever new treatment or tincture Julia had designed in an attempt to restore her son-in-law to health. But not even Miriam could stop the inevitable. One evening shortly before her fourteenth birthday, Judah fell asleep by the dwindling fire. When Martha came to rouse him to move him to their bedchamber, he was cold and still.

For Caiaphas, his son's death signaled the departure of a dream he had barely allowed himself to entertain. In the years when Judah was well, there had been moments when Caiaphas would look at him and imagine that one day he would grow strong enough to take back the high priesthood that had been lost, to reset the balance between the priests and the Romans, and to continue Caiaphas's legacy into the next generation and beyond. Although in his clearer moments he knew that Judah lacked both the temperament and the fortitude for such an assignment, Caiaphas had yearned for a miracle, even after Judah's health began to decline. Judah's passing put an end to those hopes.

The entire community of priests and other prominent families in Jerusalem greeted the loss with profound sorrow. Many came to Caiaphas's estate to pay their respects during the week of mourning. Martha, who had been Judah's devoted caretaker since they were children, was unexpectedly subdued and stoic, calmly going about her duties preparing the home for visitors and cordially receiving those who came to call. At first, Rivkah, who was besieged by her own sorrow, worried that her daughter-in-law was harboring a sadness so deep that it would consume her once she finally allowed it in. But it soon became clear that Martha had long ago made peace with the inevitability of her husband's passing, and had quietly begun to think about her future.

It was on the third day of mourning when Joshua appeared. Although he had buried his own father eight years before, Joshua continued to live in the modest home Gamaliel had established for them near the temple, where he spent nearly all of his time. He had married not long after Martha and Judah had been joined in matrimony. But his wife had been lost in childbirth a few years later, along with the baby boy she carried. He had been alone ever since. Joshua's temples were peppered with gray strands, and though lines had begun to trace across his forehead, he remained as handsome as ever. His dark eyes were sorrowful as he greeted Caiaphas and Rivkah at the courtyard entrance. Clasping Rivkah's hands in his own, he shook his head gently. "The loss of a son is a terrible thing. May God grant your family peace in this time of sadness."

It was Caiaphas who answered, his voice trembling but thick with gratitude. "I thank you, Joshua. It is a sorrow we know you share." With an effort, he smiled at the younger man, and put a hand on his shoulder. "Come, you must join us for a meal. We will try to turn our thoughts to things that may give us more pleasure. I want to hear the latest news from the temple. A rumor has reached me that there is a possibility that the high priesthood is not entirely out of the hands of the household of Annas as we had previously thought."

Joshua smiled, glad for the change of subject. "Yes, it is true. As long as Ben does not do anything too rash or impulsive, the chance is there."

At that time, the high priest was a young man named Joseph. He had been appointed by Julius, the son of Agrippa, who had after some political maneuvering been granted by Rome the authority to manage the high priesthood assignments from his palace in Tiberias. Joseph had served for only one year. While there was nothing remarkable about him, he had succeeded in satisfying the new Roman king as to his willingness to work with him and to bend to his authority. The priesthood grumbled about Joseph in private, seeing him as weak and ineffectual. But Joshua and Ben had wisely carved out for themselves prominent roles within the young man's council. Ben in particular had found favor with both Joseph and the Roman king who had appointed him, and he and Joshua had made themselves indispensable to the high priest as advisors and mentors.

More recently, a rumor from Caesarea suggested that yet another shift in the landscape might soon be upon them. After Pilate, a series of men had filled the Roman governor's position, each one more pompous and self-important than the next. The current governor, Festus, was not fond of Ben, or indeed, of anyone from the house of Annas. He had effectively blocked Annas's youngest son from pursuing the role of high priest. But Festus was rumored to be ill. There was a possibility that, if he died, there might be a vacancy in Caesarea, at least until the emperor Nero could appoint a replacement. With the governorship empty, Ben and Joshua were clearly hoping that their influence with Julius, the other local Roman authority, might be enough to sway the tide in Ben's favor.

Joshua continued. "In his last correspondence to Julius, Ben mentioned his concerns over Joseph's youth, and suggested to Julius that perhaps for the next appointment, a man with more seniority and superiority of birth might be a more fitting choice." Joshua smiled ruefully. "I do believe he and Julius are of one mind. If the news of Festus's decline is accurate, I have no doubt that Ben will achieve his aim before the year is out."

The news was a balm to Caiaphas even in his time of mourning. If it could not be his own son, he was more than happy to see a man from the house of Annas regain control of the high priesthood. Assuming his visions were to be trusted, he had always known that a future existed in which Ben would become high priest. It appeared that the moment was in fact approaching. He exchanged glances with Rivkah, with whom he had long ago shared the particulars of his dream. She smiled softly, although her eyes remained sorrowful.

As they spoke, Caiaphas, Rivkah, and Joshua passed through the courtyard and entered the main hall, where Miriam had been helping her mother prepare the final elements of the evening meal. The lamps were lit, and the firelight flickered across both mother and daughter's heads, bent over the table together. Even bound and plaited, their hair shimmered in the low light like a pair of golden ropes. As Martha turned and caught sight of Joshua, a short gasp escaped her lips, as if she had been inadvertently holding her breath. In an instant he crossed the room and took her hands in his. For a moment it seemed they had forgotten where they were, oblivious to anything else. Then Rivkah cleared her throat gently and Martha returned to herself. Dropping Joshua's hands, she bowed low, and said softly, "Thank you for coming. We are honored by your visit." She said nothing more for the rest of the night. But her eyes drifted again and again to where

Joshua sat at the other end of the table. She retired as soon as he had said his goodbyes and departed.

Judah's passing had occurred several weeks after the Feast of Unleavened Bread, just as the rains began to taper off. By the time the temperatures grew warmer and the myrtle trees bloomed in earnest, their white flowers bursting with a sweet, heady scent, the temple received word from Caesarea that Festus had in fact succumbed to his illness. A messenger had been sent to Rome with the news that a successor would need to be named. Ben and Joshua lost no time in convincing Joseph to send a delegation to Tiberias to give the news to Julius directly, so that the Roman king would receive it from the priesthood rather than from Rome. The two men volunteered to lead the party. When they returned a few days later, they carried documents ordering the removal of Joseph as high priest and appointing Ben as his replacement. Caiaphas, who had been overseeing sacrifices at the temple and praying for this outcome, was in the outer courts when they returned. He was the first with whom they shared the news.

So it was that, by the time Ben finally became high priest, more than thirty years after Caiaphas had first seen it in his dreams, the ranks of those who had been influential in his reaching such a distinction had dwindled significantly. Joazar, Gamaliel, Annas, and Tova were all gone. Although Simon still lived, he was ill and seldom left his estate. Of Annas's sons, there remained only Theo, Matthias, and Ben. Caiaphas and Rivkah, while both in good health, mourned the loss of their son.

Even so, Ben's appointment felt like a sign of hope to those who remained. It was with great pride that Caiaphas stood among his fellow priests, the hair on his head and in his beard now speckled with gray and the corners of his eyes creased with lines, waiting in anticipation for the ritual to begin. As Joseph lowered the ceremonial breastplate onto Ben's chest, all those gathered shouted in celebration. The temple musicians began to play. For that moment, at least, the music that filled the temple courts had an air of victorious joy.

Ben had been high priest for less than a month when Caiaphas received what would be his last letter from Gratus. The two men's relationship, which had spanned nearly five decades by this time, had become almost familial in nature, despite their many differences. Caiaphas had come to see Gratus, who once so intimidated him, as an anomaly among the Romans, a man of character whose integrity had more than proven itself across the years. Gratus was nearly eighty, and no longer traveled outside of Rome. But he continued to write regularly, and was always a source of information and insight. It was he who informed Caiaphas of Pilate's passing, less than two years after the former governor had been recalled to Rome.

Gratus was also the first to share the news of Saul's arrival in Rome, and that he was being held under house arrest within the city walls. Saul, the former student of Gamaliel, had unexpectedly deserted the priesthood shortly before Martha and Judah's wedding, while Caiaphas was still high priest. Much to Gamaliel's horror and heartache, Saul had shifted his allegiance from his former teacher to those who continued to rally around the slain Jesus. His traitorous actions had forced the council to expel him from their ranks, and ultimately to turn him over to the presiding Roman governor for censure. Saul had been held within the palace in Caesarea for a time, and had ultimately been sent to Rome for questioning before the emperor himself. Caiaphas, who had always been impressed by Saul's serious manner and vigilant dedication to his mentor, could not imagine what had possessed the young priest. He knew the desertion had haunted Gamaliel for the rest of his life.

But this letter contained news of a different kind. Gratus, whose health had been waning over the last several months, was writing for what he clearly assumed would be the final time. His letter held both a farewell and a warning. Caiaphas received the message just as the council meeting was about to begin. He quickly left the Chamber of

Hewn Stone, and paced the length of the Priests' Court as he read its contents.

"My dear Caiaphas," the letter began. Caiaphas could imagine Gratus, still an impressive figure with his sumptuous robes and carefully curated accessories, seated at a table in his sitting room overlooking the central courtyard of his home in the capital. "I write to you at the end of a long and rich life. As I reflect back on my years, I am thankful to you and to your family for your partnership. While I cannot pretend to fully understand the ways of your people, it has been a privilege to participate in furthering the peace and prosperity of Judea. Your temple and your god are mighty, more so than many of my fellow Romans understand. I count myself fortunate to have been a friend and ally to your father-in-law, and to you."

Caiaphas smiled, and looked over the edge of the parchment at the temple before him. The steps leading up to the sanctuary shone brightly in the morning light. Above them, the columns that flanked the inner temple reflected white and gold. It was indeed a majestic and noble place, altogether worthy of the God he served.

He looked back at the letter, and his brow furrowed as he read the next section. "But I fear that the future is not without new challenges for your people. Unlike Tiberius and those who came after him, our current emperor seems increasingly intolerant of those who follow your god. For some time now, Nero has been tightening his grip on any whose worship does not revolve around him. He is surrounded by men eager to advance themselves in his court, who will think nothing of supporting his most vicious initiatives if they believe that by doing so they can elevate themselves.

"I appreciate that you have always been willing to work with the Romans to protect and defend your people, even as you would prefer to be left in peace from our meddling hands. But a time may be coming when peace is no longer an option. Even so, you must continue to be the voice of reason among your council, and to dissuade those who might choose to take a more aggressive or radical approach. I know that, with his appointment of your brother-in-law, Julius has further restricted the authority of the priesthood, requiring

Roman approval for all but the most minor of decisions. But I know also that Annas's son is not one to be told what to do."

Caiaphas sighed. Gratus had always been an astute judge of character, and had judged his youngest brother-in-law correctly. He too feared that Ben would find it difficult to adhere to the newest rules put in place by the Roman king, who had stripped the priesthood of much of its former power. He could almost hear the sigh that appeared to come before Gratus's next sentence. "In the end it may make little difference. One way or another, the fiery temper of our emperor, which has so far scorched many within my own city, may find its way to your threshold, whether you choose it or not. But for your sake I hope I am wrong, merely an old man nostalgic for simpler times and seeing danger where there is none.

"Whatever the future may bring, I remain your friend and servant."

Caiaphas looked up again, and realized that, while he was reading, he had inadvertently made his way to Nicanor's Gate. He gazed out across the Women's Court, which was full of pilgrims, priests, and merchants, all engaged in the day's business. In one corner, a group of boys sat learning their lessons. Across the way, a handful of men who had obviously traveled a great distance were unpacking their satchels, looking for coins with which to purchase animals for their offerings. He remained there for a moment, taking in the scene.

It was as Caiaphas turned to go back to the Chamber of Hewn Stone that he saw the three men being led across the inner courtyard, with Theo ahead of them and several other members of the guard bringing up the rear. He took a step back in surprise, and had to steady himself to avoid tumbling down the staircase just beyond the gate. Theo looked up at Caiaphas as he passed. His expression was grim. The prisoners behind him were dirty and disheveled, just as they had been in Caiaphas's vision. Their expressions were less relaxed and harder than he remembered. In an instant, he realized that what he was seeing before him was the aftermath of his vision, which must have taken place while he was busy reading Gratus's letter. These men were being led away, not to be judged, but to be punished. He had missed their trial entirely. Suddenly he understood why not only Jonathan, but he himself, had been absent from his dreams.

As Caiaphas continued to watch, Theo led the men out of the northern gate nearest to them. Caiaphas, his heartbeat quickening, knew that Theo and the other members of the guard would not return until the sentence, which would take place beyond the city walls, was carried out. Gratus's letter still in hand, Caiaphas turned away briskly and walked almost without thinking toward the Chamber of the Hearth, whose warmth enveloped him as soon as he entered it. He lowered himself onto one of the stone benches, and sat there in silence, listening to the steady beating of his heart and trying to calm the rising panic he felt threatening to engulf him. With Ben skirting Julius's orders and taking advantage of his position as high priest to both try and sentence enemies of the temple, it would not be long before the ire of the emperor would be drawn to Jerusalem, especially with no governor currently in Caesarea to shoulder some of the responsibility and blame. If Gratus's warning was right, such an action would be more than enough to warrant a strong and swift response from Rome.

His heartbeat slowing, Caiaphas suddenly felt the full weight of his position as a senior member of the priesthood. Looking around the room, his thoughts flickered to Joazar and Annas, as he remembered that this very chamber and the ritual bath below had once been the key to their survival in a time of great uncertainty and chaos. The Chamber of the Hearth had also been the place where he had come upon Eleazar in pain. This memory flooded his mind with images, as he recalled the way he had worked to protect and defend Eleazar in his time of need. The priesthood had already survived so much. Yet new threats were continuously emerging, ones that threatened to shake its very foundation. Taking one last deep breath, Caiaphas rose. Without looking back, he left the chamber and came into the sunlight, his eyes briefly blinded by the glare. He blinked once, and then turned toward the Chamber of Hewn Stone. There was still so much work to be done.

CHAPTER 32

It was just after Ben had been named high priest, and less than three months since the clothes of mourning for Judah had been put aside, when Joshua requested a meeting with Caiaphas. He put forth his case eloquently and simply. Although Caiaphas put him off, saying that he would need to talk to Simon before making a determination that would affect the future of the man's daughter, it was more a formality than anything else. Martha and Joshua were betrothed in a simple ceremony at Caiaphas's estate. The guests were limited to those from the households of Simon and Annas, along with a handful of other high-ranking priests from the temple. Miriam, at fourteen, was old enough to attend her mother at the signing of the marriage contract. As soon as the proceedings were over, however, she retreated to Rivkah's side, where she remained for the rest of the afternoon, her big green-gold eyes taking in the scene with keen curiosity.

The promise of the union was of great comfort to Simon, who had with effort summoned the strength to attend the celebration, Julia by his side. As his oldest son, it was Eli who would inherit all that Simon had. With Judah's death, Martha had been left vulnerable as a widow without a male heir, despite the substantial wealth of her father and father-in-law's estates. Simon had no doubt that Caiaphas would care for both Martha and Miriam for as long as they remained members of his household. Still, the older priest was gratified to see his daughter joined with a man who had his own property and reputation, and was himself the heir of a great and learned member of the priesthood.

There had been only one concern in Caiaphas's mind when Joshua asked for Martha's hand in marriage. Clearing his throat, he chose his words with care. "Joshua, it is not unknown to me that for many years Gamaliel hoped you would one day ascend to the high priesthood." Joshua smiled a little sadly as he nodded, clearly remembering his father.

Caiaphas continued. "If our God were to allow it, a man like you could be just what we need to guide us through this dark chapter of our people's history, a leader not only learned but bold, willing to listen to reason but not easily swayed from his purpose." He sighed. "But our times are even more uncertain than they were while your father lived. Although we are fortunate to once again have a member of Annas's family installed in that position, there is no guarantee that any of us will be able to determine who next wears the high priest's robes."

Caiaphas paused, and shook his head slightly as he continued. "Still, you know the Scriptures as well as I do. You are aware that our law prohibits anyone joined in marriage with a widow from becoming high priest, no matter how prestigious her family or how virtuous her character. I do not mean to dissuade you from your petition. Assuming Simon is amenable, I am more than happy to welcome you into our family. But I do not wish for you to be hasty in choosing a bride over your duty to the temple, or in sacrificing your ambition for a decision you may later regret."

Joshua smiled again. This time there was something in his eyes that reminded Caiaphas of the way he had been when he first entered the priesthood, brimming with confidence and slightly surer of himself than his station appeared to deserve. "Yes, noble Caiaphas, I am indeed aware of the challenge my union with Martha might put on my future prospects. However, as you say, the times in which we find ourselves are not as they once were. I am confident that whatever God has for me, it will not be thwarted by my pledging myself to a woman as honorable as Martha. I am nonetheless grateful for your concern and your warning, which I know to be merely a sign of your care both for my wellbeing and for that of the priesthood." The conversation ended, but Caiaphas remained unsettled, certain that there was more to be said on the matter.

Several weeks after Martha and Joshua became engaged, Caiaphas received his letter from Gratus and found upon his return to the Chamber of Hewn Stone that an unsanctioned trial had taken place, with Ben presiding over the lives of the prisoners before him. Caiaphas lost no time in expressing his disapproval regarding these events both publicly and privately. He met with Simon, who remained too frail to attend council meetings, and shared Gratus's warning with select members of the priesthood, including Ben, Joshua, and Eli.

Ben would hear none of Caiaphas's concerns. The men in question had been scoundrels, former followers of the man Jesus, and had been stirring up division among the people of the city. Like his father before him, Ben was adamant that it was his responsibility to crush them, whatever the consequences. He had clearly decided to take full advantage of his time as high priest, even knowing that his impulsive behavior might lead to his removal or censure. He felt that Caiaphas of all people should see that his actions had been both justified and necessary.

Eli, who seemed to grasp far more than either Joshua or Ben the severity of the warning given by Gratus, cautioned Ben to heed Caiaphas's advice. A suggestion was made that Ben write a letter to Julius explaining what he had done, so that it would seem at least that he was not trying to hide his actions from the Roman king. But before a letter of this kind could be drafted and sent, a messenger arrived from Rome, this time announcing that a new Roman governor had been chosen and would be arriving at Caesarea before long. Festus's replacement, a man named Lucius, had been stationed in Alexandria, and would be traveling directly from that coastal city to the west. Assuming the traveling conditions remained fair, he would be in Caesarea within a week, and would endeavor to visit Jerusalem before too much time had passed.

Mercifully, by the time Lucius arrived, taking up temporary residence at Herod's Palace as his predecessors had done before him, Ben's tenure as high priest had already come to an end. Lucius's displeasure at the way Ben had conducted himself during his brief term, although not an auspicious beginning to the relationship between the new governor and the priesthood, was no longer a pressing concern. Caiaphas was only able to put together the events that had transpired to bring about Ben's removal as high priest after the fact. He remained astonished at the way it had been accomplished.

IT SEEMED that Joshua had been far more aware of the danger in which Ben had placed himself than he let on. After Caiaphas shared Gratus's warning, Joshua discussed the matter with Martha, who saw immediately that swift action was needed. She and Joshua went to see Simon the day after Caiaphas's own visit. While she accompanied her husband-to-be under the pretense of visiting her childhood home and paying a visit to Julia, Martha clearly had other things on her mind. Simon received Joshua and Martha in his private chamber, where they passionately bemoaned the fact that Ben's hasty actions would likely result in his deposition. Simon, who had always felt tenderly toward his daughter, listened avidly as she shared with him her fears regarding what would happen to the temple if the high priesthood was again wrenched away from the most prestigious families, perhaps for good this time. Martha painted a bleak picture of a group of priests unmoored, lost without the direction of a strong leader like Annas or Simon himself. Joshua, for his part, warned that Ben's indiscretion would only add ammunition to the Roman authorities' belief that the priesthood was in need of their increasing intervention and governance.

The two made an ardent and persuasive pair. By the time they departed, they had convinced Simon to write a letter to the Roman king Julius expressing his own concerns at Ben's behavior. The letter, which was accompanied by a number of expensive gifts, including a large quantity of newly pressed wine and several items of jewelry that had been in Simon's family for generations, questioned whether the emperor and his advisors would look kindly on a high priest operating autonomously and with inflated authority, and asked whether the inevitable disapproval from Rome might not also reflect badly on the regional king who had chosen the man. Simon's letter respectfully ended with the suggestion that the wisest course might be to remove Ben before any hint of the misconduct could make its way to either Rome or Caesarea. It put forth Joshua's name as a worthy replacement.

Ben was surprisingly sanguine when he received the official letter from Julius a few days later. Opening the parchment and reading swiftly, a rueful smile spread across his face. Ben chuckled as he looked across the top of the priests' heads for Joshua, whom he found in a corner conversing quietly with Eli. "I see you have done it, my friend." He shook his head as Joshua, looking mildly surprised, left his seat and approached Ben where he stood in the center of the Chamber of Hewn Stone, the council meeting having just ended. "It was only a matter of time before we two would find ourselves grappling for control of the high priesthood. Since childhood, I have always known that if there was anyone who could wrestle the bit and bridle from my hands, it would be you."

Joshua, who by now had reached him, took the letter from Ben's hand, and scanned its contents. As he reached the end, he raised his eyes. The twinkle in them belied his serious tone as he spoke. "Ah, but Ben, it is not a single animal we drive, but an entire temple and all those who gather within these walls. And you forget our place. We are not the masters, but the beasts of burden, pulling the weight of our people on our own broad shoulders. I only wish to share the labor, to yoke myself alongside you as we protect and defend the priesthood from forces both within and beyond the city gates."

Ben laughed at this, but Joshua's smile was small and thoughtful as he continued. "You and I will strive together to bring back the glory of the priesthood, to return Jerusalem to a time when our citizens did not feel the need to cower in corners. But we must be careful, and wait for the proper moment. We must learn from our elders, that there are ways and means of exerting power, and that often the tongue can be our most valuable weapon." He looked at Caiaphas, who stood a few feet from them, as he spoke. Caiaphas, who was not sure he deserved the implied compliment, was nonetheless impressed as always by Joshua's boldness and spirit.

Ben chuckled once more, and clapped Joshua on the back heartily. "Indeed, Joshua, it appears your tongue has done a great deal of work on your own behalf of late. I accept this news with whatever humility and grace I can muster. I pray that, as you say, your time as high priest will prove to be of service to us all."

The fact that Joshua and Martha's marriage had not yet been consummated meant that Joshua was still officially eligible for the appointment, a technicality that Caiaphas felt certain might nonetheless be a stumbling block for many members of the council. But he had not counted on the amount of respect and admiration Joshua had garnered through the years among the priesthood, nor the degree to which Gamaliel's reputation remained an influential part of his son's appeal. As Ben was willing to abide by Julius's decree to cede the high priesthood to Joshua, the rest of the priesthood followed his lead, and preparations began immediately for the transfer of power.

SIMON LIVED JUST LONG ENOUGH to see Joshua and Martha married, and to watch as Joshua received the breastplate and crown from the hands of Ben. The council had determined that, since Joshua's election by Julius was already made, and his eligibility decided, the restriction against his union with Martha was no longer relevant. Caiaphas remained uncertain as to whether this resolution, which was driven primarily by Eli and a small group of others, had been won through earnest wrestling with the minutiae of the law, or as a result of familial loyalty and strategic gifts. But he chose to keep silent. He was tempted to agree with Joshua that God had made a way, carving out an opportunity for a priest who was both capable and willing, and who had not yet offended their Roman allies. Joshua's actions, self-serving as they might have been, protected Ben from any consequences that might otherwise have come to him at the hands of the new governor. And the peaceful transition from Ben to Joshua meant that the house of Annas was able to maintain its honor and standing, if not its position of power, among the priesthood.

Although Martha had been a member of Caiaphas's household for over twenty-five years, Julia requested that her daughter's second wedding be held at Simon's estate due to her husband's failing health. It was a request Caiaphas and Rivkah were more than happy to grant. Julia and Rivkah spent the days before the wedding together from dawn until dusk, seeing to all of the details and making the necessary arrangements. The ten years between them were more obvious now, as Julia's eyesight had begun to fail. Her hands shook slightly as she examined various fabrics, feeling them between her thumb and fingers, trying to determine the best linen to be used for the matrimonial clothes. But the women's friendship, which had begun when Julia herself was a new bride, and had withstood so many births and deaths across the decades, remained strong. Upon arriving at Simon's estate on the morning of the ceremony, Caiaphas watched with pleasure as Rivkah and Julia sat together, Rivkah's dark and Julia's golden hair both intermingled with gray, the lines around their eyes crinkling with joy as they examined their handiwork.

The central courtyard of the estate had been decorated with poppies and lilies. The blooms and aromas of the scarlet and white flowers intermingled, permeating the air. The effect was wondrous to the senses, pungent even as Caiaphas knew it would be temporary. By the time the celebration ended, the wine drunk and the music only a memory, the blossoms too would have begun to wilt and droop, unable to sustain themselves away from the source of their potency. He thought of the Scriptures, which spoke of the fleeting beauty of the flowers of the field. "The grass withers, the flower fades, but the word of our God will stand forever." Sighing, he raised his eyes to the sky, where a few scattered clouds did little to shield the gathering guests from the sun's blistering rays.

It had been decided that Miriam would remain with Rivkah and Caiaphas after the wedding, to give Martha and Joshua the chance to establish their household together, and because the high priesthood would require much of Joshua, especially at the beginning of his term. An unintended benefit of the arrangement was that it also allowed Rivkah the opportunity to continue Miriam's lessons, both in weaving and in Scripture memorization and mathematics. Although Miriam had never attended school, and was past the age where a girl would normally receive such training, Rivkah felt strongly that a woman's mind needed to be honed as finely as her skill with a needle and thread. Caiaphas, who did not object, was nonetheless amused by his wife's vehemence.

"Joseph, there is no way to know what Miriam's future will hold. The more she is able to do and understand, the better. She is Martha's daughter, to be sure, captivating and lovely, with a strength of character beyond many twice her age. Losing her father was a blow." Rivkah's voice faltered for a moment. Caiaphas knew that it still pained her to think of Judah. "But I believe it will fortify her for whatever is ahead."

She sighed, and continued. "I confess I am surprised that the girl remains unspoken for, given both her beauty and her connections. But as long as I have the opportunity to keep her close, I will use it to improve her inner parts, as God has already seen to her exterior."

The three of them quickly settled into a peaceful rhythm that reminded Caiaphas of his own childhood. The house was larger and grander than the one in which he had lived as a boy, and Miriam was older than he had been before he and Hadassah lost Abel and were taken in by Annas. But otherwise the daily rituals felt oddly familiar, the quiet of the home a relief when Caiaphas returned each day from the council meeting. The temple was always full of people, with pilgrims and merchants constantly bustling through the outer courts, and priests going about the business of receiving offerings and sacrificing animals. As one of the older members of the council, Caiaphas had been relieved of many of the more arduous responsibilities of the priesthood. While he still participated in the ceremonial sacrifices during the festivals, his role had become primarily one of advisor and mentor to Joshua, Ben, Eli, and the others.

In the afternoons Caiaphas remained at home, going through his correspondence, walking the perimeter of his estate, and taking his evening meal with his wife and granddaughter. It was here that he received the news that Gratus had finally breathed his last, and also where he learned that Saul had run out of good will in Rome, and was gone, having maintained to his last breath an allegiance to the fallen rebel who had been the cause of so much trouble for Caiaphas and the priesthood.

After Joshua's appointment, Joshua and Ben quickly established a shared management of the temple that suited them both well. Whether they intentionally styled themselves after the stories they had heard of Joazar and Annas, Caiaphas did not know. But he could not help but see the similarities between the two partnerships. Joshua was equally as magnetic and charismatic as Annas had been in his prime. Within a few months he had welcomed both Lucius and Julius to Jerusalem, where his own charm, along with Martha's gregarious hospitality, was able to smooth over much of the tension with the Roman governor and king. Ben, who wisely kept his distance during these visits, tended to operate more covertly, his impulsiveness tempered by a clarity of purpose and understanding that Joazar would have appreciated.

For almost a year, it seemed that Joshua's prediction was prescient. A new era of peace might well be upon them. To Caiaphas, it felt as if the whole city was holding its collective breath. From the temple to the marketplace, people whispered that perhaps Joshua, the son of Gamaliel, was the one who would bring about freedom such as they had not seen in many generations. But then Rome began to burn, and with it, the harmony that had settled over Jerusalem dissolved like ash disturbed at the base of an altar, billowing up into the sky and mingling with the smoke's tendrils like so much dust.

CHAPTER 33

It was early summer and Joshua was still high priest when the first reports from Rome arrived that the city had been set on fire, by persons unknown. By the time a messenger arrived to say that the flames had finally been extinguished a week later, it was reported that nearly two thirds of Rome had been destroyed. Rumors in Jerusalem were rampant as to the cause of the fires. Every merchant in the marketplace and priest in the temple had their theory. Caiaphas received word that the grand house where Gratus had lived during the last years of his life had been reduced to ash. The atmosphere of fear and suspicion that spread across Rome quickly settled over Judea as well, as different factions interpreted the news of Rome's tragedy to suit their own plans and desires.

The zealots who littered both the countryside and the city had been quietly biding their time after the transition from Ben to Joshua. They saw the unrest in Rome as a sign that the Romans' power over the region was waning. They became bolder, gathering not only on street corners and in the marketplace of Jerusalem but even in the outer courts of the temple. They spoke of revolt, and began amassing secret arsenals of weapons, acquired through trade, purchase, or theft. These men were convinced that the partial destruction of Rome was a foreshadowing, and that it was only a matter of time before the tight grip that the Romans continued to exert on Judea would begin to loosen, either on its own or by force.

The priesthood as a whole continued to caution the people against any action that might appear rebellious or treasonous, maintaining that diplomacy and political alliances with the Roman governor and king were the best way to ensure the continued safety and security of the city and all who lived there. But even within the council there were disagreements as to the extent to which those in power could be trusted. Some of its more outspoken members began to ask whether a time might soon be coming when a different path would need to be taken.

Caiaphas's concern mounted steadily as he listened to those on the council bicker, both within the Chamber of Hewn Stone itself and in stolen moments in and around the temple. He had lived long enough to see the way this type of discord ended. If the Romans decided that the zealots in Judea were becoming too numerous or too rowdy, or if they saw revolutionary ideas spreading among the Jewish leadership, it would not be long before their legions would descend, filling not only the hilltops surrounding the city, but the streets themselves. His mother's words from when he was a child echoed in his ears. Only hours before they received the news of his father's death, Hadassah had cautioned that Roman soldiers brought peace at a bloody cost. It was a truth Caiaphas knew all too well. If it came to that, even the strongest fortifications would make no difference against those bent toward destruction.

He found himself thinking almost wistfully back to a time when it seemed that Jerusalem was growing stronger, not more vulnerable. Caiaphas had been deposed for a little under four years when Agrippa, who had been newly appointed by Rome, paid a visit to Jerusalem from his residence in Tiberias. While there, the king toured the city, exploring everything from the Pool of Siloam in the Lower City, to its northernmost parts, where homes had begun to be built far beyond the Second Wall as the population continued to grow and expand. At the time, Simon held the position of high priest. He and

Jonathan went to great lengths to make sure that Agrippa felt both welcomed and respected by the leadership of the temple, showering him with attention and gifts. Simon's son Eli, who was twenty-six years old at the time, served as part of this delegation along with Jonathan's brother Matthias, accompanying Jonathan to Herod's Palace where Agrippa was staying, and helping to host several dinners at his father's estate. Eli had grown into a young man of some renown, admired especially for his dexterity with the Scriptures and his ability to mend disagreements among his more excitable peers. Agrippa was understandably impressed with the young man.

Eli and his sister Martha, born four years apart, could not have been more different. Where she was determined, passionate, and occasionally stubborn, he was even-tempered, calm, and flexible. But despite their differences in temperament, the two remained close throughout their childhood and into adulthood. After Martha left her father's home to join the house of Caiaphas, Eli, who never married, found that he was often alone, as Julia and Simon both kept themselves busy with the management of their estate and temple affairs. But Eli did not mind the solitude. He spent much of his time at the temple himself, where he was one of the priests tasked with the education of the younger boys. When he was not occupied teaching or fulfilling his other temple responsibilities, he could sometimes be found walking along the perimeter of the temple, pacing the length of the walls from the Antonia Fortress to the north down to the southern end of the pathway where he could look out across the Lower City.

Caiaphas remembered well the day he and Judah found Eli near the northwest corner of the wall, gazing out at the building project taking place in the distance. Judah, at twenty-three, was still alive and thriving, a married man who had become a priest only a few years earlier. There remained a specter of weakness over him, and Caiaphas had to slow his pace slightly as they walked together. But the young man, whose curls shone in the afternoon sun, and whose hazel eyes looked eagerly at the scene before them, was clearly relishing his health and his last several years of good fortune.

As they approached, Eli turned and smiled, shifting to make room for them along the perimeter. Caiaphas followed his gaze beyond the fortress, past the Second Wall, to where he could just see in the distance the piles of rock and wood, and the columns of men hard at work, erecting scaffolding that would serve as their structure as they began construction. Their aim was a third wall of Jerusalem, which had been commissioned by Agrippa shortly after his visit. The wall would serve as protection for the city from the north, where Agrippa had determined it was most vulnerable. It was an ambitious and arduous endeavor. The sounds of metal striking hard ground, digging trenches that would provide additional protection outside the final walls, and wood being sawed apart by enormous blades, rang out and carried across the city. The din, which was undoubtedly deafening near the construction site, was soft and muffled from where they stood watching.

Caiaphas shook his head. "It remains a wonder to me that King Agrippa desires to bolster our city's defenses in this way. I would have thought that Agrippa would fear the emperor's opinion, that his master might be wary of a subject fortifying his own territory. Our previous experience has shown that Rome never looks kindly on anyone appearing to have power. Once built, this wall will serve as a sign of strength indeed."

Judah and Eli both nodded respectfully at Caiaphas. Eli looked thoughtful as he replied. "Agrippa seems desirous of harmony in our region, that much is certain. He has received our demonstrations of solidarity with gratitude. Perhaps he sees this wall as a way to further show our people that he is a friend to Jerusalem, and is confident enough in his standing with the emperor to take the risk. It may be that God has sent him to us like Hezekiah, to fortify our defenses against enemies that have not yet emerged."

Caiaphas smiled at Eli, whom he liked as well as respected. He was glad that his son had been blessed with not only a suitable wife, but a worthy brother-in-law as well. While Caiaphas and Simon's relationship remained strained after the events involving Jesus's arrest, he was nonetheless grateful that he had not allowed his own relationship with Simon to prohibit Martha and Judah's union from proceeding.

THE MEMORY CAME BACK to Caiaphas as he sat in the Chamber of Hewn Stone, listening to Eli try without success to urge the more passionate members of the council to remain calm. The news had just reached the priesthood that yet another change was being made in the governorship in Caesarea. Lucius was being replaced by a man named Florus. With Gratus no longer alive to send information to Caiaphas, the priesthood knew nothing about this new governor. They were discussing how best to welcome his arrival, worn but ready to ingratiate themselves to yet another Roman overseer of their territory.

It soon became clear that Florus's intention was not to bring about peace, but to exert his own power and demonstrate authority over his new subjects. Florus appeared to have no regard for either the temple or the priesthood. He refused to receive a delegation of priests at Caesarea. The first time he came to Jerusalem, he sent a small unit of soldiers to the temple, with orders to patrol the inner courtyards and report back on the activities going on there. Serving as representatives of the high priest, Ben and Matthias met the soldiers at the eastern gate, and explained that none but those who had been made ritually clean could enter beyond the outermost courtyard. The soldiers left after some discussion, but Florus was enraged upon their return. His retaliation was swift. By nightfall he had written to Julius demanding a change in temple leadership. Within days the response came in the form of a letter to the temple, deposing Joshua and handing the high priesthood over to another.

Florus had been governor for two years when he took the action that finally shattered the fragile equilibrium the fractured council had been fighting to maintain. In those two years, Florus had become well known for his habit of taking bribes, sometimes in the midst of a trial over which he was presiding. He released prisoners from jail in exchange for a portion of their future plunder, and continued to ignore pleas from the priesthood to allow them to meet with him to discuss how they might better work together to lead the people. In addition to his complete lack of respect for the temple, Florus appeared to have a lust for violence. Caiaphas found himself longing for the days when Felix held the governorship, as at least his assassins were discreet and targeted only those select members of society who were seen as a threat. Florus encouraged local groups across Judea to wreak havoc throughout the countryside, plundering towns and synagogues without fear of retribution or punishment from the Roman governor.

For the most part, though, Florus kept his distance from Jerusalem, and specifically from the temple, leaving the priests to continue their daily sacrifices and annual festivals in relative peace. When pilgrims flocked to the city several times a year on the holiest of days, Florus remained in Caesarea, content to smell the sea air and watch his coffers grow. But eventually his greed overcame his good sense, and he ordered his soldiers to return to the temple in Jerusalem, this time with instructions to raid the treasury and bring him back a bounty.

Like Pilate before him, Florus underestimated the resiliency and might of the Jewish people. An assault on the temple was an assault on God. As the money in the temple treasury had been largely provided by the citizens of Jerusalem, who gave out of their own purses whenever they visited the temple to worship or make sacrifices, it felt personal. The zealots found themselves flooded with new members. They rallied these troops and began plotting an attack. They sent most of the new volunteers north to Galilee, where their forces had centralized, but kept a substantial enough presence within the city to remain formidable. Caiaphas watched in horror as even priests began to abandon their responsibilities at the temple to participate in the rebellion. Those who remained began to question whether or not the priesthood should consider joining forces with the zealots in solidarity against the Roman governor. Ben, Joshua, and Eli, all of whom continued to counsel their fellow priests that a strategic alliance with the Romans remained the best course of action, found themselves increasingly outnumbered and unheeded.

Within days, the situation had become untenable. Rebels were crowding the streets, shouting at and threatening any Roman soldier who happened to pass. The entire city felt as if it were bubbling over like an angry iron kettle. Rivkah was deeply concerned that, if a fight broke out within the temple or its outer courtyards, Caiaphas would not have the fortitude necessary to escape without harm. Having just reached the completion of his seventh decade, Caiaphas was still a strong man. But he was no solider. She begged him to remain at their estate until the danger had passed. One look at her terrified face convinced him of the wisdom of this course. Ben assured him that the priesthood would keep him apprised of any news, either from the north or closer to home. Caiaphas spent his time in meditation and prayer, ceasing only to take the evening meal with Rivkah and Miriam, both of whom were anxious and on edge. Miriam's usual lively charm was dampened by the tense atmosphere, and she glanced back and forth between her grandparents, her eyes worried and dark. They ate in silence, their ears straining for any sign of a messenger's footsteps. By the second day the lack of news was stifling.

IT WAS on the third day that Eli arrived, looking haggard and worn. He sank into a seat by the fire that had just been lit in one of the courtyards, and gratefully accepted the mug of spiced wine that Miriam brought to him. He took a long drink, sighed, and turned to face Caiaphas and Rivkah, who were eagerly awaiting his news.

He spoke quietly. "The zealots have done what no one thought possible. The Romans have been removed from Jerusalem."

Caiaphas took a step back, and shook his head. "Removed? What do you mean, Eli?"

Eli looked as surprised as Caiaphas felt as he continued. "There was a riot, near the temple. The zealots have a greater force than we understood, Caiaphas. Among their number they include some of our own priests and the young men we have been training at the temple. They marched to Herod's Palace and lay claim to it, taking down any Roman soldiers who crossed their path. The Romans who survived the attack escaped through the Tower Gate and fled north. They are gone."

Caiaphas sat down hard beside his brother-in-law, and exhaled long and low before speaking again. "They are not gone for long, Eli. The Romans will not tolerate this kind of insurrection."

Eli nodded. "I know, and I agree. But there is more." He paused and looked up at Rivkah, who had drawn closer to the two men and was listening expectantly. "After the zealots routed the Roman soldiers, a delegation of them marched to the temple, and confronted the priests who remained there, dutifully continuing to pursue our obligations in spite of the chaos raging beyond the temple walls. The leader of the zealots insisted that he was now the rightful leader of our people, given his triumph over the Romans, and demanded the high priest's garments. To their credit, his own followers immediately balked at this. A skirmish broke out in the Women's Court. Theo and the rest of the temple guard quickly brought an end to the fighting. The zealot leader was killed by Theo's hand as the man tried to enter the inner sanctuary of the temple, to claim it for his own."

Rivkah and Caiaphas exchanged glances, but remained silent as Eli continued. "In the minutes that followed, it became clear that the zealots had no great love of their leader. As much as they had fought fiercely and powerfully at Herod's Palace, they seemed uncertain as they stood flanked by the temple guard, murmuring amongst them-selves and eying the priests with suspicion. Ben, who had been watching the skirmish from the southern tower, saw his opening. Making his way toward the entrance of Nicanor's Gate, he stepped forward and began to speak."

A look of wonder flashed across Eli's face. "It may be that, like the prophet Isaiah, our God put the words into Ben's mouth. Everyone from the youngest rebels, no more than boys, to the eldest members of our council grew silent and listened. Facing the destruction before him, the wounded men and the priests with their faces flushed and their robes askew, Ben spoke with power and warmth. He called for unity among our people, joined as we are against a common enemy. He cautioned that the Romans would not be content to allow this victory to stand, that this was not the end but the beginning of the battle. He proclaimed that the only way forward would be to stand as one."

Caiaphas smiled ruefully. "So he has taken to heart Joshua's advice regarding the wisdom of the tongue. And what is the result?"

Rivkah leaned forward, her hand on Caiaphas's shoulder. He could feel the tension in her fingers as Eli answered, looking at her.

"Your brother Ben has been appointed to lead the rebellion, to bring zealots and the priesthood together against the Romans, with Joshua serving as his second in command. I believe their hope in grasping power is to bring the zealots under the council's control. But I fear the damage has already been done. The Romans will pay no heed to anyone, priest or zealot, once the news of this rebellion reaches Caesarea and Rome."

Caiaphas rose to his feet as Rivkah took a step back, and together they all stood looking at the fire, which was now merrily blazing before them. Miriam, who had gone to fetch more wine, had drawn near to them in time to hear the end of this conversation. Rivkah took her hand and held it reassuringly. Caiaphas shook his head. It was lunacy, to think that the priests would be able to control the zealots, or that the Romans would be willing to listen to any kind of plea for leniency or pardon after the events of the last several days. Still, he had seen stranger things than these come to pass. Only time would reveal what God had in store. When he spoke, it was with determination. "If any men can bring these zealots to their senses, it is Ben and Joshua. We will pray for their success, and hope for a miracle."

CHAPTER 34

The miracle never came. When the Romans returned, it was with brutal and decisive force. The legions gathered in Ptolemais to the north, and struck first in the region of Galilee, where the zealots had established their base of operations. The city of Capernaum, which sat at the northern end of the Sea of Galilee, was hardest hit. Many of the rebels were captured. The slain bodies of those who fell drifted across the sea and into the mouth of the Jordan River, traveling downstream and gruesomely announcing the massacre to those who lived along its shores. Alarmed, Ben and Joshua gathered the council and the zealots who remained in Jerusalem, trying to determine the next course of action. Contentious and passionate, the two groups went back and forth as to whether they should attempt to provide military support for their allies or stand firm in Jerusalem. Joshua was ultimately able to convince all those present that the wisest course would be to remain in the city and prepare for the battle to come to them. The zealots lost no time in organizing companies of tradesmen to bolster and fortify the third wall, which Agrippa had not been able to fully complete during his reign, so that the northern border of the city would be as impenetrable as possible when the time came. Then they waited.

What they had not bargained for were the fleeing refugees from the remaining zealot forces, who reached the city within days and were ushered in and taken to the temple immediately. The men who arrived were worn and embittered, their cloaks torn and their feet bloody. Caiaphas, who continued to remain at his estate but received regular visits from Eli, could picture them as they climbed the steps leading up to the Court of the Israelites, their eyes rimmed with red and haunted by the things they had witnessed. He imagined their faces as they looked around at their fellow zealots, still healthy and whole, and at the priests who continued to maintain the regular operations of the temple, the cycle of sacrifice and offering the only thing sullying their otherwise perfectly white robes.

"They are angry, Caiaphas." Eli's brow was furrowed and he paced in short, clipped circles as he spoke. Caiaphas could feel the younger man's worry and fear as he moved, and then he stopped abruptly, turning to face Caiaphas. "They feel they were abandoned in their time of need. The dying screams of their fellow rebels echo in their ears, calling for revenge. There are even whispers among our priesthood that some of the zealots believe the council is secretly working with the Romans to suppress the rebellion."

Caiaphas raised his head in alarm, but Eli put up a hand to stop him and continued. "I know it to be a falsehood, spread by jealous, angry men. But I fear that Ben and Joshua may be in danger if enough of them are convinced. You know more than most that the priesthood has for many generations worked closely with the Romans to establish and maintain peace. Yet our true loyalty has always been with our own people. I dearly hope our former association will not be our undoing." He paused. "The temple has become a dangerous place, Caiaphas, rather than the haven of refuge and holiness it once was."

Caiaphas sighed deeply. But when he spoke his voice was resolute and firm. "Ben and Joshua are gifted leaders, Eli. Both have worn the high priest's robes, as you have, with honor. At times our people forget the sacrifices we make to follow God into the priesthood." His thoughts flew unbidden to the death of his mother, and how he had resisted the temptation to mourn her passing in favor of the obligation to complete the rites of dedication. "But we have been chosen to stand as intercessors between a holy God and the men, women, and children who fill our streets and inhabit the dwellings of our city and beyond. The temple is our home, more than any estate or land we might possess. The Scriptures tell us to guard our steps when we go into the house of God. It is my prayer that these men you speak of will adhere to this mandate, and that cooler heads will prevail."

Eli nodded, although he still looked grave and ill at ease. He did not stay for the evening meal, but returned to the estate he shared with his mother Julia, who became anxious if he was gone too long into the evening. Martha was with them, having joined her mother and brother just after the first news of the attack in Galilee. Joshua was spending most of his time at the temple, and he and Martha had agreed that she would be safest and most comfortable near her own family. Miriam, who had lived with Rivkah and Caiaphas in the years since her mother's wedding, remained with her grandparents. The arrangement suited them all well. Judah's death had created a powerful bond between his mother and his daughter. Rivkah and Miriam seemed at times more like mother and daughter themselves than women separated by fifty years and two generations. Watching them together by the fire in the evenings, Caiaphas imagined he was seeing Tova and Rivkah as they had been when he was a boy, smiling and laughing together as they bundled herbs or pressed dried grapes and dates into cakes.

That night, Caiaphas dreamed again of the girl and the mountain path. This time he thought he could almost make out the outline of her profile as she clambered up the rocks ahead of them. Although her hair and manner reminded him strikingly of his own granddaughter, he could not be sure. Nor could he fathom why the two of them would be so far from Jerusalem, unaccompanied and on foot. He tried to climb faster to reduce the distance between them. But before he could do so, the vision was gone, replaced by the one that had haunted him since childhood. As he watched the temple burning, the flames lapped the facade of the sanctuary, melting the gold that adorned its eastern wall so that it looked as if the entire front face of the building were weeping. And then he was awake, left with a sinking feeling that remained long after the dreams had faded away.

Two more days passed before Eli returned to them again. The previous night, there had been a terrible storm. The rain poured down, causing rivulets of muddy water to swirl in and around the outer courtyards of Caiaphas's estate. But by morning the sky had cleared and the sun emerged. By midday the air was warm and the ground dry. Caiaphas, Rivkah and Miriam had just finished a meal of fish and lentils, food Miriam had prepared with the herbs she and Rivkah had been drying and storing. She had become an accomplished cook under her grandmother's tutelage, and possessed a natural ability for choosing complementary and unexpected flavors. It was she who had discovered that the garlic plants that grew in one of their gardens held bulbs beneath the halo of purple flowers, which could be roasted and used to season the bread and lentils they prepared.

Rivkah and Miriam were gathering the remnants of the meal when suddenly Eli was steps away from them, having entered through one of the back gates of the estate directly behind the courtyard in which they had been dining. His appearance startled both women, who immediately left what they were doing and hastily crossed the distance between them. Eli's face was covered in dried mud. His garments were soiled, both by dirt and what appeared to be blood. He was holding one arm as if injured, and he walked with a limp. When he lifted his downcast face to look at the others, they could see immediately that his eyes were full of tears.

"Eli." Rivkah gently took his arm and led him to the table, which still held the remains of their meal. Miriam poured a mug of wine and thrust it into Eli's trembling hands. He took it gratefully, and drank deeply before putting it down on the table and turning to face them all. Caiaphas, who had been stoking the fire when Eli first appeared, still held the bronze shovel in his hand, although he abandoned the task as soon as he heard the fear in his wife's voice. He drew closer to Eli, his heart sinking with each step.

When Eli spoke, his voice was small and pained. "The temple has fallen. Ben and Joshua have been murdered. The zealots have chosen their own high priest, if you can call him that, a young man unknown to the priesthood named Phineas whom they selected themselves by casting lots." He looked up at Caiaphas, and the anguish covered every inch of his face. "We are finished, betrayed and vanquished by our own countrymen. Our people have turned in on themselves like hungry dogs. Nothing can save us now." With these words, Eli sank down, his head in his hands. The tears he had been keeping at bay burst forth, landing in large, fat drops on the ground before him.

Caiaphas felt as if a great wind had knocked him over, as if the storm that had come and gone the previous night had caused irreparable damage to his own body rather than merely to the few trees that had toppled due to the heavy rains. He found that he too was unable to stand. He sank down next to Eli, looking up at both Rivkah and Miriam, who remained rooted to the spot. The silence stretched, punctuated only by Eli's sobs, and the rustling of his cloak as he rocked gently back and forth. Eventually his breathing slowed, his tears ceased, and he was able to share with them all that had happened in the two days he had been away.

On the first day, the zealots within the temple revolted, taking over the sanctuary building and refusing entry to all but their own. Ben and Joshua immediately met with Theo and several other members of the temple guard. Although Theo was in favor of storming the sanctuary and taking the zealots by force, Ben and Joshua both argued that it would not honor God for there to be fighting within the sacred inner chambers of the temple, where the zealots would surely retreat if threatened. A compromise was reached. Theo and his guard set up a perimeter around the sanctuary so that the zealots could not go in or out. The idea was to hold fast until the insurgents realized they were trapped, and at that point to begin a peaceful negotiation.

What the priesthood did not know was that, before taking hold of the sanctuary, the zealots had sent a message to another faction of their forces that lived south of Jerusalem, calling for their help as part of the planned revolt. This group, called the Idumeans, strongly believed that the Romans were a scourge to the Jews, enemies who needed to be rooted out of the land. Anyone who sided with the Romans for any reason was considered by them to be a traitor. It was all too easy for the zealots to enlist their help against the priesthood.

Fortunately, Caiaphas's brother-in-law Matthias had continued to serve in the treasury despite the shifts in power and organization that had befallen the temple, and as such interacted with both zealots and priests on a regular basis. It was he who overheard the plot to enlist the Idumeans' aid. When the sanctuary was taken and he realized that the information was more than mere talk, he went directly to Ben and Joshua. Half of the temple guard was quickly dispatched to the southern gates of the city to deny the Idumeans entry if they arrived. The night of the storm, the temple guard was divided, with half of their number patrolling the city gates while the other half kept watch at the temple. As the storm raged, Ben and Joshua retreated to the Chamber of the Hearth with several priests including Eli, to prayerfully petition God for a swift resolution to the standoff. Ben saw the continuing storm as God's answer, demonstrating the might of his power, which undoubtedly would stand with the priesthood.

Unfortunately, the weather proved to be more of a problem for the priests than for the zealots. In the darkness, and under the cover of a cloudy and rain-soaked sky, several zealots were able to sneak past the priests keeping watch outside the sanctuary. These men made their way to a northern gate within the temple grounds, one that was usually reserved for priests leaving and entering the city, as on the Day of Atonement when a sacrificial animal was led into the wilderness. The temple guard had not thought to protect this entrance. They had no way of knowing that the zealot allies had changed course when they realized the southern gates were barred to them, and had traveled north through the Kidron Valley to this very spot. The priests did not know that there had been a breach in their patrol until the

Idumean rebels were already upon them, the enemy's weapons making swift work of the exhausted and outnumbered members of the guard.

Theo, who along with several others had been standing watch outside the Chamber of the Hearth where Ben, Joshua and Eli had settled for the night, was seriously wounded almost immediately. He managed to hold off the Idumean rebels long enough for the other priests to escape the chamber and attempt to make their escape. Eli turned back to help Theo. In the chaos, he was able to drag him to safety under the eaves at the northwest corner of the temple grounds, where Caiaphas had once overheard a stolen conversation between Annas and Simon. There they remained, shrouded in darkness and aided by the sound of the rain that continued to fall, even as the dawn began to break through the clouds. There was just enough light for the two men, huddled together as Theo tried to catch his breath, to see Ben and Joshua, who had been attempting to leave the temple through the gate just east of the Chamber of the Hearth, apprehended by the Idumean rebels and dragged out of sight toward the Priests' Court.

Eli shook his head in disbelief as he continued to relay his story, and Caiaphas could tell that he was wrestling with himself even as he spoke. "Theo wanted to keep fighting, to go after Ben and Joshua and find a way to free them. But he was injured, more than he wanted to admit. I knew that my first priority had to be to get him to safety." Eli looked beseechingly at Caiaphas, as if seeking support for his decision. "We moved swiftly out the northwestern gate and crept across the terrace toward the Court of the Gentiles, where we were able to slip down into the Upper City."

The tears returned to Eli's eyes as he continued. "The last thing we heard as we were leaving the temple was Ben's voice, thunderous and proud, denouncing the zealots and declaring that our God would contend with any who took arms against his chosen representatives. And then there was a terrible, strangling cry, and silence." Eli bowed his head.

No one spoke for a long moment. Then Eli continued, his voice shaking. "We made our way to Julia's estate as quickly as we could, given Theo's condition, and were greeted by Julia and Martha, who immediately began treating his wounds and preparing a draught for him. He has lost much blood, but I believe he will recover.

"While I waited, I paced the exterior courtyard. It was there that young Samuel, one of Theo's newest recruits to the temple guard, found me. The boy had been tasked with patrolling the upper perimeter of the temple overnight. From that vantage point he witnessed all that took place before slipping out the same way Theo and I made our escape. It was he who confirmed that Ben had been struck down, and Joshua beside him, and that the zealots had chosen a young man from among their ranks, placing on him the ceremonial garments of the high priest and instructing him to stand on the steps that lead up to the sanctuary, a profane token of their victory. As Samuel crept down the staircase leading to the main level, the surviving zealots and their allies were gathered in the temple court-yard, shouting and celebrating. He was able to slip away without anyone noticing."

Eli turned to his niece, and his voice was sad but tender. "Miriam, your mother is heartbroken at Joshua's death. But it seems that the two of them were not unprepared for the possibility. When I told her the news, she shared that they had discussed the danger of his remaining at the temple before she moved to my mother's house. They determined that his duty lay with the priesthood, no matter the outcome. She is resigned but proud of his sacrifice." He shook his head, glancing at Rivkah and Caiaphas. "Martha is a wonder. A weaker woman would have crumbled at the loss of one husband, but my sister has always been strong, in prosperity and hardship alike. Now twice widowed, I have no doubt she will endure this loss as she did Judah's passing, with grace and dignity."

Taking a deep breath, Eli slowly pulled himself to his feet and faced Caiaphas, as if remembering his own duty. "Before I came here, I dispatched Samuel, giving him the unfortunate task of delivering the news of Ben's death to his wife. The remaining members of our priesthood have scattered. Julia is prepared to house any priests who wish to remain together rather than returning to their homes, which may no longer be safe. Matthias is missing, but if he lives, I imagine he will soon make his way either here or to Julia's estate." He sighed deeply. "The threat of the Roman invasion still looms before us. Without the temple, I fear we may already be lost."

Caiaphas shook his head, still reeling. He could scarcely believe it. All his life, he had endeavored to be a man who relentlessly sought greater understanding. From the hours he had spent as a boy listening with rapt attention to Annas and other council members debate, to his years as high priest himself, some of his greatest joys had come when he was able to unlock a particularly vexing puzzle, to grasp the meaning or purpose behind a word or deed. His father-in-law had found him reluctant to act as a result, and had labeled this weakness. But Caiaphas believed his desire to fully comprehend was a gift from God, aided uniquely by the visions he had been given in order to catch glimpses of what was to come.

Yet he could make no sense of the world in which he now found himself. The Romans had been the enemy for as long as he could remember. But the way to do battle with them had always been with words, with flattery and reassurances, with wit and wisdom. The zealots, rebels, revolutionaries, and other troublemakers were also a constant, crying for freedom and proclaiming the name of one leader after another, the faces and names varying but the methods and motives remaining unchanged. Now, however, the zealots were not only warring amongst themselves but had attacked the priesthood, causing death and destruction within the temple walls, while the Romans bore down on them all like wolves hungry for a kill.

Rising as well, Caiaphas put a hand on Eli's shoulder. In his early fifties, Eli was no child. But Caiaphas still thought of him as the young man who had watched from the rooftop of the temple as the third wall of Jerusalem went up. Eli's earnest belief at the time that the fortification might be called into service against a future enemy seemed painfully prescient now. The hour was fast approaching when every resource Jerusalem had at its disposal would be required to defend against the impending threat.

When Caiaphas spoke, his voice was halting, as he grasped at a hope that felt insufficient for the moment. "I do not pretend to know God's plan in all of this, Eli. And yet, the words of Zephaniah echo in my ears. In ages past, the prophet spoke of a future time when judgment would befall those who desecrated the house of God. Remember that our Scripture tells of a day when foreigners and those who fill the temple with violence and fraud will be punished alike, when a mighty man will cry aloud, when Jerusalem will be searched and the complacent laid to waste. He warned of a day of wrath, of distress and anguish, ruin and devastation, clouds and thick darkness. And how is this not the time in which we find ourselves, with Ben the son of Annas crying out at the moment of his death, honoring our God with his last breath? The storm that allowed the zealots entry to our city may yet be a sign of a tempest still to come, one that will bring with it a new day.

"I confess I know not how this redemption might come, nor to whom we can look for our deliverance. But our God is mightier than my understanding. We have no choice now but to wait for his hand to show itself." He sighed. "Come. Bathe yourself and take some fresh clothing. Let Rivkah tend to whatever wounds you have ignored in your rush to rescue Theo. Then you may remain with us or return to your mother's estate as you see fit."

Eli looked grateful, and he nodded. The four of them turned as one to move into the inner chambers of the estate, eager to escape the midday heat that had quickly become stifling as the clouds continued to melt away.

CHAPTER 35

When the Idumean forces discovered that the priesthood had not in fact been plotting alongside the Romans, the knowledge irrevocably shattered the alliance between them and the zealots. Disgusted at the way they had been manipulated and used, many of them abandoned the cause and fled the city, leaving in their wake crippling enmity among those who remained. The surviving zealots and members of the priesthood were left to pick up the pieces, to attempt an uneasy but essential fellowship, as the threat of a Roman invasion continued to loom large. The following months crept slowly by, the peaceful blue summer sky and bright sunlight incongruous with the constant worry that at any moment the Roman legions might descend from where they had set up camp in Caesarea. Priests and merchants became soldiers overnight, and were pressed into service as the city readied for an attack. Amidst the heat and fear, a rumor began to spread that the emperor Nero, who was said to have become increasingly unhinged and manic since the fires in Rome, had taken his own life. The Roman general Vespasian, who had been placed in charge of the assault against Jerusalem, appeared to fall back, awaiting orders until he knew to whom he would now be pledging his allegiance and his sword.

During these uncertain months, the surviving members of the priesthood set up their own headquarters at the former home of Annas, where Theo and Matthias still lived with their families. Matthias, whom it was revealed had been smuggled out of the treasury by a handful of zealots loyal to him, remained in hiding for several days. He eventually resurfaced as Eli had predicted, at the doorstep of Caiaphas's estate. Matthias was weak with hunger, and heartbroken to learn of his brother and Joshua's deaths, especially because their bodies, which had been dragged from the city by the Idumeans, had not been recovered for burial. But he was far too practical a man to allow his grief to get in the way of what must now be done. Within weeks he and Theo and their wives had turned their estate into a place where the priesthood could gather to meet, pray, and plan, and where those with nowhere else to go could remain for as long as was necessary. A dozen priests, including the young man Samuel, joined them. In the evenings, the estate's courtyard was filled with the boisterous sound of voices and the pleasant aromas of bread, stew, and wine. Matthias's wife Hannah was kept busy replenishing the plates that emptied almost as soon as they were filled. The roof was lined with sleeping mats, as the younger priests found spare corners to settle in for the night. Caiaphas was gratified to know that his father-in-law's estate had again become a place of refuge, as it had been for him so many years before.

Once Theo recovered, one of his first acts was to meet with the zealots who still held the temple, in an attempt to see if they might be able to reconcile their differences and reach an agreement that would allow them to work together against their common enemy. Despite the atrocities that had been committed against the temple and the priesthood by the zealots' hands, there was no question that the only possible chance for victory against the Romans lay in a unified effort. Theo was determined to honor the memory of those who had been lost by finding a way forward. The zealots, who had suffered casualties as well, and had been made significantly more vulnerable by the loss of their Idumean allies, were willing to negotiate.

Eventually, Theo and the zealot leaders came to an agreement. The priests would be allowed to empty the temple of its most sacred resources, including the majority of livestock, grain, linens, and select items from the treasury. The zealots, who were not willing to relinquish the temple itself, agreed to remain only in its outer parts, leaving the sanctuary itself unoccupied and undefiled. On the appointed day, Theo and Matthias brought a small delegation to the temple. While the zealots watched, they wrangled sheep and loaded bull calves with bolts of fabric and sacks of barley, along with precious instruments that had been fiercely protected by members of the priesthood since the temple had been consecrated. All of this was taken back to Annas's estate, where it was dispersed across several of the great houses still remaining.

Eli took most of the items from the treasury, which he and Martha put away in an underground room of their estate normally intended for stockpiling food and wine. They packed the most precious pieces, including the golden lampstands and ornaments, into reed baskets and stone water jars, in the hopes that a raiding army might overlook such commonplace vessels, giving them a greater chance for recovery should the worst befall their property. Julia, who was now nearly blind and in failing health, nonetheless sat by them as they worked, offering advice and ideas for further concealment.

Caiaphas was given the livestock and feed, and turned two of his estate's four exterior courtyards into pens for the animals. After several days, he and Rivkah became accustomed to their presence. The change to their daily routine was negligible, other than the feeding and clearing of muck, which had to be removed regularly. Miriam was especially charmed by the lambs, and the way they cavorted together until chastised by the rams in their midst. It was a small pleasure to have milk readily available, to which Rivkah added honey and spices. The soft bleats and snorts of the young calves reminded Caiaphas of the goats and sheep his mother had once tended and cherished. The grain and wine from the temple remained with Theo and Matthias and their households. Small amounts were dispersed as needed to any who required them.

So it was they remained for almost a year, as the seasons came and went, and with them the festivals that had once consumed the priesthood's entire existence. Without access to the temple, the daily rites of sacrificial offering became impossible. Still, each morning, a group of priests gathered in the courtyard of Annas's estate, where they would make a single grain offering, praying to God to return them to the temple as soon as possible, so that another day would not go by without them performing the sacred responsibilities to which they had been assigned.

In the year that passed, no fewer than four men wrangled bitterly for the emperor's crown. All the while, Vespasian remained in Caesarea, training his troops and biding his time. As the rainy season began in earnest, turning the skies of Jerusalem a murky gray that seeped into the hearts and minds of the city's inhabitants, it seemed as if there would never be an end to the waiting, to the dreaded anticipation of what was to come. Then the news came that none other than the Roman general himself had been selected as emperor. A heightened sensation of terror spread throughout the city as the news passed from priest to merchant to midwife.

Vespasian was the father of two sons, the younger of whom remained in Rome and had been instrumental in leading the forces that championed Vespasian's selection as emperor. His elder son was a soldier named Titus. Titus had fought boldly alongside his father in Judea, and was known for his determination and skill with a weapon. It was to this accomplished and impassioned young man that Vespasian gave over his troops as he departed for Rome to fulfill a different kind of destiny, leaving behind orders to waste no time in finishing what he had started.

The first attack came in the spring, just as the poppies began to bloom. The tiny, blood-red blossoms dotted the landscape surrounding the city, their petals curving gently toward the sun. It was the time of the Feast of Unleavened Bread. After some negotiation, Eli had convinced the zealots to allow the priests to use the temple for the sacrifice of the lambs. Many pilgrims who had been keeping away from the city journeyed to Jerusalem for the festival, to find comfort in the familiar scent of roasting meat and to see the priests in their holy garments, sacrificing and worshiping within the temple walls. Their prayers had an increased sense of urgency this year, as they raised their voices to the heavens, calling on God as the people's help and shield, crying out for deliverance.

And then the news came that the city had been closed without warning, that soldiers stood guard at every gate prepared to kill or capture any who tried to escape. Roman legions gathered north of the city, their battering rams aimed at the third wall. It took fifteen days for the invading army to break through, compelling the city's forces to withdraw behind the second wall and abandon the northern part of the city, where the Romans quickly set up camp. Every able-bodied man in Jerusalem was now armed. It was not uncommon to see zealots, priests and tradesmen patrolling together, daggers at the ready.

Another week and the Romans breached the second wall, although this time the forces that met their attack were ready for them. The battle was fierce, the clanging of swords and the cries of dying men ringing out on both sides of the barricade. By the end of it, two of Theo's three sons were among the fallen. It was hard to find a household in Jerusalem that did not mourn at least one among their number, and the Romans suffered profound losses as well. By the time the second wall had fallen and the citizens of Jerusalem were forced to retreat to the Upper City, Titus determined that it would take more than merely weapons to complete his mission.

Undeterred, the Roman general quickly shifted his strategy. While those within the city tended to the wounded and mourned the dead, and Matthias and Hannah continued to mete out supplies to those whose resources were running low, Titus ordered his Roman legions to construct a temporary wall around the entire perimeter of the city. The wall, which encircled both Jerusalem and the neighboring hills and valleys, was heavily guarded, effectively cutting off both communication and commerce with those outside Jerusalem. Titus's plan was to starve the city of both food and resources, weakening the people's defenses before embarking on a final invasion. The strategy proved to be brutally effective.

As the weeks wore on, the days bled into one another. The heat radiated through the dry, dusty streets, permeating even the underground ritual bath where Caiaphas regularly sought solace. Each day brought news of a skirmish or death from injuries sustained in battle. Rations and other supplies began to run dangerously low across the city. Rivkah was down to her last few measures of grain, which she and Miriam attempted to stretch by preparing porridge made of ground barley, water, and salt. The livestock they continued to tend had become greatly reduced in number. The animals that remained were thin and haggard, as even their feed was in short supply.

On the tenth week of the siege, the Antonia Fortress, the mighty stronghold that had been built by Herod the Great himself, and that now sat directly between Titus's camp and the temple, was attacked by Roman soldiers. The battle began under the cover of darkness, and continued into the day as the zealots fought fiercely to push the foreign army back. Eventually the zealots were forced to abandon the attempt and retreated into the temple, determined at least to keep the Romans from making any more forward progress.

That night, Caiaphas and Rivkah sat beside a dying fire, quietly conferring as they watched the embers glowing before them. Miriam was already asleep. The night seemed unnaturally peaceful, a summer breeze flitting across the courtyard and gently rustling the folds of their tunics. Rivkah was shaking her head, her face anxious as she looked at her husband. "We are nearly out of food, Joseph. We must go to my brothers and ask for more, while it is still possible to do so."

She put up a hand to stop him from interrupting. "I know they are wisely holding grain and wine in anticipation of a longer siege. But we will not be here to see it if we waste away from hunger ourselves. If not for me, or for yourself, think of your granddaughter. Miriam does not complain, but her body gives her away. I have heard her stomach grumbling morning to night as she goes about her chores. Her face is pale and pinched. She needs more than just gruel to sustain herself."

Caiaphas sighed. He worried that the streets were not safe, and that at any moment the fighting to the north and east might spill into the Upper City, threatening all who were not sequestered safely in their homes. But he knew his wife was right, and that they were more fortunate than most, with relatives willing to share what they had. He sighed again, resigned. "I do not disagree, Rivkah. For what use is bread but to feed the hungry, wine if it is not consumed by those who thirst?"

He patted her hand, and smiled. "In the morning I will take two of our calves and go to your brothers, bringing one as a gift and the other to carry back my bounty. I will not return until I have ample provisions for our household."

She returned the smile and took his hand in hers. "Thank you, my love. You must know that I long to see my brothers with my own eyes, to greet their wives, and to hear the latest news directly from their lips. I have been penned in for many weeks now, and would relish the chance to walk freely through the streets on this errand. But I know that in these perilous times, one of us must stay behind with Miriam." She pressed his hand to her lips, holding it tightly and closing her eyes as she kissed it, her mouth soft against his skin.

The next morning, Caiaphas awoke to find that Rivkah was gone, having taken the two calves herself. She had begun to make her way through the streets between her brothers' estate and their own just as the sun broke over the horizon. Shaking his head at her tenacity and stubbornness, he relished the thought that Theo and Matthias would surely chide Rivkah when she arrived alone. He was comforted by the fact that he knew they would not send her home unaccompanied.

Caiaphas smiled ruefully as he thought of his wife. Though the years had turned Rivkah's raven hair a silvery grey, she remained as beautiful as ever, her dark eyes deep and rich as the finest wine. He imagined her walking purposefully along, the top of her head shimmering in the glow of the rising sun, happily anticipating a reunion with her brothers in the house she had once called home.

By MIDDAY, it became clear that something was happening in the city. Shouts could be heard echoing from the north, and a distant smell of smoke wafted in through the open air. Miriam and Caiaphas were just sitting down to a meal when they heard the voice, the strangled cry of a young man, and hard footsteps pounding against the ground. Samuel broke through the central entrance of the estate, gasping for breath, his tunic covered in soot and his eyes red and streaming. He bent over, coughing heavily, and as soon as he could catch his breath, he retreated back through the doorway. When he returned a moment later, he was leading one of the calves that Rivkah had taken, a rope tied loosely around its neck. Slung across the animal's back was Rivkah, her body bent and slack, her hair hanging loose and her tunic scorched and torn.

Samuel looked up at Caiaphas, and Caiaphas saw for a moment his own pain and disbelief reflected back in the young man's face. Behind him, Miriam let out a choked sob. She rushed forward to her grandmother's body, placing her hands on Rivkah's back as if willing her to rise up, to be revived. Caiaphas, who had not moved from the spot where he stood, looked beseechingly at Samuel, his eyes asking the question his lips could not form.

When Samuel spoke, his voice was hoarse and raw. "Noble Caiaphas, the house of Annas has been destroyed, set ablaze by Roman soldiers who have breached the northern wall of the Upper City. I do not know where Theo or Matthias or any of the others are. I had been sent on an errand and returned to find the estate in flames, one wall already collapsed and the others in danger of crumbling."

Another coughing fit overcame him, and he paused to collect himself before continuing. "Over the sound of the crackling fire, I thought I heard a calf's terrified bleating. As I tried to make my way closer, I saw through the smoke and rubble a woman's body, lifeless but preserved just within the front vestibule of the estate. I was able to pull the body to safety, the calf following me as I emerged from the building just as the front entrance fell." He stopped again. His eyes were filled with tears as he gazed at Miriam, her head now bent over Rivkah's body, silently weeping. "When I saw who it was I carried, I knew I had to bring her to you, to grant you the privilege so many of our people have been denied, to bury your dead." His voice broke. "I am so sorry I was not able to save her." And then he was weeping himself, his tears flowing freely, as he looked at Caiaphas with regret and dismay.

Caiaphas stood staring at the young man before him, at his granddaughter stretched across his wife's lifeless body. It was as if time had frozen, the sun suspended in the sky like it would never move again. He felt numb, unable to breathe or even think.

The end was upon them now.

CHAPTER 36

Caiaphas was not sure how many minutes had passed. Samuel, who had taken him gently by the arm and led him over to the table where the porridge and dried fruit cakes remained untouched, had left him there and returned to Miriam. The two young people gently lifted Rivkah's body from the back of the calf. Samuel removed a sheath of white linen from a pack he had been carrying on his back. Together, they wrapped the body in the cloth, as delicately as if they were swaddling a newborn. As they worked, Samuel spoke in low, urgent tones to Miriam. She nodded, taking in all he said with wide eyes.

When they were finished, they lifted the body onto the calf's back, and tied it tightly, making sure that no amount of jostling would cause it to slip from its position. Miriam shot a last anxious look at Caiaphas and then retreated into an inner chamber. Samuel made his way back to the older man, sitting gently beside him and looking nervous but resolute.

"Noble Caiaphas, I wish I could tell you there was time to grieve. But that is a luxury we do not have. The Romans who have entered the city are few in number for now, but they have obviously been given orders to find and destroy those whom our people see as leaders. We have been hearing for weeks that there are spies and defectors among them. I have no doubt that their information regarding the whereabouts of those who have held power within our priesthood is sound. You are not safe here. You and Miriam must leave immediately."

He nodded toward the entryway through which Miriam had gone. "I have sent your granddaughter to pack food and supplies, and to clothe herself in garments suitable for traveling. You must gather yourself as well, collect any money or belongings you do not wish to leave behind, and prepare yourself for a long journey. With the gates still guarded and the Roman wall surrounding Jerusalem, there is still one possible chance for you to flee to safety. But we must make haste."

Caiaphas, who had been listening to Samuel without any indication that he had heard anything being said, stirred at last. "A way out of the city? How?"

Samuel grimaced. "It is not an easy path, nor one that I would wish on a man of your age and stature, nor on a young woman traveling without a husband or brother to accompany her. But there have been whispers of those who have made their way to freedom through the aqueducts, traveling the opposite path of the flowing water away from the city and past the walls built by our enemies. I believe it may be the only means of escape, before the Romans break through our last defenses and pour into the city. But we must go now."

As he said these last words, Miriam emerged. She was dressed in a thick traveling cloak and had bound her hair tightly into one long braid. On her back, she carried two woven sacks, which Samuel helped to tie on top of the calf alongside Rivkah's body. Miriam's face was ashen, but she appeared determined as she approached Caiaphas.

"Come, grandfather. Prepare yourself, and Samuel will show us the way. It is time."

When they were ready, Samuel led them to one of the back entrances of the estate, and they slipped away, with barely a moment to look around one last time at the estate that had been Caiaphas's home for nearly five decades. As they sped down the street, they could hear shouts and cries in the distance. More than once they had to stop and wait, to make sure the way was clear before they continued. Samuel led them south, leaving the Upper City and traveling through the Lower City, where Hadassah and Abel had once made their home. Skirting the southern wall, they came finally to the Pool of Siloam, the place where Caiaphas and his father had walked so many years before, the place where he had first told Abel of his visions.

The pool was an expansive body of water, clear and smooth, with stone steps surrounding it on every side. Caiaphas felt a pang as he looked into its depths and saw the cool, peaceful water lapping gently at the pool's edges, oblivious to the turmoil that was taking place throughout the rest of the city. The water that filled the pool came from a tunnel at its northwestern corner. It was to this spot that Samuel led their small party, the calf straining slightly under its load but continuing on, as if somehow it sensed the precious nature of its burden. When they reached the entrance of the tunnel, Samuel handed the rope to Miriam. He turned to Caiaphas.

"This is where I must leave you. I know not what has become of the rest of the priesthood or their families. But if any of them still live, they will need assistance. I cannot abandon them." He took a deep breath, as if readying himself for whatever was to come. "I intend to make my way to the house of Eli, assuming it still stands." His face was solemn as he turned back to Miriam. "If I find your mother or uncle, I will reassure them that you and your grandfather are on a path to safety. And I will pray that like our people in the days of Moses, you will be granted safe passage through the waters, and will emerge on dry ground, far from this place."

Miriam's look of gratitude and admiration was unmistakable. The smallest smile flashed across her face just before she lowered her eyes. As Caiaphas looked at the two of them, the willowy young woman and the handsome young priest, standing a breath apart, his heart lurched with pain, at what might have been, at what could no longer be. He nodded, and said simply, "God be with you, Samuel. You are a credit to the priesthood, and we will remain forever in your debt." With that, Caiaphas and Miriam entered the long, dark tunnel, the water flowing at their feet immediately soaking their sandals and the hems of their garments, with the calf clambering after them, its hooves slipping over the wet rock.

THEY WALKED on in the darkness for what seemed like hours, the trickling water the only sound apart from the animal's soft panting and their own soggy footsteps. At times, the tunnel opened up so that they could walk side by side. But for the most part it was narrow enough for only one person at a time to pass. Miriam took the lead, with the calf marching doggedly behind her. Caiaphas brought up the rear, sure that at any moment they would hear the sound of soldiers behind them in the tunnel, their escape foiled. As the incline of the rock floor began to shift upward, and the water grew slightly warmer, he began to allow himself to think that he might once again feel the sun's rays on his face, to kindle hope that this tunnel was in fact merely a passageway and not a watery tomb.

It had been several hours when the tunnel took a sharp turn to the right, and the air shifted, the stale dankness replaced by something that smelled almost sweet. And then they saw ahead of them a sliver of light, which grew as they trudged forward, their pace quickening even as their legs ached. Within minutes, they found themselves at the opening of a tunnel, much like the one where they had begun their journey. This time, the pool before them was more than double the size of the one they had left in Jerusalem, surrounded by pine and cypress trees and gleaming in the late afternoon sun.

At the side of the pool, they took a moment to rest their bodies and to allow their eyes to adjust to the light. After so much darkness, the colors surrounding them seemed somehow more alive. The verdant treetops undulated gently, their branches whistling softly as they swayed in the wind. Caiaphas took deep, long breaths as Miriam unwrapped some bread and pulled a wineskin from one of the woven sacks, taking care not to disturb the linen bundle that lay beside it. They sat in silence, eating and drinking, until they had both had their fill. Then Miriam rose to her feet, wiping the crumbs from her lap, and looked at Caiaphas.

"If you are ready, we must continue our climb, grandfather. Samuel told me that if we were to make it this far, we should follow the sun west and then turn north, up into the mountains and away from Jerusalem. There is a small village there called Ein Kerem, which we may reach by nightfall if we do not tarry. Samuel lived there as a boy before he began his studies at the temple. According to him, it is a modest place. But a small spring provides water for both the people who inhabit it and the olive groves and vineyards they tend. He believes we will be received by his relatives with hospitality."

Caiaphas looked at his granddaughter in awe. At twenty-two, Miriam had limited experience with the world outside her own home. In many ways Caiaphas still thought of her as a child. But here she was, leading him like a seasoned soldier, shouldering death and grief and the loss of everything she had ever known with determination and grace. Surely this was the great-granddaughter of Tova, the granddaughter of Rivkah, the daughter of Martha. His heart seized as he looked at her, young and vibrant, standing beside the unmoving body of his wife, whose spirit she had so clearly inherited. He was overcome with both sorrow and pride. He nodded quickly, not trusting himself to speak.

They went on, the road becoming rockier and more treacherous, climbing higher with each step. After they had been traveling for some time, Caiaphas stopped to glance behind him. He was not surprised to find himself looking at a familiar scene. He saw the pool from his vision in the distance, its waters just barely visible through the trees. When he turned, there was Miriam, her back to him, the calf behind her being led along the path, the bundle it carried now painfully recognizable to Caiaphas from his dreams. His head ached, and his legs threatened to buckle beneath him. But he forced himself to keep moving. The sun, which still shone brightly, had already begun its slow creep toward the horizon.

When next they stopped to rest, they found themselves on a high crest of rock, the entire valley opened up before them like a piece of parchment. Below, they could see the tops of olive trees. Beyond that, the Roman perimeter wall curled like a serpent before them, encircling the city of Jerusalem within its deadly coils. With the sun just beginning to set behind them, there was an eerie glow to the landscape, as if the air had become suddenly tangible and thick. And then Caiaphas saw the flames, rising from within the city itself. He gasped.

Even from this distance, he could see that the temple was on fire, blazing just as it had been in his dreams for decades, stark and clear against the twilight sky. The temple walls rose white and cold despite the heat of the plumes that licked at their bases, threatening to topple them. He could tell by the amount of smoke rising from its center that the entire sanctuary was on fire. He knew that the Holy of Holies, in which a single flame had burned without ceasing for generations, must be engulfed. As he watched, unable to tear his eyes away, the southeast tower of the temple crumbled in a heap, its turret collapsing in on itself like a beast wincing to avoid the lash, disappearing from view in a cloud of dust and rubble that billowed skyward.

From where he stood, no sound could be heard but the evening wind whispering through the trees. But Caiaphas did not need to hear anything to know exactly what it would be like if he were there in the midst of the destruction. He had experienced this vision too many times to be ignorant of the sounds and smells it carried, the choking, pungent smoke, the searing heat of the flames as they danced around the temple mount, the desperate cries of those trapped by both Roman soldiers and by the fire itself.

Trembling, he tore his eyes away from the scene and saw that Miriam was looking at him in horror. Her lip quivered. "If the temple has fallen, then the city is lost." He knew she was thinking of all those left behind, for whom no relief would now come. He understood how she felt. It was as if the entire world were on fire, everything Caiaphas had ever known or loved going up in smoke, its tendrils weaving their way up to the sky like shrouds billowing on a windy day. He looked down at his garments. Far from the rich linen clothes he had worn as high priest, the tunic that now covered him was rough and course, well-made but humble. No longer were his robes at risk of defilement from being pulled apart. And yet he did not have the strength or desire to tear them. He felt dazed as he stared at the flames now licking the tops of the remaining towers. His eyes blurred with hot tears as he bowed his head.

As they stood there in silence, his mind flew to those who had come before him, and their faces passed across his memory like shadows. His mother Hadassah, who fought with every feeble ounce of strength she had, from the moment she brought him into the world until her final blessing on the day he left to be dedicated at the temple as a priest. His father Abel, a man of integrity and bravery, who more than once put his own life in danger to protect the priesthood, and whose ultimate sacrifice had been in service to the temple that now lay in ruins before them.

And Annas, his father-in-law, larger than life, a man who had welcomed him into his home like a son, giving him the gift of his daughter as a bride, and preparing the way for him to become a priest. Annas, who had seen potential in a small, lonely boy, and had taught him nearly everything he knew, orchestrating events so that his son-in-law would go on to wear the high priest's robes for nearly two decades. Caiaphas felt ashamed that he had ever taken this attention and care for granted, that he had nearly destroyed the relationship out of a desperate desire to make his own way. He saw now, too late, that he had always been a part of something bigger than himself. He was one member of a holy priesthood that had at its center the temple, the place where God was worshipped, where sacrifice and offering led to blessing and honor, where the future of the people was determined by the diligence and discipline of those who served them. But now all of that was gone, shattered like glass into a million shards, broken and irretrievable.

"Grandfather." Miriam's voice brought him back to the present. Tears slid down her cheeks as she took a shaky breath. "With the temple destroyed and Jerusalem overthrown, what will become of us?"

Caiaphas sighed deeply, his head heavy and his heart hollow. "I do not know. There is nothing for us now but to continue on, to find a welcoming corner of these mountains where we can make a home for ourselves, where we can bury Rivkah." He choked on these last words, forcing them out as if saying them was the only way he could convince himself that it was really true, that she was gone. Everything was gone.

He fell silent, returning his gaze to the scene before him. The air around the temple undulated with heat, and the flames rose higher than before. A second tower had just fallen, leaving even more ash in its wake. The sanctuary was no longer visible. Miriam drew closer to him, and softly leaned her head against his shoulder. She smelled of sunlight and lilies. For the briefest of moments Caiaphas was reminded of his wedding day, and of the blossoms that Rivkah had worn nestled in her hair. Gently, he rested his head on top of his granddaughter's, and together they stood side by side, watching the temple burn.

ACKNOWLEDGMENTS

Writing may be a solitary act, but creating a book requires a tremendous amount of cheerleading, support, encouragement, and patience. I've been incredibly fortunate to have all the best people in my corner from the beginning.

Thank you to the scholars, academics, historians, and writers whose research I found invaluable to this endeavor. Scott Korb's *Life in Year One*, Jodi Magness' *Stone and Dung, Oil and Spit*, Mirian Feinberg Vamosh's *Daily Life at The Time of Jesus*, and Samuel L. Adams' *Social and Economic Life in Second Temple Judea* were instrumental in helping me to bring this world to life. Dr. Randall Price's *Rose Guide to the Temple*, Lester L. Grabbe's *An Introduction to Second Temple Judaism*, and Joachim Jeremias' *Jerusalem in the Time of Jesus* provided valuable insights into the lives of the temple priesthood. James Alexander Thom's *Once Upon A Time It Was Now* gave me the courage and direction I needed to attempt a book of this scope in the first place. *The New Complete Works of Josephus* translated by William Whiston provided a direct line to the original source, and the meticulous research of James C. VanderKam's *From Joshua to Caiaphas* helped to breathe life into the legacy of high priests before and after Caiaphas. I am especially indebted to Adele Reinhartz and Helen K. Bond, whose books on Caiaphas were the first I read, and to whose pages I returned repeatedly during the research and writing phases of *The Gospel of Caiaphas*.

Thank you to my fellow writers. To my L.A. Inklings, you kept me going when I got stuck, and inspired me to keep plugging away. A special thanks to Paula Sword Orr, for being not only a wonderful friend but an incredible editor. Turns out there are some benefits to being quarantined together. To the 6th floor, thank you for believing in me and giving me some of my very first positive feedback. To Danica Tucker for the gorgeous cover and illustrations, and for talking me off the ledge more than once.

Thank you to my agent Kate Garrick. You are tenacious, honest, and brilliant, and your embrace of this manuscript from day one was a gift. Our journey together has been a long one, from coworkers and colleagues to friends and more, and I'm forever indebted to you for your editorial feedback and clear-eyed direction.

Thank you to my parents Shari and Stewart, who have been my editors all my life, long before I ever thought to bring Caiaphas to life. You have supported me as a writer and a thinker, and both my writing and my mind have been shaped and improved by your example and input.

Thank you to my husband Reggie, who has been my biggest fan and most loyal supporter. I couldn't have done this without you. Thank you for encouraging me to dream big, to take a leap, and to press on. There are no words for how much I love you.

Thank you to my children, Adina, Maya, and Sam, who inspire me every day. You keep me tethered to the brightest, most joyful parts of myself.

This book would not have been written if I had not felt the tug of a calling, a still small voice that beckoned me to revive the eight-year-old little girl who declared herself a writer, a whisper from the past telling me there was a story aching to be told. I'm so glad I listened.